MW01627181

NEXT, PLEASE!

JERUSALEM
PUBLICATIONS

EFRAT SINGER

NEXT, PLEASE!

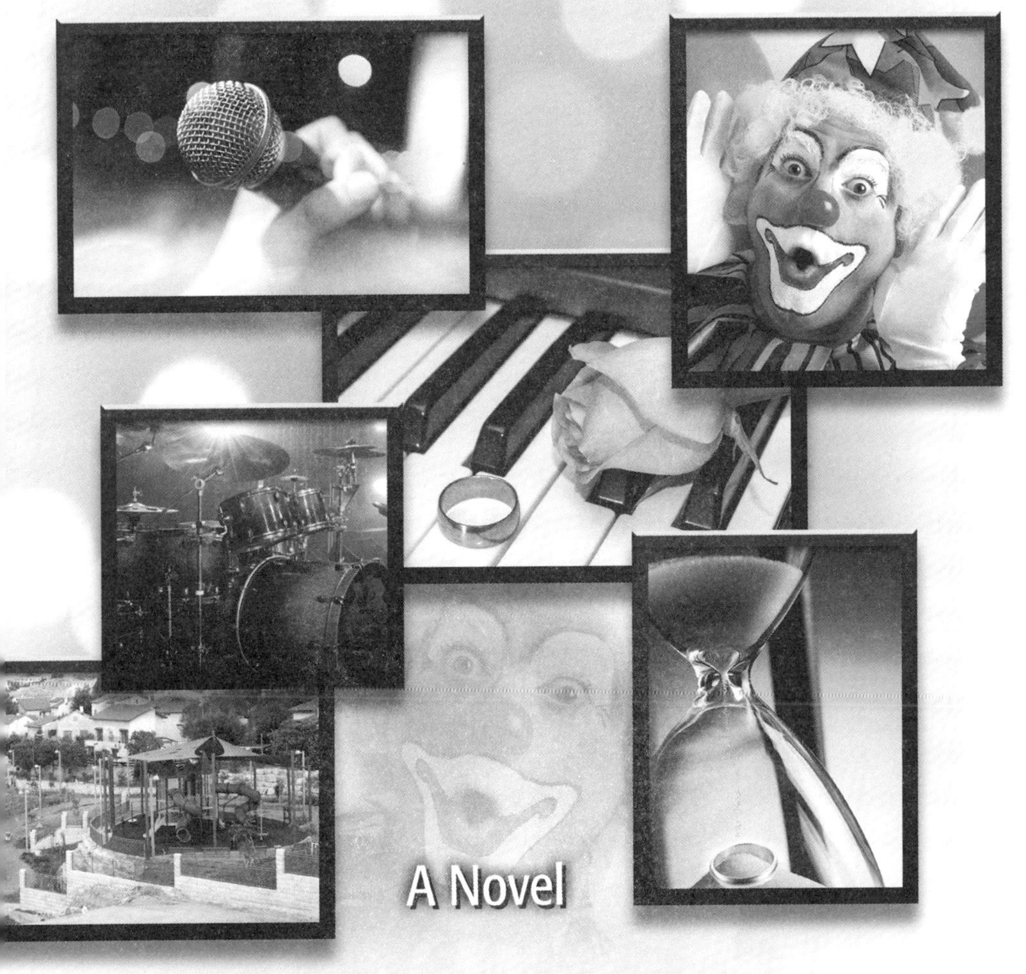

Copyright © 2018 by Jerusalem Publications
ISBN 978-0-9987055-4-5

All rights reserved.

No part of this publication may be translated, reproduced, stored in a retrieval system, adapted or transmitted in any form or by any means, such as but not limited to electronic, mechanical, photocopying, recording, or otherwise, without permission in writing from the copyright holder.

This is a work of fiction. Names, characters, places, and incidents either are the product of the author's imagination or are used fictitiously, and any resemblance to actual persons, living or dead, establishments, organizations, or events is entirely coincidental.

Cover Design by David Yaphe
Typesetting by LG Studios

Distributed by Feldheim Publishers
POB 43163 / Jerusalem, Israel

208 Airport Executive Park
Nanuet, NY 10954

www.feldheim.com

Distributed in Europe by:
Lehmanns
+44-0-191-430-0333
info@lehmanns.co.uk
www.lehmanns.co.uk

Distributed in Australia by:
Golds World of Judaica
+613 95278775
info@golds.com.au
www.golds.com.au

Printed in Israel

To my mother:

This, too, is for you.

1 Empty Spaces

Sheila Leipzig walked up to the office building and put her dainty bronze bag on the metal detector.

The guard opened it, looked inside, and waved her through.

She ran her eyes over the business listings on the large metal sign. There it was: Shalom Bayit Realty, eighth floor.

Stairs or elevator?

Stairs.

Her bronze slingbacks slowed her down. At the third floor, she stopped and listened. The stairwell was empty. She kicked off her shoes and, holding them in one hand, raced up the stairs.

On the sixth floor, she stopped, winded. Her new schedule, while enjoyable and challenging, was grueling. With substitute seventh-grade homeroom teacher at Machon Atara now added to her regular teaching hours, it left her with no time for her usual workouts at the gym.

She felt like turning around and going home. No one knew of her appointment except the receptionist. She could cancel.

It was Rosh Chodesh, a time for new beginnings. But it felt less like a beginning than an end, the end of a cherished dream.

She pressed the up elevator button, slipped her shoes back on, and ran her hands through her hair. After a moment's thought, she pinned it back.

Inside the fashionably decorated gray-and-cream office, she stopped in surprise. What was Menucha Shalom, the formidable head of the PTA at Machon Atara, doing sitting behind the desk in a real estate office?

In a flash, it clicked. Halleli Shalom, the uncontested class leader of her seventh-grade class, was Menucha Shalom's daughter.

What now? She'd never knowingly mix her two worlds. In the game of older singlehood, she played a vastly different role than she did as star teacher in Machon Atara.

But it was too late to back out. Menucha had seen her.

"Sheila, hello. Why do you look so shocked?"

Sheila regained her poise. "I don't know why I didn't realize that you're the same Menucha Shalom. Halleli told me that her mother doesn't work, but I usually have great voice recognition. I'm surprised I didn't recognize your voice from the times we've met at PTA meetings over the years."

Menucha smiled. "I only started working for my husband at the beginning of this year. Halleli probably doesn't think of it as a real job. I double as both his receptionist and his partner. Please, make yourself comfortable."

Sheila sat down on one of the two leather chairs in front of the desk. "You must be super busy between heading the PTA and a full-time job."

"I like keeping busy. It makes me feel alive." Menucha leaned forward conspiratorially. "I know I shouldn't be asking you this, but before we get down to your real reason for being here, how's my Halleli doing in your classes? She adored Yocheved Sutton—the entire class loved her, for that matter—so I hope you aren't having a hard time filling in for her. How long has she been out, a month?"

"Just about," Sheila said. "I like teaching this age. I enjoy the way their minds work. They really think, you know?"

"Not always, but I'll take your word for it. You seem to have the girls under control. I'd have heard if there were any major problems. They're learning a lot, which is definitely to your credit, especially as a substitute."

"I've been teaching them Jewish history for the past two years, so I'm hardly a stranger. We've had two years to get to know each other and learn to work together."

"Still, being their homeroom teacher is an entirely different kettle of fish."

"That's true."

"Well, good for you! You've never been a homeroom teacher before, have you?"

"No."

"I'm sure the principal knew what she was doing when she chose you. You have the right idea, show those kids who's boss! Don't let them walk all over you."

"I try not to. Thanks for the vote of confidence."

"You deserve it. Do you have any concerns, or"—Menucha winked—"complaints about Halleli?"

"None whatsoever. Halleli's doing well. I wish I had another couple of pupils like her." At Menucha's expectant look, she added, "She's accomplished, talented, bright, and friendly." *Why not give credit where credit was due? Menucha and her husband must have invested a lot of time and thought into their only child.*

Menucha glowed with pleasure. It was common knowledge among Machon Atara parents that Sheila was a strict teacher whose compliments had to be honestly earned.

Though if she hadn't praised Halleli, it wouldn't necessarily mean all that much. After all, she didn't have any children of her own yet, so how much could she know about children? Some of the girls were actually scared of her. Maybe not *scared*, but they all knew she definitely wasn't a teacher to cross.

"Thanks. I must tell you that Halleli talks about you all the time, compliments only. She's an only child, you know, which makes her an anomaly in the class, so I worry. You know how it is."

Sheila smiled understandingly.

"Enough about my daughter. You didn't come to the office to discuss her. Well, here we are. What exactly did you have in mind? Tell me again what you told me on the phone. Something about edging into property ownership? Not buying right away, but maybe later on? Do I have that right?"

"It's probably an unusual request." Sheila twisted the sapphire ring that matched her eyes. "Everyone keeps telling me that what I have in mind isn't realistic, so I came to you for a professional opinion." Avoiding eye contact, she began telling Menucha what she wanted.

Menucha nodded intently, clicking away on her computer.

Sheila felt a surge of embarrassment. What must Menucha think of her, walking in without knowing if what she wanted even existed?

But what were her choices?

Even being here feels like a giant step. I just don't feel emotionally ready to buy a home as a single woman. With a husband, yes. Yes! On my own? That's so sad.

"Let me see if I got this right," Menucha said at last. "Your parents are willing to buy you a one-bedroom apartment within walking distance of them here in Neot Yaar. You, on the other hand, feel that since you've always lived at home, it's too much of a leap to buy, so you'd prefer to take things slowly, step by step."

"Exactly." Sheila nodded. Without a husband to help her think and decide, without a husband to build a life with, she couldn't face moving out on her own. But tomorrow, or the next day, she'd get fed up living at home, and she'd kick herself for not leaping at the opportunity her parents were offering her.

"You want me to find someone who's willing to rent out their place for six months or a year and then maybe sell it to you, correct?"

"Y-yes. I hope I'm not asking for something that doesn't exist."

"Not at all. Rentals with an option to buy exist," Menucha said. "I'm glad I understood what you're looking for. Now we can move on. You've told me your price range, and it's definitely enough to purchase a really nice place in this size range. Your parents want you within walking distance, which rules out another neighborhood. How about if you and your parents start looking at available properties, and I'll keep my eyes and ears open?"

Sheila tuned in to what Menucha was saying.

"Nothing goes so fast when it comes to buying a home. You do need to be on the ball, but we're talking months, not weeks. Maybe in the meantime you'll see a place that will sing to you."

"Sing to me? What does that mean?"

"It means," Menucha cocked her head, "that it will call out to you, saying, 'Sheila Leipzig, I am your home!'"

"We can start looking," Sheila said, "but don't count on that happening to me." She paused thoughtfully. "But then again, maybe something will sing, as you so poetically put it, to my mother."

"I understand your reluctance to take on an enormous responsibility like buying a piece of real estate, but it's a wonderful investment. People do it every day!"

"Single women too?"

"Not too many. Here and there. Mostly couples. You won't be as alone as you think. Your parents will be behind you the entire way, and so will I."

"I appreciate that." Sheila stood up. "I'll be in touch after I speak with my parents."

* * *

I took the first step. I went to a real estate agent. Too bad I didn't connect

Shalom Bayit real estate with Halleli Shalom. Not the best idea, having the mother of one of the most popular girls in my class as my real estate agent, but there isn't any graceful way to back out now.

Sheila got behind the wheel of her car, which had been her thirtieth birthday present from her parents two years previously.

Going to a real estate agent was the right thing to do, even if I still feel ambiguous about moving out of my parents' home. When I asked Estelle Bruner—whoops, Hacohen...got to get used to that one—who found the apartment that she and Elchanan bought, she told me that Shalom Bayit real estate did an excellent job for them. I guess she thought I knew that Menucha Shalom works for her husband there.

It doesn't really make a difference who helps me in this area. A person has to keep on moving. I need to do what I need to do. How I feel will just have to fall into place. I'm a grown-up now.

She put her key in the ignition. *No one's kicking me out of the house. Abba would be thrilled if I changed my mind and decided to stay.*

A person has to keep growing, changing, moving, building.

Sheila swallowed hard, past the lump in her throat. *I don't want to buy a home all alone. Besides, I don't have to do this alone. Renée Lowenstein has hinted, more than hinted, any number of times that she'd love to join me in this venture, as a roommate. I don't want to insult her, but I don't see it working out. We're just too different. Friends, yes. Roommates, no. In any case, I want a husband! I want a family to fill our home! Buying a home on my own is such an older single thing to do. How did this happen to me, Sheila Leipzig?*

She put her head down on the steering wheel, struggling to keep her tears at bay. *So empty. What good is an empty home? I'm still me, even if I'm an older single. What's wrong with being an older single? It's nothing to be ashamed of!*

What good do all these questions do me? Enough! Leipzigs do what needs to be done. And they never cry in public! She started the car.

As Sheila drove, she thought hard. *Many things are beyond my control, but there's one thing I can control, and I will. No one will pity me. People will continue to admire me.*

I will function at top capacity. I will be the best teacher, the best volunteer, the best daughter and aunt!

Estelle told me that Menucha Shalom used to be an older single not so long ago. Halleli is only twelve years old. Menucha, you of all people should have some tact.

What a heedless remark: "You know how it is." No, I don't know how it is! I don't know how it is to have a child, only or otherwise, and if you had any sensitivity, Menucha Shalom, you'd realize that! And all that comparing me to Yocheved. What was the point? You should think before you speak. Your problem, not mine, but does it hurt? Sure does, and that's the point.

You, Menucha are uber-tactless! I know you mean well, but who's hurt? Me! I am! Who forgot the entire conversation as soon as it ended? You. I, on the other hand, feel put down and dumb. All that has to change. I need to let thoughtless, silly remarks slide right off me. I'll learn to do that. I will!

I'll never be an object of pity. I never have been, and I never will be, no matter how I feel, even if I never meet Rabbi or Mr. Right.

Don't say that! I will meet Mr. Right or Rabbi Right or Dr. Right!

Until then, I'll make my life work for me.

She was on the block, almost in front of her parents' beautiful villa, but she wasn't prepared to face them. Not yet. Not when her mother was still urging her to forget about meeting Yerachmiel Kantor. Not that she was sure what her final decision was going to be, but she had enough internal pressure eating away at her now without any help from the outside. And her mother was desperate to help her, no question about that. Her way of helping though...well, that was another story.

Sheila's lips curled into a wry grin as she recalled her mother's reaction to her sister Michal's suggestion that she meet Yerachmiel Kantor. Yerachmiel was at least forty and headed Rina-O-Mangina, a very popular and successful *simchah* band. To say that Professor Leipzig had been taken aback was an understatement.

"Sheila! I don't understand you at all. Please explain this to me. Are you doing your best not to get married? Do you lack a father figure in your life?"

"The same answer goes for both your questions, Ima. Not at all."

"Then why are you considering a wild suggestion like this one, way out of left field? I'm going to have a talk with Michal. I'm surprised at her. You're extremely eligible, even if you are twenty-nine years old, and you are very far from being desperate!"

I'm thirty-two. "He's also extremely eligible."

Until then, her father had listened silently to their conversation, but now he intervened.

"I'm sure that Yerachmiel is a fine individual, with many special qualities."

She'd turned gratefully to her father. "Yes, he is! He's successful! You know how everyone always says that a woman builds her husband? He's built himself. He's already made something of himself. He's already done something important with his life."

"You want someone who's already fulfilling his potential."

"Yes!"

Her mother had shaken her head gloomily. "You've always had a way with words, but I'm not convinced. All this talk about potential. Yaakov Stone is in your age bracket. He's a successful lawyer. He's been begging you for a second chance. So he made some mistakes on your first date. Are you perfect?"

"No."

"You can still call Nechama Rotter and tell her that you thought it over, and—"

"I'm not dating Yaakov Stone again, Ima. End of story."

"End of story? Who gives you the right to say that?"

Sheila's mother had turned to her father. "It's almost as if she's dating just to get us off her back. Then, when it doesn't work, she can tell us that she tried."

"Sheila's a grown-up, Miriam. It's her prerogative to decide who she wants to date and who she wants to turn down."

Sheila pulled herself back to the present. Her grin faded. Her mother's question was a good one. Obviously, she was wrong in her assessment of Sheila's motivations, but the fact remained that she brought up the subject whenever she saw Sheila and—

I have no strength to argue with her. Should I just drive around in circles until I calm down and I'm ready to go home? Her lips curved up involuntarily as it occurred to her that if she had her own place, that particular problem, at least, would be solved.

Where should I go now?

I could visit Michal, play with Batya, hold her, and free up Michal to do some housework. Holding Batya always makes me feel better about life. Sheila smiled eagerly at the thought of her sweet six-month-old niece. After a moment, she nixed the thought. Michal was sure to pressure her about Yerachmiel, though her pressure would come from the opposite direction. They would argue, get into a fight about it.

I don't want to get into another fight with Michal.

And if I do? We'll fight, we'll make up. I need to hold my yummy baby.

Deftly negotiating a U-turn around the cul-de-sac that led to her parents' home, she drove the short distance to her sister's house.

I refuse to become one of those bitter complaining older single types that everyone pities. I don't want anyone feeling fake regret for forgetting to invite me for Shabbos when they never really wanted my company in the first place. I don't want to be the older single who, nebbach, makes people feel awkward, because how many times can they discuss her job and hobbies when the mainstays of most women's discussions are their husbands and kids. And if and when they do invite her, everyone wonders what she's kvetching about again. Let her stop being so picky and settle, the way everyone else does!

The way they did?

Did they? Does everyone?

I never thought I'd end up in this position, but now that I have, no one will ever hear me breathe a word of how much I hate this part of my life, and how it's starting to consume all the other parts of my life until nothing is left of me.

Older single, marriage, children, when, when—

WHEN!!!!!!

If I only knew when this whole ambiguous hurtful period would be over, even in a year, or two, or five, it would be so much easier to accept it now.

* * *

"Talk about serendipity." Michal Feller opened the door of her apartment and smiled indulgently as Sheila made a beeline to pick up Batya, who was whimpering on the play mat. "I keep trying to put her down for her nap, but she just won't fall asleep."

"She knew I was coming. You knew Aunt Sheila was coming to visit, didn't you, Batyale? Come to Aunt Sheila," Sheila cooed.

Sheila sighed blissfully as Batya cuddled against her. "Smart kid. She doesn't want to miss out." *I needed this. I really needed this.*

"Sheila? Did you hear what I said?"

"About Batya's nap?" At her younger sister's serious expression, Sheila sat up straight, still holding Batya close. "Serendipity? Uh-oh."

"Yup. Serendipity. Do you realize you haven't dated anyone, no one at all, since the Yaakov Stone fiasco? That was six weeks ago!"

"So what?"

"*So what?* You're thirty-two years old!"

"Fine, fine. Just to get you off my back."

"Not just to get me off your back! Because you want to get married!"

"Same thing," Sheila muttered.

"I heard that. No, it's not the same thing. I'm doing this for you!"

"I know that, Michal. It's… I appreciate it. I know. Believe me, I know."

Her sister relaxed. "Sorry. I just got off the phone with Avital Kantor. You aren't being fair to Yerachmiel. If you said yes, and then said that your new subbing job has you drained and you need to adjust to your new schedule, well, time's up on that excuse. It's been over two months since you started substituting in the seventh grade."

Sheila said nothing. She hugged her niece closer to her.

"I think it's only fair to everyone if you decide what you want. Say yes or say no but—"

"*Okay!* Tell Avital to tell Yerachmiel that I'm available any evening this week. He can choose a time and place."

"Really? So simple?"

"Why not? Other than the age difference, which is a real concern, he sounds like someone I'd want to meet."

"True, but…?"

"But?"

"I hope your sudden attack of flexibility doesn't mean that you're just going out to get the whole thing over with," Michal said suspiciously.

"That's insulting."

"Maybe. But maybe it's also true?"

"I hope not." Sheila sighed deeply. "I've heard that he has a very deep spiritual side, but at the same time, he's grounded enough to lead the most successful *simchah* band in Yerushalayim. I'm going to do my best to overlook the age difference." *Am I being honest with myself, or just grasping at straws to avoid facing reality? Who knows?*

"I'll give Avital a call right now."

"Not now, Michal. Please. Wait until I leave."

"Why?"

"I came here to cheer up."

"Getting the show on the road is the best way in the world to cheer up."

"Michal."

"What happened? Why are you upset?"

Sheila spilled out the entire story, omitting Menucha's identity. Michal listened attentively, expressing sympathy and indignation in all the right places.

"You're so brave, Sheila. I have no idea how you cope."

"Oh, come on. Lots of older singles manage beautifully with much worse situations."

"Don't call yourself that."

"That's what I am."

"No, you aren't."

"What am I then?"

"Just"—Michal hesitated—"just temporarily unmarried."

"Plenty of wonderful people are in that position, both male and female."

Michal threw her arms around her. "They aren't my big sister."

The moment Sheila's car pulled away, Michal picked up the phone to call back Avital Kantor with the newest development.

How can anyone as brilliant as Sheila not realize that if she'd just be open to settling a little bit, her problems would be over and she could finally be like everyone else? Why is she so fixated on his age? No one's perfect. Besides, everyone says that he looks very young.

* * *

When Sheila got into her car, feeling a lot better, she saw a message on her phone. Noa Lewin.

"Hello, Sheila. I know that you're very busy with your seventh graders, but just a friendly reminder. Yocheved Sutton will be returning from maternity leave soon, and you'll be finishing the school year in my class. You'll be pleased to know that my girls miss you very much, even though they adore Aviva Lavie, who's been subbing for you in the meantime. I had an idea about that. Please call me as soon as you get this message. I urgently need to discuss my idea with you."

Sheila smiled wryly. Nothing like a dose of Noa Lewin to bring a person down to earth. Noa was the proud homeroom teacher of a first-grade class that Sheila had found extremely challenging. Sheila had taught them or tried her best to teach them a weekly Jewish history session, with scant success. How she'd come to dread her weekly dose of humiliation! And that remark about Aviva Lavie. How typical of Noa not to realize that perhaps it might be a little bit insulting to be told that she'd been replaced, even temporarily, by a nineteen-year-old teaching assistant with no real experience in the field.

Though, if I'm painfully honest, Noa has a point. Aviva has much more patience for first-grade shtick than I do. Experience is great, but she's got a flair for that age group. It isn't just patience. She's good at it.

Better than I am. Much better.

When Sheila had been offered a full-time job in the seventh grade, she'd been unspeakably relieved to flee the torturous feeling of failure. Imagine, a teacher with over a decade of experience being unable to manage a group of unruly youngsters fresh out of kindergarten. Perhaps they'd matured during the time she'd spent substituting for Yocheved Sutton, the seventh-grade homeroom teacher. She hoped so. It was kind of Noa to say that they missed her. It had to be true if Noa said so. She never lied. But why would they miss her after her disastrous interactions with a few of them and her strict discipline? Little kids were strange.

Noa had something urgent on her mind. Sheila hesitated. Her relationship with Noa, who had begun her teaching career in Machon Atara at the same time as Sheila, wasn't a smooth one. In fact, during the time they'd worked together, she and Noa had almost quarreled more than once. On the other hand, Noa had been very supportive of Sheila in the face of criticism from some class parents.

She took a deep breath, braced herself for a discussion that would probably be awkward at best and acrimonious at worst, and called her colleague back.

"Hi, Sheila. Thanks for calling back so promptly. I have an idea I'm going to run past you. I have one request."

"Which is?"

"Please don't react right off the cuff. You probably will have some sort of gut reaction, but I really want you to give this idea due consideration."

I shouldn't have called her now. I have zero strength for Noa. I hope, hope, hope she's not calling to suggest a shidduch. "If you could just tell me what this is about?"

"I told you. It's about Aviva Lavie."

"Aviva?" Sheila could feel the beginnings of a strong headache.

"Yes," Noa said, a bit impatiently. "Didn't you listen to my message?"

"Yes."

"Do you agree to my conditions?"

"Noa?" All at once, Sheila's head was pounding. "I have a terrible headache. Could I call you back later?"

"You could. Feel better. Only, it takes just two seconds to tell you what I have in mind, and then, I don't even think you should react."

"Go ahead." Sheila sighed.

"So..." Noa suddenly sounded hesitant. "My idea's like this..."

After the first sentence, Sheila bolted upright. She heard out the rest of the monologue in utter silence. Finally, Noa finished.

"Sheila, are you still there?"

"Yes."

"Will you think about what I said?"

"Yes."

Please, Yerachmiel Kantor. Please be the one. I meant what I said before about not being a nebbach case, but I don't know how much more of this I can take.

2 At Face Value

"Ah. *Ta'am Gan Eden.* I love this couch." Yehudit Sapir sank into the black leather living room couch, tucked her legs under her, and shut her eyes. "It's been a looong day."

"Ditto, and it's not over yet. Remind me one more time," her roommate Devora Levin said as she lifted a dining room chair and moved it to the side of the room. "When did you say that— what's her name? Renée? Right, Renée. When did you say that Renée Lowenstein is coming to look at the apartment?"

"Eight-ish, I think. Maybe a little bit after that. Look, I marked it clearly on the calendar," Yehudit murmured. "Didn't you notice? It says, '8 p.m., Renée Lowenstein.'"

"So it does." Devora finished pulling the chairs to the side of the room and began moving the table.

Yehudit opened her eyes. "Devora? What are you doing? Why are you rearranging the furniture in here again? Didn't we just do that last week, last time we interviewed a prospective roommate?"

"Yes, but apparently it didn't work. She was probably put off by how cramped this place is, so I'm trying to make the room look bigger. Not that it will make much difference. This place is tiny, and that's that. But I want to try. I liked the potential roommate last week, and I bet she would have said yes if this place had looked larger. Can you help me with the rug? It's heavy."

"Sure." Yehudit got up from the couch and picked up one side of the faded Persian carpet. "I doubt it was that, though. She would have had an hour's commute to work every morning."

Devora smoothed out a corner of the rug. "Thanks for your help. Yeah, that's what she said, but I personally wouldn't allow an hour's commute to stand in my way if I were apartment hunting. Especially if I had no idea where I was going to be living the following month. Not if I liked the people and the place."

"I see no reason not to take what she said at face value." Yehudit took a tissue and dabbed at her forehead. "Whew, it's hot. The fan's not doing all that much to cool this place. Let's turn on the air conditioner."

"I'm not hot, but if you need it, fine. Just remember, the two of us are stretching to pay three rents." Devora switched on the air conditioner. "Go sit down. I'll manage."

"Are you sure?"

"Uh-huh. I'm moving everything back the way it was. It's a hopeless task. Let's just roll up the rug and put it behind the couch."

"Why?"

"It's heat-producing."

The two roommates rolled up the heavy rug and dragged it behind the couch. Yehudit sank down again as Devora continued rearranging the room.

"She should be here soon," Yehudit said. "Are you positive you don't need my help? I feel guilty letting you do it alone."

"I'm fine. It was my silly idea."

"Not silly. Why do you seem so uptight?"

"Because I am." Devora stood stock still in the middle of the room. "Next time, instead of writing a name, just write 'Next, please.'"

"What are you talking about?" Yehudit asked. "What's 'next please' supposed to mean?"

"Prospective roommates. We've been interviewing for a full month. They all begin to sound the same after a while. Same with dates. We've both been dating for close to twenty years. Next, please! No? Oh, too bad. Sure you aren't doing something wrong? Next, please! Still no? Oh, that's terrible! Next, please! What? Still no? How could that be?"

"You're in a bad mood."

"I'm fed up. We could each have husbands, children, homes of our own. Instead, we're still stuck in slummy apartments, perpetually seeking, searching, grasping at straws with no end in sight."

"Aren't you being a little negative?"

"Am I? Maybe I'm just having a normal reaction to this unbearable instability we're forced to live with. Upheaval after upheaval just has a way of getting me down. I can't take the stress anymore. Chaviva moved in with us barely a year and a half ago. Now she's married, and here we go again. I'm not being negative; I'm just being realistic." Devora moved the glass coffee table into the center of the room, backed up a couple of steps to assess the effect, and moved it back to the far corner of the room alongside the couch.

Yehudit wasn't sure how to respond to Devora's outburst. Out of habit, she tried to put a positive spin on a situation she personally didn't care for much, either. But wasn't having a good attitude preferable to kvetching about a situation she had to live with whether she liked it or not?

"This room looks much bigger now that the rug is rolled up," Yehudit ventured.

The corners of Devora's mouth turned up in a faint smile. "Nice try. Didn't you tell me that Renée lives in Neot Yaar? If so, then she's used to normal-sized rooms." She sank down onto the small secondhand easy chair that was covered with a velvet throw patterned in vivid shades of red, orange, and yellow. "She said she was leaving work early at seven to get here at eight. She must be a workaholic."

"Probably. She just got this job after three months of being unemployed."

"What does she do?"

"She told me that at this point in her life, she's working as an interior decorator, but she's actually a qualified architect. The company she worked for downsized, so they had to let her go."

Devora grimaced. "More instability! More uncertainty! More being in limbo!"

"It's her, not you."

"It makes me feel so vulnerable! I can't even take hearing about it in someone else's life. I am so not in the mood for this. Let's call Renée and reschedule."

"We can't do that to her!"

"Why not? What's the difference between today and tomorrow? I need a break. First, Chaviva left. To get married. Wonderful, but it's not so great for the two of us left behind. I know that's not the world's most popular point of view."

Yehudit looked at her roommate intently, nodding in comprehension. "A lot of people think the very thoughts you're thinking, but I wouldn't go around saying them. Doesn't sound all that altruistic. But I know where you're coming from, so you can say it to me. Just be careful with other people."

"Yes, Mom."

"Hey! Quit that!"

"I was just teasing you, Yehudit. Don't worry. I know I'm not supposed to say things like that, but I can't pretend with you. If I can't tell *you* how I feel, who can I tell?"

"You can tell me anything. We feel the same way."

"We do?" Devora's amber eyes opened wide.

"I also feel an empty space. We both miss her very much. I don't think there's anything wrong with saying that. It's not as if you're begrudging her her happiness or anything like that. You would never begrudge anyone's finding their *bashert*. You just wish it could happen to you, too."

"The way I feel has nothing to do with missing Chaviva." Devora's face crumpled. "It has everything to do with another interview. A real, live person with preferences, and quirks, and all kinds of needs and opinions is coming to meet us. I'm scared, okay? I don't feel up to making the decision about whether some stranger will move in with us. It could turn out to be a disaster."

"We don't even know if she's going to want to move in with us."

"But she might."

"Only if we like her."

"Don't tell me that's not risky. Do you realize that we could end up wrecking the entire atmosphere of this place if we choose the wrong person? Tell me that's not scary."

"Never said it wasn't, but at least we're in it together." *Please snap out of this negative mood before Renée comes.*

"How do *you* take it so calmly?" Devora asked.

"That's life! There's always something to deal with. What's the alternative?"

"That's *so* soothing."

Yehudit checked her watch. "Renée should be here pretty soon. I can't do this alone. I need you to be on the team."

"Team? What team? Fine, I'm on the team, as you put it, just worn out."

"That's good. Devora?" Yehudit's stomach twisted in a tight knot. It was now or never. She wished she hadn't put off the discussion, but there was never a good time to have it. She had a good feeling about Renée. "It's just that I wanted to kind of mention one point before she gets here," Yehudit said.

"Go ahead."

"But before I start, let me just say that you know how much I value and appreciate and respect and like you. You know that, don't you?"

"You're making me nervous."

"Before Chaviva got married, she and I were, uh, talking?" Yehudit shifted uncomfortably in her seat.

"About…?"

"We were talking about someone we both care about very much and appreciate and respect, and like, and want the best for, and—"

"Were you discussing *me*?" Devora's eyes welled up. "You were! I don't believe this! Nice to know I can trust you not to gossip about me behind my back!"

"Don't think that was our intention."

"Why should I care what your intentions were? How would *you* feel if one of the few people you trusted decided to gossip about you?" Devora swiped angrily at her eyes.

"That's not what happened at all."

"The two of you have some nerve passing judgment on me. I thought…I hoped that at least here I'd be safe from being gossiped about by well-meaning people who don't have the slightest idea what I'm all about."

"We care! It wasn't gossip! We wanted…want to help you."

"Thanks for your concern." Devora's voice shook. "Help me with what?"

"You have to admit that your tendency to, um, be very, very cautious and scrupulous about, well, take *kashrus* for example. Not that it's not very, very important, but it really caused so much conflict." Yehudit looked at her desperately. *Throw me a lifeline! Don't make it so hard to talk to you.*

"Are you *punishing* me for taking halachah seriously? What's your issue? *Kashrus*? Not *treifing* up the kitchen? Chaviva was a *kallah*! Her head was in the clouds! She wasn't sleeping nights! Do you even know how many mistakes she made in the kitchen when she was talking to her fiancé on the phone? How many times I had to take the *milchig* ladle out of her hand, for example, just before she stirred the chicken soup with it? That girl seriously needed a *mashgiach temidi* at that point in her life. I'm sure she's back to herself now. I'm not implying that I wouldn't eat in her house."

"Why didn't *I* notice a problem if things were so drastic? I live here too. Wouldn't I have picked up on something?"

"Not necessarily. You never cook. You're allergic to the kitchen. When was the last time you made yourself more than a cup of coffee?"

"Anyway, that's all we spoke about, I promise you. I just explained to Chaviva that sometimes, different people have different standards and it can potentially lead to misunderstandings. It happens in the best of homes."

"I can't believe you're trying to downplay it."

"I don't think I am."

Devora stood up angrily. "I'm not going to be present at the interview, Yehudit. Do it yourself."

"Please don't do this!"

The doorbell rang.

"Give me a single good reason why not. I'm devastated."

"I know. I feel terrible. You're taking it the wrong way, and—"

The doorbell rang again.

"Please. We'll continue later. Come on, Devora. You know I'd never do anything to hurt you. Please, let's present a united front for Renée. Let's not spoil this opportunity." She eyed her roommate anxiously as the doorbell rang again.

* * *

I made it! Renée Lowenstein sighed in relief. The carved olive-wood sign on the door read "Y. Sapir and D. Levin." Interesting that the third roommate's name wasn't listed, but maybe they'd put up the sign after she moved out. Whatever. It really made no difference.

She rang the bell.

For six entire months, she'd been working to make this moment possible. For half a year, her main goal when she got up in the morning had been to do what she was doing right now: look at a potential place to move into, starting as soon as possible. If this new place looked okay inside—just okay, nothing more—and the women seemed normal, she was going to say yes. Yes, and then cope with whatever came up later. Anyway, what could possibly come up that she hadn't encountered and dealt with successfully in the eight years since she'd been on her own? She wasn't looking for friends. Not anymore. This was pure business as far as she was concerned. She rang the bell again.

I'll make it work for me. Anything is better than having my mother on my back. I know how to take care of myself. Always look out for number one. What do Chazal say? If I'm not for myself, who will take care of me? No one.

What's taking them so long? I hope they didn't forget that I'm coming.

She rang the bell again. *Where are they?*

A woman with sleek brown hair opened the door. Renée noted with relief that she didn't look a day over thirty. *No old-looking roommates for me. Not good for my image. People are liable to think I'm the same age. Though beggars can't be choosers. I'll go bananas if I live at home one second longer!*

The woman ushered her into a tiny living room where another woman, petite with curly reddish hair, nodded a greeting.

"Hi," the first one said. "I'm Yehudit Sapir, and this is Devora Levin. Come on in! Welcome to our humble abode."

3
Balancing Act

Estelle Hacohen, who had been Estelle Bruner for the first forty-two years of her life, rubbed her tired eyes. She'd been reading compositions, writing comments, and inserting corrections in the margins for the past three hours. Her concentration and her patience were both running dangerously low.

It's not fair to the girls to be marking their work when I'm in a grouchy mood, but when else am I supposed to do it? As it is, I'm way behind schedule. Maybe just a ten-minute catnap to lie down and recharge?

No. I'm not a baby. I can tolerate a little discomfort. No stopping till I'm done, and that's that, she decided. *I'm a professional. I'll transcend this grumpiness. It won't affect their grades. What I'll do is*—she flipped through the pile of papers, looking for the work the stronger students had handed in—*I'll mark the better ones first. That will put me in a better mood, knowing that the girls, at least most of them, absorbed most of what I put in so much thought and effort to teach.*

She worked steadily for the next half an hour or so, but the pile, which was comprised of the literary efforts of the fifth, sixth, and seventh grades she taught, looked the same: gigantic.

Groaning aloud, Estelle reached for the—was it the twenty-ninth paper that morning? Sarah Roth? Good. Poetry? Good, nice and short. It shouldn't take long.

After a moment's reading, she put down the paper.

"Safe"

Here I am
Safe
Your claws won't rip my heart.
Here.
Where it's safe.
I wish it were true.
Even here there is
No one to save me from
You.
The poison you leave behind
Echoes in my mind.
Your words
Your looks
Cut me down.
Your frown.
I ask why?
Why do you hate me?
What did I ever do?
Why do you see me
As an adversary?

Suddenly queasy, Estelle put her head on her desk, trying to think clearly.

This is a cry for help.

She marked the paper with an enormous red "100%" that sprawled across the entire first paragraph. After sketching a rose alongside it for good measure, she wrote, "Sarah, this is a powerful poem. It touched me deeply."

She put the composition on the pile of marked papers and reached for the next one, but her concentration was shot. She still had hours of work left to do. Visualizing another veiled rebuke from the administration, she tried hard to concentrate on the next offering, which was neither interesting nor well written. Whether a pupil got an 80 or an 82 on her report card seemed laughably trivial. There were real problems in the world.

Whoever thought up the concept of grades has a thing or two to answer for. So much unnecessary stress. Who can truly give a mark that reflects what each student invested, or failed to invest, in her work when they are so different one from another? When their abilities are so different? What an unfair system! But even more than that, what a dishonest system. How can I compare work that, let's say, an only child like Halleli Shalom does in utter tranquility in her beautiful private room at home with her devoted mother Menucha hovering at her shoulder, ready to answer any question, with this poem, wrenched from Sarah's heart under who knows what circumstances?

Estelle closed the file.

What I'm doing now is a total waste of time. Machon Atara is demanding that we, the teachers, waste our time now, at the end of the year, giving grades and more grades, as if anyone is going to do anything about them during summer vacation. As if our efforts will change anything at this point of the year. The good students will be happy with what I give them; the poor students will think I hate them. That's definitely a worthwhile accomplishment. Yay. What a waste of time. Too bad I'm so busy. Too busy for busy-work.

She shut down the computer, and sat, eyes closed, head on her hand, thinking.

How is it that a thinking, intelligent woman like Rabbanit Sudri hasn't come to these realizations on her own? Machon Atara ought to start a trend. Whatever happened to the concept of learning for its own sake? No comparisons, no competition, simple trust in ourselves and in our talmidos, and of course, in the relevance of our subject material to our lives. All we have to do is treat them like mature adults, and not hold the threat of grades over their heads. We don't need to flaunt our power over them. We simply need to make what we teach interesting enough to keep them engaged and then watch them blossom. Yes! And then...

And then... I don't want to know what would happen to the entire school system if grades were abolished. Unfortunately, human nature is human nature.

"Not happening," she said out loud, her face mouth twisted into a wry grin.

I'll take a break, and after that, it'll be back to the salt mines. Now then, Estelle. Break time does not have to equal snack time. Keep out of the kitchen if you know what's good for you.

She went into their living room. The stack of Shabbos magazines beckoned. She ripped open the plastic covers, but virtuously refrained from reading.

"You are my special Shabbos treat for long Shabbos afternoons," she informed them strictly. "You are my safeguard against mindless, unwanted snacking. See you later."

She couldn't relax. The poem had shattered her concentration.

She and Elchanan were eating all the Shabbos *seudos* home this week. Preparations had been unexpectedly time-consuming, which was the reason for the backlog of schoolwork that morning.

This is not how I operate. No free time, every minute accounted for. Not my speed at all. In spite of that, I'm always catching up. She winced. She'd already received one notice from Rabbanit Sudri about missing the first deadline for submitting her grades in a timely fashion. She'd been mortified.

What am I doing wrong? Why is this so hard? This shouldn't be hard. I've lived on my own for twenty years. Why can't I manage to carry just one more person?

Her feet carried her to the kitchen. She stopped short.

Oh, no. Unfair. Elchanan, how could you do this to me?

Plenty to do around here, she thought sourly. *Why didn't he keep his word?*

Her disappointed glance fell on the fleishig sink piled with dirty pots and containers she'd left for her husband to do, at his urging, after her cooking marathon the night before.

Elchanan said he'd do the dishes right after minyan this morning. Why does this keep happening? I told him last week that it bugs me to have dirty stuff piled up until almost the zman on Friday.

Soon, no doubt, Elchanan would come rushing in, all smiles, holding a bunch of beautiful roses, or carnations, and she, of course, was supposed to melt with pleasure and thank him, as behooved a wife of under six months. He was a doll, really he was, and what were a couple of dirty dishes, after all? Right? Wrong. They were a big deal, a very big deal, because they were Elchanan's job, one of the very few housekeeping jobs he actually had any idea how to do properly.

Today, she wouldn't wash the dishes to surprise him, the way she often did. No, she most definitely would not spoil him that way. Why hadn't she stayed up till she finished reading her students' work instead of having a cooking marathon?

I wanted to be a good wife.

It was just the two of them. Who needed so many side dishes? Soup. Five kinds of salads. Fish. It all took time—to buy, to prepare, to clean up after. Elchanan didn't seem to realize that he was developing a paunch. Didn't he care about his health?

Unless a miracle occurred, she was due for another written reprimand from Rabbanit Sudri, disguised as a reminder, the following week.

Some perspective here wouldn't hurt, Estelle, she chided herself. *Look at poor Sarah. If it's true… I hope not.*

What are a couple of dishes? Ten minutes, and this will all be a nonissue. You yourself said you needed a break from hunching over the computer screen. Be a good sport and just do it. Some elbow grease, soap, hot water. Build your home, your marriage, your future…

No! Who said that's called being a good wife? He doesn't even realize half the time that he says he'll do something and then it just slips his mind, and I end up doing it. It can't become a pattern around here. No way.

The key turned in the lock. Elchanan was home, holding an armful of tulips.

"Estelle! Hi! How's the grading going? Almost finished?"

Giving builds love. When does the mechanism click to On? I'm not feeling very affectionate at the moment, and don't tell me that washing the dishes is the secret.

"Is something wrong?"

"Yes. The dishes. You promised they'd be done this morning." She dabbed at her eyes. "I'm sorry. I'm being a baby, but we discussed this. I care about this more than I care about fl—"

"Than you care about what? Estelle, are you crying?"

She sniffed. "It's not important. These are beautiful. Let me put them in a vase. I love tulips, especially these beautiful yellow ones."

Elchanan seized the *fleishig* sponge remorsefully, then turned on the hot water full force.

Water splashed on the floor she'd mopped so meticulously the night before so that the entire house would be clean and ready for Shabbos. She'd have to either ignore the inevitable footprints or *sponga* the whole kitchen again.

I don't have time for this.

"It's probably women's work in your house, right?" she said to Elchanan. "You probably never had to wash dishes before you married me."

"No, I didn't," he admitted. "Even when I was living here on my own, before I met you, let's just say that putting paper plates in the trash was as far as I got in terms of housekeeping. Now, it's different. Before you start feeling guilty, I promise that I prefer it this way."

"It's just that I'm not in the mood to get another impersonal notice that I'm holding up the entire system because of my disorganization. I'm not the type to lose it over a bunch of dirty dishes."

"Do you want me to read some of those compositions for you?" he offered.

"No, the girls write these papers for my eyes only. I'm running into some very personal stuff."

"Aha."

"Unless maybe...if you don't mind... You don't know any of these students, so maybe you could work with me on calculating the averages and entering the results into the computer, let's say at around ten on *motza'ei Shabbos*?"

"Deal." He beamed.

She put the vase of flowers in the middle of the dining room table.

"Estelle, I forgot something very important. I'll be right back."

"Can't it wait till after Shabbos?"

"No."

What could possibly be so urgent? Estelle wondered.

After he left, she hastily redid the kitchen floor.

4
Today's Generation

"Why are you running yourself ragged in this heat when you have big girls home to help you? Why are you washing the kitchen floor? The work in this house can be divided three ways. Sarah is not nearly as incompetent as she pretends to be. She's very capable when she chooses to be. I don't know why you coddle her or why you encourage her laziness. You aren't doing her a favor. She's a big girl already, past bas mitzvah, and—"

Bubby went on and on. Sarah knew the speech by heart. Her stomach lurched. She fled to her room and shut the door as quietly as she was able to.

I'm not home. Please, Mommy. Say that I'm not home.

At the sound of footsteps coming down the hall, Sarah cringed and tried to make herself as small as possible. There was a knock on her bedroom door. Her mother stood there, face drawn.

"Sarah, please come and dust the living room furniture again. Now! Is it really too much to ask a big girl like you to do a good job the first time around?" She turned to leave.

"Mommy?"

Her mother turned around.

"Is Bubby still here?"

"What kind of a question is that?"

"But is she?"

"Yes, she is. She's in the kitchen. She and Zeidy are coming for Friday night."

"Please, Mommy, can I dust again after…she goes home?"

It was on the tip of Adina Roth's tongue to say, "No, absolutely not. You'll come into the kitchen and say hello like a *mensch*." Looking at her daughter's crumpled face and hunched posture, she couldn't say the words. She couldn't condone Sarah's behavior, either. True, her grandmother tended to be harsh with her, but why was Sarah so sensitive to the slightest hint of criticism?

"Do what you think is right," she told her daughter. "But when you do it, try to do a very good job."

"Because Bubby will check up on me?" Sarah asked bitterly, flopping down on her bed.

Her mother sat down next to her. "No. Because if you do a job, you should do it well."

Sarah sat up. "I don't understand why the furniture needs to be dusted every week. It's not a floor. No one walks on it."

"Do a good job." Her mother went out of the room, leaving the door ajar. Sarah could clearly hear the conversation taking place in the kitchen.

"*Nu*, where is she?"

"She's lying down for a little while."

"Why? She just got up. Why junior high school students need to have Fridays off is beyond me. They barely work in school anyhow. Every day another activity. But if she is off, she ought to be helping you prepare for Shabbos."

"She doesn't feel well."

"What's wrong this time?"

"She has a headache."

"Yes, very convenient. Last week it was a sore throat. She's lazy, that's all."

When she heard the front door close, Sarah emerged from her room. She plied her rag. Who cared about a little dust? *She* did, which meant they all did. Dust was so powerful. Whatever *she* cared about was powerful. So, if *she* came on Friday night, she'd be sure to notice if any surfaces were dusty. Sarah couldn't imagine what difference a little dust made, but it wasn't worth risking *her* criticism.

So scary, when she looks at me with so much disapproval. How am I different than all the other grandchildren? Mommy says that it's just my imagination, but it's not. It's not.

Sarah heard the phone ring in the kitchen, and her heart lifted. Mindy. Right, Mindy Lavie was supposed to call.

"I'll get it," she yelled, flinging down the rag. She raced into the empty kitchen. "Hello?"

"Hi. Sarah?"

"It's me."

"Sarah, my mother just had a great idea."

"Go ahead."

"It's like this." Mindy's voice bubbled with excitement. "Aviva's not home for Shabbos, and it's just my parents and me. I know it's Friday afternoon, and I know that your parents don't love it when you sleep over at friends, but could you please, please just come for tonight? And then, maybe I could come to you tomorrow?"

"I don't know." Sarah paced nervously, her ear pressed tightly against the phone. "I want to. It sounds great. I really want to, but I'm pretty sure that my parents won't let me come. Shabbos is in an hour. It's not the way we do things in my house. Maybe, just maybe, they might allow me to invite you, though it is at very short notice and my mother doesn't go for that."

"Your mother doesn't go for what?" Mrs. Roth rushed into the kitchen. "Sarah, don't you see the soup bubbling over? Is it too much to ask you to turn down a flame? Please get off the phone now. It's too close to Shabbos to be wasting your time on phone calls."

"Mommy, listen."

Her mother grabbed a roll of paper toweling and began mopping up the spilled soup.

"Look—it's all over the floor. Why must you live in your own little world, the one with no one but you and Mindy Lavie? I'll listen a different time. Please get off the phone and go get the pail and squeegee."

Sarah sniffled. Her mother looked at her in exasperation.

"Sarah, please. You know our house rules. You knew I would say no. Why do you insist on asking me for what I can't give you?"

5
Second Best

When does something become a problem? he wondered as he turned the key in the ignition. The streets were mostly empty at this hour, and he reached his destination quickly.

Elchanan entered the supermarket, which remained open late on Friday afternoon, and glanced around. Fruit. He'd look for some mouthwatering summer fruit. Now, where was the fruit aisle?

Some of the time, sometimes, but only sometimes, not most of the time, but, yes, I feel…it's almost as if she doesn't like my company all that much. But how could that be? She married me, didn't she? Why would she marry me if she didn't like spending time with me? Makes no sense. Why am I creating problems? It's wrong of me, wrong and ungrateful. Look at me, feeling bad for myself when my dreams have come true. Look at me, shopping for a Shabbos to be spent with my wife—my wife!

The one I traveled across the ocean to find. And I found her. I did. Hashem rewarded my efforts, my mesirus nefesh, if I want to use a giant term for a small deed, leaving all my loved ones behind. He gave me a chance to build my life.

You did that for me, Ribbono shel Olam, and I thank You. I thank You! I thank You a million times for the paltry struggles I have now, that I'm not still single, still searching. If not for Your chesed, I would be.

Watermelon. Big luscious-looking watermelons. No, they weren't on sale, but... Delicious ice-cold bright red watermelon *l'kavod Shabbos*. Could anything be more appropriate for their shared Shabbos meals?

He selected the largest watermelon he could find. Large was economical, right? Estelle liked him to be thrifty, which was a beautiful trait. He wouldn't want to be married to a woman who wasted money.

He sighed a little under his breath. Surely there was a middle ground to be found, somewhere. He wasn't poor, not after saving money by living at home for most of his life. Sure, he'd helped out with expenses here and there, and bought his parents gifts, but they didn't need to pinch pennies, either. He and Estelle were in *shanah rishonah*. Surely they could afford to indulge themselves just that little bit. And speaking of indulgence, there were a couple of bottles of fresh fruit juice that he knew Estelle adored. He put them in his shopping cart.

He paid for his purchases, and emerged from the air-conditioned supermarket, blinking in the blinding sunlight. He caught a glimpse of himself in the mirrored windows of the supermarket. Short, balding, rumpled clothing. Not very impressive, he had to admit, but then he never had been too impressive physically.

She didn't marry me for my looks, that's for sure. Estelle's a deep, thinking person, so I'm certain she doesn't care.

Maybe she does still care, a tiny little bit, but not much. No enough to make a difference.

It's not that she doesn't have warm friendships or good relationships with her family and colleagues. She does, which means that we will too. She has the capacity to connect and to care. It's one of the reasons I married her. She just needs to get used to me, that's all.

I waited over twenty years to find her. What's another month or two?

* * *

It was only three. Working in tandem, she and Elchanan had done the impossible. Everything was ready for Shabbos. Amazing.

Unbelievable what one hour of daylight savings time accomplished, how it completely altered the feel of every day, and most of all, Friday afternoons. What should she do during the three-and-a-half hours before candle lighting? Definitely no grading until she did something about getting Sarah Roth the help she needed. No more doubts about whether the poem was true. It was.

Who to call? Sheila Leipzig was subbing as the seventh-grade homeroom teacher. The fact that she was single might mean nothing in this context, but it also might mean that she was at loose ends on this long Friday afternoon and wouldn't mind a school-related call. As a matter of fact, Estelle's long years as an older single had taught her that Sheila just might be feeling disconnected from the world out there. She might be feeling superfluous. Or maybe not? Sheila was reserved. It was hard to tell. Who else could she consult with?

Sarah's homeroom teacher, Yocheved Sutton, was returning from maternity leave in less than two weeks, but Estelle wouldn't dream of disturbing her now. She could try Avital Salamonte—oops, Kantor—Machon Atara's dedicated guidance counselor, but she too was a relatively fresh newlywed.

Like me, Estelle realized with a start. Somehow, she had never thought of herself in those terms.

So, Sheila it will be. Estelle looked up Sheila's number on the school listing. Surprisingly, Sheila's cell phone number wasn't listed. Sheila lived with her parents. An *erev Shabbos* school-related call could be awkward unless it was truly urgent. Was Sarah's poem a cry for help? She wasn't sure. Was it urgent? Also not sure. Maybe whatever it was didn't qualify as an emergency. Important, very, but urgent, no.

One more day won't make a difference. I'll look for Sarah in school on Sunday, and also notify Sheila then. We'll take it from there.

The sound of Elchanan's key in the door startled her. She put away the class list and went to greet her husband.

If I'm a newlywed, and I guess I probably am one, I want to do it right. He's not exactly my dream husband, but…even so. Maybe I just need to get used to being married.

I hope it's that.

"Hi. I bought us a little surprise here, *l'kavod Shabbos kodesh."* Elchanan hefted the watermelon onto the kitchen counter.

Estelle's jaw dropped. "Elchanan! How could you! Watermelon is thirty shekel a kilo! No…more!"

"I remember your telling me that watermelon is your very favorite summer fruit."

"It is, but—"

"But?"

"Extravagance makes me so uncomfortable," she blurted.

Instantly, his expression of delight faded.

"Maybe…just this once, *l'kavod Shabbos kodesh,"* she added hastily.

Mollified, Elchanan smiled at her and began rummaging in the pantry for plastic containers.

"What are you doing?"

"We need to cut this up and put it in the refrigerator," he explained.

"Go, I'll do that. We don't keep the containers in that closet, and that knife hardly cuts butter. I'll do it."

He handed her the knife. "You *are* pleased, Ess? I do remember your telling me how much you look forward to summer and watermelon."

She relented. "Of course I'm pleased. Thank you so much."

After Estelle finished cutting up the succulent fruit, she

rearranged the contents of the refrigerator to make room for the containers.

An entire watermelon for two people! A whole watermelon at top price. Why does he insist on doing these things?

6
Comfort Zone

Elchanan sang Kiddush in a tremulous voice. He still couldn't believe that here he was, in a home of his own, in Yerushalayim, with a wife standing opposite him concentrating intently on his words. It was almost too much happiness to bear, especially when he reflected on the fact that he'd almost despaired of ever reaching this moment.

Intuiting his feelings, Estelle smiled at him understandingly as she drank the rest of the wine in the silver goblet, a wedding gift from Machon Atara's linguistics staff.

"You actually enjoy the sour white stuff," she told him, grimacing comically. "I would never have believed you to be a dry white wine type of guy."

He chuckled. "I never would have believed that you never drink anything but grape juice."

"Even that's a bit much for me. Too sickeningly sweet. Orange juice, pomegranate juice—now those are real drinks."

"I know. Just a moment." He went into the bedroom, where he'd hidden two plastic bottles. "Voilà, Madam."

Estelle looked down at the table, struggling to adjust to Elchanan's demonstrative way of relating to her. She blushed. "So that's where you went so late this afternoon. I didn't see any bottles left in the corner grocery. Don't tell me you schlepped to the supermarket!"

Elchanan nodded, his eyes dancing.

"That supermarket is a zoo on Friday afternoon! How long did you have to wait in line?"

"What difference does it make? It's my pleasure. I know it adds to your *oneg Shabbos.*"

"It does. Thank you. But why get both? They're so expensive. Even one is too much. You don't need to spoil me, Elchanan. I'm a big girl." She poured the pomegranate juice into crystal goblets, admiring the way the light sparkled on the ruby-red beverage, and added ice cubes from the silver bowl on the table, another wedding present from the school, this time from the general staff administration. *Just last year,* Estelle reflected, *no one on that staff had dreamed that I'd have my own home, my own Shabbos table, and…a wonderful husband. Chasdei Hashem.*

"Let me enjoy myself," Elchanan said. "I like making you happy."

Estelle nodded and felt her cheeks flush. "I know. Thanks. Let's save the other juice for *shalosh seudos.* I'll serve the soup." She stood up. "It's fine, no need to help me," she added hastily as Elchanan rose to his feet.

She returned to the dining room carrying an expensive china tureen, a wedding gift from Menucha and Eliezer Shalom. Menucha, Estelle's former roommate and still best friend, had spared no effort in encouraging Estelle throughout her dating period and subsequent engagement to Elchanan.

"Tell me when it's enough," she said as she ladled soup into his bowl.

"I love soup!" Elchanan said.

Humming under her breath, Estelle filled his bowl and then hers. She moved the bowl of soup nuts nearer to him and sat down.

"What did your parents say when you spoke to them on *erev Shabbos*?" she asked. "Anything special? Did you tell them I'd already lit candles, so I couldn't come to the phone?"

Elchanan put down his spoon. "Definitely. And I sent them your love. This soup is delicious, and it feels great on my throat."

"You didn't tell me that your throat hurts! When you're done, there's tons more in the pot."

"It just started this afternoon."

She poured him another glass of pomegranate juice.

"Thanks. News from my parents? Nothing major. My father mentioned that there's a youngish couple who are close to my parents, the Rubinoffs, who are coming to Israel sometime this month."

"Hmm."

"My father thought maybe it would be nice if we had them over for a Shabbos while they're here." At Estelle's blank look, he added, "Don't you remember them? They were at our wedding, came especially from the States? Avigdor and Kayla Rubinoff?"

"No, sorry. I met a lot of people that day, your brothers and sisters were there, and your parents. A lot of it was a blur."

"Understood. It was an intense day for both of us."

"They came especially for the wedding? That's nice of them. What did you say to your father?" she asked as a sudden tight feeling came over her. "Elchanan? I hope you said yes."

"I told him that it was probably okay, that I'd check with you because you're under a lot of pressure from school at the moment. Isn't that what you wanted me to say?"

Estelle frowned. "I don't want them to think that I can't manage a simple Shabbos meal without getting all bent out of shape."

"Who would think that? My parents?"

She nodded silently, not trusting her voice.

"No way. My parents aren't the critical type at all."

Not of you.

"Please don't worry, Estelle. When the Rubinoffs come, they'll give us a call. I'm sure we'll be able to work something out—if they're not too busy touring to spare us anything but a phone call. If they can't clear their calendar for a Shabbos meal, maybe they can drop by for dessert during the week."

"When are they coming?"

"Monday." Elchanan cleared his throat. "My father also asked if I could meet them at the airport."

"What did you say?"

"I said yes. My parents have taken the two of them under their wing."

"I have a bad feeling about this," Estelle blurted.

"A bad feeling? About what? My father said they'll be staying at one of those posh hotels downtown. Maybe we'll get a gourmet meal out of it." He chuckled.

"It's not funny. I'm serious."

"Sorry." He leaned forward. "Why do you have a bad feeling?"

"I'm going to have to prove myself to your parents, and I don't have the time right now. I'm barely managing as it is."

Menucha would tell me to take it step by step. She'd probably tell me to invite them to stay with us. She'd tell me that this is my chance to give to my new husband, to build our marriage. I'm inundated with opportunities to give to him. Elchanan's nice about my limitations. He accepts them, so whatever Menucha thinks is kinda irrelevant, even if she does imply that Elchanan deserves more from me than what I give him. Maybe he does.

"You'll see, Estelle. They're coming to daven at *kivrei tzaddikim*. They're going to be so busy we'll be lucky if we can snag them for a meal."

"Oh. Well," she said hesitantly, "if we do host them, try to let me know as far ahead of time as possible. I'm not a last-minute person."

"Will do."

"I'll bring in the fish." She collected their soup bowls and was soon back with a steaming platter of salmon baked with potatoes and carrots. "I made that recipe we had at the *shevah berachos* Menucha and Eliezer held for us. I noticed that you liked it a lot. I hope it came out okay."

He smiled gratefully. "Everything you make is scrumptious. Soup and salmon at one meal. You're spoiling me, Estelle. And these salads! Why did you make so much food when you're under pressure? But thanks! Salmon is my favorite fish, especially sweet and sour."

"I know. That's why I made it. Tell me if it's good. How many slices do you want?"

"Easy does it. I'm full from that delicious soup. Orange soup, you called it? What's in it?"

"Sweet potatoes, pumpkins, carrots, a few white potatoes, onions, a touch of cinnamon, ginger, and pepper. That's all." She served herself some salmon.

After the fish, Elchanan began to sing *zemiros* in his pleasant tenor voice, and Estelle joined him.

At a break in the singing, she asked him, "Do you want more salmon?"

"It's delectable, but I'm saving room for the main course."

Silence.

"That *was* the main course," she said finally, in a small voice. "Shabbos comes in so late... But, if you're still hungry… Remember we spoke about eating lightly so late at night?"

"Right, we did." He held out his plate. "I'd love some more potatoes."

Later, when Estelle was reading by the light of the Shabbos lamp in the living room, he took three slices of turkey roll from the platter in the fridge, rearranging the slices carefully after he did so. Could he take just one more slice? He wasn't hungry exactly, but his stomach didn't feel full. Carefully, he lifted one more slice off the platter. Nah. Estelle would notice, and her feelings would be hurt. Sighing lightly under his breath, he found himself wishing there was some good *mezonos* around to munch on. In the course of their six-week engagement, he'd noticed that Estelle never ate cake or ice cream.

"I battled my weight for so many years," she'd explained. "Nosh is the easiest thing for me to give up, and I find that it makes a big difference. I try hard not to have it around. If I have it in the house, I eat it, and, bye-bye weight loss."

She'd never asked him not to bring home the sweet and salty junk food he loved, but it was a small sacrifice he made for her.

He arranged some peaches and apples on a platter. He thought fleetingly about adding some watermelon slices but decided not to. Estelle hadn't seemed as thrilled with his purchases as he'd hoped she'd be.

Was she just stressed due to the combined pressures of running a home and finishing up the school year?

7
Moving On

"Did I make a mistake with the time?" Renée asked.

Yehudit and Devora glanced at each uneasily.

"No, not at all," Yehudit said. "Something came up last minute."

"I wrote down the time we agreed on, right after we spoke. Still, after I rang your doorbell so many times without getting an answer, I thought that maybe I got the time wrong."

"No, you were right on time," Yehudit repeated.

There was a pause.

"Thanks so much for being prompt," Devora said quietly, not wanting to torpedo the meeting despite her hurt and anger over what she considered Yehudit's betrayal. "You didn't have a hard time finding us, did you?"

"Not at all. I'm familiar with the neighborhood."

"That's good," Yehudit said.

"Something to drink?" Devora offered, indicating a pitcher of water on the table.

"No, thanks." Renée looked around. "Maybe later. This place is cute. On the small side, like you told me on the phone, Yehudit, but definitely livable. It has potential. It's a lot nicer than some of the dumps I've seen. I don't know how some landlords have the nerve to charge rent for their so-called apartments."

Yehudit nodded. "Unfortunately, I know exactly what you mean. Would you like to get down to business? Business before pleasure, I always say."

"Totally."

Yehudit opened a door directly off the living room to reveal a small room, empty save for a bed and wardrobe. "This is the room that's currently for rent."

Renée walked in, opened a closet door, then looked out the window.

"I know it doesn't look like much, so empty," Devora said apologetically from the doorway. "Chaviva, the girl who got married, just vacated it." She looked at the tall, stylishly dressed girl who had gone silent once again and added, "It's also a little too small, maybe? I know you live in a villa in Neot Yaar. Here in Shikun Shoshan, we live more simply. I guess you could put it that way."

"My *parents* live in a villa in Neot Yaar," Renée corrected her, turning around to face her. "I personally have learned to lower my expectations. I'm paying my own way. I've been living in rental apartments since I turned twenty-four, and most of them were right here in this neighborhood. Thankfully, in the new part, not where the shacks and dumps are. The room's small, no getting around it. Still, as an interior decorator and licensed architect, I do see that there are ways to make this space look larger. I see a lot of possibilities."

"You say you've lived here for years?" Devora asked. "I thought I recognized you, but I couldn't remember from where."

"Who knows? Probably just from around. It's great to be in a place where a single person's the norm. Since I was laid off from my job a couple of months ago, I've been living at home. Don't ask. Not a single around for miles. I felt like a freak. My mom is at me constantly, pressuring me about dating and all that stuff. I'm sure I don't have to give you all the gory details. I was out of there the moment I started to earn a decent salary."

"Let's go back to the living room," Yehudit suggested. "Unless you're not done here?"

"I'm done. There's not much to see."

The three women returned to the living room.

"I've looked at five different places," Renée stated, "and this is the nicest one. I like the way you set it up, so that it looks like a home, not a dorm."

Yehudit smiled at her frankness. "Thanks. We like it. We do try to make it homey. We've been here for five years. But why are we all standing? Sit down. Have a drink." She gestured at the dining room table.

"Lucky you. I've moved seven times in the past eight years," Renée said as she took a seat.

Devora waved at the crystal tray holding tulip-shaped glasses, cold drinks, and ice cubes. "Water? Cola? Apple juice?"

"Just water. Thanks. You don't have to serve me." Renée poured herself a full glass of water, quickly said a *brachah,* and gulped it down thirstily.

Yehudit waited a beat before pouring apple juice for Devora and cola for herself. "Let me tell you about us," she said. "I work as a tour guide, woman's groups only of course, and Devora is a school librarian. She's also a professional pianist."

"Don't exaggerate," Devora corrected her. "There's no space here for a piano, so I'm completely out of practice. Do you like music, Renée?"

Renée, who wasn't especially fond of any sort of music, faked an enthusiastic nod.

"We live low key," Yehudit continued. "No parties past ten. We did host a *shevah brachos* for our roommate, Chaviva, who just got married, and it went on a little later, but in general."

"Got it. Sounds good to me." Renée nodded approvingly. "I'm tired of living in happening places. When I finally get home from work at night, I want peace and quiet. Maybe when I was in my twenties I appreciated the action, but not anymore. Before I forget, Sheila Leipzig told me to give you her regards, Devora. She says you used to be next-door neighbors."

"Sheila Leipzig! That's a blast from the past. How do you know her?"

"We were classmates in high school. Too many years ago to remember, but she and I kept up, and in the past year, we've gotten to be good friends again."

Maybe not so good though, Renée thought. Why doesn't she want me to move in with her, if and when she gets a place? What does she think, that I'll steal the silver? So lame, to tell me that she's afraid it will hurt our relationship. She's selfish, that's all. Too bad. Any place she buys will be much nicer than this. Well, her loss. I could show her the ropes, as I've been on my own for the past eight years, while she's been living it up in her parents' villa. The Leipzigs must know how to let her live, unlike some parents I could mention. In any case, she's dragging her feet. At this point, there's nothing to discuss.

"Small world. What's she up to nowadays? Where's she living?"

"Home. Her choice," Renée said. "Her parents are willing to buy her an apartment, in Neot Yaar, where they live." She felt like adding, *don't waste your pity on her. Where is she and where am I? Imagine—a place of her own! That would be a dream come true, but I don't dare even dream it. I'd change places with her anytime.*

* * *

"Do you want to go first, or should I?" Yehudit asked, picking up the tray of drinks. Renée had just left, promising to be in touch by the following evening. "You weren't too comfortable. I'm sorry."

"I'm just fine. Let's approach this without emotional involvement."

"You're not serious, are you? Forget it, Devora. Let's talk later. You're still feeling hurt by what I said before."

"I am."

"So forget discussing this now."

"I want to. Let's get it over with. She's not fresh from home, she's lived in similar situations, she can pay the bills. Finished. So she's young. What difference does it make? I'm certainly not planning on being friends with her. That being the case, what's the point of looking endlessly? We'll never find anyone perfect. We'll never find anyone even near perfect. It's all business this time around, as far as I'm concerned."

"I suppose sounding tough *could* be her defense mechanism against being hurt." Yehudit nodded slowly. "I'm trying to visualize Renée participating in all sorts of situations here with us. I can sort of see it. Can you?"

"Who knows? Maybe. I can't say I care that much, either way. I don't see any glaring red warning signals. I say, go for it."

"This is no way to make a major decision," Yehudit said helplessly.

"It's up to you."

"Should we call back another couple of candidates?"

"Your choice."

Yehudit sighed in defeat. "Let's see what she says. I personally think that she'll want to move in with us. Didn't you get that impression?"

"Whatever. It makes no difference to me one way or another."

Yehudit's patience snapped. "Devora Levin! Would you mind stopping that right now?"

Devora's voice was dangerously low. "Would you mind not yelling at me? Don't you think you've done enough damage for one night? Don't you realize that gossiping about me and lecturing me, giving me *mussar* about my behavior might be just the slightest bit off-putting?"

"I told you. Or I tried to tell you. We weren't gossiping."

"I disagree." Devora's fair cheeks were pink with insult. "Not only did you and Chaviva go behind my back, but you also condemned me without a trial. So..." She stood up. "I need some space. I need some time to absorb all the—" She choked on her tears and ran out of the room.

Yehudit heard the door gently close. Pure Devora. She would never slam a door, no matter how she felt.

More than anything in the world, Yehudit longed to knock on that hermetically sealed door. She didn't, though. When Devora said she needed space, it was final.

Yehudit wondered if things would ever be the same between them.

8
The Right Choice

I shouldn't even be thinking this way, Geula Leibowitz warned herself. *Thoughts lead to deeds, and deeds lead to being broke, and being broke leads to no place I want to be. Which is why I'm not spending any more money today. Not a single shekel!*

Enough is enough. Tomorrow is another day. I don't have to stuff everything into one day. On the contrary, when it comes to spending money, procrastination pays off, big time.

She had just finished her weekly shopping at the neighborhood grocery, conveniently located across the street from her ground-floor studio apartment. Outside, she hefted the four bulging bags of groceries, smiling in satisfaction.

Ah. Such riches. Fresh, delicious-looking peaches, the first of the season. They were prohibitively expensive, but she'd only bought three instead of the seven that were in the box. She'd also gotten a sweet-smelling, great-for-the-hair brand-name shampoo, and fancy paper goods, all so pretty. *Abundance.*

Having a full pantry felt so good. The grocery was the only place where she bought on credit, the one place she allowed herself to spend money she didn't have in her purse or in her bank account. This single dispensation she permitted herself was the only way she could splurge for Shabbos and *Chagim*—and both were a mitzvah to spend lavishly on. Plus gifting. It all added up, shekel by shekel. So, here she was back to—what else? Money.

Yes, money. A full wallet, nice and full for the first time in two weeks.

Lighthearted with relief that she actually had financial means, even disposable income, to—yay!—dispose of without calculation, she came back to earth with a thud. Her relief was premature. The inconvenient facts were that her winter electric bills were *way* overdue, and they were extremely high. Purim and Pesach had both been very expensive. This was the first month she could even contemplate covering both bills.

No, she had no disposable cash this month either. What a disappointment!

I've got over a thousand shekels due anytime I want to fork it out. Why did I use so much heat? On the other hand, was I supposed to freeze? And, with this head cold, which just won't quit even though winter was months ago, saving on heat wasn't an option. Even though—she mopped her damp forehead—*it's close to impossible to imagine being too cold now, in this burning heat early in June. On the other hand, with the money I've earned—my own, through hard work—shouldn't I be able to go beyond the bare essentials? Will there never be any room in the budget for extras?*

She put away her groceries, which included six bars of expensive Swiss chocolate—Schmerling's, to be precise—and shook her aching arms in relief. Then she sat down to contemplate how to spend her luxurious free afternoon.

She'd merited an unexpected day of vacation. Four grades of

the girls she taught were on one- or two-day trips, depending on their ages, and miracle of miracles, she'd been given the afternoon off rather than being kept in school to substitute. She yawned. She could take an early afternoon nap, a treat she dreamed about during her long teaching days as the clock hit just around now, one thirty in the afternoon.

No. Not a nap. If I were exhausted, that would be another story.

I could finish up calculating my grades. No. I have no patience to be holed up with the computer. I'll stay after hours in school tomorrow, do it then. Maybe.

I'll walk, get some exercise. And buy something small and fun. A minor purchase, but not a necessity.

She switched to her sneakers, grabbed a water bottle, crammed a hat over her thick, shoulder-length graying curls, and locked the door.

Freedom! I need—no, I want… (Who cares about the terminology?) Well, fine. For honesty's sake, I'll be accurate: I'm treating myself to a special something. Maybe one of those flowered cotton sweaters I saw on sale in Zara and have been eyeing all month.

No! I can't afford clothes now. Maybe some perfume.

Something.

After last month's ridiculous privations, enough is enough! I've been under the weather and working anyhow. If I were still at my old job, I would have missed a day or two of work, but as a new teacher, I want my attendance record to be as perfect as I can manage.

Now, I deserve a little pick-me-up.

I deserve? No one deserves anything.

So…I really want something new and exciting,

I won't go to an expensive place. If there's nothing in the industrial center, then forget buying anything at all. If there are sales, I won't get two for the price of one, I'll get only one.

Plus, I'll walk there. The whole way. It's at least half an hour, which is healthy for my blood pressure.

Geula set out at a rapid pace, pausing every so often to cough and blow her nose. *Maybe I'm too run down to take a long walk. But everyone says that exercise is like medicine, good for body and mind. Anyhow, it must be an allergy, because no cold lasts this long. I should get it checked. Summer vacation's coming. I'll do it then.*

She soon found herself across the street from her favorite craft store.

Remember this morning's decision! This store is beyond your budget this month. Even if it's your favorite place in the entire world to buy jewelry crafts.

I knew I should have taken a nap after I got what I needed in the grocery, but no harm done. I can still leave, and at least I got in a walk. I'm a full-fledged adult. I can delay gratification. I most certainly can.

She turned on her heel, heading determinedly toward the bus stop. The digital sign showed that her bus home wasn't due to arrive for another twenty-eight minutes.

Twenty-eight minutes!

A wave of exhaustion swept over her. Her stomach was growling. *I should have eaten breakfast.* She took another sip from her water bottle and then another, but her stomach was not appeased. She wondered if she should get a cup of coffee in the small restaurant across the street. She decided against it. Three times what it would cost her to make it at home, and besides, she'd already drunk enough coffee that morning. No need for more caffeine.

Twenty-five minutes to go. She jiggled her foot restlessly.

It's boiling out here.

A cab passed by and slowed. She shook her head regretfully.

I can't afford a cab. I'll just go back to the store, look around, and if I see something cheap, then maybe…

It's wrong to go into a store if I'm not planning to buy anything. Besides, if I spend, let's see, around forty shekels, that would be the equivalent of what a cab would cost, and it will be a quality purchase that will last me a lot longer than one little cab ride. Twenty-four minutes left to wait for this bus, and I won't even get a seat when it comes.

Slowly, Geula retraced her footsteps and headed toward the air-conditioned interior of the store.

Forty shekels. That's my outer limit.

No impulse buying now, she cautioned herself. *You went overboard the way you spent your summer bonus last year, buying that area rug and easy chair for the apartment. Okay, you're not sorry about it. You need to live in a normal-looking place, with decent furniture.*

Am I rationalizing? Could be, but should a forty-five-year-old woman be agonizing over spending a measly forty shekels? Yes, if she just took a job that offered a full day's less work than she had before.

Did I have a choice? The other school that was hiring would have been a disaster for me to teach at. No way could I have been anything but a policewoman there, and not even an effective one at that.

So, even if my former school did close, and I desperately needed a job, any job, I still need to feel satisfied with what I do every day.

I'm very lucky there was an opening at Machon Atara. Pure siyatta diShemaya. It's a good place to teach.

In addition, I have a free day to pursue my interests and hobbies. That's the price I agreed to pay. Hah. Price to pay. Very apt phrasing. Here's the equation.

On the plus side, enjoyable employment, more free time. On the minus side, less cash. Simple math. Five hundred shekels less every month.

I hate math.

No one could believe I landed a job there, but their art teacher moved to another city, and Hashem arranged for Rabbanit Sudri to interview me before anyone else applied, so what's a little poverty compared to working in a nice school? They couldn't give me all the hours I had at my last job, but I promised myself I'd live frugally.

She circled around to the store's window and peered longingly at the display.

There's a "buy one, get one free" sale, and it ends tomorrow.

I save if I buy those unique Swarovski beads in all the colors I'm missing. None of the other chains sell those colors.

Nechama Rotter asked me to design a necklace for her to wear at her daughter's wedding. She usually wears blue or turquoise to accent her eyes. She'll be impressed and probably recommend me to family and friends. It's an investment.

I'll more than cover the cost of whatever I buy. Whatever I spend here will earn me money in the long run.

Geula shifted her weight on her aching feet.

It's almost summer vacation, a little over a month to go, and we get all kinds of bonuses then. If I permitted myself to buy on credit, I'd never be making all these petty calculations. If I had a husband, he'd buy me the occasional gift, right?

But I'm all by myself. No husband, no kids, never will be. I'm feeling down. I can't shake this cold. Who am I kidding? Myself? It's irresponsible to spend what I don't have, no matter what the reason.

I can still get out of here before I do something I'll later regret. Next time I'm leaving my money at home! Why struggle with temptation?

She looked at her watch. *Fifteen minutes isn't that long to wait for a bus, even in the heat. It won't kill me to stand on a crowded bus, either, but I am tired.*

She drained the rest of her water bottle, feeling slightly woozy.

The guard at the craft store door looked at her curiously.

He's probably wondering why I'm standing outside instead of entering or moving on. I shouldn't make his difficult job even harder. That's it. I'm going back to the bus stop this very minute.

Instead, her feet carried her into the store. She hastily made her selection, and, casting one more yearning glance around, headed reluctantly to the checkout counter. On the way, her eye caught sight of a stunning gold-and-amethyst ring, marked down to seventy percent of its original price.

It's mine! I love it! I'll get it for myself as an end-of-the-year present. This will enhance everything I own. It's rich looking, feminine, and gorgeous. I could never afford it at its usual price. Besides, if I don't buy myself jewelry, no one will. I'll save it for Eliyahu's bar mitzvah next week. I didn't buy anything new for that, and I'm his aunt.

Gingerly, she placed it on her long, tapered index finger. *Gorgeous! Oh, forget it. Not today. Maybe it will still be here in a month.*

As if.

She replaced the ring in the display case and steered herself resolutely toward the checkout counter. There were only two other people in line. She checked her watch. Seven minutes to pay and still make the bus.

"Excuse me." A woman who had just walked over to wait behind her cleared her throat. When Geula— engaged in calculations, trying to figure out if maybe, just maybe she could afford the ring—didn't respond, the woman tapped her on the shoulder.

Geula turned around. Her interlocutor was tall. Her brunette windblown *sheitel* was held back by a boldly colored bandana.

I'd never combine magenta and burnt orange, especially not in such, um, striking patterns, but apparently, she has the self-confidence to carry it off.

"I can't believe you missed it, with those lovely amethyst earrings you're wearing. There's an absolutely phenomenal ring someone's going to grab if you wait one more second. It's a match made in Heaven, I tell you. And cheap. Go for it. You only live once."

"I tried it on. It's exquisite and cheap, but…"

"Grab it!"

"I'm, ah, temporarily on a tight budget." Geula flushed. "It's been, um, kind of an expensive month. I need to be prudent about spending."

"It's good to stick to a budget, but sometimes you have to spend in order to save. Don't you know that? I know what I'm talking about. I'm a *sheitel macher*. I can't allow you to let this opportunity pass you by."

Geula's eyes widened in surprise. "That's kind of you, but I don't think I can afford—"

"I make *sheitels*. I design clothing. I also do color consultations, makeup, and hair. I must tell you that if I had your long, elegant fingers, and your lovely silvery hair, not to mention your beautiful gray eyes—or are they hazel?—I wouldn't hesitate for a second. You'll look marvelous. Grab it now, before someone else does. Go for it. I promise you you'll never regret it. I was in yesterday, and that piece wasn't here. And let me tell you something, I doubt it will be here tomorrow."

Geula capitulated, pushing her qualms aside to be dealt with later. It was so simple, after all. So simple to be pushed in the direction she was longing to go.

As the cashier wrapped up her 210-shekels worth of purchases, her bus chugged noisily past.

Half an hour's wait till the next one. A cab home was only forty shekels. She had no more strength to do battle with herself.

There goes my money, bit by bit, as usual. Now I'll have to spend my savings to cover the 700-shekel electric bill.

Why did I do it?

I ought to march right back into that store and return this ring, that's what. I should do that, but…at the moment, I can't. It's just too humiliating.

A fool and her money are soon parted, but I'm no fool.

Or am I?

No, just maybe a bit impulsive, and I love this ring. I've been working so hard. I'm not giving it back. No way. They would probably just give me store credit anyhow.

To make herself feel better, she unwrapped the gift box and stuck the ring on her finger. It really was special.

The woman from the store sat down next to her at the bus stop. Geula looked up.

"I see that you took my advice," the woman commented approvingly. "Good for you. If you don't mind my asking you something personal…"

"Yes?" Geula said warily.

"That is your hair, isn't it?"

Geula blinked in surprise. Whatever she'd been expecting, it wasn't that. She nodded.

"Like I said, I'm a *sheitel macher,*" the woman continued. "Your hair would make a gorgeous *sheitel*."

"It would?"

"Yes. That shade of silvery gray, with streaks of chestnut and dark blond. And besides, your hair is so thick and healthy looking."

"Thank you," Geula stammered.

"If you ever want to sell it, if you ever find yourself in need of a bit of spare cash, feel free to give me a call. Here's my business card."

* * *

At her nephew Eliyahu's bar mitzvah, all the assembled female relatives exclaimed admiringly at her perfectly matched, creative ensemble.

"You always find the nicest clothing!" her teenaged niece exclaimed. "Where do you buy it all? I never see stuff like that when I go shopping. You must go shopping every day. Take me with you next time you go. Can I try on your ring?"

Geula slipped the ring off her finger and handed it over.

Her parents live frugally. They are the real deal. No cabs or takeout for them on a kollel budget. I don't want to make her long for a lifestyle that will be beyond her reach if her life goes the way they daven it will. She'll marry a guy who wants to learn long-term, no money for luxuries or extras. Perhaps if they budget very carefully? How should I answer her?

"Penina, none of it's expensive. It just looks like it is." She smiled. "I keep my eyes open for bargains. You know how I enjoy the challenge of shopping in vintage shops. Plus, jewelry-making is my hobby."

"Still..." Penina's mother, Leah, joined the conversation. "Everything costs something, and any money spent in one place is money not spent or not available elsewhere."

"Guess I'm spoiled, but I love pretty things."

"No, you aren't, so stop apologizing for nothing. It's not a crime to have a stunning wardrobe if it makes you happy."

"I don't want anyone to think that I'm…uh…self-centered. Even if… Who knows? Maybe I am." She laughed self-deprecatingly. "By the way." She dug around in her purse. "*Afikomen* presents for the kids who didn't steal the *afikomen*," she explained as she handed over the six Schmerling's chocolate bars, still in the grocery's plain plastic bag.

"That's silly. We all love your style. Why do you feel that you must tell us if something's a hand-me-down or from a *gemach*?"

"I told you already. I don't want to give the impression that I'm materialistic and spend tons of money on myself," Geula explained.

"You're worth it," Leah said warmly. "Every shekel."

See? Geula said to herself. *Everyone thinks it's okay if you treat yourself once in a while. But who will cover the shortfall? Whatever. I'll just be extra careful for the next two weeks.*

* * *

Home at last.

Leah Leibowitz, the proud and exhausted mother of the bar mitzvah boy, sank into a kitchen chair and slipped off her heels. Geula had remained at the *simchah* until the end, the last guest to leave, in spite of the fact that she worked the following day and it was already midnight.

She looked beautiful. Not a day over thirty. But why doesn't she dye her hair? That gray is so aging. It adds at least ten years to her age. Her face is still so young. If she'd just dye her hair, she could easily pass for under forty. Should I suggest it to her? She doesn't have sisters, and it's not the type of suggestion a brother is likely to make. The problem is, I can't think of a tactful way to bring it up, and she'll be hurt no matter what I say.

I wish the idea would occur to her without my saying anything. That would definitely be the best. She's aware that nowadays the younger a woman looks, the better. Especially a woman who still hasn't established a home of her own.

Leah's eyelids began to droop as the tension and exhaustion of the preceding weeks took their toll.

She can't be serious about what she keeps telling us, that we shouldn't suggest anyone new, that she's through with shidduchim. Forget her hair. How can she just give up the most important parts of life?

I hope she's just temporarily burnt out.

9 Take a Chance

Yerachmiel Kantor picked up the phone on the second ring.

"Hi. Avital just spoke to Sheila again about when she can meet you," Menachem Kantor said to his older brother. "Sheila can make it tomorrow if it works for you. Or any day this week."

"She has nothing planned for the entire week?"

"She makes dating and marriage a top priority. Good for her."

"Good for her, but *I* can't make it this week. Sorry. She certainly took her time to decide. A month! Well, now it's my turn to be unavailable. I'm all booked up. People are getting married right and left before *Sefirah* starts."

"Okay, okay. You don't have to get so worked up. We can discuss this calmly. You don't need to yell."

"Spare me the lecture. I'll try to speak softly. Are you sure you didn't have to twist Sheila's arm to get her to date someone my age, eight years older than she is?"

"I told you, but I'll tell you again. The answer is no. Where's your self-confidence?"

"In my pocket." Yerachmiel paused. "Is there anything I should know about Sheila that you aren't telling me, just that single detail that changes the entire picture? Something that will jump up and bite me on the date or during the dating process? If, by some miracle, there is a dating process instead of one date and goodbye."

"No, there isn't. Don't you trust us?"

"Trust you and Avital? I trust both of you. My question has nothing at all to do with trusting you. I guess I've run into some unpleasant surprises over the years."

"Sheila has nothing to hide," Menachem insisted. "Avital told me that you're afraid to get your hopes up."

"How deep. I suppose, once a guidance counselor, always a guidance counselor, even if I don't happen to be in elementary school anymore."

"Hey, no fair," Menachem protested. "We really want to see you settled."

"I know that. I apologize. It's simply upsetting to be the subject of discussion."

"We care."

"You and Avital are both very kind. Please don't think I don't realize that," Yerachmiel said with difficulty. "In terms of Sheila Leipzig harboring some deep, dark secret…well, we Kantors tend to err on the side of being naive and trusting. In the alternate universe called *shidduchim,* bitter experience has taught me to modify that trait."

"It's better to be naive than to be paranoid and suspicious," Menachem said firmly. "I don't think you should call it an alternate universe. It's not. Plenty of people are normal, and lots of girls would want to date someone just like you. I can't figure out why you're so negative and insecure. She liked what she heard about you, and she's also not twenty or twenty-two or even twenty-five. She's already thirty-two years old, and she wants to get married."

"Why *isn't* someone as eligible and well-connected as Sheila married already?

"Maybe she's just waiting for the right guy, and maybe that's you?"

"You really are still in *shanah rishonah* dreamland," Yerachmiel teased. "Get real."

"You never know unless you try," his younger brother said. "Look at me and Avital. She's almost a year older than I am, she works as a guidance counselor. That's hardly the glamorous *shidduch* profile of many of the other of girls I dated, and look—it worked."

"Gotta go," Yerachmiel said hastily. "Uh, sorry. There's knocking at the door." He went over to the door of his small but tastefully decorated Neot Yaar apartment, knocked on it so that he'd be telling the truth, said a hasty goodbye to his brother, and sat down at the kitchen table, breathing heavily.

I had to get off that phone before I said something I'd regret.

When you give me advice from your vast storehouse of shidduch experience, Menachem, it really pushes my buttons. Did you know that, Menachem?

You, at the advanced age of twenty-seven, agreed to meet someone who was twenty-eight. What self-sacrifice.

I'll meet Sheila, but I'm calling her right now. Yes, it's kind of Menachem to advise me, his older brother.

Kind, well-meaning, and degrading.

Things have changed since he was my kid brother who looked up to me, who, let's be honest, worshipped me. I was his big brother, and I could do no wrong.

Times have changed, but I'm still the same Yerachmiel Kantor I always was and always will be. I want the same things in a wife. I need the same things.

Good for me.

I want, and I need. Very user-friendly. That's gotten me to where I am now, and gotten Menachem to where he is now.

Good for him. I mean that.

Now he and Avital, barely married six months, are expecting their first kid, and I couldn't be happier. I mean that. I plan to be the best uncle around.

And I'm still at square one.

Here goes nothing...

Yerachmiel picked up the phone to call Sheila Leipzig.

Ten minutes later, he put down the phone, smiling. That had been much easier than he'd expected, much easier. Far from the jarring, acrimonious, difficult exchange he'd half expected and wholly dreaded, it had actually been a nice conversation.

Sheila was a pleasure to talk to. She had easily accepted his explanation that he was all booked up with back-to-back weddings. They'd made up a time to meet early the following week.

He found himself wishing he wasn't caught up playing at other people's happy events so that he could meet her earlier. They would probably have a harmonious date and emerge with their dignity intact.

At my stage of the game, I don't take even that much for granted.

He hurried out of his apartment, a song on his lips. Within moments, he was seated behind the wheel of his silver Lexus. He didn't want to keep Rabbi Henry waiting.

Rabbi Henry Eisenberg had been his choir director long ago when Yerachmiel had been in high school. They'd kept up a warm relationship over the years. Now his former mentor was retired.

Rabbi Eisenberg had never married, and time hung heavily on his hands. He relied on his biweekly three-hour learning sessions with Yerachmiel for many things, among them, the feeling that he still mattered to someone, that the world hadn't forgotten him. Yerachmiel hadn't missed a session yet and did his best always to arrive on time.

An hour later, he rang the bell of Rabbi Eisenberg's apartment. He heard the slow, shuffling footsteps of the elderly gentleman as he carefully negotiated his walker to the door.

As always, Yerachmiel winced inwardly at the sight of his former mentor. Rabbi Eisenberg, who'd helped him launch his career as a professional musician, had been a natty dresser, a tall, impressive man who'd radiated confidence and success.

Not anymore.

Now he was old. Osteoporosis had cruelly bent him over. And as far as personal grooming was concerned, at best, it left a lot to be desired. Not that it made a difference to Yerachmiel. He still cared deeply about his former teacher. He still held him in high esteem. But...the rabbi wasn't what he'd once been. Yerachmiel felt a pang of sorrow that he always felt when he saw his teacher standing there at the door of his apartment, lonely and sadly diminished.

"Yerachmiel! Hello! How are you, *bachur*?"

"Good! Good."

The dining room table bore various *sefarim*, as well as a bottle of seltzer and two glasses.

"Do you want a drink? Did you have breakfast?"

"I'll drink soon. Sure, I ate before I came."

"Then come." His *chavrusa* gestured at the table. "Let's get down to business."

"My pleasure." Yerachmiel hesitated. "One sec, okay? I just need to use my phone for a sec."

"Take your time, Yerachmiel."

"I'll go into the kitchen in case I need a little privacy."

"Whatever you need."

While checking his voicemail, Yerachmiel walked into the kitchen. It was immaculate. The Indian cleaner who came in twice a week must have come that same morning. No garbage in the can, no dishes in the sink.

But he'd missed the stove. Grimacing with distaste, Yerachmiel tore off a paper towel, sprayed on cleaner, and wiped the stovetop clean.

He surveyed the kitchen once more and opened the refrigerator. Well stocked with all the basics. Excellent.

"Yerachmiel? You almost finished?"

"Coming, Rabbi Eisenberg. Right away."

People take advantage of him. It's terrible to be old and alone. Naturally, Ima keeps hinting, and Abba keeps threatening that if I don't get a move on as far as shidduchim are concerned, I could end up in his position.

As if I don't realize that.

What should I do? Create something that's not out there?

Maybe Sheila Leipzig will be different.

A couple of hours later, the two men were finished learning. *Baruch Hashem,* Rabbi Eisenberg's mind was as sharp as ever.

Rabbi Eisenberg leaned back in his chair. "So, Yerachmiel. What's the good word? Anything new in your life?"

Yerachmiel smiled and stretched. He reflected for a moment before answering. Rabbi Eisenberg had asked him that question hundreds, perhaps thousands of times over the five years they'd been learning together. Never before had the query been a source of anything but pain, which he'd hastily hidden under a casual answer forced through a constricted throat. But this time…

He savored the moment, the flare of hope that made him smile. Then, he moved his chair closer to the table and told Rabbi Eisenberg about his conversation with Sheila Leipzig.

10
Discretion

"I didn't copy it from anyone, Morah Estelle. I promise I'd never cheat." Tears formed in her expressive blue eyes. She turned away from Estelle and buried her head in her arms.

Oh, my. How did this happen? I should have told Avital and let her handle it. She's the professional. Or Sheila. She always knows what to say. What do I do now?

"Sarah. Sarah, please calm down," Estelle said helplessly. "I don't think you copied anything from anywhere. I'd never suspect a wonderful girl like you of cheating. Never. Why do you think that's what I meant?"

Sarah lifted her tearstained face. "What *did* you mean?"

"All I said was that this is an excellent poem. Really special and powerful. Look, that's what I wrote on top." She indicated the paper lying on the desk between them. "Do you think I'd give a hundred to someone who cheated?"

"No." Sarah hiccupped.

Estelle passed her another tissue. "You know I wouldn't." She breathed a sigh of relief. Now for the hard part.

"About the content of the poem. The subject matter, about someone who seems to be the target of a lot of disapproval, even criticism..."

"What about it?"

Estelle braced herself. "It's very real."

Sarah nodded, looking anywhere but at Estelle.

I was afraid of this. Estelle forced herself to continue.

Sarah wiped her eyes with the back of her hand.

"I could put it more strongly and say, more than a target. Even...a victim." Estelle swallowed hard. *Do I want to know this information? No, I do not.* "Did this actually happen? Maybe to someone you're close to?"

Sarah shrugged. "You could say that."

"To you?"

"It's not a secret. My mother told me I can speak to Morah Sheila if I want."

"Will you?"

"Maybe. Soon."

"Should I tell her, or give her this composition?"

"*No.*"

"But... You will speak to her, won't you? Or should I tell her that you're having a hard time?"

"No, don't speak to her."

"Sarah, if you wrote all this, you wanted someone to know what's happening in your life. Here. I'm giving you back the poem. It's yours to keep, and, by the way, you got the highest grade in the class for your final grade, if you want to know."

Sarah looked her teacher straight in the eye. "I read this poem to my mother, and she cried. Then I asked her if I should hand it in."

"You showed your mother this poem? You did? She knows about...all this?"

"Yes," Sarah said tersely. "No secrets."

"What did she say? Did she like it?"

"She said it was well written. She didn't say she liked it."

"I can understand that. But what did she say about showing it to me?"

"My mother suggested the idea."

"She did? Why?"

Sarah fidgeted.

"You don't have to tell me if you don't feel comfortable," Estelle said quickly.

Sarah shrugged. "She said that it was a very good idea to let you see it because you know that life doesn't always work out the way we think it will."

"You can tell me anything you want if that's what you want to do," Estelle offered sincerely. "But you will speak to your homeroom teacher also, won't you?"

"Yes. I don't want to tell you personal things about myself. That was my mother's idea. I like you, but…I really, really like Morah Sheila. She's so special. No offense, Morah Estelle, but you're old. Older than Mommy. Morah Sheila cares about me. I just feel it. I mean, she cares about all of us, but maybe, just maybe, she likes me a teeny bit more than everyone else?"

"Do you have her number?" Estelle asked.

"Morah Sheila's? Yes. She gave it to us."

"Good. Wonderful." Estelle paused. *This is awkward.* "You do realize that if you want to talk, I'm always willing to listen."

"Thank you," Sarah said politely, but her mind was clearly elsewhere.

Well, obviously she prefers Sheila to me. I would too if I were a student. It's not about either of us, in any case. This is strictly about Sarah. I'd better go look for Sheila, in case Sarah changes her mind.

Wow, that was touch and go. Imagine, one wrong sentence and Sarah thought I was accusing her of cheating. How could she think I thought that?

* * *

Once safely in the teachers' room, Estelle looked for Sheila. To her relief, Sheila didn't seem too busy to talk.

"Sheila? Do you have a moment?"

"Pull up a chair. What's going on?"

"Sarah Roth."

Sheila sat up alertly. "Sarah? What about her?"

"I'm not supposed to say anything, but keep an eye out for her, okay? There seem to be some… Look, she asked me not to say anything to you. She promised me that she'll speak to you. In any case, there seem to be some not great things going on in her life."

"How do you know all this?"

"She wrote a poem."

"Can I see it?"

"I gave it back to her, but in any case, it's not mine to show."

"All right."

"She needs help, Sheila. I'm very concerned. I feel out of my depth. I never read anything like that before. Not from a pupil, anyhow."

"Estelle, I'm telling you this in confidence, but Sarah's reached out to me on a number of occasions. I'm aware of her circumstances. I'm trying my best to be there for her. You're absolutely right." Sheila sighed heavily. "I wish I could tell you that you're wrong, but unfortunately, she has more to deal with than any child her age should."

Noa Lewin, one of the first-grade homeroom teachers, stood in front of them for a moment, paused, and went back to her seat.

"*Oy.*"

"*Oy* is right."

"Sarah told me that her mother is aware of the situation," Estelle said tentatively. "So, that's good, isn't it?"

"Her mother is certainly aware of the situation at home. At the moment, there's little that she can do to change it. Is she aware that Sarah talks to me? I'm not sure."

"*Kol hakavod* to you for being willing to face the situation, whatever it is, head-on."

Noa passed by again.

"Sheila, I think she wants to talk to you."

"Who?"

"Noa Lewin."

"Noa? I'll be with her in a second. This is more important. Where were we?"

"You were saying that Sarah's mother is on top of the situation."

"I didn't say that at all," Sheila corrected. "I just said that she knows about the situation. That's very different."

"Oh! That's awful. In the poem, Sarah mentions feeling unsafe."

"She meant emotionally safe," Sheila said. "You don't need to worry about that."

"Don't you feel out of your depth?"

Sheila smiled sadly. "Comparatively speaking, Sarah's situation isn't so bad."

"But is she right to be so upset, or is she being overdramatic?"

"No, she's not overreacting."

"Oh." Estelle was crestfallen. "That's too bad. For a moment there, I really hoped—I thought that maybe you were implying that she is."

"I wish." Sheila shook her head. "There are so many problems to deal with right here in Machon Atara. So many complex situations that I've been made aware of since I became a homeroom teacher. So many kids who have been dealt a tough hand, though you'd never know it by looking at them. And you know what? Even the girls without any blatant issues need so much."

"But her mother knows."

"Knowing about the situation does not equal knowing what to do about the situation. I try to help Sarah see things from a different perspective, but it takes two to tango, and when a family member treats a child harshly, even for her own good, it's very unpleasant. It leads to a lot of unhappiness. Out of my depth? I don't allow myself to think that way when my girls need help. I became a teacher to help wherever and whenever I can." She hesitated. "Sarah's a good kid, a terrific kid, in a very tough situation. I like her. It's easy to want to smooth her path."

"But you told Avital, didn't you? It seems to me that the guidance counselor should know about this kind of stuff."

"Of course."

"Estelle, aren't you finished yet? Sorry to interrupt. Tell me you're finished." It was Noa Lewin. "Sorry for interrupting. Sheila and I have been playing phone tag. Sheila's not too easy to reach on the phone, you know."

"I think we're done." Estelle stood up. "Thanks, Sheila."

"Thank *you*."

What a relief. Out of my hands and into your capable ones, Sheila. Better you than me. So much responsibility. I wouldn't know where to start. I never saw myself as the savior type, anyhow. Poor Sarah. I'm going to keep her in mind when I daven.

Noa sat down near Sheila. "Did you think about what we discussed?"

"About having Aviva continue taking over for me as a sub for the Jewish History hour, even after Yocheved returns?"

"Yes," Noa confirmed.

"First of all, I don't even know if that's legal. Aviva doesn't have a teaching degree, as far as I know." Sheila tried hard to keep her tone businesslike though she found it extremely difficult to mask her burning hurt and seething fury. How dare Noa have the chutzpah to go behind Rabbanit Sudri's back with her interfering, unprofessional, and unnecessary suggestions. How dare she make her preference for smiley, malleable, *young* Aviva Lavie so obvious. Just because Aviva could be manipulated into doing whatever Noa wanted, whereas, she, Sheila Leipzig actually had a mind of her own?

How dare you, Noa?

"It can be worked out," Noa said. "I discussed the situation with colleagues from another school, leaving out names and changing some details. I'm just trying to help you out. You have so many talents and skill sets. First grade just isn't your thing. You never taught first grade until this year. The entire set-up was not good, on many counts. You did your best. Why not admit that and move on?"

Sheila bit her lip, hard.

"I'll square it with Rabbanit Sudri," Noa urged.

Sheila found her tongue. "How, precisely, are you planning to do that?"

"Trust me. Aviva needs to rake in X amount of teaching hours in front of a classroom. Technically speaking, you could be the one observing and grading her, instead of me. You could be doing it as a favor to me, while I take care of the million details I need to finish this year successfully. Complete win-win."

"No."

"Why are you being stubborn about this? Isn't it a shame not to give our girls the best teacher possible? We didn't go into teaching to feed our egos. In any case, we shouldn't be doing that, ever. It's unfair to them. They trust us. We're only talking three short weeks."

"No."

"No? Why? I promise you that I have your best interests at heart. Why must you be so…so…" Noa paused.

"Did you want to say so rigid? Egotistical?"

"No, I didn't."

"Well, that's good. Thanks for judging favorably." Sheila's cheeks were burning. Was it anger? Humiliation? She wasn't sure. "That's not where I'm coming from. Absolutely not. I appreciate your concern for your students. It's very commendable of you to want to look out for their best interests, but no. I'll finish what I started. What we started together. I'm sorry you feel I was doing such an awful job. Allow me to remind you that Rabbanit Sudri has never, ever approached me about my performance in your class. Therefore, I'm going to assume that this little scheme of yours is your idea exclusively." Sheila was breathing hard.

Noa remained silent.

"This entire year, until I took over for Yocheved, you sang a different tune, so forgive me if I'm a little taken aback. When we prepared together, and when I consulted with you when you so kindly carved time out of your super-busy schedule to do me those two favors—I know Rabbanit Sudri asked you to help me out—I thought that I understood your evaluation of me differently." Sheila's voice grew colder and more formal with every word. "I was under the impression that my errors were simply a result of never having taught such little girls before. If you said that only to be encouraging, I have to tell you that I don't appreciate false praise. Not at all. I prefer the truth. I'm not a baby. I'm not one of your first graders."

Sheila didn't notice that her voice had risen.

Estelle gazed at them curiously but forced herself to leave the room. Whatever Sheila was so upset about was none of her business.

"It wasn't false praise." Noa tugged agitatedly at the edges of her short brown *sheitel*. "It was true. Your errors were a result of the fact that you've never taught first grade, or even second or third grade before. Could very well be that with a couple of years of experience, you'd pick up a knack for it."

"But in the meantime, in your opinion, not, I repeat, in Rabbanit Sudri's opinion, these poor girls suffered so much from my amateur efforts that anyone at all is preferable to me. They were rescued from me when I took over the seventh grade and my schedule changed, and you, as their protector, need to ensure their continued safety. Sorry, Noa Lewin. I don't buy that. I'll finish the year. I'll finish what I started."

What Rabbanit Sudri trusted me to start. I tried so hard. Maybe I didn't do a perfect job, but I certainly didn't do a terrible job either. Noa has some nerve, putting me down like that. The kids learned about Rabbi Akiva, about Rashi, about all the gedolim I was supposed to teach them about. The classroom was definitely quiet enough for even the kids who sat in the back to hear my voice.

Even if I did have to yell.

11
Fitting In

"Ima, I don't need so much food for just one week. All that matzah gave me a massive stomachache. I was up most of the night after the Seder."

"I heard you." Tzipora Lowenstein's face creased with concern.

"Well, excuse me. I'm so sorry that I felt sick and it kept you up. Next time, I'll try to be quieter."

"That's not what I said at all, Renée. Get that chip off your shoulder. I can't say anything without stepping on your toes. Are you feeling better now?"

"Maybe."

"What kind of an answer is that? You're either feeling better, or you aren't."

"Ima, please. I told you, I'm *fine*. Stop putting food in that bag because I'm not taking it with me. I'll end up tossing it into the garbage."

"No, you'll eat it during *chol hamoed*. I know you didn't stock up. What's in your fridge, diet yogurt?"

"That's all I want. I don't want any kugel or matzah. I avoid carbohydrates during the week."

"That's ridiculous," Tzipora Lowenstein retorted, removing another mysterious package from the massive refrigerator.

Renée peered rebelliously at the bulging shopping bag her mother was filling at the *fleishig* counter, which was covered by a glistening slab of custom-cut black marble in honor of Pesach. No foil or linoleum coverings for the Lowenstein family, thank you very much.

In the apartment she'd moved into three weeks previously there hadn't been any cash to spare for such luxuries, not after they'd hired *bachurim* to scrub the oven and stovetops, but you can't have everything.

Too bad. The kitchen looked like a spaceship gone haywire. Renée couldn't bear the sight of it. What was completely crazy was that Devora had gone over the stovetop *again* on *erev Pesach* with bleach and a toothbrush because Renée had eaten a slice of pizza at the kitchen table after the stovetop had already been cleaned. True, the kitchen was small, and true, the table was right next to the stovetop. But, come on!

It got worse. The foil was yuck, and someone—guess who?—had insisted on pouring boiling water on the countertops while Yehudit squeegeed it into the sinks. The two of them had then double-covered both sides of the sink with thick foil until every inch of the *chametz* counters were completely hidden. Ugly—and a waste of time and energy—but, whatever made the two of them happy. After all, Renée was the newest roommate, and this was her first Pesach in her new place. She'd go along with the program, not make waves.

She frowned. All in all, Devora had been even more controlling before Pesach, and unfortunately, Yehudit had sided with her.

It was still easier than living at home.

Was it? Maybe. Most of the time. Whatever. Another hot dating topic. Do you get all hysterical before Pesach? You do? Goodbye, and good luck.

She ran her fingers through her shoulder-length hair and grimaced. Too dry. It was the weather. How annoying was this *chamsin,* just in time for Pesach? Very, very annoying. Her skin was super dry too. Her mother moved over to the *milchig* side and started ladling soup into a big container.

"Ima, do you like it when I ignore you? I asked you nicely to stop. Then you complain that we have no communication."

"We don't." Her mother turned around. "Stop hollering. This isn't for you. Calm down."

Renée doubled over as a sharp pain pierced her stomach. "How can I calm down when you keep stressing me out?"

"In the shape you're in, I don't think you should go back to that apartment tonight."

"I'm going. This stomachache—it's all stress." *And the stress is all from you and the way you treat me. I'm thirty-two, okay? During the entire chag, last night and this endless afternoon, you remembered that so well—even going so far as to drag me out on a stroll, force me to get up when all I wanted was to sleep, just so people could see me and remember that I exist.*

Now you're forgetting it. Forcing me to take food or you'll tattle to Abba that I'm not taking care of myself. Trying to force me to stay here when I can't wait to leave.

I'm either a grown woman or a little kid, Ima. You can't have it both ways.

I thought you'd drive me insane during these past two days. The only reason I didn't explode at you more than I did is because Abba especially asked that I keep the peace.

I did my best, but you kept picking on me. "If only you'd put on that gorgeous yellow suit and go to shul."

"Let your nieces help me serve the soup. How will they learn, if you always jump up and clear the table? You had your turn for so many years, now let them work a bit." Good. Rub it in that I've been sitting at your table for so many years.

Well, you're done, and I'm out of here. I can always give all those calories to Devora, she's so slim, or Yehudit. Both are super lucky to be able to eat whatever they like and never gain a pound.

Renée's irritated expression brightened. *I'll write a note saying that the food's there to be shared. Yehudit will be overjoyed because she hates to cook.*

Maybe not. People are paranoid when it comes to eating other people's food on Pesach. I don't get it. Kosher is kosher. Why do people create problems where they don't need to?

Renée began braiding her hair. Braids were very in. She took her pocket mirror out of her shoulder bag to assess the effect. It looked good.

Her mother placed the bulging shopping bag on a kitchen chair and sat down next to her daughter.

"Stop fiddling with your hair. How many times have I told you not to touch your hair in the kitchen? You listen to me on this subject the same way you always do. Why am I surprised? No, you won't throw out a single thing. Not after I slaved over it in our Pesach kitchen when my feet were killing me. You'll eat it, every single morsel."

"You could have let Marianna do the cooking," Renée pointed out. *Who asked you to make yourself into a martyr? Why do you always do this? You kill yourself and then kvetch and make everyone else feel guilty.*

"What does a *goya* from the Philippines know about the love and *tefillos* a Jewish mother puts into the food she makes for her family? Not while I still have strength in my hands and feet. It's a privilege to have loved ones to cook for, Renée, and it's my privilege to make the special Pesach foods that have been in our family for generations, just as you'll do for your family soon."

"Riiiiight. Did you forget that I think it's a waste of time to cook, stuck in the house slaving over a hot stove on a hot day with all the great takeout places around?"

"It's not the same as homemade."

"Who says? I never taste the difference. As a matter of fact, sometimes it's even tastier. Besides, I hate being *fleishig*. You know that. Why do you always ignore me?"

"I ignore you when you shoot yourself in the foot. If you insist on going back to your apartment instead of staying here for *chol hamoed,* I won't have you living on ice coffee, gum, and salads. You're buying into secular values with this constant deprivation. You're skinny enough as it is, and that's unhealthy."

"I know what you think, Ima. It's not even attractive, right? Wrong. This is the way I like to look, and plenty of people agree with me."

"Yes, whoever is a slave to the secular media. Big *chachamim,* all of them. Which reminds me. You love *charoset,* and we have plenty left." Her mother sprang up and took a small container from the fridge. "There." She crammed it into the bag. "I can only try to help you take care of yourself at this point. Now it's up to you." She sat down and sighed. "I did my best. Eat it after Pesach. Share it with your roommates."

"Maybe. Yehudit will adore your almond schnitzel."

"Eat some yourself," her mother urged. "I didn't slave over a hot stove for your roommate, you know. I wish you'd rest up and eat proper meals for a change. I don't know why you insist on working on *chol hamoed.*"

"I'm not risking this job I finally landed, not after hunting for it for a billion years." Renée shuddered.

"Aren't your roommates taking off from work?"

"They weren't just hired."

"Could be." Her mother sat down next to her again. "I don't appreciate this workaholic lifestyle you've chosen for yourself. Any dates penciled into your busy schedule?"

Renée rolled her eyes. "You know there aren't. Can't just pluck them out of thin air."

"Tell me the truth. It's become a side issue for you, getting married, hasn't it?"

"No."

"Yes, it has."

"Why do you say that?"

"You're too comfortable living on your own."

"Do you want me to be miserable until Mr. Right comes along?"

"Don't settle for half a life."

"I have no idea what you're talking about."

"You know exactly what I mean. Living on your own, becoming set in your ways, forgetting how to be flexible and get along with people, it's so destructive. You'll have a lot of self-centered habits to unlearn when you finally meet the right one."

"Ima, I'm not alone." Renée felt her patience about to snap. "I have two roommates, in case you've forgotten."

"Yes, you do. Two over-the-hill older singles who have convinced you that you should be just like them."

"Stop it. I thought you said you liked them when you and Abba helped me move my stuff in."

"I did say that, and I do like them, but do I want you to end up like them? Never."

"What's so bad?"

"A year ago, you wouldn't have asked me that. Half-lives. Not what I want for you, Renée. Get a move on now, while you're only thirty-two, and the world's still open to you. How will you learn from two confirmed bachelorettes how to manage in life? You won't. At least when you were living with younger girls, you had some incentive to move on in life, but now, I see you just letting yourself waste precious time like those poor girls you live with probably did when they were your age. What were the parents thinking, I want to know? Even though maybe both girls were as stubborn as you. Can't blame their poor parents, I suppose."

"Women, Ima. They are women, and so am I. Yehudit told me she hates being called a girl. She's a woman, a grown woman. So is Devora, and *so am I*."

"There's no need whatsoever to yell, and I wish you'd stop repeating yourself. When you speak to me, keep a civil tongue in your head. Pretend I'm someone you're interested in impressing. Your boss, or one of your roommates." Tzipora stood up and cleared away the crumbs on the counter. "Girls. I call them girls. I call you all girls because that's what you are. Until you live with the natural responsibilities any grown woman has, in my book you are older girls."

"Could you get off my case?"

"I don't like this new living situation of yours one iota. Last year you lived in a normal situation, with girls who were just taking a little longer to get married. Who asked you to move to this older singles apartment? You know I was completely against it."

"I'll explain it to you for the billionth time, and then, can we please never, ever discuss this again? I was sick of being the oldest wherever I lived, as if thirty-two is pathetic. I was fed up with having to have to search for new roommates each time someone got engaged and flew the coop, and maybe, just maybe it's not so much fun always being left behind?"

"Maybe you are fed up with constant transitions." Her mother looked at her thoughtfully.

"I am."

"All it takes is one good guy."

"Ima, is there anything in this whole speech you're going to give me that I haven't heard yet?"

"Maybe something will finally penetrate. You don't have a contract in this new place. I want you to back out."

"No way." Renée rose from the table, signaling that at least as far as she was concerned, it was the end of the—conversation? Fight? Loaded discussion? Argument? She wondered why her mother was so hard to get along with, why she insisted on picking fights about every little thing, but that was just the way she was. No point getting all worked up.

"Could you please explain to me again why you can't just stay here over Shabbos, or even till Sunday, when there's nothing special going on in your life? Don't tell me, I know. You think I'll keep nagging you. Well, if you'd just act a bit more responsibly, I'd have no reason to nudge you, but no, you just grow more entrenched in your ways."

"If you'd invite normal guests instead of weirdos, maybe I'd feel like eating here sometimes.

"They are not weird. They are simply bruised by life. How can you be so callous? Are you suggesting that you prefer eating alone in your apartment to suffering their company? Don't you realize how fortunate you are to be in the position of a giver? Besides, can't you look past the exterior to see the soul within?"

"Can I help it if they make me feel uncomfortable? I have to get going." Renée draped her violet-and-cream shawl around her. "It's getting late. *And this conversation—I've heard you say this a million times, okay? I've had it with these topics. Why can't we just agree to disagree? You have your point of view, and I have mine, okay? Besides, calm down.* "Yehudit will also be home on Friday night, and I never like to eat much for the afternoon *seudah*. I don't know why you and Abba insist on having these three-hour ordeals. Bye. I have a bus in five minutes."

"It's not even nine thirty. That's not late for a person whose normal bedtime is one or two in the morning," her mother pointed out. "It doesn't help to run away from reality. The world isn't a playground. It's full of suffering, and we try to help in any way we can."

"Whatever. I'm out of here." Renée hefted the shopping bag and turned to leave.

"Just a second."

"Ima, I really have to go."

"Go home tomorrow."

Renée's control almost snapped. She managed to choke out, "See ya. Bye."

* * *

"Not a word of thanks." Tzipora opened the Pesach closet and started to put away the *fleishig* china.

"Here, let me give you a hand," her husband Yechiel offered.

"Thank you." She handed him a stack of dishes. "She did live here for almost two months this year. And does she think that the Seder she participated in is not something to acknowledge? The time, the expense, the effort. We didn't bring her up to be ungrateful, yet not a single word of thanks. Not one offer to help clean for Pesach. I let it go. She's slaving away for a pittance at her new job. She thinks it's a good salary for a newbie, so I don't want to take the wind out of her sails, but when she keeps fleeing this house as if someone's chasing her, it hurts me very much."

"It's not about you." He closed the closet. "All done."

"What kind of nonsense is that?" Tzipora flushed guiltily. "Sorry. That was way out of line. I didn't mean to snap. Tell me what you're thinking." She arranged slices of melon on a plate and set them before her husband.

"Forgiven. What I meant to say was that she's fighting for survival now. She's not giving too much thought to how her actions affect anyone else."

"*Survival*? She's not a homeless person. This is her home, where she grew up."

"Exactly. She needs to spread her wings, one way or another."

"I never said a word, all the years she lived away from home. She's moving backward. I feel like I'm dealing with a sulky adolescent, not with someone who could have an adolescent daughter herself. I'm starting to think that she didn't internalize a single value I tried—we tried—so hard to teach her. Also, doesn't she think that maybe I'm a human being with sensitivities and feelings of my own? She hurt my feelings when she put down our Shabbos *seudos*. I try to make them the highlight of the week, and she calls them ordeals."

"She didn't mean it that way," her husband soothed.

"Then why did she say it?"

"She's expressing her discontent with the way things are for her. She needs a home, a husband. When she gets married, and she sees how efficiently you manage a home, she'll learn to appreciate you for the accomplished *balabuste* and *baalas chesed* you are."

"I'm not so sure. I wish I could be," Tzipora said, brooding.

"We made the wrong choice of high school for her, and it's been downhill ever since."

"Come on," Yechiel Lowenstein objected. "She's thirty years old."

"Thirty-two," his wife corrected.

"High school was ages ago."

"Makes no difference. Her education, in the years that her character was being formed, determined the shallow choices she's making now."

"Could be."

"I tell you, she needed a school with warmth, with heart. An idealistic place, even if the academics weren't tops. If she'd gone to a place that emphasized *Yiddishkeit* and *hashkafah,* maybe she'd have her own home by now.

"Or maybe not," she said after a moment's thought. "It's all conjecture. All her sisters went to that very same school, and they're all happily married, *baruch Hashem.*"

"One day, when she visits with her ten kids, and they wreck the house, we'll laugh about this together," he offered wistfully.

"No. We won't. Even if she finally gets a bit of sense, the memory of these years will hurt."

"Tzipora?"

"Hmm?"

"Please remember what I told you."

"Which part?"

"Renée is suffering too."

"That's true, but it still doesn't excuse her behavior. No one is exempt from the obligation to act like a *mentsch.* Talk to her. Please. She still listens to you. She values your opinion." Tzipora's voice wobbled. "Me, she's shut out of her heart."

"She still loves you."

"She hides it well. Forget about my relationship with her. When is she going to grow up? I know you think I sometimes exaggerate, Yechiel, but I'm very worried about her. She's self-absorbed to the exclusion of everyone and everything that doesn't fit into her narrow little view of the world."

Yechiel sighed heavily.

"She's a nice-looking girl. She knows how to be very nice too when she wants to."

"Those aren't bad things. Why do you sound as if those are things to regret?"

"I'm her mother, but I'll say this anyhow. She'll meet some nice, naive boy who won't see past her exterior. Would you want someone like Renée to marry one of our sons?"

He swallowed uneasily. The silence stretched on. Finally, he cleared his throat. "None of what we see is the real Renée. She'll meet the right man, she'll be happy, and with the *Ribbono shel Olam's* help, he'll bring out the best in her."

"Amen."

* * *

Seder night had been okay

Bubby and Zeidy had been there, as expected. Sarah had made herself as inconspicuous as possible. Aside from redoing the entire table Sarah had set, there had been no criticism.

What would I say to Morah Sheila if I called her? She has such a perfect life, even if she is a grown-up. I don't want her to think I'm some sort of nebach.

What's she going to do about it, anyhow? What can she change? Nothing.

What's she going to do, adopt me? Take me away from all this? Besides, what good will more talking do? I talk enough to Avital Salamonte.

Sarah rubbed a dish angrily.

Her sister Shalhevet, younger by two years, looked at her. "What's wrong? The Seder wasn't so terrible with Zeidy heading it. It was even kind of nice."

"Easy for you to say. Bubby doesn't pick on you for every little thing."

Shalhevet looked cautiously at the open kitchen door. For good measure, she lowered her voice. "Look, Sarah. We all know it's true. Bubby does have it in for you, sort of."

"Sort of?" Sarah rolled her eyes.

"I told you so many times. Mommy keeps telling you, but you won't listen. You ask for it. You start up with her."

"*I* start up with *her*?" Sarah flung down the dishtowel angrily.

"Shhh. Keep your voice down. Yes. You do."

"Give me one tiny example," Sarah said.

"Tonight. Tonight, you were setting the table with forks on the wrong side."

Sarah rolled her eyes.

"That's just it. For you, it's no big deal. For Bubby, it's the biggest deal in the world. You know how to do things her way. Why must you do things that will upset her?"

"Who asked her and Zeidy to practically move in with us? We don't need them."

Shalhevet glanced anxiously in the direction of the dining room. "Keep your voice down," she hissed. "And don't be a baby. We do need them. Do you want Mommy to cry all the time the way she did when Abba was first *niftar*?" She swallowed hard.

"No..."

A slight older woman in an elaborately wrapped turban entered the room. Both girls fell silent.

"Thank you both for your help. Your mother says good night. She fell straight into bed, she was so exhausted from all the Pesach preparations." She paused. "Shalhevet, thank you so much for your help all week. And Sarah? It's good to see you pitch in. I hope you realize that your mother can't do it all on her own."

12 Beginners

Their apartment had never looked so good. She'd arranged and rearranged the furniture, dusted, swept, and mopped. She'd shined the mirrors and even swiped halfheartedly at the windows before changing her mind.

Estelle's stomach was a tight knot of nerves. "You're overreacting," she reassured herself, speaking to herself out loud, the way she had done so often in her single days. "Repeat after me: the Rubinoffs are not a threat."

She sat down on the couch. After a moment she sprang up again. "I'm too restless to sit, but why? They're going to be very busy. They've only got a week here. No one's expecting a gourmet supper every night, or hours upon hours of conversation and advice. Just a simple, friendly gesture of welcome, some cake, cookies, even store-bought, hot drinks, and then off they go to their hotel, and off I go to choir rehearsal.

"I need a break from trying to build us as a couple. Does that make me a bad wife? I hope not. It's just been overly intense lately, trying to please Elchanan's parents long distance." A sudden vision of them appearing at her door made her giggle nervously.

"They aren't here, but in a way, they are. Right here, in my house—sorry, our house, our home—walking in with the Rubinoffs. Talk about being evaluated.

"So what, though? I'm being a supportive wife, just the way I'm supposed to. I'm being a devoted wife, helping Elchanan look good for his parents, helping to entertain their friends.

"I wish those Rubinoff people would just stay far, far away. They'll be here soon, and then I can be polite, sweet, and leave for rehearsal. He's being a dutiful son, hosting these people he hardly knows, but they can hardly expect me to hang around when I have a prior commitment."

She looked in the hall mirror and flinched.

"I look the way I feel, and the Rubinoffs will be here any minute. What should I do? No time to change into something more flattering. Elchanan always thinks I look nice, but he's wrong."

She opened the refrigerator and stood there looking at the contents. They were out of yogurt, out of summer fruit, though there were a couple of carrots and cucumbers. Momentarily, she thought of peeling and cutting up some vegetables to place prominently next to the pastries. She decided that it didn't pay to go through the effort. She wasn't planning to eat, and Elchanan, though he should know better, would diplomatically ignore the vegetables. She was his wife, not his mother, or worse, a policewoman. There were cookies, cake, and *bourekas* on the table, all store-bought, and she just had to accept that Elchanan would partake heartily of all of them. He was a big boy, and it was his decision. Especially after that innocent but stinging comment about the main course on Friday night, and the way he'd rummaged in the kitchen afterward when he thought she wouldn't notice.

She'd tried to help him avoid overeating. Long years of struggling with her weight had taught her how easy it was to gain, and how difficult it was to lose. But never again.

It made no difference how clean the house was if there was nothing good to serve them. Why was she lazy? For that homey feeling, they'd be checking out to see if she treated him right.

"You should have baked," she chastised herself. "There's nothing like the smell of freshly baked bread, cake, or cookies to make a house smell like a home. Too late now. What good does it do to agonize after the fact?

"This *shanah rishonah* business is exhausting. I wish we were an old married couple already. My trivial actions and choices that never made a difference to anyone before are now super significant."

She looked in the hall mirror again, noting that she still looked pale and grim.

"Elchanan, how could you put me in this position? I wish they'd already come and gone. I hate being under a magnifying glass."

She could hear his answer. *They aren't mind readers, Estelle. They can only see your actions. Besides, they're coping with their own issues.*

"But why do they have to come and spy on me so that his parents will know if I'm treating him the way I should? He's pleased with me. Very pleased. He's told me that too many times to count."

At the sound Elchanan's familiar knock, she pasted a welcoming smile on her face and rushed over to open the door. Her husband stood there grinning, flanked by a tall couple in their early thirties. Behind them were four enormous suitcases.

"Estelle! This is my wife, Estelle." His smile broadened. "Let me introduce you to my dear friends, Kayla and Avigdor Rubinoff."

His dear friends? That's not what he said, not at all. He told me that the connection is through his parents. Here I am, no makeup, wearing school clothing and a snood. Great, just great. Fabulous. They'll think he married a shlump. Why didn't he tell me the truth? And what's the story with those suitcases? Why didn't they drop them off at the hotel before coming here? Please don't be staying here. Please don't be staying here.

"Come in," she said, opening the door wider. "You must be exhausted from your flight."

"They are," Elchanan said. "Exhausted and what's more, starving. The airline forgot to order *mehadrin* meals for them. That's what you get, using a computer to arrange your flight plans rather than a real live human being," he joked good-naturedly, draping an arm around Avigdor's shoulder.

"Your husband is exaggerating," Avigdor said to Estelle. "We're fine. Kayla packed more sandwiches for the flight than any two human beings could possibly eat in such a short time."

"I for one, can't eat a thing," Kayla said, picking up his drift. "A cup of tea or some Coke would be fine if you have it. I hope you didn't go to the trouble of making us something fancy, Estelle. Elchanan was boasting about what a whiz you are in the kitchen."

"A whiz? Hardly. Just the basics."

"Modest as always," Elchanan said. "But why are we standing here in the entrance? Let's get the show on the road. Step right up, folks. The kitchen's right ahead," he urged proudly.

"Um, Elchanan?" Estelle indicated the carefully set table. "I set up for us in the dining room."

"Wow, fancy," he said, eyeing pastries, snacks, and cold drinks arrayed carefully on the dining room table. "Come sit down and dig in. You'll start with a snack, and Estelle and I will bring in the real food from the kitchen. Come on, don't be shy. Come, Estelle. Let's give these people some privacy so they won't feel shy eating in front of us."

"Start? Real food?" Estelle whispered sharply to Elchanan when they reached the kitchen. "I have to leave in under an hour."

"You do? Why?" Elchanan looked dismayed. "Where are you going?"

"I told you, Elchanan. I have choir rehearsal for the play I'm performing in. I have a duet, and the pianist's traveling in specially from outside of Yerushalayim."

"Oh. What can I tell you, I didn't realize that if you canceled, it would put out so many people."

"It's not that. They'll manage."

"Oh, good."

"No, you're not listening to me. If I miss one more rehearsal, my duet goes to someone else. Menucha's giving me a ride."

"I see."

"If I explain that we have company, I'll be back so soon no one will know that I even left. Tell them I went to a neighbor. It's not a lie. Menucha is our neighbor. We live in the same neighborhood."

"It's so important to you?"

"Yes, it is. Very. How long are they staying here?"

"I don't know exactly. An hour, two hours? You wouldn't feel like… It's out of the question, right?"

"What?" she asked impatiently. "Come on, Elchanan. The sooner I go, the sooner I'll be back."

"Would it be so hard to skip rehearsal just this once more? If you explain that an unexpected family obligation came up?"

Estelle glared at her husband.

"Or how about this? Maybe the pianist hasn't left home yet, and you can reschedule?"

"She definitely left home already. Didn't you hear me say she's traveling in from outside of Yerushalayim?"

"I'll take care of it since I see you can't skip choir. No problem. I'll tell them you have an urgent job-related meeting you can't possibly miss. No, that would be dishonest. Hmm."

"Take care of what?"

"They looked so tired and hungry and forlorn when they got off the plane. No family to meet them, either. So I promised Avigdor that we'd give them supper tonight." In an undertone, he added, "We can just make omelets. Or…maybe we have some Shabbos leftovers?"

"We finished them last night, and, sorry, but we have only three eggs. How do you plan to divide three eggs among four adults?"

"My mother adds milk and cheese if she's short on eggs," he ventured.

Estelle glared. "Why don't they eat at the hotel?"

"I wanted to give them a warm, homey welcome. They've probably missed supper by now, in any case."

I can do this. He's not being inconsiderate or trying to make me look bad. Why would he want to make me look bad? We're a team, right? He thinks food jumps from the fridge onto the table, without effort.

"Elchanan, I wish you had told me ahead of time. You know I hate surprises."

"It was a snap decision."

"But it involves me. This puts me in a very awkward position. I wasn't expecting company."

"Three eggs is great. Any tuna? Cheese?"

"Yes. The tuna's where it always is, in the cabinet above the sink. Three eggs, the remains of a container of cottage cheese, that's all."

"That's my *balabuste*," he kidded, hoping for a smile, but Estelle didn't soften. "So, here's the plan. You whip together some tuna while boiling the eggs and potatoes. I'll fry onions. We'll have tuna, egg salad, mashed potatoes, and fried onions—what could be better?"

"Plenty of things," Estelle hissed, not bothering to hide her annoyance. "Plenty of things, Elchanan. Such as being given a little advance warning if I'm to serve your dear friends a meal worth eating. I'm not going to just throw some potatoes in a pot. It's not the way I do things."

"Estelle, don't make this into more than it is," he protested. "Believe me, all they want is something that doesn't taste like cardboard. That, and a chance to sit in a real room, in a real house, and catch their breaths."

"I can't believe you forgot my choir rehearsal. I thought that what's important to me matters to you too."

"Oh, it does! I guess you could leave while we're still eating, but—"

"We? You and the Rubinoffs are we, and I'm on the outside?"

"Estelle." Elchanan put down the can opener to stare at her in horror. "What are you saying?'

"Nothing. It's nothing. Forget it. And keep your voice down. They'll hear us. Put the covers on those pots. It will take forever to cook that way. You can't seriously mean that I should leave while you're hosting company."

"Stay. Of course you should stay. Only if you want to," he said helplessly.

"Out of the question. Go, Elchanan. Go talk to them before they think that all we do is fight. Wait! Don't leave the flame under the soup so high. Let it simmer."

Estelle busied herself in the kitchen, refusing to discuss the issue further. When she heard Menucha honk, she rushed outside. Menucha rolled down her car window.

"Go on ahead without me, Menucha. I can't make it tonight."

"This is the third time in a row… Wait. Estelle, is everything okay?"

"Yes. No. I— Whatever. It's no big deal." Her eyes filled with tears. "Go, don't be late. One of us should live up to her obligations."

"What's going on? Is Elchanan okay? Is he home?"

"He sure is. He and his dear friends, who dropped by for a surprise invasion"— Estelle caught herself —"for a quick dinner."

"Aha. Say no more. Fine, I'll tell the teacher that you had a family emergency. Enjoy, Estelle. Enjoy being the gracious hostess."

"And if I'm feeling anything but gracious?" Estelle asked rebelliously.

"Fake it, sweetie. That's the name of the game. It's not really faking at all. It's your *shalom bayis*."

"He offered to host them on his own."

"*Don't you dare*." Menucha got out of the car, slamming the door behind her. "I can't believe you."

"I'm sick of giving up myself. Do you hear me, Menucha Shalom? Anytime I want to do anything the slightest bit different from what he wants, you start threatening me with *shalom bayis*. Tell me, is that normal? Do you give into every single one of Eliezer's whims? No, you don't, and you never have, not even in *shanah rishonah*, so why do I have to bend myself all the time? Is there any reason you're implying that I don't value my marriage when I do?"

"You get all tangled up in knots by the most trivial stuff. He's not the best housekeeper. Big deal. He forgot that you had a rehearsal. So what? He wants you to help him host his parents' friends. He waited a very long time for this gift—a wife, a home, a chance to feel like a *mentsch* in the world—and you're concerned about a choir rehearsal?"

"He's putting his parents' needs before mine, and they're not even here! Long-distance pressure. I don't fit into the meek little wife role you keep trying to stuff me into."

"For your own good only. I promise."

"I know. I'm going in. He'll be wondering where the meal is."

"No, he'll be wondering where *you* are." Menucha gave her a quick hug. "Go, show him what a good wife he's landed. It's all worth it. I promise. Even if you do lose your part in the duet. I'll try to advocate for you. Maybe the pianist can rehearse with a different group."

"I'll be very upset if I lose my duet. I haven't sung in public in a long time. I was looking forward to it," Estelle grumbled, but she was smiling. A wave of laughter greeted her as she opened the door.

Misses me? He's just fine with his friends around.

Mustering up her best acting abilities, she marched into the dining room with a fresh plate of chocolate chip cookies, smiled grimly in all directions, while avoiding all eye contact, and said, "Real food's coming right up."

The kitchen looks like a wreck, I look like a fat shlump, my husband doesn't care about me, and I'm not allowed to have a life because of shalom bayis, which is exclusively my responsibility, even though theoretically, it's about both of us.

"Elchanan? Could you give me a hand with serving?"

"Sure."

In the dining room, Avigdor and Kayla eyed each other uncomfortably.

"I don't think we came at the best time," she said.

"Maybe she's upset about something else entirely," Avigdor said hopefully.

"I didn't say it's our fault, but obviously, they need privacy. Let's make this quick."

* * *

Later that evening, Elchanan slowed the car to a crawl. Where had that sign been, the one advertising medical clowning? The sign had caught his eye that morning on the way to Shacharis. Now, on the way to Maariv, he felt desperate.

He didn't want to be overdramatic, but he felt a strong need to alleviate the harsh disappointment he felt over the way the evening had gone.

Where was that sign? To the best of his recollection, it had featured big clown shoes, along with a brightly colored logo saying something along the lines of "Not just clowning around." Clowning around wasn't his thing, but it seemed that medical clowning was about helping children endure difficult medical treatments. The idea spoke to something deep inside him.

Along more self-referential lines, he allowed himself to hope. Perhaps, *halevai*, taking the course would teach him to respect himself more. Then, maybe, just maybe, he could dream of an additional outcome: that his wife would respect him more, too.

He didn't seem to know which buttons to press. Estelle, bless her, was still acting distant. Not distant, exactly, but… Distant. His mind was blank. He couldn't think of any other word to describe her treatment of him. Not cold, not mean, not angry but distant. That was that word. So if, as a result of his taking a course that might enhance self-respect, Estelle would jump on the bandwagon, it could be a good choice.

He permitted himself to dream further. Wouldn't it be unbelievable if his short stature and slightly awkward presentation, the bane of his existence for so long, were to become an asset?

Now, where was that sign? The sign of hope. Where was it?

Ah, there it was. Right after Maariv, he'd save the number in his cellphone.

* * *

The following morning, the Rubinoffs were enjoying a lavish hotel breakfast.

"Kayla, when I first told Elchanan's father about this trip, which I knew was not going to be easy for either of us emotionally, he assured me that we'd be staying at their place. Now I realize why he never brought it up again," Avigdor said bluntly.

"You're hurt."

"I'm disappointed."

"Don't be," his wife responded. "The timing's to blame. It was too soon after their marriage for this kind of a visit." She reached for the apricot jam. "Estelle's a good match for Elchanan. She's probably a perfectionist."

"What makes you say that?"

"The way she thinks, and this is just conjecture on my part, is that if she isn't perfect at all aspects of marriage, then she's failed."

"Sounds like a business venture or a job, not a marriage."

"In a way, though, being a perfectionist will work in her favor."

"How so?"

"She'll make a successful marriage a top priority."

"I certainly hope she will. I would hate to see him throw himself away on a self-centered woman who doesn't know how to appreciate him."

"Don't worry. She'll learn to care about him, but she needs time."

"We weren't like that." Avigdor smiled.

"No, but plenty of couples are. Not everyone gets as lucky as you did."

"I'm a lucky man," her husband said sincerely.

13
First Date

"Nowadays, when you play at weddings, do you feel the *simchah* of the occasion, or, I guess I ought to say, do you still feel the *simchah* of the occasion the way you did in the beginning, or has the feeling dulled with time and repetition?"

Sheila took a sip of her iced cinnamon tea and leaned forward waiting for Yerachmiel's answer. She and Yerachmiel had been on their date for about half an hour and had exhausted all the polite, getting-to-know-you airplane talk.

Practice makes perfect, I suppose, she'd thought, stifling a nervous giggle, and plunging into her first real question of the evening. Let's see how he would repsond

Yerachmiel raised his eyebrows. "Why do you assume that I ever felt the *simchah* of the occasion? Are you convinced that at least in the beginning of my career, before I became jaded, I felt that way? That's flattering."

Sheila blushed.

"Do I ever feel the *simchah* of people I've never met other than when they employ me? Other than on a purely business level? Do I feel more than the accomplished feeling of a job well done? That's what you're asking, to make a long story short?"

"Well, yes." She looked at him expectantly.

"No, I don't," he said flatly. "Other people's *simchahs* have never affected me deeply one way or the other. Not at the beginning of my career and not now."

She sat back, trying hard not to look as deflated as she felt. Her thoughts raced. Avital had promised. He looks so put together. He makes a great first impression. It can't all be packaging. The package can't be empty. I don't think I could bear the disappointment. Not again. Not after I bowed to all the pressure and agreed to date someone so much older than I am just to demonstrate that I'm willing to stretch my comfort zone. Just to show Mommy, and the world, that I do want to get married.

Just to show myself.

"Honesty is always appreciated," she said.

Yerachmiel laughed appreciatively. "That's kind of you to say. Sorry, I'm just not on that level of *ahavas Yisrael*. I'm an ordinary guy. I'm an ordinary guy trying to make an honest living. That's all." Yerachmiel sat up straighter in his soft armchair.

Please don't be ordinary. Make it easy for me to like you. Make it easy for me to respect you. Make it easy for me to agree to another date. Please. You're the first guy I've dated since the Yaakov Stone fiasco. Please. Don't let me lose faith in myself. Don't let me lose faith that someday soon I'll move on to what everyone calls real life.

Please be someone special.

Sheila shifted in her seat, glad that Yerachmiel wasn't a mind reader. She wondered if he too was listening intently to an inner dialogue. *It would be cool to ask him.*

Cool, and super gauche. I've already made a fool of myself.

But he doesn't seem to mind.

Yerachmiel Kantor was intrigued, but his face was inscrutable.

The interrogation has begun on an interesting note this time. I'm lucky that she didn't ask me how much I make when I play at a wedding, which is what the last lady asked. Ten thousand shekels for four hours, but it was none of her business.

Sheila asks probing questions, too, but this time I don't mind at all. It's a sign of interest on her part, like Aunt Eva tried to convince me was the case last time.

He smiled. *She's trying to find out who I am, what makes me tick. Good. I'll tell her. She's not pulling any punches, so neither will I. It was a strange question, though. Who does she think I am? What inflated information did my dear brother and his wife feed her that could have prompted that question?*

Maybe it's not anything they said. Maybe that's the way Ms. Sheila Leipzig thinks.

What regular person is at the level she seems to expect? Only an adam gadol could possibly be at that level of empathy, of selfless love for a fellow Jew.

"My band is a passion," he said, trying to explain. "An avocation, a calling. It's much more than a job, but nothing like you're describing. Not at all."

"You say you don't feel that way, but I don't believe you. It's obvious that you do."

"It is?" *How's it obvious, Sheila? I'll play along. Play along, ha, ha.*

"Well…um… How should I put this? Your band, Rina-O-Mangina is special." She paused. "It has something very special, something that's hard to put into words."

"Why, thank you. That's always good to hear. How, if you don't mind my asking, is it so special? Sounds like I'm fishing for compliments, which I am." He grinned. "Just kidding. I want to know what we're doing right, even if it wasn't our intention."

"It's not what you intend to accomplish? That feeling of *tzibbur*, of community, of sharing in the joy of a fellow Jew? I took it for granted that it is, so let me think for a second."

He smiled expectantly. "Don't rush. This band is like a child to me. I love to hear praise about my child." He waited a beat. "Sheila? Do me a favor and laugh. That was a joke. I try."

She laughed obligingly but pressed on. "So, about your kid."

"Very good," he complimented her.

"The sound of your band is contemporary. Your selections are a nice balance of all the newest hits, so people don't get bored, together with all the golden oldies everyone expects to hear at a *simchah*."

"I like the sound of that." He grinned, but this time she was prepared.

"I know. *Sound of that*. Joke." She smiled.

"You're a quick study."

"Thanks. Everything I just mentioned is true, but that's not what I'm referring to when I say that Rina-O-Mangina is unique."

"I'm all ears. Sorry, I'll stop with the puns. Don't keep me in suspense."

"All the people I know who hired Rina-O-Mangina felt like the band was… I guess the best way to put it is that they said the band shared their *simchah*. Everyone loves that. That's not ordinary at all." She blushed again. Yerachmiel looked like he was trying to hide a smile. "Is that too idealistic?"

I sound gauche. It's not like me at all. Avital was insistent that he's not just a talented individual, like so many other pleasant but unremarkable guys I've met over the years. She told me that he's got a lot of hidden depth.

I want that.

I need that.

Mommy keeps telling me that I shouldn't expect to get it all. She's been telling me the same thing for years. I know she's right, because here I am, sitting opposite the who-knows-what-number-date of my life, but it doesn't help me to know that she's right. I need a guy who's charismatic and dynamic, who has big plans. At the same time, I need one who has a lot of inner depth. It's not fair of her to tell me that I can't have it all. She got it all, in Daddy. And she was only nineteen. Shouldn't all my years of stifling my dreams in hotel lobbies count for something in the cosmic scheme of things? It was one of the main reasons I agreed to meet him, age difference or not, because he's not just plodding through life, waiting to get married, surviving from day to day. How did she put it?

"You hear his longing for a home of his own in the way his band plays," Avital had told her. "When he picked up that microphone at our wedding and sang the first song of the seudah, my mother told me that he has a special neshamah, Sheila. That's what she told me, and my mother is not the mushy type. But it wasn't just at our wedding. After all, the chassan, Menachem, was his younger brother. Yerachmiel was bound to have strong feelings about that. A lot of people tell me that they hire his band specifically because the whole range of emotions experienced at a simchah come out in that special Rina-O-Mangina sound.

"He's the head of the band," Avital had concluded. "That special ruach… it's all him."

"Maybe it is, but I happen to find idealism refreshing. In small doses, that is."

Sheila smiled.

"We do put our hearts into our playing. If we don't like a selection, out it goes. There's that aspect of the band, plus incessant practice. We don't rest on our laurels, ever. We upgrade all the time. We are professionals. We keep our skills sharp."

"That can't be all. You can't be telling me that the sincerity, the heartfelt sound of Rina-O-Mangina is all a matter of dry technical skill?"

"Why dry? Technical skill is extremely important in music. Can't get sloppy. Menachem told me that you appreciate music."

Sheila smiled. "You could say that."

"Then you fully appreciate the importance of consistent practice."

"Certainly."

"We do a job, we try to do it well so that people will be pleased. We put in a lot of effort toward that end."

"Is that good enough?"

"Why not?"

"For the *baalei simchah,* these are peak events in their lives. They feel that they are realizing their dreams. Well, hopefully, anyhow. It cheapens the whole experience if some of the people involved don't share that feeling. Okay, maybe not the waiters, but otherwise, shouldn't everyone present share the feeling of having received a wonderful gift from Hashem?"

Yerachmiel gazed into space for a moment. "I'm trying to visualize what you said. You put it so eloquently, but is what you said true? We live in the real world, not in a perfect universe. Would you expect the photographer, if he weren't a family member, to feel the deep feelings the siblings do, for example? I'm afraid you'd be very disappointed if you could read his mind. Doesn't mean he wouldn't be a top guy, doing a great job, or that the family won't enjoy the pictures later, does it? Come on." He folded his arms.

"When you put it in those terms… But I always felt that your band had something different. A mission. But if you don't, forget it. I guess I misunderstood."

"What does everyone think our mission is?" Now he was smiling openly. "What lofty intentions is everyone, whoever they are, giving us credit for? What's the mission statement of Rina-O-Mangina? I can't wait to hear." He laughed at her dubious expression. "No, really."

"You're not being sarcastic, are you?"

"Not at all. I promise."

"Your band's goal is to make each and every *simchah* unique. Your band's goal is to demonstrate through your music that you know and feel that you're playing to celebrate, well, a miracle. It's not just another cookie-cutter wedding, bar mitzvah, or whatever. Something unbelievably important is going on. Worlds are being built. It's a gift from Hashem."

"That's beautiful," he said softly. "*Halevai* we should reach a fraction of that level of *chesed,* of caring."

She leaned forward again, determined to find the depth she was seeking. "You probably do possess some of that, but you're just used to it, so you don't realize it. You're the head of the band. You're its… soul, I guess. So many people I spoke to feel the way I do, that the uniqueness of the band and the reason so many people vie for your playing is the *neshamah* you bring to your music." Sheila stopped. "Forget it. Sorry. I don't mean to belabor the point." Feeling her mouth dry, she drained her cup.

I'm being very open for a first date, but he doesn't seem to mind. He doesn't agree with me, though. This is so embarrassing, to have rushed in with a bunch of mistaken assumptions about who he is. I'm probably being annoying at this point. He probably feels as if I'm putting him down. Time to change the subject, pronto.

But her mind was completely blank. She opened her mouth to say something, anything at all, when he spoke.

She believes what she's saying. Forget whether I feel that way or not. That's beside the point. She's telling me something important about herself, her values. Interesting what idealism hides behind that sophisticated exterior. I like it. I like it very much.

"I'll get you a refill."

"No thank you. Maybe soon. Yes, maybe I am describing a high level. A lot of people tell me to try to lower my standards and expectations."

Yerachmiel caught a passing waiter's eye. "Absolutely not. That's bad advice. Don't do that. Let other people raise their expectations to meet yours."

She smiled.

The waiter came over.

"A hot chocolate for me," Yerachmiel said.

"And for the lady?"

"Hot chocolate sounds good."

Yerachmiel waited until the waiter was out of earshot. "Just, theoretically speaking, can't you believe that even if we're without a mission or a message, what we do will work its magic? It does, from what you tell me. People always place their own interpretations on everything, on all communications. Anyhow, just to change the subject for a moment, I have a pet peeve about *simchos* in general."

"What is it?"

"In my opinion, the only people who ought to be invited to a *simchah* are those who want to be there, who would never want to be anywhere else that evening, who wouldn't dream of making different plans. Anything else is a waste of everyone's time and money. When I see people rush in, stay five minutes until they're sure that the *baal simchah* notices them, and then leave, it gets on my nerves."

"I don't feel that way at all," she objected. "I don't think it's the norm. I think it's the exception to the rule. People care a lot. They're very busy."

"Tell me about it."

"I teach sixth and seventh grade."

"World history, isn't it?"

"Yes. Actually, I'm also doing a three-month stint substituting for the seventh-grade homeroom teacher, but she's coming back in two short weeks, right before the end of the school year."

"You sound like you love teaching."

"I do. It's the best job in the world."

"Good for you. I don't hear that very often, about any job at all. What were you saying before?"

"I go to every single bas mitzvah party I'm invited to, even if only to say *mazel tov*. Sometimes five minutes is all the time I have, but I want each *baalas simchah* to know I care enough to come."

"Wow."

"It makes the girls so happy. Personally, I find it very touching, to witness them becoming Jewish women, precious members of our nation embarking on the first steps of their life journeys."

Yerachmiel whistled. He leaned forward. "That's very impressive," he said quietly. "I'm very impressed."

Sheila decided that it was time to slow down the momentum of the date. Enough intensity. Enough self-revelation. It was only a first date.

"I heard that you play the oboe."

He nodded. "It's my mother's favorite instrument. I started lessons as a kid. When I came to Israel as a seventh grader, I went to a *frum* music school. It made aliyah so much easier. My Hebrew wasn't great, but music was a common language. Then I went on to study piano, keyboard, and voice."

"Do you perform anywhere but in the band? In a men's choir, or as a *baal koreh*, or a *chazzan*?"

"No, I don't sing in a men's choir, but I am the lead singer for the band, and I hope this doesn't sound like boasting, but I get a lot of invitations to sing at various occasions. What else did you ask? I do *chazzanut*, and I'm a *baal koreh* as well. All the Kantors are. As a matter of fact, our family name was Chazzan. My great-grandfather changed it to Kantor when he immigrated to the United States. My father has taught bar mitzvah boys for years, and so do I. My brother Menachem and I are both *baalei koreh* for our shul. Menachem already received an offer to be a *baal tefillah* for Rosh Hashanah, now that he's a married man. He has a terrific voice. He just needs training, and he'd be tops."

* * *

"I'm surprised at you," Shlomo Kantor told his wife, Elisheva. "I'd think you'd be over the moon that he finally likes someone."

"It's not ringing true. Who comes back from a first date in a state of euphoria? He's going to crash, Shlomo. I don't have a good feeling about this. Two grown-ups, both of whom have been dating basically forever, don't just find each other in a single evening. It's not realistic."

"Why not?"

"Because. Because it isn't. Do you know what he told me that he likes about her, once he was calm enough to analyze his feelings about the evening?"

"Nu? When did you go to sleep last night, two in the morning?"

"Just about. Why?"

"You're a good mother, that's all. First, to stay up waiting for him, and then to spend hours discussing the date with him on the phone. He's forty years old. I don't know where you get the emotional energy to invest in his relationships, especially since they always fizzle out in the end. After all, let's face it, what's a first date?

"Exactly."

"Also… Well, you're overtired. That's coloring your judgment."

"You mean I'm being crabby, refusing to see the bright side. True. But Shlomo, there's no balance here. When I spoke to Yerachmiel on the phone before the date, he was skeptical that anything could come of it. He was positive that Sheila was coerced into meeting him. He's a lot older than she is. Then, a brief six hours later, he calls. You have no idea—he hasn't sounded like that since Ilana Cohen."

Both parents fell silent, remembering Yerachmiel's brief engagement almost eighteen years previously.

"I understand that you don't want him to get hurt again, but that's the name of the game," Shlomo said finally. "What does he like about her?"

"About Sheila Leipzig? Supposedly, he likes her idealism."

"That nice. What's wrong with that? I would think it would balance out our son's cynicism."

"You know he's all heart, and it's all a shell to protect himself from the world."

"Could be, but it's a pretty thick shell at this point."

"I'm afraid for him. Sheila's very sophisticated, very attractive, and she has high standards. What if she were short and not all that appealing? Ugly? Do you think he'd still find her idealism to be a selling point?

"He's met other girls with the assets you're describing," Shlomo said dismally.

"This new relationship looks and sounds and feels like it's based on infatuation. Infatuation! I just can't begin to understand him. He's not a kid anymore, some young boy who's just beginning to date. How on earth is he permitting himself to make the same foolish mistake? Who is going to pick up the pieces this time? Doesn't he realize that the two of us won't always be able to put Humpty-Dumpty back together again? We aren't getting any younger."

"I know. I know that," Shlomo said. "And I agree that he's taking a risky path."

"What was wrong with Estelle Hacohen and other girls like her that he dated over the years and rejected after one or two dates?"

"Estelle Hacohen? I don't recall an Estelle Hacohen."

"She was Estelle Bruner then. She's married now. Eva was furious when he threw that shtick. She was one of the poor women that he dated for under an hour."

"What was wrong with her?"

"She was plump."

"Why did anyone bother setting them up in the first place? He'll never go for a heavy girl. That's a real no-no in his book."

"It was just a silly excuse," she insisted. "I'll tell you what was wrong with them. They were attainable. They were available. He actually had a good chance of establishing a nice warm relationship and a nice stable marriage with them, any one of them."

Shlomo threw her an astonished glance. "You've certainly changed your tune. Whatever happened to your understanding and acceptance of his dreams?"

"Menachem and Avital happened. Avital is nice and sweet and all that, but is she glamorous or extraordinary in any way? Yet look how happy they are together. What more does he need?"

"Yerachmiel isn't Menachem. Yerachmiel follows his heart. He always has."

"Yes, and look where it's gotten him. Living all alone," she said morosely. "And it makes it much worse to see him on the artificial high. Like drinking salt water to quench thirst. When is he going to grow up? So Sheila's glamorous and attractive enough to suit his pie-in-the-sky standards. Will that make her a good wife and mother? No."

"Honestly, Elisheva, now who's being so idealistic that she's out of touch with reality?"

His wife stared at him. "Me?"

"Yes. He's human."

"Looks are so...surface."

"I feel like we've changed roles completely. I'm saying your lines, you're saying mine."

"And it gets us nowhere. He's the only one who can help himself, and he doesn't want to."

"How about—" Shlomo stopped short.

"Therapy?" his wife supplied. "Maybe, but it won't work unless it comes from him. Anyhow, he never takes advice he doesn't agree with. Too smart for his own good."

"You sound just like your sister. It's fine on her, but it doesn't suit you to be so cynical."

"Well, she's usually right now, isn't she? Admit it."

"Don't give up hope so fast. Maybe this time will be different."

She took pity on her husband, but the thoughts echoed repetitiously in her mind and heart. *Nothing will change for Yerachmiel unless he does.*

* * *

Sheila opened the door of her home as silently as she was able to. She'd been astonished to note the time Yerachmiel dropped her off: already close to midnight. Her mother was a morning person who started to yawn after nine at night, probably because she habitually rose before five. Sheila didn't want to wake her up. She'd be asleep, which was phenomenal. Her mother was in the habit of asking penetrating questions, intelligent questions, and...

She couldn't handle them right then. She wanted to revel in the feeling of being very special. Later, she'd analyze what was going on, but Yerachmiel was a pleasure to meet and very good company. That's all she wanted to take away from the evening. She hadn't enjoyed a date so much in...forever.

Why? Because.

Perhaps her father had gone to sleep as well? He was also an early riser and went to bed before eleven. It would be much simpler if both her parents were sleeping. She needed time to sit with her feelings, to clarify how she felt about this date.

Yerachmiel.

She didn't want to share the evening's conversation with anyone, even her beloved father. Not until her thoughts and her pulse slowed down. Though if he *was* up, she could tell him all that, but he'd be hurt.

"Sheila?" Her father looked up sleepily from the couch where he'd been dozing while trying hard to stay awake. He sat up, rubbing his eyes. "It's too late for any real discussion, but your mother asked that I greet you when you return. She also said that lately, you haven't wanted to analyze your dates. Can't say I blame you. Just one question. Was meeting him worth your time and energy? We heard terrific things about him."

"I-I enjoyed spending time with him," she confessed. Confessed? Yes, because that was a sure conversation starter, the very outcome she was trying to avoid.

Why was the date so enjoyable? For starters, Yerachmiel listens attentively to everything I say. It's a pleasure to talk to someone who seems to want to hear what I have to say, who doesn't contradict or interrupt, though he does have his own strong opinions.

"Good." Her father rose. "I'm glad it wasn't a negative experience."

"Not at all."

So much for avoiding analysis of the date. I guess it's too ingrained a habit to break.

All the things I take for granted, all the middos I try to develop in myself are news to him, things he's never thought about too much. At all. What does he value? How does he grow as a person?

I talked about myself a lot tonight, even if it seemed as if we were talking about his band. He knows a lot about me. Next time, if there is a next time...

Do I want there to be a next time?

Yes. I want him to say yes. I think…I hope he will.

"Abba? I was thinking about this whole apartment search business."

"Go ahead."

"So, I'm going to take a little break from looking for a place to buy, because I can't concentrate on starting a relationship and that at the same time."

"Sheila. Sheila, no one is pushing you out."

"It's not that, Abba."

Her father rubbed his eyes. "Finish what you started, Sheila. You embarked on a search for a place of your own. It wasn't a decision any of us arrived at lightly."

"But if I do that, then…"

"Then?" He looked at her intently, waiting for her to continue.

"Then, you know…" She faltered.

"Tell me."

"This is so hard for me to say."

"Sheila, you're a strong woman. You're my strong, put-together, capable daughter."

"It's such an older single thing to do. Getting my own apartment, when I'm not even dating anyone seriously. It's plunging into the world of older singles. I don't want that for myself."

Her father sighed heavily and tugged at his beard. She'd never noticed that it was completely gray. He was getting older. They all were.

"Take the ball and run with it, Sheila. It's what grown-ups do."

She shook her head miserably. "I don't want to. It's too hard. Maybe he's the one. Maybe it will be unnecessary. Why can't I wait and see what happens? Don't you think that could work? Tell me you think it could work."

Another heavy sigh. "You can stop, wait and see. It's up to you."

"You think it's a bad idea."

"I'm glad you enjoyed yourself on this date."

"You are?"

"Of course."

"Then…"

"No one's pushing you out, but you started the process for a reason. You're a grown woman. You deserve your own space. You want your own space."

"I'm not sure it's worth it…" Her voice trailed off.

"Take things one step at a time," her father said firmly.

"I should keep looking for an apartment? Even if we get serious?"

"It's wonderful that you enjoyed your date. Keep on looking for an apartment."

"But why?"

"Because he's forty-two years old, and he's never been married."

"First of all, he's forty, and second, maybe he never met the right person."

14 Odd Couple

"Home sweet home."

Renée put down the heavy shopping bag while speaking to Sheila on the phone. "So that's the story, Sheila. My mother and I spent much of today and yesterday arguing. I don't think she gets that I'm not a little girl anymore. It feels like she doesn't even try *not* to push my buttons. It's so hard for me to spend time with her."

"*Chaval* that you had an unpleasant *chag*," Sheila said sympathetically.

"Unpleasant," Renée snorted. "Unpleasant, she calls it. I don't know how you can stand living at home with your parents."

"It's not so bad. My parents give me a lot of space."

"That's not what you said earlier this year," Renée countered. "Then you were all about, 'I'm getting my own place, and no one can stop me.' What happened?"

"Oh, I don't know. Depends. It comes and goes. I like cleaning for Pesach, and so does my mother. We had a good time tackling the house together."

"You are absolutely not normal."

Sheila laughed.

"Are we on for tomorrow?"

"Definitely. Are you sure I can't bring anything to eat?"

"Positive. You know how it is. My mother sent me home with the entire refrigerator. I couldn't stop her."

"I think it's very nice of your mom to take care of you that way."

"Well, I don't. I don't want all this stuff."

"Hmm," Sheila murmured noncommittally.

"Not hmm. Your mother is very different from mine." Renée rolled her eyes in exasperation. "Whatever. I'm going to put the stuff in the fridge. I'll be in big trouble if words gets out that I let it spoil."

"I doubt that."

"I'll never hear the end of it. Don't say hmm again. See you tomorrow."

"Bye."

Renée went over to the fridge that Devora had scrubbed compulsively before Pesach. Fortunately, it had withstood the abuse, and since Devora's parents had given her the fridge secondhand when they bought a new one, Renée supposed that it was hers to abuse as she saw fit. At the moment, it was shining, sparkling with cleanliness, and empty of anything but produce and milk products. Her roommates had requested that only specific *hechsherim* be used. Renée had acquiesced, rolling her eyes only slightly.

If it makes her happy, though a hechsher is a hechsher is a hechsher. I thought they were normal. I guess no one's normal at their age. Ima thinks I don't want to get married. When I see the two of them sharing a kitchen at their age, being chesed guests even when they're with their families, I promise myself I'll never let that happen to me. She has no idea how wrong she is. If only I could get my own place, like Sheila… Lucky Sheila.

Renée began unloading the numerous containers of chicken, meat, fish, *kugels*, and salads that her mother had insisted on sending with her, setting them down on the foil-covered counter. She grimaced in distaste. Foil was so low class.

Wait. Our family doesn't use the hechsherim that the two of them want here. Or do they eat those hechsherim? How should I know? Well, too bad. Kosher is kosher. Enough is enough. What she doesn't know can't hurt her. Uh, wait. I'll use my own pots. That's not so hard to do. See, Ima? I do know how to get along with other people. It just depends on which other people.

Her mother had sent so much food that there wasn't enough room on the two shelves allocated to each roommate in the large fridge. After a pause for thought, she hesitantly placed two containers on Devora's shelf, planning to remove them instantly if her roommate objected.

After unpacking her clothing, she wandered back into the living room, at loose ends. She wanted to do something special, something festive and out of the ordinary, but what?

I should go for a power walk, but nah. Chol hamoed. It used to be a blast, all the trips we used to take, Pesach hotels with all the entertainment, until Ima and Abba got these ideas about staying home for Pesach, quality family time, blah, blah, blah. They just got cheap. I hate when they get all cheap for no reason. When I'm married, Pesach hotels here we come, the more luxurious, the better. Or maybe a cruise. Fine, but what about tonight? Gotta kill some time here. I'll sleep late tomorrow before I hit the gym. At least the gym is open. She drummed her fingers restlessly.

Off to the mall. There's always something to buy. Retail therapy, woo-hoo. You never know what might be out there if you don't look. Cheered by the prospect of action, Renée went to check her makeup in the mirror. The doorbell's ring interrupted her. It was the downstairs neighbor, whom she knew only slightly, holding foil-wrapped packages and looking hopeful.

"Finally, someone hears me ringing. Nice and quiet in here. Everyone has kids running around and screaming, even though it's way past their bedtime. My kids were always asleep at eight thirty sharp even during vacation, and I barely ever had to take them to the doctor. I know children in this building who live in the *kupat cholim*." She shook her head disapprovingly. "Three single ladies, not home for the first or last days, I thought you might have some room in your fridge."

"Oh, no thanks. I have plenty of food."

Her neighbor looked embarrassed. "I actually was wondering if you might have some storage space in your fridge for over the week."

I'll just stick the stuff Ima gave me in the freezer. I didn't want it in any case. Then, she can use my shelf. Wait! The freezer was sold to a goy. So? It's clean. I cleaned it myself. My nails were disgusting, even though I used gloves. No open chametz in there, so no crumbs will fall on anything.

Renée took the packages from the neighbor, who thanked her profusely and left.

Eager to be on her way, Renée peeled the tape off the freezer door and crammed the containers from her mother inside. She placed the packages from the neighbor on her shelf and then saw that the freezer door had opened. Probably overstuffed.

Ima slaved over the food on her aching feet. Her choice, but still. Right, and maybe she sent some brownies. Mmm. Though I really shouldn't.

Renée opened the freezer once again, took out two big containers, and placed them on the counter for just a moment to check the contents. No brownies, but there was fruit salad and coleslaw. Not bad. She replaced them on her shelf in the fridge. There. Now her roommate had her precious shelves back, plus she'd done her neighbor a favor. *I'll even eat some of what Ima sent since it's on my shelf and all. Why didn't she send brownies? She knows they're my favorite.*

She heard a key turn in the lock. Seconds later, Devora strode into the kitchen, smiling broadly.

"Renée! How was your Seder? Mine was fantastic. Inspiring. You should have heard my two-year-old nephew say Mah Nishtanah. Who said it in your family? Renée? Why is that freezer door open? The freezer's *chametzdik*." Devora backed away. Her face turned pale.

"Whoops." Renée closed the freezer door. "Chill, it's nothing. The whole business of selling to a goy, never understood it, but all

I did was put in some stuff my mother forced me to take, so relax. There are no crumbs in there, just wrapped packages."

"Whoops? Relax? I…I can't believe this. I thought I could trust you. Didn't we have an agreement?"

"Yeah, but so what? I'm human, maybe I sort of forgot? Or maybe not. Who says you can't trust me?" Renée defended herself. "Stop overreacting. All I did was put some stuff in the freezer, to do a favor for the neighbors."

Now her roommate looked ready to faint. "A favor? Which neighbors?"

"The Ben-Yashars. What difference does it make who needed space in the fridge?"

"Did you ask them if their stuff was *kitniyot*? No, you didn't." Devora opened the refrigerator and gasped. A container of *techinah* had opened and was slowly dripping onto the shelf. "Oh no!"

She ran to the bathroom and grabbed a rag that she saturated liberally with bleach, and threw it on the spreading pool of *techinah*.

"Stop! Are you crazy? Bleach in the fridge? Are you trying to poison us? It's just *techinah—kitniyot*, not *chametz*."

"I can't let it get into my food," Devora choked out, busying herself with a mound of rags that she placed gingerly in a garbage bag. Were those tears in her eyes?

She's nuts, Renée concluded, swinging her designer bag over her shoulder. *Just my luck. Semi-decent apartment, one normal roommate, and one who is…nuts! Great.*

The mall had lost its appeal, but what else was she supposed to do? Visit family and eat Pesach cake? Visit married friends and pretend to be happy for them? Visit other singles and listen to them vent?

Her phone buzzed insistently. It was probably her mother. Without checking the screen, Renée turned her phone to silent.

Once in the bustling, brightly lit mall, soothed by the bright lights, action, loud music and the sheer abundance surrounding her, she calmed down. She didn't have to act like a baby, even if Devora seemed to think it was an appropriate way to act.

Tears, for a simple human error. Was she for real? It's probably because she doesn't have a life and probably will never have a life. She's thirty-six. She'll never find a normal guy at this point.

Feeling proud of her magnanimity, Renée decided to buy Devora a small gift.

I really didn't intend to upset her. Too bad she's paranoid, but it takes all sorts to make a world, right? She completely overreacted, for a change. Story of my life. Between Ima and Devora, I'm glad at least I'm normal.

To her delight, along with big gold hoop earrings for herself, she found delicate filigree earrings with small amber stones that perfectly matched her roommate's eyes.

I personally go for a more striking look, but Devora goes for understated, almost dowdy. If you ask me, these are what she'd like. No accounting for tastes. Renée had the earrings gift wrapped.

15

Gift Wrapped

When she returned home, well after midnight, Devora was nowhere to be seen. Renée was disappointed. *Chaval. I wanted to give these to her right away. Clear the air. It's so annoying when she looks at me as if she's afraid of me, or threatened by me. She definitely has a problem, but someone has to make the first move. Besides, these were buy one, get one free, but she doesn't have to know that.*

Yehudit was sprawled on the couch, munching on potato chips and reading an ArtScroll Haggadah. She sat up.

"Hi."

"Hi. Why are you reading a Haggadah? The Seder is over, you know? Unless you have two Sedarim, since you're used to it? When did you come on aliyah, ten years ago?"

"Five," Yehudit corrected her. "So, no, I'm not used to two Sedarim anymore, but yes, sure I miss having two Sedarim. There's absolutely nothing like my father's Sedarim. He has a special tune, a *nusach* for the Haggadah that means Pesach to me. I love being here in Yerushalayim for Pesach, and as you know, my mother's entire family is here, but I love my own family Sedarim.

"You do?" Renée exclaimed, amazed. "Even one drags on and on, as far as I'm concerned. Last time I enjoyed *leil haSeder* was the last time I hid the *afikomen.* I was nine. Take a look at what I got for Devora. I was shopping, and these were so her I just couldn't resist." Renée untied the silver ribbon on the small box and held it open for Yehudit's inspection.

"That was very nice of you. They *are* her. Renée, listen. She went to sleep, but she asked me to apologize to you for what happened earlier this evening. She also requested that in the future, you please be more careful, especially on Pesach."

"She was pretty uptight," Renée retorted. "About basically nothing, if you ask me."

"She's a very sensitive type of girl, but it's more than that. We need, all three of us, to be able to trust each other."

"Trust each other? Why are both of you making a big deal over some *techinah* that spilled?"

"We all agreed on which *hechsherim* we'd use over Pesach."

"Was I supposed to tell Geveret Ben-Yashar that she couldn't store her overflow in our fridge?"

"Nooo."

"What did I do that was so terrible?"

Yehudit thought hard. "Nothing, even though it wasn't the best idea in the world to open the freezer. It's more…attitude. I wasn't there with the two of you, but…"

Renée retied the silver ribbon on the dainty box, stood up, and looked at Yehudit through narrowed eyes. "Yes?"

"Renée, until now it's been great between the three of us, except that—look, I don't blame you, *erev Pesach* is stressful in the best of homes, and we appreciated your pitching in, doing the freezer even though you hardly used it—"

"Get to the point."

"I didn't discuss this with anyone, so whatever I say now is only my own opinion."

"Yes?"

Yehudit sighed. "I can see that you feel accused, unjustly so. It's not what I have in mind, at all."

"I'm listening." Renée folded her arms.

"I hope so because I know it's not your style keeping all these *chumros,* as you see them."

"You could say that."

"I'm sure that all three of us would give a lot to be in our own kitchens, making our own Pesach, in the way we feel comfortable."

"You got that right."

"So, the story is that for whatever the *Ribbono shel Olam's* reasons, it's not the case for any of us this year. We're sharing this and a lot of other things. It's not all bad."

"It's not?"

"We can give each other the gift of support. We can give each other friendship and trust. That may be all we can do, to help each other through, but it's a lot."

"I'm not following you at all," Renée said. "I'm not into all this deep philosophical stuff at all."

"I'll try to be clearer. See, I could tell you thought we went overboard making Pesach. Maybe we did. Once the kitchen was clean, we all agreed not to bring any *chametz* in, even wrapped, even though we're adults and eat neatly."

"Right. We did agree on that, but come on. No one brought in *chametz*. I can't waste my life being controlled by the fact that Devora's neurotic."

"Hey! You can't say that."

"Well, sorry if you're in denial, but she is."

"Stop talking that way. You hardly know her." Yehudit began pacing. Back and forth. Back and forth. "How dare you?"

"How dare I? Someone needs to tell the truth. She needs help. As in real help. Psychological help. That's right. Don't look at me that way. It's nothing to be ashamed of." Renée warmed to her theme. "The two of you have been living in the same place for so long that you don't see it. Either that or you're taking her side because the two of you have lived together for longer. Either way, it's getting really annoying. I have no idea how you've put up with her for so long without saying anything."

Yehudit stopped pacing. She was silent, concentrating intently on what Renée had said. She was quiet for so long that the younger woman shifted uneasily. Finally, Yehudit spoke, slowly and quietly, measuring her words.

"I hope I don't sound like I'm lecturing you or giving you *mussar* when I say that what you just said was completely uncalled for. Number one, it's not true, not at all. As for what you said about Devora, that's a gross exaggeration. You're completely twisting the facts, misinterpreting them for some reason I can't understand. Devora's sincere. She's sensitive. She and I are friends. Close friends. I'm sorry if we've inadvertently made you feel left out."

"Don't waste your pity on me. I have plenty of friends," Renée snapped.

Yehudit drew back, stung. "And she's never been like this. So… jumpy. Not in general. Maybe you moved in at a bad time, right before Pesach and all. In general, first of all, that word *neurotic* is very unkind. It's insulting. And secondly… Secondly, I don't go for discussing anyone behind their back, and I'm sure that you don't, either."

"I can't believe what I'm hearing. The entire situation is my fault."

"No. I told you that now she's very sensitive."

"So you just allow Devora to control you because she's so sensitive, and all." Renée's sarcasm was unmistakable.

"Control?" Yehudit shook her head in disbelief. "She's not controlling me at all. Devora and I are on the same page as far as Pesach goes. A lot of people go a little overboard when it comes to Pesach, but do you know what? It's preferable to being negligent, to having an overly casual attitude, the way some people do. At least, that's the way I see it."

"An overly casual attitude the way I do, for example?" Renée's voice rose. "I suppose that's not insulting?"

"I didn't mean you."

"You could have fooled me there."

"No, I didn't mean you specifically. I was talking in general."

"If you say so."

"I say so. It doesn't look as if we're getting anywhere with this discussion. Both of us are tired. I'm very sorry if I insulted you. Let me start again. Nothing happened." Yehudit took a deep breath. "All that happened is that on *erev Pesach* you didn't realize how serious Devora was about every single limitation she put down, because to you it seems unnecessary."

"She was being completely…going completely nuts, making the rest of us crazy, and still, *I* apologized."

"You did, and she accepted. But I think that the whole incident made her nervous."

Renée's nostrils flared.

"It's harder to build trust than it is to break trust," Yehudit said.

"Especially if you have issues to start with."

Yehudit gave her a look of warning.

"I'm allowed to have an opinion. Fine, have it your way. Anything not to rock the boat, is that the way it is?"

"If you want to put it that way."

Another silence.

"All this talk, talk, talk is so not my style," Renée grumbled.

Yehudit looked at her seriously. "I know. You probably should have moved in after Pesach, at a less intense time. But nothing so terrible happened. Let's not get carried away here. Maybe be extra careful for a while? We all adhere to our agreements, and that's what creates a feeling of trust. Of safety, and of trust." Yehudit took a deep breath and looked at Renée hopefully.

Just what I need, more micromanagement of my life. Sheila Leipzig, count your blessings. This discussion is pathetic. I wish I were Sheila. Anytime she decides to, she can have her own place, be her own person.

A thought struck her full force. She couldn't believe that she had such insensitive parents. Why was she any different than Sheila? They were the same age. They were in the same position.

Ima and Abba aren't poor. Why are they so stingy? Why aren't they offering me the same thing, to buy my own place and be my own person? Don't they care about me? Don't they care about my happiness? Why am I still stuck fighting with Ima, or coping with neurotic roommates and their strange ideas? Why didn't I ever think of this before?

She checked her jeweled wristwatch. It was way too late to call Sheila tonight, but she was coming over the next day. *We need to discuss this. I can't stand it here anymore. Too bad. I already paid a full month's rent up front. Maybe I can get some of it back. Meanwhile, though, I obviously play it safe. Come on, Renée, you're a good actress. Go, Renée, go!*

She smiled at Yehudit. "I need to think about everything you said."

"I appreciate that. Sorry if I came on strong, but—"

"Oh, it's fine. Totally." Renée went into her room. She tossed the box with Devora's earrings on the table. They weren't going to Devora, that was for sure. What had she been thinking? If Devora was off the wall, she, Renée, ought to be steering clear of her, not giving her presents.

Too bad I wasted money on them. They are so not my taste. I went to the trouble of choosing something she'd like, I had them gift wrapped, but she's not getting them.

She brightened.

Sheila's coming tomorrow for lunch. She's always buying presents for her family.

Maybe she'll buy them off me.

16 Roommates

At two in the morning, Renée woke up retching. She barely made it to the bathroom before she threw up the entire contents of her stomach.

Good for you, Ima, forcing me to eat the seudah today when all I wanted was a cup of cocoa. Good for you, Devora, stressing me about absolutely nothing. Thanks a whole bunch, Yehudit, for taking her side, instead of mine.

No sooner had she staggered back to bed when she was bowled over by a new wave of nausea.

What's going on with me? she wondered, with the first twinge of fear. *I hope I don't have food poisoning.*

There was a gentle knock on the bathroom door.

Leave me alone...

"Renée? Are you all right? Is there anything I can do?" Devora asked.

"No, I'm fine."

"You don't sound fine."

"It's just something I ate."

"Let me know if there's anything I can do."

Renée didn't answer. She waited until she heard Devora return to her room. Then, she ran to her own room and closed the door hard behind her.

Did you think I want to talk to you now?

* * *

It was almost noon the next day. Renée's door was still shut.

"She may have fainted," Devora said nervously.

"Or maybe she's still asleep," Yehudit said. "She made it clear that she wants to be left alone, so let's leave her alone. She's a big girl."

"Still…she may need help. She could even be dehydrated."

"Mmm." Yehudit knocked gently on Renée's door. Was that a voice she heard? It was. She was fairly sure it was.

"You don't need to be so nervous, Devora," she reported. "I hear her talking on the phone."

"That's good." Devora breathed a sigh of relief.

"So, let's go on with our day. See, she's fine. Put the whole thing behind you. She and I talked last night."

Devora froze.

"It wasn't what you're thinking. I simply tried to explain the difference between living with a family and living with more mature roommates."

"Did she hear you?"

"I hope so. She moved in here with us. She's the one who has to make the adjustments around here, not you. Look, I won't lie, Devora. It's not an ideal set-up. She's not the best match for us or we for her."

"Please don't be angry with me."

"Angry?" Yehudit said incredulously. "At you? Why would I be angry at you? What did you do?"

"I wimped out, get it? I let you make the choice of who should move in with us on your own."

"Not true. Just at the end."

"Yeah, and look where it got us. I can't imagine ever feeling comfortable around her."

"Stop looking for her approval and maybe you will," Yehudit suggested.

"Who says I want her approval?"

"Who says so? Me." Yehudit pointed to herself. "I do. Me, your roommate and good friend. Come on, smile. You know I think you're the greatest."

"You do?"

"Stop fishing for compliments. Didn't you say you wanted to go to the *tayelet*?

"Yes, but what if she's really sick?"

"Stop feeling guilty, Devora. It's not your fault that she has an upset stomach."

"Maybe it is? At least let's make her a thermos of tea."

"And then, let's go."

"I hope we're doing the right thing." Devora bit her lower lip anxiously.

"We are," Yehudit assured her. "She's not Chaviva. She wants a business relationship. Nothing too close. She has other friends. That's what she said last night. If we leave her alone, give her her space, that's how we show friendship."

"I hope you're right."

"I am."

"I hope she's not sick because of me."

"Devora, quit it. I just told you she's not."

* * *

It was the first day of *chol hamoed Pesach*. Sheila had spent an hour and a half engrossed in research on a new topic for the *shiur* she gave every Shabbos summer afternoon at the Yanavov's home. It was a heavy topic: destiny versus free choice. The subject matter was enthralling, but she wished she had someone to study with. Her parents were out of the house, at the zoo with Michal and David's kids, while Michal and David escaped, as Michal had said only half-jokingly, up north for two days. Naturally, Sheila had been invited to join the expedition to see the animals, not to mention the crowds of fellow zoo visitors.

"Please join us, Sheila," her mother had urged early that morning over a breakfast of *matzah brei* and freshly squeezed orange juice.

"Maybe not. I'd love to get a head start on my *shiur* prep, clean this place up, even go back to bed and curl up with a good book."

"That sounds wonderful," her father commented enviously. "How about *you* go with Mommy and the kids, and I'll adopt your plan."

"No way," his wife said adamantly. "I'm looking forward to a day with you, and so are the kids. Sheila, you can start your research another time. It's a long *chol hamoed*. The zoo's a zoo on *chol hamoed*, as you well know, but it's a crime to keep the kids cooped up inside on such a gorgeous day. Another sane adult around with a spare pair of hands to help would be more than welcome."

"You'll manage without me, won't you? Gila's already a big girl, and she's used to helping with Batya."

"That's true. We don't need your help so badly, but I wish I understood why you feel the need to shut yourself up in the house on such a beautiful day when you have a family who loves you and is eager to spend time with you. What if you were company, visiting from the States? Wouldn't you consider it to be a special treat to spend a family day with all us?"

"I'm not, though."

Sheila had declined the invitation because she felt increasingly awkward and out of place on these public family outings,

"Everyone who couldn't think of other *chol hamoed* plans and their relatives will be there. My pupils and their families will be there. Sorry, Ima, I don't think it's my speed. I'll join our family picnic tomorrow, all right? While you're gone, I'll make some potato salad," she offered, trying to sound lighthearted.

"Why not do both?" her mother said. "Will you join us tomorrow at the science museum?"

"Um, probably not."

"Why?"

"I feel like a third wheel, tagging along with you and Abba and the kids."

"I don't see why you need to feel self-conscious. It's no crime to be unmarried," her father commented.

"It's not that. Not entirely that."

"What else could it possibly be? What other reason would you have for being so obstinate?" her mother asked. "Besides, running away from reality never works.

Obstinate. Sheila turned the word over in her mind. It had an unpleasant ring. *Running away from reality* didn't sound much better. Maybe she was being obstinate, perhaps she was fleeing reality, but there was more to her refusal than a desire to evade discomfort.

But I don't know how to put it into words. Something about...my own...

The house was quiet. The silence was tangible. She could hear various families who lived in her building leaving noisily on their own *chol hamoed* outings, an occasional child whining or sobbing in vociferous protest at something or another, neighbors welcoming company into their homes.

And I'm all alone. It was my choice. What if I had a baby sleeping in another room and my husband was out of the house, learning? I'd be alone then, also. I'm doing a mitzvah. I'm doing something meaningful. I'm not just filling my time. I'm building. That's what will fill the void within me best, to build. Who said it's supposed to be easy? Michal and David are building their marriage, Abba and Ima are building their relationship with the grandchildren, and I'm building my neshamah, and knowledge of Hashem's world. I'm lonely, but I'm accomplishing. Right?

She decided to take a break. After she finished cleaning up the kitchen and put a plastic tablecloth on the table, she began peeling potatoes.

Yerachmiel Kantor was at a Pesach hotel somewhere in Teveria with his parents and the entire Kantor-Goldenberg extended family. He'd asked her if she wanted to go out on Pesach, but she'd urged him not to make the trip back to Yerushalayim just for that. Instead, they'd arranged a date on *Isru Chag*.

Abba would have loved to spend the day at home. It was a gift to have time alone—sorry, private time—to delve into such a fascinating subject. Who says I'm doing anything superfluous? Just filling time? Why think negatively?

The phone rang.

"Hi, Renée."

"Hi."

"You don't sound good."

"I have some kind of nasty stomach bug. No work for me today. My mother will be happy about that. I just called in sick. They weren't pleased."

"It's *chol hamoed*. I'm sure a lot of people aren't coming in this week. I'm sure they understood."

"I'm not so sure, and besides, I'm bored stiff. I'd prefer to work."

"Where are your roommates?"

"Gone, thank goodness. I need some space. They made me a thermos of tea. I hate tea."

Sheila laughed. "Come on, Renée. They can't know that. It was sweet of them to do that."

"I guess."

"How's it going? Are you still in the mood for company?"

"Don't you dare cancel on me, Sheila. I'm going crazy here."

* * *

Sheila whistled. She looked at the silver foil-covered kitchen. "Whoa. Serious Pesach. Good for you guys. Hey, Renée, you look pale."

"Gee, thanks."

"No, really. You don't look so great."

"Stop it, okay? I'm fine. Are you hungry, Sheila?" Renée gestured at the platters covering the kitchen table. "Help yourself. Take it home. I have to get rid of all this food."

"You're not anorexic, Renée, are you?"

"Strange question."

"I didn't think so, but why aren't you eating anything? Your mother is right. You're too thin."

"No such thing. Thanks for the compliment."

"It wasn't one. You're welcome. I feel awkward, eating a three-course *seudah* while you eat nothing."

"I'll be sitting here drinking cola," Renée pointed out.

"That doesn't count. You're so pale."

"Sheila, do me a big favor. Don't you dare join the millions of people who are trying to run my life. I can't eat anything at the moment. I don't want to start throwing up again. My stomach was killing last night. I thought I was going to die from the pain. It was scary. I'm telling you, it was scary."

"Spare me the details. I got the picture. Don't worry about my running your life. I can barely run my own life," Sheila pointed out. "Sorry, but you really don't look like you're going anyplace tomorrow, either."

"We'll see. What's new with you?"

"Not much. I like teaching seventh grade. I told you about that?"

"Only a million times. I'll never understand why you became a teacher. Anyone can become a teacher."

"I've told *you* a million times, that's absolutely false. It's not a glamorous career like being an architect, but it's real. It's working with people. It's very fulfilling."

"I'm glad you enjoy babysitting. *Not* for me."

"Let's agree to disagree," Sheila suggested.

"Fine, fine. I wasn't asking about that anyhow."

"Dating?" Sheila started shaking her leg, a nervous habit she thought she'd dropped. "Not much."

"Rumor has it that you're going out with Yerachmiel Kantor."

"Who told you?" Sheila asked, astonished.

"I don't remember. Word gets around. Sheila, he's like tons older than we are."

"Don't remind me. Anyhow, it's eight."

"More than that."

"Not really. Age isn't everything, Renée."

"If you say so. Have you gone out with him yet?"

"Once."

"And?"

"I wanted to go out again."

"Oh. Well, in that case… Let me tell you something."

"What?"

"I also went out with him."

Sheila's eyes widened. "You did?"

"Yes."

"No! Who in their right mind would put the two of you together?"

"Well, it just goes to show how much thought people put into setting other people up," Renée said. "As in, none. The two of us are so, so different, and what do you know? Yerachmiel Kantor, the one-size-fits-all guy. We ought to advertise. Have you run out of guys in your age group? Move up a decade or so. Try it out, you never know."

Sheila laughed reluctantly. "Let's change the subject."

"Tell me," Renée wheedled. "All the juicy details."

"No way." Sheila pushed her chair away from the table. "Whoa, am I full. When you speak to your mother, tell her that her schnitzel is out of this world. Do you have the recipe?"

"Are you kidding? I never go anywhere near the kitchen if I can help it. Stop trying to change the subject."

"Number one, I never discuss my dates," Sheila said firmly.

"Goody-goody."

"No, it's *lashon hara*. Serves no purpose."

Renée raised her eyebrows. "Tell me, since when are you into that stuff?"

"Since forever."

"Not true. We were in high school together, and I don't remember you being so…" Renée waved her hand. "Fanatic. So in-your-face *frum*."

Sheila reddened. "Do you realize how many years ago high school was? Ever hear of growth? Maturity?"

Renée waved her hand. "Kidding. I'm teasing you. Stop taking yourself so seriously. Lighten up. What's number two?"

"Huh?"

"Number one, you never gossip." Renée held up a finger. "Number two is—"

"Not everything is a joke," Sheila said stiffly. "I only said that I try."

"Number two?"

"Number two, we only went out once. Subject closed."

"Keep me posted. That would be hysterical. You and Yerachmiel." Renée pursed her lips thoughtfully. "I can see it. Maybe. Ooh. You're blushing."

"You say one more word, and I'm out of here."

"No. Don't go. Sheila, nothing's working out for me. I can't stand my life. I'm having a hard time getting along with my roommates. I thought it would work out here, but it won't. I hate my job as an interior decorator. I'm an architect. My mother… No decent dates. My life's a total mess, Sheila."

"Oh, Renée. I'm so sorry. I know how you feel."

"No, you don't. Don't tell me that you do. You can't because there's no way that you know how I feel. You like your job, you have a chance to get your very own place, you—"

"Okay." Sheila cast around for something to say. "I've never seen you so upset. I wish there was something I could do to help."

"Oh." Renée took a careful sip of her cola and clutched her stomach. "There is."

"Tell me what."

"I told you already once, but you said you were afraid to ruin our friendship."

"Renée! Renée, that's not fair."

"Why isn't it fair? We're supposed to be friends, right? What's so horrible about me that makes you afraid that if you got your own place, and we were to become roommates, it would ruin our friendship? You're the one being not fair. Can't you see that I'm desperate? Can't you see that I'm so upset that I'm literally sick to my stomach?"

Sheila got up from the table and began to stack the dishes. "Which sink is *fleishig*?"

Renée shrugged. "You don't have to do that. I'll do that later. I'm surprised at you. I thought I could depend on you. But whatever. No is no. I'm not going to beg you."

Sheila turned around. "I don't even know if I want to get my own place. We're talking about nothing."

"Don't tell me that. You yourself told me that you've been going with what's her name, Menucha Shalom, to look at properties."

"I don't like any of them." Sheila sat down.

"I have no clue why you're stalling," Renée said frankly. "I think you're crazy. I'd compromise, just so my parents wouldn't change their minds."

"Mine won't."

"How did you convince them to buy you your own home?"

Sheila seized the opportunity to change the subject. "It was my mother's idea."

"Your mother's idea?"

"Uh-huh. She said I was stagnating at home. You know my mother. She convinced my father that moving out on my own would contribute to my maturation process."

Renée's shoulders slumped. "Forget about it. My mother will never say that, not in a million years."

A key turned in the lock. Renée leaped to her feet. "It's them.

They're home! Can't stand either of them. Come, let's go to my room. Now."

"But the dishes," Sheila protested.

"Leave them."

Sheila hurried after Renée to her room. Devora and Yehudit entered, chattering animatedly. They came into the kitchen. Yehudit stopped short at the sight of the messy table, still cluttered with containers and crumbs. Her eyes narrowed as she took in the dishes in the sink.

"This was not what we agreed to when she moved in."

"Forget it." Devora was already cleaning up.

"Why are you doing that?"

"I told you. I feel bad about last night."

"Don't be ridiculous."

"So, I'm doing a little *chesed*. Big deal. Maybe she doesn't feel well enough to clean up after herself."

"Could be. Here, I'll give you a hand."

"I'm finished. Takes longer to talk about than to do."

I'm not sure that was chesed, Yehudit thought. *Not sure at all. But, I can't keep on mediating. The two of them are going to have to learn to get along with each other. Either that or Renée's going to have to move out.*

I hope something changes soon. I'm not looking forward to having that conversation with Renée. She's not afraid to say what's on her mind, and she uses some very strong terminology.

17
A Perfect Morning Drink

Unfortunately, Geula disliked her schedule. This year, the year of two brand-new beginnings, major beginnings, was a lot harder than she'd ever dreamed it would be. Did she regret the choices she'd made? She didn't know. Maybe she did.

Three afternoons a week she taught some of the most restless and inattentive children in all Machon Atara. The hour right after lunch break, when their motivation and will to cooperate were both at their lowest ebb, were a test of her patience and, presumably, theirs as well. There was nothing she could do to change the situation.

Although a veteran teacher, she felt like the new kid on the block in Machon Atara. As such she couldn't complain. The way her schedule had worked out was nothing personal against her. Nechama Rotter and Hadassah Noleman, the team responsible for the teachers' schedules at Machon Atara, both possessed an innate sense of fairness. They were even more scrupulous than usual when it came to arranging the yearly schedule. Geula knew that. There were probably teachers who knew how to work the system to their advantage, but Geula had never been one of them.

Today, when her alarm was ringing, horribly, shrilly, and compellingly, completely ignoring her urgent need for sleep, it was hard to remain calm, objective, and rational. Those three afternoon hours weren't her favorite, but Mondays and Thursday mornings were the worst.

Every Monday morning and Thursday morning Geula had to be up at six fifteen or six thirty at the very latest. Latest? Six thirty wasn't late in Geula's opinion, but the fact was that she had to be in school at eight sharp, so six thirty was pushing it if she wanted to daven properly before the hour-long commute to work.

It shouldn't matter, the main thing was that she had a satisfying job in an excellent school, and yet, it did. It just did. She couldn't help it. In Bnos Naomi, where she'd taught for twenty-five years until the big switchover this year, she'd never started school before nine forty-five in the morning. It was a huge difference. Not that she minded the early wake-up time, at least not in principle. She hadn't thought it would be an issue, and under normal circumstances, it wouldn't be. She was usually a morning person. However, now that the doctor had told her to stay away from coffee, even decaf, that had changed. It wasn't just the taste she sorely missed. It was also the caffeine jolt that formerly had gotten her going in the morning. The chicory blend she'd found wasn't bad at all, but it just wasn't the same.

The sun wasn't bright yet, but it was already light outside, and there was a cool breeze blowing through the window. She groaned out loud. These cool Yerushalayim early mornings at the beginning of the summer were a gift. She actually enjoyed waking up early to experience them. Usually, but not today. Today, she was just too tired, and just too upset to enjoy anything. Washing her hands, she found herself remembering a conversation she'd had with Helen Tauber one rainy, wintry Monday morning earlier in the year.

* * *

For whatever reason, Geula had slept poorly the night before. It happened sometimes. Pulling herself out of bed hadn't been simple, but with no other choice, she'd done so, rolling her eyes at the storm raging outside her kitchen window. It looked like nighttime. The sky outside had been as dark as her mood. It was pouring rain that was bone-numbingly cold. When she'd left, extra early, planning to get to school early and daven there, her umbrella had turned out to be completely ineffective. She was soaking wet before she even got on the bus. The overcrowded buses crawled sluggishly, and despite her early start, she'd gotten to school barely in time for the first bell. Her throat was parched. She still had ten minutes. *Baruch Hashem*. Ten whole minutes. Not enough time to daven, if she didn't want to be late to class. She'd have to daven in the classroom, with the students. It was something she tried to avoid doing because it interfered with her *kavanah* even if she didn't speak to anyone while she was doing so. In addition, she felt guilty. How could she trust the girls to daven instead of fooling around, when there was no adult to supervise? She couldn't. It was slacking off her job, it was poor *chinuch*, and it would be her fault if some girls stared into space, doodled, or talked. Rabbanit Sudri claimed that the main thing was personal example, that the girls see an adult davening, and with no other choice, today she'd have to fall back on that and hope for the best.

Today, she'd have to make an exception and hope that no child would urgently require her attention or rebuke. Ten minutes. She could make herself a cup of hot coffee—no, hot chicory—and *baruch Hashem* for that. She could sit down and catch her breath. Thus fortified physically and even more so emotionally, she'd be better equipped to face the third graders, not all of whom were a hundred-percent cooperative or in the best of moods when she saw them in the morning.

She walked into the teachers' room with a fervent hope: *Please let there be milk. Please, please let there be milk. The chicory tastes terrible without milk.*

She opened the refrigerator. No milk. Her heart sank. She looked hopefully at the counter next to the sink. No milk. She'd have to drink her bitter beverage black, which in the larger scheme of things was absolutely no big deal, but at the moment, to Geula, it felt like the biggest deal in the whole world. She needed the comfort that a splash of milk would give her. She craved it.

Noa Lewin had closed her siddur. She instantly made a beeline for the refrigerator, opened it, and shook her head in annoyance. "No milk? Again? Still no milk? I'm going to speak to Nechama Rotter or Helen Tauber. They have to be more on top of the milk situation. I hate drinking coffee without milk. Oh, well. Beggars can't be choosers," she muttered. She took a cup from the dish rack and rinsed it out.

The milk situation? That sounds funny, but it isn't. Are we spoiled, or just human?

Helen Tauber swept into the teachers' room, holding a dripping umbrella and smiling widely. "*Boker tov, boker tov lekulan, boker tov, morot yekarot.* Good morning to all."

I have no koach for her. She makes me feel so inadequate. That good mood, well, good for her. But I hope she doesn't talk to me. I have no strength to pretend to be in a good mood. Not the way I'm feeling.

Geula took another gulp of her drink. Bitter. Bitter. Coffee was just as bitter without milk, but somehow it tasted better. Why couldn't she just have coffee like everyone else?

Helen hung her soaking wet coat over the back of a chair and headed straight for the sink. Not bothering with a spoon, she shook a liberal amount of coffee into her cup, which was emblazoned with the slogan "World's Best Teacher."

"No milk? Oh, dear. Too bad."

"Too bad?" Noa said. "Come on, Helen. Why isn't there any milk in the mornings this week? Did the teacher's committee run out of money?"

"As a matter of fact, yes. The coffers are empty," Helen answered, unruffled, as she poured boiling water into her cup. "If you teachers would just pay your dues on time, this wouldn't happen."

"Helen, you and Nechama have to be on top of the situation. I paid. Geula did you pay?"

Geula nodded her assent.

"See? It's not fair to deprive those of us who do what we're supposed to do when we're supposed to do it." Noa moved away.

"Complaints, complaints," Helen commented to the room at large. "There's always something to complain about if that's what a person chooses. Always something to kvetch about. It's a matter of choice. Look at the weather. Such a beautiful day. Such a *brachah* this rain is to us. Oh, Geula. What's that you're drinking?"

"Chicory."

"How interesting. Why?"

"I can't have coffee."

"Why not?" Helen asked, finishing her first cup, and shaking out more coffee for a second one. "I didn't get a chance to have my coffee at home this morning. I'm not human without my coffee."

"Blood pressure. No, rapid pulse. The doctor told me no coffee at all."

"Oh, dear. At your age?"

"Yes."

"Good for you, taking care of yourself. You don't need high blood pressure, not at your age. It's a simple enough solution not to drink coffee. What about decaf?"

"Not that either. It's not so simple for me. Actually, I'd far prefer a cup of coffee once in a while," Geula had retorted. To her distress, her tone of voice was sharp. Why did Helen consistently bring out the worst in her?

Helen's eyes had widened. "Coffee is nothing but a drink. You have your health in exchange. It's a beautiful day."

The bell rang. Hadassah Noleman, the assistant principal, entered the teachers' room.

"*Morot,* the bell rang," she announced. "Whoever is teaching now, the girls are waiting for you."

Slowly, with varying degrees of alacrity, the teachers began moving toward the exit of their haven to begin a day's work. Soon enough, the room was empty, except for the two or three teachers who had a free period. Discreetly, Hadassah approached her colleague.

"Helen, a number of teachers have been telling me that there's no milk in the morning."

"They told you about that? Please. Don't people have coffee, milk, and hot water at home?"

"Well, they do, but some of the teachers travel a long way, and, oh, I don't know. It's a concern that needs to be addressed, that's all. It's part of the ambiance to offer our employees a good cup of coffee when they come to work. People appreciate the small details. It shows that we care."

"Oh my, such a tempest in a teapot. A coffee pot."

Hadassah smiled politely. "Coffee pot. Good joke."

"I thought so myself."

"Only, let's not lose sight of the fact that for our staff, a good hot drink when they come in for a long day of work is no joking matter," Hadassah said seriously. "I'm sure if a survey were taken on this, a teacher who had her cup of coffee would prove to be far more productive and motivated than one who did not. The teachers' committee is providing an essential service to everyone in the school, the kids, the teachers—everyone.

"What happened to a simple sense of mission?" Helen waved her hand dismissively. "People get down in the mouth about the most foolish issues instead of counting their blessings. We are a spoiled, coddled generation, Hadassah. The reason there's no milk is that not all the teachers paid their dues to our teachers' committee, which means there's no money to buy milk or coffee. Or cups for that matter. So far, Nechama and I have been laying out the cash from our own pockets, but there's a limit."

"I didn't realize that. You'll be reimbursed," Hadassah said apologetically.

"No, no, that's not necessary. I was just explaining."

Geula had to go to class, so she missed hearing the rest of the conversation, which she imagined was predictable enough.

Helen wasn't accusing me, in particular. She wasn't referring to me personally when she said spoiled and coddled. She was speaking in general. And even if she was, who appointed her to be my judge? I don't think I'm spoiled or coddled.

What does Helen Tauber know about me or the circumstances of my life? Even though, looking at the situation from a mature perspective, getting so worked up about milk isn't very flexible or mature.

Maybe I am spoiled.

"What a fuss about nothing, I tell you," Helen said after Geula left. "Don't people respect themselves? Milk, no milk, what are they, babies?"

"No, they aren't," Hadassah agreed. "But if there's one thing I've learned in my years of working with adults, it's this." She paused.

"I'm listening."

"Number one, having a properly equipped teachers' room is far from being a small matter. You and Nechama have always done a superlative job as far as that's concerned."

Helen inclined her head. "Thank you. We care."

"I know you do. We all know that you do. And second—"

"Yes?"

"When a reasonable person makes a fuss about nothing, it's because something big is bothering them."

"So something is bothering them? We all have a *pekel* to carry, don't we?"

"So they make a fuss about something small."

"That may be true, but it still doesn't excuse rude behavior,"

Helen told her. "We all carry burdens, and there's no justification for rudeness."

"I agree, but isn't making sure that the teachers' room is a welcoming place a small price to pay to avoid unpleasantness?"

"The whole thing rubs me wrong." Helen shook her head disapprovingly. "It smacks of entitlement."

"Why do you say that?"

"Teachers don't pay their dues, yet they expect the services."

"Number one, many teachers do pay." Hadassah sighed. As was so often true in her job as an administrator, no one was wrong, everyone was right, and yet the main thing was not to get trapped in a net of opposing points of view, and instead to actually get the job done. So often someone ended up feeling unheard and misunderstood.

"We'll reimburse you for the expense," she repeated. "Give the receipts to Yonina Nachum."

Helen shook her head disapprovingly.

* * *

Geula caught sight of her alarm clock and snapped back to the present. Much as she hated to go to work when she was feeling almost sick with exhaustion, she had no other choice.

It's not the kids. I can handle the kids. It's my colleagues. When I'm feeling this awful, I can't take having to look on top of things, optimistic, happy, and upbeat. I feel like curling into a ball and avoiding the world until the pit in my stomach and lump in my throat both disappear. Maybe I shouldn't have started a job at a new place at this stage of my career. No one knows me. I always have to be at my best.

Geula selected one of her favorite outfits, a swirling, flowing skirt in various shades of purple, with a silky violet-colored tunic. For a finishing touch, she slipped her new ring on her finger. There! At least she looked her best.

I thought I'd make a fresh start. I thought I was stronger. I thought I'd make new friends, get away from the whole image as the only older single on staff.

It was just past six. The sun was already shining outside, but the air was still cool. The quality of the light and the early Yerushalayim morning breeze were normally a delight to her soul. Ordinarily, even sans coffee, this was her favorite time of day, replete with possibility, opportunity, and the promise of fresh starts. But not today. Not today, and in some ways, maybe never.

What is there in my life other than work, work, work? What fills my life? What gives it meaning? What gives it purpose? What gives it a center? Where do I belong? What's my role in the world? Who can supply me with satisfying answers, answers I can live with?

Sometimes she thought that the answers simply didn't exist, or that they were too lofty for a person at her level. Unconsciously, she gritted her teeth. It had been her choice to move to Yerushalayim.

Her school, Bnos Naomi—her bastion of security, accomplishment, and companionship—had closed down.

At first, she'd been literally shell-shocked. The entire staff had seen it coming, but still, she was shocked. They all were.

When the dust settled, she'd discovered that it was liberating as well. The sole reason to continue living in the small suburb near Yerushalayim had been her job. That reason no longer existed. She had no children to uproot, no husband to take into consideration. And… Yerushalayim. Her entire immediate family—mother, siblings, nieces and nephews—lived there. Not that she would move in with family, not at her age and after so many years of living independently, but her mind was made up. She was moving back to Yerushalayim, and Hashem would help her find a job there.

Despite the doomsayers, she'd pushed past her comfort zone, gone out on a limb, and, heart in her mouth, she'd applied independently for the job at Machon Atara. They didn't need another homeroom teacher, but Geula's art background proved to be her trump card. The art teacher was retiring. Geula's principal provided glowing recommendations. In short, a match made in Heaven—at least a match of a certain kind, or so Geula had thought then.

Naturally, she had to compromise. Her new job offered fewer

hours. That translated into a reduced income, especially as she'd fulfilled another lifelong dream by buying a tiny ground-floor studio apartment that opened onto a patio and a minuscule garden. At the beginning of the year, she'd been on top of the world. She, Geula Leibowitz, owned land in Yerushalayim. Could life get any better?

That's how she'd felt then, seeing her dreams come to fruition. Now, the school year was almost over. Real life was far grittier and required far more endurance than she could summon up on this beautiful, smiling summer day.

Maybe all the doomsayers weren't wrong. I'm lonely. On the other hand, I was lonely in my former school as well. Maybe I'll always be lonely. Painfully lonely. Maybe it's part and parcel of being single at my age.

I'm calling Hadassah right now and telling her that I'm way too depressed to deal with other human beings.

Yeah, right.

Maybe in another gilgul.

Geula schlepped lethargically through the rest of her morning routine and headed out to the bus.

It was the day after the eighth-grade graduation at Machon Atara. Geula had attended the graduation and stayed until eleven thirty to help clean up the auditorium, making sure she was constantly within Rabbanit Sudri's line of vision. Now she was paying the price, but surely her low spirits couldn't be due only to lack of sleep. The eighth graders and their respective homeroom teachers had the following day off, but Geula didn't. She watched thankfully as the bus chugged up noisily, right on time. Her heart sank when she looked through the window and saw that the bus was filled to capacity.

Why was I born?

All the seats were taken, occupied by yawning teenagers. Most of them looked as if they'd just crawled out of bed moments before.

Why in the world do kids their age have any reason to be exhausted? They stay up all night, that's why. At least their fatigue is keeping them quiet. Otherwise, the rest of us would be subjected to high-pitched shrieks and giggles, not to mention some of the silliest conversations I've ever heard in my life.

I'm not being very nice. I was just as flighty at their age.

How long ago was that?

There was hardly room to stand, much less sit. Geula placed her briefcase and laptop on the floor.

I wish someone would get up for me, but I have no right to ask anyone to do so. I'm not elderly or expecting, and these kids are beyond wiped out.

It's their fault. It is exam period, true, but the facts are, they have no idea of time management. None. Why aren't their parents more on top of them?

I bet that at least some of these kids encountered whatever they're being tested on today for the first time this year at ten last night. Not that I did much better with scheduling at their age, but at least I listened in class and took notes. What do these kids think they're doing, setting themselves up for failure? It's so simple to succeed in school.

Geula took a deep breath, berating herself for being critical, judgmental, hostile, irritable, and—

I'm sad.

The thought flashed through her mind, but she dismissed it.

What do I have to be sad about? Even if I am sad, what can I do about it, other than learn to live with it? I've made my choice. There's no way I'm continuing with shidduchim, which means there's no way I'm getting married. But does that mean I have plans for how to create a rich, meaningful, full life for myself? A life that will leave me nourished and feeling cherished?

No.

No, and the yearning for a partner in life never quit.

I can make up my mind, but how can I quiet my heart?

I can't.

Not that I want to stop existing, chalilah, but why was I born? It just can't be that I was born solely to teach art to young Jewish girls. Sure, many of them love the break from more intellectual pursuits; sure, most of them enjoy their creations. I know it affords them the outlet that many of them need.

So what?

I don't want that to be the only reason I was born.

All the people who look at me aghast when I tell them that I've stopped dating. I haven't stopped longing. Just...dating was a dead end that offered no hope.

So now, I have no hope.

One of the girls conferred briefly with her friends and offered Geula her seat. Smiling gratefully, Geula accepted the offer. She sank into the seat, leaned back, and shut her eyes.

I look old. Old enough to be offered a seat.

Who cares?

The bus stopped. Most of the students exited.

This depressing mood is a drag, and so not like me. It's not who I am. It's not who I want to be. I'm being horrible company for myself. Bad mood, go away. Leave me alone.

I hope I'll cheer up soon. I know I should count my blessings. I live in Yerushalayim, Ir HaKodesh. I'm healthy. I have a good job. When I go home, I'll go right back to bed. No husband to cook supper for, no whiny, kvetchy kids tugging at me. I can eat when I want, I can sleep when I want...

See? There are definite advantages to being single.

Geula shook her head despondently, thinking of all the times she'd staunchly repeated that very statement to her colleagues and friends at Bnos Naomi. It had been true, then. For the first five years after she'd shed the irksome, pointless burden of dating and tried to build her life in other ways it had been absolutely true. Now, though? It was hard to discern what was simple loneliness and living in a new place, and what was...

I'm not going there ever again.

18

Inner Resources

To her vast relief, by the time Geula got off the bus, her bad mood had faded.

"I guess I'm not late," Aviva Lavie said breathlessly to Geula as she rushed into the teachers' room with only moments to spare before the eight o'clock bell rang. "Do I have time for a drink? Tell me I have time for a drink. I also need to wash my face and fix my makeup. I totally cannot go into class like this. If you're still sitting in the teachers' room, that means there's time till the bell rings."

"Why does it mean that?" Geula asked. "Here, sit. Catch your breath. I'll get you something to drink."

"Because you're always one of the first teachers to get up after the bell rings. You, and Noa, and, of course, Sheila."

"Where is Noa? I haven't seen her yet, come to think of it. She's always the first one here in the morning, after Rabbanit Sudri."

"So, that's just it. I'm subbing for her first hour, while she goes for her end-of-the-year evaluation with Rabbanit Sudri. They're both in the office right now." Aviva gulped down the glass of water Geula offered her, draining it in a single gulp. "Wow! Thanks! I needed that."

I really should offer to take over for Aviva for just a couple of moments, until she gets her act together. Isn't that the kind of person I want to be? Warm, caring, giving—regardless of my life circumstances. Isn't being a kind person my core value?

She didn't even ask. I'm also exhausted, and besides, why should I serve someone young enough to be my daughter?

I refuse to be petty. Just open up your mouth and make the suggestion.

I can't. I won't. I don't want to. Noa's class is too challenging this early in the morning. Even Sheila Leipzig couldn't handle that bunch without screaming her head off. Never knew she could scream. I can't imagine how Noa copes with them, hour after hour, day after day, when I breathe a sigh of relief after having them for my solitary hour a week. Come to think of it, how does Aviva manage them so beautifully? I've never heard her raise her voice.

"Why are you staring at me?" Aviva asked self-consciously. "Do I have a stain on my shirt, or what?"

"No, no, not at all. Actually, that was a look of admiration you just spotted."

"Admiration?" Aviva fidgeted. "Why?"

"You must be a natural. You must just be one of these naturally talented teachers."

Aviva's mouth curved into a smile. "I wish. I love teaching. I adore the kids. Why do you say that?"

"Well, for one thing, the way you handle Noa's class. You have to admit that some of the kids there are, um…"

"Normal kids? Not robots or soldiers? Why should they be? They're so little. They're so young. They don't see their mommies all day. Why do we have such high expectations of them? All they really want is our attention. Don't you think that they deserve at least that much from us?"

"Wow!" Geula was impressed. To her chagrin, she also felt a touch of envy, which she hastily suppressed. Oh, to be young, with her entire life before her. Though she had to admit that she'd never had Aviva's fiery enthusiasm for teaching at any age. "Good for you. That's some answer."

"Is there any other valid way to feel about the subject?" Now Aviva had her hands on her hips.

"To feel? Look, Aviva, people have lives that make heavy demands on them."

"So what?"

"They get tired."

"Is that the kids' faults? A good teacher should be able to soar above all that and give her all to the kids."

Noa Lewin walked in to hear the tail end of Aviva's speech.

"Good for you, Aviva. You'll go far. So, the way it turned out, Rabbanit Sudri is calming down one of the parents who just came without an appointment. I came to get a drink. No reason for me to wait around in the office. Yonina knows where to find me when she needs me." She went over to her big beige pocketbook and took out a water bottle filled with milk.

"I won't say who's in the office with Rabbanit Sudri, but boy, did she look upset. Now, where did I put that can?" She drew out a small can of Elite coffee. "My emergency kit. What was I saying?"

"You were giving Aviva some well-deserved compliments," Geula offered.

Noa shook some coffee into a cup. She held out the can. "Anyone want some?"

Geula and Aviva shook their heads.

Noa made a *brachah* and took a long sip. "Ah...mark my words, with your abilities and wonderful attitude, you have what it takes. I wouldn't be surprised if you followed in Rabbanit Sudri's footsteps."

Aviva blushed a deep scarlet.

To her acute dismay, Geula's pangs of envy sharpened. *What's with me? I don't want to be a principal. I never wanted to be a principal.*

"Milk delivery, ladies. Your milk is here," Helen Tauber announced with a flourish, depositing three bags on the table. "You can breathe easy. Drink to your heart's content. Plenty more where it came from. Noa Lewin? Did you hear me?"

"Thanks, Helen," Noa said. "I'm sure the other teachers will appreciate your efforts, but personally? I've learned not to take chances." She shook the small bottle. "I bring my milk from home. Forewarned is forearmed. I learned my lesson this winter."

"What happened this winter?" Aviva asked.

"Don't ask." Noa waved her arms dramatically. "It was pouring outside, and you were home with the flu, so I had to cope with our little angels single-handedly. I was feeling absolutely awful. I was coming down with strep, but who had time to think about that? Who had time to go to the doctor?"

"*Oy*. I'm so sorry!" Aviva gasped.

Noa looked at her blankly. "Sorry? Why? You were sick."

"I'm sorry for letting you down."

"You didn't let me down." Noa drained her cup. "You were sick, sweetheart."

"So were you."

"I'm a mother. A mother gets used to sacrificing her own comfort for her children. She gets used to putting her own needs last. You'll see. When you become a mother yourself, it will become second nature. In any case, I dragged myself to school, longing for something hot to soothe my throat, and there was no milk for the third day in a row. I barely made it till ten o'clock recess, when *baruch Hashem*, Hadassah Noleman did something to remedy the situation. Since then, I come equipped."

"Have it your way," Helen retorted with a shrug. "As you wish."

Aviva chuckled aloud, putting her hand guiltily over her mouth.

"They do this all the time. It's their little routine," Geula explained. "It's all in good humor, so don't worry."

"Avivaleh, are you laughing at us old fogies?" asked Noa, who was all of thirty-two. "Wait until you're our age. Then you'll see how essential a good cup of coffee can be to starting off the day on the right foot."

"Who are you calling an old fogey here?" Helen waved her hand dismissively. "Bah. You're babies, both of you. Wait until you're a grandma several times over like I am, pooh, pooh, pooh. Then you'll have earned the right to term yourself an old fogey."

"A baby with seven kids, *bli ayin hara*," Noa objected.

"You're still a baby."

And what am I? Aviva's a glowing nineteen-year-old with a sparkling future. Where do I fit in? Noa's a settled mother and a very successful teacher. Helen's the school's official one-woman chesed committee and a savta to boot. Who am I? What am I?

Where do I get to shine?

"Okay, Aviva, enough kidding around. Let's review what I want you to do with the class while I meet with Rabbanit Sudri. I have at least five, ten minutes before I need to go wait again. Let's not waste the time. Menucha Shalom never takes less than twenty minutes—oops!" Noa covered her mouth with her hand, looking chagrined.

Both Geula and Helen glanced at her alertly, but neither woman commented.

Fortunately, Aviva was fairly oblivious to the internal politics of Machon Atara, and Noa was grateful.

The first-grade teacher and her assistant bent over a pile of papers, their heads close together.

"You look very nice," Helen Tauber said to Geula. "What you're wearing is stunning. It takes at least five years off your age. And that ring!"

"Thank you."

"I think you lost weight. Did you?" Helen asked, looking Geula up and down and nodding approvingly.

"I try," Geula replied, sounding terser than she wanted to. She wasn't sure why Helen got under her skin, but remembering her resolution to open up more about herself, she made an effort.

"Thanks for noticing. It's a lot of work."

"Anything worthwhile takes effort. Sure it's work, but so worth it. In any case, I find that after a week or so on a diet, my stomach shrinks. It's all a matter of willpower. How do they say it nowadays? Won't power. In this hot weather, I find myself a lot less hungry than I am in the winter."

"I don't," Geula informed her. "I always like to eat. Winter, summer, it makes no difference to me."

"I wouldn't cook at all if my husband wasn't fond of a well-rounded hot meal. Tuna sandwiches would be just fine. Now you can go back to fitted clothing. Much more becoming."

"Thanks."

Helen leaned closer to Geula. "Did you ever think of dying that gorgeous hair of yours? It would make you look so much younger, and it would be a lot easier than losing weight."

Geula's mouth dropped open in shock. She drew away, blushing furiously.

"Why are you so embarrassed? I dye my hair too, and it's always covered."

"Um."

"I most certainly had no intention of offending you. I'm sorry if you think I did."

Geula found her voice. "It's fine, thanks."

"It's important for an individual at your stage of life to present herself to her best advantage. I'm an old bubby, so after all is said and done it's just vanity on my part. I have an eagle eye for even one extra pound on myself. Straight into a weight-loss regimen I go. No bread, no cake. You look excellent. Now, you need to get married. I want to give you a *brachah* that you should be married, this year. That you should have twins, and not have a single moment for yourself."

She means well.

Think of her annoying comments as a cough, annoying but harmless. Just words, that's all.

She means well. It's just words.

I know she does, but it doesn't help. At. All. But…mazel tov! I think she reached a new low in intrusiveness today. Or should that be a new high? I know this is how she shows closeness and caring, but I wish she'd get off my back. Until now my weight wasn't a topic of conversation, nor was my hair color.

No one's home to talk to even if I'd want to tell her how her comments make me feel. She'd be so hurt, so bewildered.

Repeat seven times: she means well. She's trying to be nice.

Why does she assume that I still want, still long for all that, after so many years? Can't she stretch her mind to encompass the possibility that I've moved on?

Have I?

Can't it occur to her that maybe normal human beings learn to live with other realities, even if it's not their first choice? Search for other ways to fill their lives with meaning and positive content with whatever resources they have at present? How long am I expected to yearn and pine? Forever?

Even if I do.

Even if I do yearn and pine with no end in sight.

She's not doing me any favors by constantly bringing the subject to the forefront. Emphasizing what I lack. What's the point?

Isn't there any other way to show caring?

"In any case, whatever the reason, don't sabotage yourself," Helen continued, oblivious to the raging inner dialogue taking place inches from her head. Her kindly face brightened perceptibly. "I just thought of something! I can't believe I never thought of this before."

Uh-oh.

"This is so *min haShamayim,* Geula."

Tread carefully. Think before you speak.

"I want to tell you about a wonderful individual, sixtyish, who's a *ben bayis* by us. He davens with my husband, Nachum. Never married. Excellent conversationalist. He's also fed up with being a guest. So many times my heart aches for him, Shabbos after Shabbos, *chag* after *chag,* sitting at someone else's table while time keeps passing. What do you think?"

"It's not simple to have to do that all the time," Geula said, pretending not to understand the question.

"No, what I meant was, how about joining us for a meal next time we invite him?"

"Oh. Um, Helen? Listen, I can't see that kind of thing going anywhere."

"Why?"

"Well, um..." Geula stammered. "I...you said he's sixtyish?"

"Yes, but he's youthful looking, fit. Very *makpid* on diet, healthful eating, exercise. See, now? You already have something in common. Would you believe that he never touches dessert?"

"That's nice."

"Are you free next week? We just assume he's coming to us unless he tells us otherwise."

"That's sweet of you."

"No, honey, it's my pleasure."

"I'm not accepting your invitation. I just meant that it's wonderful of you to open your home to him."

"Why not?"

"Didn't you mention that he's sixtyish? Almost eleven years older than I am?"

"That's no reason not to try."

"Helen, it doesn't sound up my alley. Nothing personal, no offense."

"As you wish." Helen's demeanor screamed outrage.

Should I have told her that I'm not planning on going down the shidduch route ever again? That would have been a bombshell, and I fear her disapproval, no matter how unwarranted. No matter how ill-equipped she is to understand, or judge, it's foolish, dangerous even, to make myself vulnerable. No, instead I get to merit labels like "picky," and "unwilling to try." Why is that fair?

Who said it is? It just goes with the territory.

"Was that the bell?" Geula said. "My girls start fighting over who is going to be the *chazzanit* if I'm not there to referee."

"I didn't hear the bell," Helen protested.

"I think it rang. We'll talk. Thank you for thinking of me." Geula trilled her fingers at Helen and fled the teachers' room.

Helen stared after her, nonplussed and more than a little insulted.

That's how it goes, sometimes. I extend myself to her, go out of my way to show her that she belongs, and she repays me with a slap in the face.

When Geula trudged lifelessly into her third-grade classroom, her bad mood was back full force. Listlessly, she went through the motions. She refereed a fight over a chair that two girls hotly claimed was theirs. She appointed the loser in that dispute to be the *chazzanit*. When the students were settled into their seats, she took out her siddur and began to daven.

After *tefillah*, one of the third graders approached her. "Who were you talking to, Morah Geula?"

"When?"

"When you were davening."

"I was talking to someone while I was davening?"

"Yes. You were standing in the corner, and you looked like you were talking to someone real."

Porcupine

"I want to talk about someone. Pure *to'eles,* I assure you. Geula Leibowitz."

"What about her?" Nechama started the car.

"It's hard to shout past that chip on her shoulder," Helen told Nechama Rotter, who drove her home whenever they finished teaching at the same time. "I realize how difficult it must be for her to switch jobs at this stage of her life. I try hard to make her feel a part of things."

"Very commendable," Nechama commented encouragingly.

"I have to work so hard just to have a normal conversation with her. It's impossible to know ahead of time what will make her angry or upset. Can't talk to her about her kids, she doesn't have any. Marriage? That's one major topic that's taboo."

"Estelle used to discuss her nieces and nephews," Nechama ventured. "I, personally, don't find Geula hard to talk to."

"Estelle was an easy older single. She never made the rest of us feel uncomfortable for having more than she did, and see? In the end, Hashem rewarded her for her *ayin tovah*. But Geula? She's impossible. None of the normal topics people talk about fit. So much energy just to find a subject where we share common ground. Toes all over the place. I don't think she even wants to get married. But then why doesn't she stop complaining about having to be a guest? If she's not willing to put forth effort to improve her reality, what does she want from the rest of us?"

"Maybe nothing?" Nechama suggested. "She has a family, friends, hobbies, a job, a life. Maybe she's happy continuing on the way she is. I happen to get the sense that she's made peace with her situation. Good for her."

"I don't get your point," Helen said stiffly. "Stop trying to justify her reactions. There's a limit to everything. I offer her a place for Shabbos, a wonderful opportunity to meet someone—don't you think it's our responsibility to convince her to give my suggestion one evening of her time?"

"She's a big girl."

"I suppose. I pride myself on my perceptiveness about other people, my sensitivity, but somehow, with Geula, it's never good enough. She manages to take offense at the most innocuous remarks. It's exhausting. What does she think, that the rest of us have problem-free lives?"

"I doubt that she thinks that. She wants to be treated as an equal, Helen."

"But is she? A free bird, no one to please but herself."

"I think that you're answering your own question."

"Not at all. She has the power to change if she wants to. One meal, one small effort is all I ask. I'm handing her an opportunity on a silver platter, and what does she do? She turns up her nose."

"Helen?" Nechama uncharacteristically hesitated, then spoke

her mind, as was her habit since she could remember herself. So what if Helen lost her temper? She'd get over it. "Would you want to accept anything from someone who thought you were a *chesed* case?"

"Why are you defending her? She *is* a *chesed* case. At the moment. I'm the one who's willing to stick my neck out to get her out of her situation. *Miskeinah*."

"What exactly makes her a *miskeinah*?"

"Isn't it obvious?"

"Remind me?" Nechama asked.

"There you go again, trying to turn black into white. You know why." Helen heaved a heartfelt sigh of frustration.

"Humor me."

"I don't know why you insist on making everything complicated. Geula lacks all the most basic blessings and obligations every Jewish woman should want. If that doesn't make her a *miskeinah*, I don't know what does."

"I still don't grasp why."

"She's half a person. She has half a life."

"She just may have chosen to opt out of an area that's given her no satisfaction," Nechama hazarded a guess.

"Stop speaking in riddles, will you?"

"She may have chosen to remain alone."

"Does she have a right to that choice if she may still be able to marry and raise a family when there are so many older men *chalishing* for a home and a wife? I happen to be suggesting a quality human being, never married, no baggage, no hostile children. She can't do better than that at her stage of the game."

"It takes a lot of energy to take on another person," Nechama spoke slowly. "Could be that she's tired of trying, or that she's reasonably content as she is."

"She certainly didn't sound that way when she spoke to me before. Tell me, Nechama, who will take care of her when she's older? Ever think of that? She'll be sorry then that she wasn't willing to take her chances—no, make that grab her chances—while she still had them, but she'll have no one to blame but herself."

"Are you so sure that she's mistaken in her life choices? How well do you know her, after all is said and done?"

"Not that well, but she's all alone. She looks so lonely and woebegone sometimes, it just breaks my heart," Helen said. "I wish I knew someone who has influence over her. Someone who could convince her to stop wasting her life on foolish fantasies and instead make correct choices for herself. Adult choices. How long can she live in a fantasy world?"

After Helen got out of the car, Nechama sat thinking for a long time. She was over her head in wedding preparations for her daughter. The details were endlessly time-consuming. The other side wanted a big, fancy affair for their only son, while the Rotters tended toward something more low key. That meant hours on the phone trying to arrive at a compromise that would please everyone. With her natural people smarts, Nechama was the main negotiator.

Still. She took her job as head of the teacher's committee very much to heart. Resolutely, she picked up the phone to call Rabbanit Sudri. If Geula was indeed part of the Machon Atara family, it was time for all of them to play a more active role in making her feel like a valuable member.

"Hello? Maya? Where am I catching you?"

"Nechama? Hello. Still at school, where else?"

Both women laughed ruefully.

"That's the end of the year for you," Nechama said. "I know that you're in over your head with work, so I'll cut right to the chase. I'm calling about Geula Leibowitz."

"Geula? I'm pleased with her work. She's extremely successful in the classroom. The girls like her, and she's actually got them enthused about art history. Why, just the other day one of the mothers was telling me that she went with her daughter to an exhibition, and her daughter was pointing out various techniques that the artist had employed. A fourth grader, mind you."

"That's impressive," Nechama said sincerely. "But I'm calling about her social situation."

Rabbanit Sudri sighed. "So many bright, capable women and men are suffering. It's beyond sad. Why?" Her voice brightened. "Do you have a suggestion for her? I don't know her that well, but if you want someone who does, I can give you the phone number of the former principal of Bnos Naomi as a reference."

"No, no suggestions. I don't really know anyone in her age bracket."

"Perhaps Estelle Bruner does," Rabbanit Sudri said thoughtfully. "Or perhaps Estelle's husband does. I'll suggest the idea to her. Now, there's a miracle for you."

"Yes, *baruch Hashem*. Though why it should have taken a miracle for a wonderful girl like Estelle to find her *zivug* is anyone's guess. Look, Maya, Geula keeps to herself. She's very pleasant to everyone, friendly and all that, but..."

"But what? What's the problem?"

"She seems to be feeling down. Maya. As far as I can see, the only person on staff she has any real friendship with is Aviva Lavie."

"Aviva? But she's half her age. Now, Aviva's a lovely girl. You know I think that."

"We all do," Nechama said.

"I set her up with my son Aharon earlier this year. Did you know that?"

"I heard something to that effect," Nechama admitted. "I take it that nothing came of it?"

"Very unfortunately not," Maya Sudri said indignantly. "He turned her down because he said that she's too American for him. A silly reason like that. I told him that it would pass. After all, Aviva wants nothing more than to live here. I told him that she'll become more Israeli as time goes by. I told him that they'd grow together. But did he listen to me? No." She sighed again. "Now, every time poor Aviva sees me in the halls she turns beet red, poor girl."

"Still, at her age, she'll receive a plethora of suggestions and so will he," Nechama said. "Soon, the whole story will be in the past. While Geula, on the other hand… I don't have a *shidduch* for her, but I so wish there was something we could do to give her a boost, to make her feel more at home."

"I'll think about it," Rabbanit Sudri promised. Later, as she scrolled through her e-mail messages, she thought about Nechama's request. Who could she enlist in the cause? Estelle Bruner? Good. Sheila Leipzig? Now that was a good idea. Sheila was warm and personable. She was easily a decade younger than Geula, but surely the age difference was insignificant at their age. After all, the two of them were both mature, accomplished adults. She sighed for the third time in ten minutes. Surely, they shared common ground other than being older singles. For one thing, both women were excellent teachers.

She opened an e-mail and prepared to respond. Her last thought, before plunging back into work, was that she gave no credence to Menucha Shalom's thinly veiled criticisms of the way Sheila was handling Yocheved Sutton's seventh grade. Yocheved, too, was an excellent teacher, but no one was perfect. She'd been far too soft on the girls, and now, as her substitute, Sheila was dealing with the inevitable consequences. Sheila was a bit on the strict side, but what of it? It would do the girls good to demand a bit more of themselves.

She frowned. Now, the story with Morah Noa's first grade was far more problematic. To tell the truth, she was disappointed in Sheila. The girls were a handful, true, but surely a weekly hour with them was nothing that a gifted and experienced teacher like Sheila couldn't handle if she just put her mind to it. Why, even young Aviva Lavie taught them more calmly and effectively than Sheila had managed to do before she took over for Yocheved Sutton and gave up the hour. Yes, Aviva was doing a superlative job with those children, while Sheila's tutelage had been mediocre at best. She shook her head ruefully. She didn't want to think that a dedicated teacher like Sheila had decided that a single hour in a primary grade wasn't worth the investment of her very best efforts, but what else was she supposed to think? It was obvious.

She shut her eyes in thought. Perhaps there were mitigating factors of which she was unaware. She certainly hoped that was the case. Hopefully, at Sheila's end-of-the-year evaluation, the entire situation would become easier to comprehend.

20
A Perfect Life

"Hello. This is Miriam Leipzig. Is your mother home?" Miriam asked the young voice at the other end of the phone.

"No, my mommy's not home."

Miriam stifled a sigh. Rebbetzin Glassman had a perfect right to be out of the house or unavailable every time she called, but it was definitely exasperating, particularly as she didn't have her cell number.

"You sound like a big girl. Can you take a message?"

"A message?"

Miriam shut her eyes in mild exasperation. "Is anyone older than you at home now?"

"Yes, my abba."

"Oh." Briefly, Miriam debated whether to disturb the Rav. He probably had set times to receive calls from the public. Concern for her unmarried daughter won out over her natural diffidence.

"Can you ask him to come to the phone?" she said. "Tell him my name is Miriam Leipzig."

"Yes." There was a sound of the phone being dropped and the child—Miriam couldn't tell if it was a boy or girl—hollering, "Abba! Abba! There's a lady called Likey or Lipey on the phone."

"Who?" Rabbi Glassman picked up the phone. "Hello. Who's speaking please?"

"Hello. My name is Miriam Leipzig," Sheila's mother introduced herself. "I'm very sorry to disturb you. I'm actually calling for your wife, but if I could leave a message, it would be a great help. I've been trying to reach her for quite some time with no success."

"My wife's not easy to reach," he agreed. "She's extremely busy. I'm babysitting, as you may have heard, so perhaps I can help you instead."

"I'm calling about my daughter. My daughter, Sheila, is a senior teacher at Machon Atara. Have you heard of it?"

"Very much so. Three of my nieces went to elementary school there. Is Rabbanit Sudri still the principal?"

"Yes. Yes, she is, and she can be called to get a recommendation for Sheila."

"A recommendation? For what?"

Miriam took a deep breath. "I'm sorry for not making myself clear. I read that the shul is looking for a lecturer to substitute for a women's *shiur* given on Shabbos afternoon."

"Yes, we are. Where do you live?"

"In Neot Yaar. Across the street from the shul, actually."

"Leipzig. Yes. The name sounds familiar. You and your husband aren't members of our shul, are you?"

"No. My husband walks to a minyan at the Kosel every Shabbos."

"I see. Quite a walk." There was a pause. "Has your daughter given lectures to adults before? This *shiur* is on a high level. Our regular lecturer is a tough act to follow. The women are very educated, very knowledgeable. Many of them taught or currently teach *limudei kodesh*."

"My daughter is more than up to the task," Sheila's mother assured him. "She herself is extremely well-versed, and eloquent as well. Why not call her principal? I don't expect you take my word for it."

"I think my wife's been in touch with Rabbanit Sudri in a professional capacity, so we have her number. I'll pass on your information to my wife. Thank you for calling."

* * *

"Miriam Leipzig?" Rebbetzin Glassman asked her husband. "Is that what she called herself?"

"Yes. Why?"

"Nothing, just that she and her husband are both professors."

"Really? Of what?"

"I'm not sure. I think she teaches linguistics or something like that. Her husband does something big in the Weizmann Institute in Rehovot. I'm just surprised that she didn't introduce herself as Dr. Leipzig. They're well-to-do people. Big *baalei chesed*. Involved in the community. Any daughter of theirs is probably very well educated and has good values, at the very least, growing up in a home like that. Yes, I think I recall that they have an older daughter. She must be at least thirty by now. It's worth a try. I'm going to call Rabbanit Sudri right now."

21 Unfair

Sheila was wrapping up her *shiur*. The small audience of young girls still seemed receptive, but she was in a rush to get back home.

"In summation, we all try to do our best to build with what we have, to create with what Hashem put in front of us. To run with the ball, if you want to put it that way. A lot of times, we don't necessarily choose our givens, but we can choose our attitude and what we accomplish, in our own unique set of circumstances."

She looked over at Julia Yanavov, who hosted the *shiur* in her modest Anfei Ilanot living room. Mrs. Yanavov smiled approvingly. The group of preteens remained silent. Sheila was surprised. She'd been anticipating an onslaught of questions. Perhaps they hadn't understood the material. Maybe she hadn't presented it clearly enough, or perhaps the terms she'd used had gone over their heads. After all, their knowledge of basic Jewish concepts was meager, though she'd tried hard to fill in some of the gaps in the previous four-and-a-half months since she'd begun to give the *shiur*.

"Any questions? Comments?" she asked. "Anybody out there, or did I put you all to sleep?"

Some muffled laughter spread through the room, but silence fell again.

"Let me put a question to you," Sheila began.

A hand shot up. Sheila stifled a sigh. *Not you, Rika. I don't need you to puncture a hole in what I said before the other kids have a chance to absorb my message.* Seeing no other show of hands, with no other alternative, she bowed to the inevitable.

"Yes, Rika. What do you think?"

"What do I think? I don't think you want to know what I think, but that's not going to stop me."

An uncomfortable titter spread through the room. Mrs. Yanavov half rose out of her seat, but Sheila motioned to her as if to say, "I'm on top of this."

"What you said makes sense, *if* I want to ignore the obvious," Rika Sonolevitch commented sarcastically. "As long as I do that, ignore the fact that's life's totally unfair, that there are people who have nothing and people who get it all. Sure. Have it your way. We all get *exactly* what we need. Look around you. It's just obvious."

"I never said it was obvious."

"Right, it's not obvious. It's about *trust* and *faith*. Tell us a neat little story about someone who had zilch, nada, nothing, and fooled himself that he had everything." She snorted derisively. "Let's see you trade lives with me, get it?" She glared at the others, daring anyone to disagree with her.

Now Julia Yanavov rose to her full five feet. "Rika, what a way to talk! Where is your gratitude to Sheila for all that she's done for us the past few months? Speak with respect. This is a teacher, not one of your friends."

But Rika's flow of words was unstoppable.

"Morah Sheila, *your* life is perfect. Totally perfect. Forget your life. *You're* perfect. You have it all, okay? Who gave you any right to barge in here and lecture us about free choice and making the best of what we have?"

"I… No one has it all," Sheila began.

Rika raised her voice, and Sheila fell silent.

"So, you'll excuse me for being just a little bit skeptical when you tell us all about Hashem and how much He loves us, and that thing you said, *hashgachah*, great, terrific idea." Her blue eyes, magnified by her hot pink glasses, flashed defiantly. Her friend Vicky tugged at her arm urgently, but Rika shook her off.

"Come on, people, open your mouths instead of sitting here like a bunch of dead fish, and tell her what you really think."

The small group seated around the Yanavov's dining room table gazed at her stoically. Finally, Sabina broke the awkward silence. She toyed with long her feather earring.

"Hey, Rika, cool it. It's just a bunch of ideas. It's just words. Take it or leave it. What are you getting all worked up about?"

"She's here to help us." Rika pointed at Sheila. "But she's not helping. She's not helping at all. She just makes everything worse with her fancy ideas that she says are from our *heritage*. Our *heritage*! She comes here from her fancy neighborhood that none of us could ever afford to live in, not in a million years, dressed in her clothes that look like she's going to a wedding, and you're all like, wow."

"Morah Sheila is here because she cares about you. *All* of you," Julia Yanavov said firmly. "We owe her our gratitude."

"I'm not grateful. She's not giving me anything to be grateful for. Nothing. I'm on my own." Rika shrugged dramatically, but there was genuine pain in her voice. "On my own, against the world. As usual. Good, if *you're* all a bunch of cowards, *I'm* not afraid to tell the truth. My father's working in a dead-end job, get it? What a boring way to spend Saturday afternoon. My mom's so depressed, she's barely functioning, so naturally, she's thrilled to have me out of her hair one afternoon a week. This way, she's got one less problem to deal with. Believe me—" Rika's voice cracked. "The only reason any of us are here is for the free food and an indoor place to hang out. Admit it, everyone, why don't you?"

There were one or two reluctant nods.

Anna spoke up, twisting a strand of her hair around her finger. "It's not true. Maybe that's why I came in the beginning, but... Sheila's teaching us about our own heritage. Our own history. I happen to think I owe it to myself to explore this stuff even if it's irrelevant to real life and all."

Rika pounced. "That's just my point. No one here thinks that any of this Jewish stuff you keep pushing at us has anything to do with real life. How dare you try to tell us lies? No one knows, no one cares, and the only one who'll ever take care of me is yours truly. Me, myself, and I is all *I* have to rely on. Say something, guys. You're such a bunch of fakers. Why don't you say all the stuff you say when she's not around to hypnotize you?"

Rika sprang up and pushed back her chair. "I don't even know why I keep coming. If the rest of you want to listen to nice, comforting Jewish stories, you can waste your summer. I'm out of here."

Sheila opened her mouth to reply to the heartfelt outburst. Rika was unusually articulate, not to mention very bitter. She was mature and perceptive, but her open resentment made it hard for Sheila to like her. Her comments were not unexpected and had been visibly simmering within her for months. Though she was somewhat thrown off balance by the force of Rika's outburst, Sheila had prepared a number of possible responses ages ago. The only question was why now? Rika had held back for so long. Something happened to set her off, but what?

Her attacking me in public doesn't bother me. Much. That's about her, not about me. What is difficult is that she sounds as if she dislikes me. Really dislikes me. Why? What did I do to her? Is she correct? Am I really so patronizing?

I don't think so. It's not about me. It's part of dealing with a wider public.

No matter how hard I try, no one can possibly get through to everyone or please everyone. I'm sure everyone else in this room is happy that I make the effort to come here every Shabbos. I'm sure that they've learned a lot. She's a lone voice.

I hope this doesn't take too long. Ima will have my head if I'm home late.

Without meaning to, she glanced discreetly at her watch.

"Rika, you brought up a number of good questions. Questions I'm sure many of us here share but are afraid to ask. You did us all a favor. Right, everyone?" Sheila looked around the room, smiling.

No one met her gaze.

"Don't you want to hear my answers?"

Vicky folded her arms and leaned back, feigning nonchalance, but Sheila had been a teacher of preteens for too many years to be fooled by her pose. Sabina edged forward in her seat.

So, Rika is voicing the way the others in the group feel. She's not a lone voice, though probably the other kids would have been gentler with me. It's fine. I can take it. I know it's not personal. Still, I thought I was doing a better job of getting through to them. Other than Rika, I was sure they knew that I care about them, and…I thought my feelings were reciprocated.

Her heart sank. *Chinuch isn't only about imparting information. Am I losing my touch?*

Here I am, schlepping out in the heat against opposition, and it turns out that they don't even like me all that much. I thought we were connecting so well. Turns out I was wrong. The only one to defend me is Mrs. Yanavov. Yes, and Anna. One girl. They say that one person is enough to justify the entire effort, but it's hard for me to feel that way.

Sheila knew no one could discern her thoughts by looking at her face. Later, when she was on her own, she'd allow herself to fully feel her hurt and disappointment, but now, facing her audience, she showed no weakness.

"Sorry I'm not pimply and fat and cross-eyed and maybe badly dressed and poor in the bargain," she began, deliberately exaggerating to make a point.

Anna giggled and then guiltily clapped a hand over her mouth.

"Would it be easier for you to trust me then? If you felt you could look down on me? Would you rather pity me than look up to me?"

Someone else in the group giggled. Sheila glanced around quickly, gauging their reactions. They were still staring at their laps. No one was willing to make eye contact with her.

Rika lashed out in response. "Stop making fun of us! How dare you mock us to our faces! Calling us poor and badly dressed? Who do you think you are?"

"I didn't say that," Sheila said evenly, with a calm she was far from feeling. "You said that I'm perfect, which you're old enough to know yourself, even without my going into details, isn't at all true. I'm not perfect, and neither is my life. You said I'm feeding you stories. I'm just asking you if you think what I say would be truer if I were, let's say, cross-eyed and ugly, or if even then what I'm trying to teach you would be completely false. I think that's a fair question. Does anyone want to try to answer it?"

"Stop being so *calm* all the time! Who needs you to come here anyhow? Go back to your perfect world and *get out of our lives!*"

Julia Yanavov was furious. "Enough! We've been very patient with you, Rika, but you've gone too far. Now be quiet and sit down, or leave. No one forces you to come here, and no one's forcing you to stay. Where are your manners? Stop feeling sorry for yourself, young lady. Sit down! Sit down this instant! Apologize!"

Rika clamped her lips together in a thin, tight line.

"You owe Sheila an apology for attacking her in front of everyone. A gigantic apology. It's extremely impolite to imply that she's selling you a pack of lies. It's very unkind to attack her, to embarrass her in front of the group. After all she does for us. It's not like you to be so rude to a guest. I'm surprised at you. Apologize this very instant."

"No! I'm not sorry that I told the truth."

"She doesn't need to apologize," Sheila said. "I'm fine. We all need to, um, express ourselves at times."

"Of course she's going to apologize!" Julia declared vehemently.

"Venting has no place here. Rika, we're all waiting. Sheila prepared a beautiful lesson, and it's unfair for all of us to miss out."

Rika shrugged sullenly. There were tears of rage streaming down her face.

"Mrs. Yanavov, please let it go. It's not necessary. Her reaction is understandable. She's in a lot of pain, and I understand, and"—Sheila lowered her voice to an urgent whisper—"she's just a kid. Let her go calm down. She'll calm down and then later..."

Julia looked at her quizzically. "Excuse us," she told the group. "We're taking a small break. Girls, help yourselves to refreshments."

She ushered Sheila into a small side room and closed the door. They could hear the girls get up from their frozen positions and begin to talk in low tones.

Discussing me, most likely, Sheila thought, and a dull flush rose from her neck and spread to her face.

"She needs to apologize," Julia said to Sheila forcefully. "She's a well-brought-up young lady, even if right now it's hard to see it. She owes it to herself to apologize, and you should respect her enough to need her apology."

Sheila blinked rapidly. Julia's rebuke stung. Now even Julia was taking sides against her.

Stop that. You're not a baby. This about helping the kids. We're all on the same side.

Had she been feeling a secret sense of superiority to these kids? The question shook her. No. Her intentions were sincere. She genuinely wanted to help these kids, enhance their lives, draw them closer to their heritage.

There was a knock on the door. Rika stood at the head of the group, red-faced.

"I'm sorry," she muttered. There was a visible exhalation of relief.

Julia Yanavov nodded approvingly. "That took courage."

"It most certainly did," Sheila concurred.

Rika wasn't finished. "It still doesn't mean I'm ever coming back here again. Maybe what Sheila is saying is true for her and people like her, but it has nothing to do with us, and you all know it. And yeah, Sheila. It would help if you had some struggle in some area. You say you do. Maybe share it, you know? Maybe then it would be easier to believe that what you're telling us actually has some validity?"

She ran out of the room and the apartment, slamming the front door behind her.

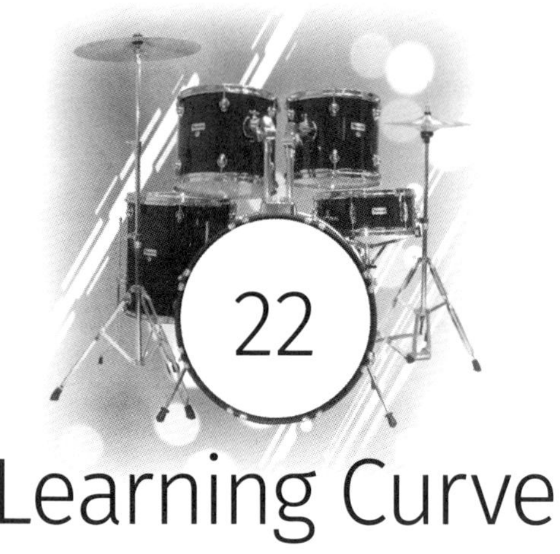

22 Learning Curve

Perfect. My life's perfect, huh. What a scene. What a waste of time. What a waste of an afternoon, and I have a date tonight. I put myself out, week after week; I try to help people, and they throw it in my face. Perfect. Just phenomenal.

Sheila could feel a headache starting to work its way toward her left eye. She had no time for headaches. She had a date tonight.

She gulped down half the contents of her water bottle but forced herself to stop, though she was still thirsty. Now, at five thirty in the afternoon, on her way back home, the sun was a lot less hot than it had been when she'd left her parents' home in Neot Yaar to embark on her weekly trek to Anfei Ilanot three hours previously. As usual, she'd tried to be super quiet when leaving the house. But, as always, her mother had woken up from her

Shabbos afternoon nap. The scene replayed itself as she walked, taking her back against her will...

Here we go. Please, Hashem, help me not to lose my temper.

"Sheila? You're going in the middle of the day, in this heat? No sunscreen, because it's Shabbos. Not a very good idea, is it? Do you realize how unhealthy the sun is at this hour? How aging?"

"I have a hat, and see?" Sheila held up the water bottle. "Water." She edged toward the door.

Miriam Leipzig sighed. "I'm sure they'd understand if you didn't show up just this once."

"Ima, the truth is that you're not crazy about my going, no matter what the weather is."

"You aren't a twenty-year-old, that's all."

"What does that have to do with anything?"

"You're an experienced, professional educator. I see no reason for you to sacrifice your entire Shabbos afternoon, for months on end, walk for over an hour in each direction just to give a forty-five-minute *shiur*. Let someone who lives closer do it. They'll find someone. Believe me, no one is irreplaceable."

"I don't see anyone lining up, and I made a commitment. Bedsides, Ima, remember what I told you on *chol hamoed* after you came back from the zoo?"

"Yes, that you need to accomplish and to build. I agree with you that you need to do that, but why be so extreme in the way you go about it?"

"How am I being extreme?"

"You made a big mistake by turning down Rebbetzin Glassman's offer to give a *shiur* here, right here, only five minutes away. So, you would have skipped a month with these children. You already gave them three months of your time."

"Four and a half." The corners of Sheila's mouth turned up.

"Five. It's more than anyone else would do. Enough."

"Ima. I don't need everyone staring at me, looking me up and down, scrutinizing my clothing, my hair, my everything, and wondering why I'm still single."

I need my own place. This is insane, having to explain my every move. But all the places I've seen are dumps compared to here.

"Unkind, inaccurate, and most of all, immature," her mother said flatly. "I'm surprised at you, but I appreciate that you told me what's on your mind. These women are coming to hear a *shiur*, not to gossip. They are women who want to grow, women seeking inspiration, women whom you'd do well to judge with a far kinder eye. That's first of all. Second of all, any and all discussion of you is only for the best and most caring of reasons."

"I'm sorry."

"It isn't I who needs your apology. You're harming yourself, closing doors you ought to be keeping wide open, and that hurts to see. When you have children of your own, you'll understand how I feel. I would like this week to be the final week that you teach those children."

"They need me more than the women in the shul do," Sheila declared adamantly. "I go where I'm needed, not where it's easier and more comfortable. Being comfortable doesn't cut it for me. I need meaning. I need to know that I'm making a real difference in the world. Otherwise, my life is flat. You get that, Ima, don't you?"

Her mother gave a faint, reluctant nod. "I know that, Sheila. Allow me to remind you that aside from your natural idealistic tendencies, which can be used for good or not so good, the reason you are so enthused with having a meaningful life is that your father and I brought you up to be that way. We gave the same upbringing and *chinuch* to all your brothers and sisters, but they—"

"But they?"

"Never mind." Miriam Leipzig turned aside. "It's not important. I never compare my children to each other. You are each your very own individual person."

"But they what?" Sheila persisted.

"You are all individualists in your own way." Her mother was unyielding. "Please don't put words in my mouth. It won't work, Sheila. You know that."

Sheila did know it. After a pause, she continued. "Besides all that, Ima, it gets to be very annoying. The single stuff gets in the way all the time."

"What on earth are you talking about? I don't understand what you're trying to tell me."

"I can't take knowing that, let's say I did give the *shiur*, no matter what I'd say, no matter how deep or inspiring a thought I'd present, no one would ever forget that I'm single. Single! At least with the kids, it's a non-issue."

"I completely disagree. You are displaying poor judgment. If you don't want to be single, do something to change it. Running away is never the solution to any problem. Your father and I have tried to teach you that."

Sheila kept her temper in check, knowing exactly what her mother was going to say next.

"You have a date with Yerachmiel tonight, don't you? Second date, isn't it?"

"Yes," Sheila said shortly. "I do. But I cannot put my life on hold for dating, not anymore."

"No one's asking you to do that, but must you use up all your energy walking in the heat? You'll be exhausted. No one says you have to put your life on hold, but please keep your priorities straight. I hope that's not too much to ask."

"He's got enough momentum for both of us," Sheila blurted.

"What's that supposed to mean?"

"Um, Ima, we said no postmortem, no discussing the date endlessly for more time than the date actually took, remember?"

Almost no one my age who's unmarried lives with her parents anymore. Even though Abba and Ima offered to buy me a place of my own, which is incredibly sweet. They are the best parents any girl could want. But still...

"Is that a bad thing, that he's interested?" her mother persisted.

"You must see something you like if you agreed to have a second date two days after the first one."

"I don't know if it's a good thing. Sometimes it is, sometimes it isn't. This time, it's okay, because I do like him. Ima, don't look so excited. I like him enough to meet him one more time, that's all I said."

"Sheila, everyone finds dating hard, some more than others, but no one denies that Yerachmiel's a very special, quality boy who just hasn't found his one and only, so…"

"I know. 'Good boys don't grow on trees.' But Ima, I thought that you don't want me to date anyone who's so much older than I am."

"I didn't, but Abba told me that when you came back from the first date, your face was shining. Just be careful." Her mother sighed anxiously.

"Don't worry, Ima. I'm going to do my best not to look for something that may not even exist."

"Do more than that."

"What should I do?"

"Try to like what's right in front of you. I've made quite a number of calls checking him out. From all I hear, this is a boy, actually a man, who is easy to respect. He's accomplished, good-looking, good-hearted, provides a beautiful service to the Jewish community, and has not a bad *parnassah*."

"I know all that."

"Yes. I know you do." Her mother sighed in frustration. "We should have married you off before you became so strong-minded."

"When was that?" Sheila asked, her hand on the doorknob. "When I was an infant?"

"Probably not even then." Her mother laughed reluctantly and pecked her on the cheek. "Leave that neighborhood as soon as you can. Should we wait for you to come home for *seudah shelishis*?"

"Please."

I'm calling Menucha Shalom right after Shabbos to see if she's heard about any new properties. Even though…if something does take off with Yerachmiel…

I can't put my life on hold for dating.

But I never thought I'd be thinking of buying my own home, all alone. Welcome to my perfect life.

* * *

"I called Rebbetzin Glassman to call Sheila and ask her to give the Shabbos *shiur* to the women in our neighborhood, substituting for Rebbetzin Safra. Did I tell you about that?" Miriam Leipzig said to her husband, who had ambled into the room in search of a cool drink, a Gemara under his arm. "Did I tell you about Sheila's latest decision?"

"No. What happened to Rebbetzin Safra?"

"She's giving a series of lecture tours in New York for the next month." Miriam poured her husband a tall cup of lemon seltzer and went to the freezer to get some ice cubes. "That's why I jumped at the idea of suggesting Sheila to fill in during her absence."

"Thank you. Wonderful idea, in many ways, including all the exposure she'll get to some very well-connected women. Good thinking. When is she going to start?" Her husband took a long sip." Ah. *Gan Eden*. Don't you want any?" He moved the pitcher toward her.

"Thank you." She poured a full glass and drank. "I hope she took enough water with her. She was in such a rush to leave. So, are you following me? Rebbetzin Glassman called Rabbanit Sudri to see if Sheila was up to giving a high-level *shiur* to a group of educated women."

"And? Yes, I'm with you. What happened?"

"As expected, Rabbanit Sudri gave Sheila rave reviews. She thinks the world of our daughter. A lot of good that did."

"I'm not following. They found someone else?" Sheila's father frowned. "Sheila refused to try?"

"Exactly. Yes, she turned down Rebbetzin Glassman. Can you believe it?"

"Why did she turn down such a good offer? Was she that nervous about filling Rebbetzin Safra's shoes?"

Miriam shrugged. "Could be. That's not what she told Rebbetzin Glassman."

"Doesn't she realize how many women would have seen her doing something she does superlatively, on a weekly basis?"

"That's how I see it, too." His wife put her glass down hard. "However, Sheila has a different perspective.

"What a shame. I would have helped her to prepare, though she's perfectly capable of doing it on her own."

"She is," his wife affirmed.

"Have you noticed that lately, it's getting to be a pattern. She doesn't seem to have the same drive as before."

"What makes you say that?" Miriam bristled. "She's doing a sterling job substituting for the seventh grade."

"Yes, but remember how she struggled to hold her own with that first-grade class she tried to teach earlier this year?"

"She's never taught that age before. She did her best."

"But she quit in the middle," he said, still shocked at the thought of a Leipzig doing such a thing. "She stopped when the going got rough. That's no way to behave."

"I think you're operating under a misperception."

"That's what I understood from what Sheila told me."

"You must have been preoccupied when she spoke to you."

"I don't think so," he said, shaking his head. "That's the way she sees it. The job in the seventh grade simply served to extricate her from a sticky situation."

"First of all, there's nothing wrong with that. Second, I told you. There was a scheduling conflict with the seventh grade where they'd asked her to substitute for Yocheved Sutton. Sheila is far better suited to teach that age than a bunch of unruly infants."

"If you say so. I believe that had she wanted to continue in the first grade, the school would have accommodated her wishes."

"Well then, I guess you'd agree with Sheila on turning down

Rebbetzin Glassman, telling her that she has a prior commitment." The mother's face twisted in anguish. "I'm so worried about Sheila. What will be with her? Neither of us is going to live forever, and she keeps on making harebrained decisions."

"Sheila has a good head on her shoulders."

"About everything else, but not about the most important part of her life."

"About that too, Miriam."

"I pray you are correct."

"I am," he assured her. "Is she still giving that *shiur*?"

"She is. She went hiking over there this afternoon when she has a date tonight."

Her husband's face brightened. "I thought she finished. She told me that the last *shiur* was right before Pesach. As for her date tonight, she's not an old woman who needs to rest after every exertion. She should be making the most of every opportunity, and living her life to the fullest."

"The *shiur* was supposed to end, but that Julia Yanavov convinced her to continue."

"That's very good to hear. I know that the children in that *shiur* give her a hard time. I'm glad she's not yielding at the first signs of trouble."

"She's always had a lot of initiative. Why take one first-grade glitch and magnify it?" Miriam said.

"Don't you see my point? I was concerned, because how hard could it be to teach first grade? But now I realize that she's capable of trying new things. It's not good for her to rest on her laurels. She needs to grow."

"That's all fine and well, but I'm sure you'll agree that now Sheila's main priority has to be to do whatever she can do to ensure her future."

"I think she made a commitment to the Yanavovs, and I see no compelling reason for her to break it. Good for her," Sheila's father said proudly. "A *mentsch* sticks to his or her commitments. She kept her word. That's the way I'd hope any child of ours would act."

"Yes, and who's going to notice her and think about her and maybe, please Hashem, find her a *shidduch* over there? Julia Yanavov?"

Her husband was silent.

"There's a time and a place for everything. Now is the time for as many people as possible to see her and make appropriate suggestions."

"You said she has a date tonight, a second date."

"She does."

"So?" He looked at her questioningly.

"Do you realize how much older than her he is? I want you to speak to her about calling back Rebbetzin Glassman and offering to give the *shiur*."

"Let's wait and see." Her husband stroked his short-trimmed gray beard. "Let's wait and see how it goes for her tonight. Didn't you tell me you heard wonderful things about him?"

"I did, but all the same, it's hard for me to feel calm about this. He's reached his age, and he's still unmarried. Why?"

"People ask the same thing about Sheila."

* * *

Here goes.

Sarah Roth clutched Mindy's cell phone in a hand slippery with perspiration.

I wish I had my own cell phone, or at least my own home line. Sarah winced, recalling the conversation with her best friend.

"Some people would at least feel that they owe me an explanation. I am lending you my precious personal property," Mindy had hinted broadly.

"Some people would at least be nice enough to respect other people's privacy," Sarah had countered.

"Ooh, privacy. Fine, I can take a hint."

"So, can I borrow it?"

"Just like that? No payback?" Despite her intense curiosity, and more than a touch of jealousy, Mindy's innate good-heartedness won out in the end. "Fine. Don't tell your best friend anything. When do you want it?"

"Um..." Sarah turned her face away, stammering. "I need to think when's a good time to call this person. I'll let you know."

Mindy wondered anew who on earth her friend could be calling. Other than Mindy, Sarah had no close friends, though she was friendly with everyone in her class. What was going on with her?

"Are you okay?" she asked with sudden concern.

"Just fine. Why do you ask?" *You won't ever understand me, not if you tried for a million years. Look at your relationship with your Bubby Beatrice. She adores you to pieces. You're her most absolutely favorite grandchild. Maybe you're even her very favorite person in the whole wide world. Look how she came rushing across the ocean from seven thousand miles away because she thought you were sad when you came on aliyah. Imagine having a grandparent who loves you so much.*

While I have my Savta Marilyn, who I think can't stand me.

Why? What did I ever do to her?

It can't be what Ima keeps telling me, that if I would just do things her way and not "defy her"; that's not enough of a reason for her to hate me. Ima says she doesn't hate me, but she does. She does!

After days spent agonizing over what would be the very best time to call her teacher, Sarah had decided on an hour and a half after Shabbos. That Friday in school, Mindy handed over the phone without another word.

Two obstacles still loomed. The first was privacy. Where should she make the call? Not in the room she shared with her sisters. Not the kitchen, or the living room. She'd whizzed through all her post-Shabbos chores davening for a solution.

"I'm going for a walk. Okay, Ima?" she said finally, praying that her mother wouldn't question her sudden need for exercise at 9:30 p.m.

"Good for you," said Mrs. Roth, eyeing her daughter's somewhat rotund figure. "Are those Shabbos shoes comfortable for walking? Didn't you tell me that the right shoe rubs your heel? Take a minute to put on sneakers. You'll be more comfortable that way, and you'll stay out longer. You need to keep moving at least twenty minutes for it to count."

"Half an hour at a brisk pace," came a familiar, decisive voice.

Sarah froze in dismay. *Bubby Marilyn is still in the house. Didn't I hear her leave right after Havdalah?*

"Sarah's about to go out for a walk," her mother said. "She'll walk off some of that Shabbos food."

"Some of that excessive Shabbos nosh, I would add. Is that safe? A seventh grader all alone in the dark? Maybe she ought to get up early tomorrow morning instead."

Sarah held her breath. *No. Please, please.*

"Well…" Her mother wavered.

"I'll stick to our block and just the next block over," Sarah quickly promised.

"Okay."

Sarah let out her breath.

"Sneakers really would be preferable for an exercise walk," her mother reiterated.

"Uh, I'm not going for a long enough walk to change into sneakers. Just once or twice around the block." Sarah groaned inwardly. Now, she'd have to actually walk. A real walk, instead of pacing around the building's lobby, as she'd been planning to do. She didn't feel like walking. At all. Plus, her shoe really was rubbing her heel. But she couldn't take the time to change. She couldn't call close to ten at night because the time limit written on the sheet the school had distributed for times that teachers were available to take calls stated clearly: "*Sheila Leipzig*. Not after 10:00 p.m."

Once outside, Sarah took the downhill route from her home. It would mean an uphill hike on the way back, but with any *mazel*, she'd catch Morah Sheila right away. It would be too mortifying for words to be panting while she talked to her teacher.

She stopped and stood next to a wall, far from windows or doorways where someone might overhear. Carefully, she punched in the phone number she'd memorized.

To her keen disappointment, a man's voice answered. Another gauntlet to run. She almost hung up, but she persevered.

* * *

Sheila found herself looking forward to the date with Yerachmiel Kantor, which was definitely a nice way to feel. Very nice. Perhaps it was because he so clearly admired her, which was—yes, she admitted it—flattering. She knew Yerachmiel had high standards for himself and for other people. It was a compliment that he thought she made the grade, because she admired him too. Yes, she did, and she wanted to get to know him better.

However, she reminded herself, all that didn't mean anything. Or rather, it was all intriguing but neutral, as mutual admiration didn't mean anything. No, if it wasn't followed by more substantial, though perhaps less exciting essential components for marriage, nothing doing and goodbye.

She hoped it wouldn't be goodbye.

She took a last look in the full-length mirror and decided to go for a more sparkly pair of earrings. She picked the gold-and-garnet ones, to match her silk scarf with its swirling shades of pink. Good. Good enough. If she were honest, much better than just good enough. Her eyes were sparkling, despite the fact that she'd returned for *seudah shelishis* in a very different state. Three hours earlier, she'd been hot, discouraged after Rita's blowup, and short on both temper and hope, with her head pounding. She'd tried hard not to burden her parents with her bad mood. After all, she was a grown-up and responsible for her emotional state. Plus, she didn't want to have to deal with any reactions or advice. She'd seen her mother glance at her father in dismay. The look had broadcasted, as if on a loudspeaker, her disapproval of Sheila's choice to hike to Anfei Ilanot, especially on a hot afternoon, and especially when she'd turned down a far more suitable offer, and *especially* when she had a date and needed to be at her very best—if she had any sense, which, unfortunately, wasn't a given.

Sheila gave her parents credit for holding their peace. It couldn't be simple. Her father had gone to shul to daven Maariv, and Sheila had felt her mood lighten. A second date, with someone she was curious about, who didn't bore her. Wherever it led, that much was undeniably true.

"Ima, is it okay with you if I go lie down for about twenty minutes just until Abba gets home for *Havdalah*? The walk back wore me out. I'll dry the dishes tonight."

"You won't do anything but get ready for your date. Straightening up from the three of us shouldn't take me more than an hour, even less."

Sheila entered the dining room to say goodnight to her parents. By mutual agreement, she and Yerachmiel had decided that he'd pick her up outside her home, rather than come in and chat with her parents. Her parents had been amenable to the arrangement. His parents moved in the same circles as did hers. Yerachmiel Kantor was a well-known individual, even if they weren't acquainted with him personally.

"You look ten years younger than you really are. I don't know how you do it. You don't look a day over twenty-one, twenty-two at the most," her father complimented. "Isn't that right, Miriam?"

"Sheila always looks beautiful." Her mother nodded. *That's never been the problem. I don't know what is. I wish I did. A known problem can be dealt with, somehow.*

"Sheila," her father continued, "now's not the time for this, but you had a phone call from a pupil. Her name is"—he consulted a small piece of paper—"Sarah Roth."

Sheila's face brightened. "Sarah Roth?"

"Yes, that's what I wrote. She sounded quite anxious to speak to you, but I told her that you'd be unavailable for most of tonight. She actually left instructions that you call her within the hour, if at all possible. Can you imagine?"

His wife shook her head disapprovingly.

"I'm sure it was more of a request. She was probably very nervous."

"Possibly, but let me ask you. Is it customary for students to call their teachers at home, especially on *motza'ei Shabbos*? I wouldn't have dreamed of calling any *rebbi* or teacher when I was in seventh grade. Contacting teachers out of school? That was strictly my parents' department, and only when absolutely necessary. Is this a discipline issue?"

"No, not at all. Sarah is a far from being a troublemaker. I'm very happy that she's reaching out for help. It's terrific that she called. Did she leave a number?"

"Yes, but why are you so pleased? Your students call you all the time. Convenient, inconvenient, *erev Shabbos, motza'ei Shabbos*. Don't their parents realize it's a nuisance?"

"Did she leave a message saying what she wanted?"

"No. She only asked that you return her call within the hour, as I told you before. She was very uneasy to have gotten through to me instead of reaching you. She made that only too obvious. Does she think you live alone? Doesn't she realize that you live with your parents?"

"Why would she? I don't discuss my private affairs with my pupils."

"I'm glad to hear that your relationship has some normal boundaries," her mother said.

"Maybe I *should* have given the kids my cell phone number, so it doesn't put you out."

"I hope you meant that facetiously."

"Not at all. I was serious."

"Absolutely not." Her mother flared. "It's enough that they have your home phone number. They see you four—no, five days a week. Besides, didn't you specify on that list that you gave the students when it was more convenient for you to receive calls? Who calls at nine thirty on *motza'ei Shabbos*? Isn't she mature enough to realize that you may have a date?"

"Ima, Abba, she's only in seventh grade." Sheila tried to decide whether she had time to return the call before Yerachmiel arrived to pick her up. She'd been waiting hopefully for Sarah to reach out. Sarah Roth was not the type to disturb her at home even to get some badly needed attention. Since she'd begun substituting, Sheila had definitely dealt with a number of such calls. Her parents weren't entirely mistaken in their general assessment of the situation, but this time was different.

When she'd taken over teaching the seventh grade, almost three months previously, their homeroom teacher, Yocheved Sutton, had sat with her to give over essential information on several students who might need more than the usual amount of guidance.

"One more child. I left her for last. Sarah Roth," Yocheved had told her while gently stroking her newborn daughter's head. "She's a straight-A student. Maybe not super popular, but well liked."

"Didn't she sort of adopt Mindy Lavie when Mindy came on aliyah at the beginning of the year?"

"Yes, that's her. I can't figure her out. On the one hand, she's respectful. Attentive. Quiet, but not afraid to speak her mind. Not at all spoiled. She comes from a good family, you can just tell. Her older sister, Malki, graduated Machon Atara two years ago, and she has a younger sister, Shalhevet, in fifth grade. All well brought up, good kids."

"But?"

"But sometimes, out of nowhere, Sarah makes remarks that are… bitter, I guess you'd call them. She says things that are just too old for her age. Her father passed away after an illness when she was little. I'm not clear on how old she was then. Her mother never remarried. They have grandparents who live on the same block. I got the impression that the grandmother spends a lot of time in the house helping the mother."

"That sounds good. I'm sure she could use all the help and support she can get."

"Yes, it's good that the *savta* helps out, but, and this is hard to believe so take it with a grain of salt, Sarah feels that this grandmother is very critical of her, to the point that… And again, this is her perception, but…"

"But?"

"Sarah avoids her grandmother as much as she can. She thinks her grandmother hates her. It affects her self-esteem badly."

"How could it not affect her? What a tough way to start life." Sheila pictured Sarah's clear, smiling blue eyes, and her heart lurched. She'd always had a soft spot for Sarah. "Poor kid."

Yocheved hugged her infant daughter more tightly. "I know. When I think of my *bubbies*, my cheering squad, it's hard to imagine. As you mentioned, she took Mindy Lavie under her wing before Mindy starred in the play, when she was just a new little immigrant that no one noticed or cared about much. It's not as if she's dysfunctional or anything. Just…I don't know. Something. Maybe."

"I didn't know any of this. Don't you think I should have been given this information when she became my student in fifth grade?"

"Probably." Yocheved patted the baby's back.

Sheila's stomach lurched again. Taking over as homeroom teacher of the seventh grade was very exciting, but how could it compete with having her very own baby? It couldn't. She could guide, teach, even nurture, but… *I want my own children to give to. Why not? Why not me? Hashem! Why not me too? Don't You think I'd be a good mother?*

"I'm just calling Sarah back for one second," Sheila said now. "I want to let her know that it's great, um, fine that she called, even if I can't speak to her now."

"I told you not to tell her about the call." Her mother looked at her father for a moment and shook her head slightly. "You'll see her in school tomorrow."

"I would leave it for tonight if she had just a touch more self-confidence, but this may be important. If she calls me, she must really need me. She's reaching out to me, Ima. She's not the type to call a teacher."

"Tomorrow at eight in the morning you can reach out in return," Miriam Leipzig said tartly.

"If it's an emergency, I'm sure her parents are on top of it," her father said. "Come on, Sheila. You can't rescue the entire world. You're only one person."

"You don't know her. I can't do that to her. I just know that she's torturing herself now, reviewing every single nuance of every word she said, agonizing about the fact that she called me in the first place. I'll just let her know that I received her call, so she doesn't feel totally rejected."

As Sheila left the room to make the call, she heard her father apologize to her mother. Her mother's response was loud enough to make it clear to Sheila that it was intended for her ears as well.

"I admire her dedication to her students, just as you do, but if she's not careful to prioritize she'll end up a career teacher. A superb one, but I want more than that for Sheila."

The phone rang. Sheila picked up.

"Hi, may I speak to Morah Sheila?" a wavering young voice inquired hesitantly.

"Speaking. Is that you, Sarah?"

She heard a gasp.

"Who's speaking, please? Oh! Is this…is this Morah Sheila?"

"Yes. Sarah, listen, I really can't talk now, but I'm so glad you called. Tomorrow, in school, we'll make up a time to speak about whatever's on your mind. Okay?"

"Morah! Please, just one second. It will only take a second."

"Fine, but not much more than that," Sheila warned, her voice gentle. "We'll speak tomorrow. We really will."

"You know the final project in Jewish History that's due in two weeks and you said we could work in pairs?"

"Yes?"

"And then you told us that anyone who handed it in late, even with a note from a parent, would have ten whole points taken off her final grade?"

Sheila glanced at her watch. In five more minutes, she was supposed to be outside.

"Mindy and I started, we did the outline, I mean we're working on the outline, but it's due tomorrow, and we're not ready to hand it in, and—"

"Slow down. What happened?"

"We"—Sarah swallowed hard—"we can't work from my house, and my Ima doesn't understand why I have to go over to Mindy's all the time, and we just...we just fell behind, that's all. Not because we were being careless or anything like that."

"We need to discuss this, Sarah. It's not really a discussion for the phone. Thank you for letting me know that you're having a problem. As I said before, we'll talk tomorrow in school, but in the meantime, don't worry. I'm sure you have a good reason for the fact that you're behind schedule, and I'm sure we can work something out. Is tomorrow soon enough?

"Yes. Thank you!"

They hung up.

Sarah Roth stared at the phone, speechless with joy. *Morah Sheila wasn't angry. She was so nice. See? She likes me, too. I've been getting up the courage to call her forever. Mindy was right. She told me that Morah Sheila likes me. Me! Me, especially! Even more than the really popular girls in the class.*

Smiling dreamily, she felt her heart thudding in her chest, and not just because she was climbing the steep incline back home. At the entrance to her home, she put the phone carefully in her pocket and patted to see that it was tucked all the way in.

"You took a nice long walk," her mother commented. "Take something to drink. Your face is all red."

Sheila slipped her phone into her purse and smiled contentedly. Finally, finally, Sarah Roth was reaching out for help, for support, and, no less gratifying, for warmth and affection.

I really hope I can help her.

23 Second Date

Yerachmiel had arrived fifteen minutes early for his date with Sheila. Now, ten minutes past the designated time, he was growing nervous. No way she was standing him up, was there?

He made up his mind.

In the Leipzig home, the doorbell rang. Throwing an "I told you so" look at her husband, Miriam went to open the door.

"Shalom. You must be Dr. Leipzig. I'm Yerachmiel Kantor. I have a meeting with Sheila?"

"Yes. Please come in," Miriam Leipzig said cordially, masking her irritation with her daughter. "Sheila was delayed for a moment by an urgent call from a student. She's so dedicated. She'll be ready any minute now. Please come in."

Where is she? Miriam thought in exasperation as she ushered

Yerachmiel into the living room. *Why is she playing around with her future?*

* * *

The cool night air, the gentle summer breeze, the twinkling stars above, all were refreshing and calming. Sheila found herself telling Yerachmiel about her confrontation with Rika that afternoon.

"Disgusting!" Yerachmiel declared. "How dare she give you *mussar?* Some angry mixed-up kid lashing out at the world? Who does she think she is? You ought to leave and never go back. You don't owe those people a thing. Where's their gratitude?"

"I'm a big girl, Yerachmiel. I didn't melt. As you yourself just said, she's just a mixed-up angry kid. I felt bad for her," Sheila said lightly, reflecting that it was sort of touching to be defended so strongly. How many people did she know who would rush to her defense so staunchly?

"She had no right to lash out at you just because she has a hard life."

"Par for the course nowadays, unfortunately. Respect for one's elders isn't always a given."

"I wasn't talking about the kid, though she had no right to speak to you with such chutzpah, I was talking about Mrs., um, you know, the one who came to your school to beg for volunteers for her project. How could she let anyone to talk to you that way? Why didn't she put that kid in her place right away, the minute she opened her mouth at you?"

"She did insist that Rika apologize."

He grunted. "Too little, too late. Will you go back there?"

"I don't see why not."

"What?" He was incredulous.

"It's a growth experience. They gave me food for thought, you know? Maybe they do have a valid point."

"What, that you don't care about them? That you feel superior to them? Oh, please."

"I'm not being patronizing on purpose. Really. It's too long a trek to take just for the pleasure of being patronizing," she joked.

Yerachmiel laughed.

"But if that's the way I'm coming across, I need to change my approach. I want to give to these kids. I want to teach them all about who they are and where they came from."

"After what they did to you today? You're not for real."

"But I am."

"You know what? Let's go inside, get a drink or something to eat. Come, let's have *melaveh malkah*."

Yerachmiel and Sheila entered the brightly lit hotel lobby, blinking in the sudden glare. They found a table in a far corner and sat down. A waiter hurried over with menus and left.

Yerachmiel looked at Sheila expectantly. "Do you like gazpacho? It's my favorite summer soup. It's really good here. They serve it in a bread bowl with crispy whole wheat rolls on the side."

"Well…"

"I had a big lunch, but I hardly ate anything for *seudah shelishis*. I'm starved. You too?"

"Not really. So-so."

He looked disappointed.

"But I want to try that gazpacho soup."

He brightened. "It's very good. You don't need to be hungry to enjoy it. At least, I don't need to be hungry to enjoy it. There's no accounting for tastes." He winked.

Sheila laughed.

Yerachmiel signaled to the waiter, who promptly came to their table. "Two gazpachos, please," Yerachmiel told him.

The waiter nodded and scribbled on his pad. "Will there be anything else, sir?"

Yerachmiel looked at Sheila. "Would you like a soft drink? Cappuccino?"

Sheila shook her head.

"Not right now, thanks," Yerachmiel said to the waiter, who smiled and left.

"Where were you for Shabbos?" she asked. *Good, safe second date topic. We were getting a bit intense back there.*

Yerachmiel smiled. *Does she really want to know? Maybe. I'll follow her lead for a while.* "Oh, all over. Let's see. Friday night, my parents and I walked over to my mother's older sister. We do that all the time. Almost every week, in fact. There were a bunch of people. Everyone was there for the meal."

"Everyone?"

"Yes. My grandparents on my mother's side. They have a unit in my aunt's house. Like a small apartment."

Sheila nodded.

"My brother Menachem was there, with his wife who, uh, who…" He cleared his throat. "Who set us up?"

Sheila smiled.

"They slept over at my aunt's house because it's pretty far from Neot Yaar to the Old City. Then, we walked home at about midnight. I slept over at my parents' house instead of going home, though I live about ten minutes away."

The waiter appeared, balancing a loaded tray. He set a brimming bowl of soup in front of Sheila, and another in front of Yerachmiel.

"Thank you. That looks great."

"Anything else?" the waiter asked, setting down a basket of steaming rolls with flavored butter on the side.

Yerachmiel looked at Sheila. She shook her head.

"No, thank you. Not at the moment." To Sheila, he said, "I'm going to wash for bread."

Sheila inclined her head. She sat watching him walk away. She was feeling somewhat breathless, as if she were on a treadmill set to high speed. It was simultaneously both exhilarating and exhausting.

I shared a lot about myself. She looked down at her nails, trying hard to be in the moment, to stop her thoughts from racing. She tried not to think about anything at all.

"How about you?" He was back, swallowing his first bite of roll. "Are you going to wash? It's a mitzvah."

"I'm really not hungry, but if you put it that way." Sheila pushed her chair away from the table. "Where is the washing station?"

"Over there." He pointed. "You know what? You'll get lost. I'll show you." He got up mid-chew.

"No need. Just point me in the right direction."

Yerachmiel walked her down the length of the lobby and indicated the sink.

"Thanks."

He went back to their table.

Sheila washed for bread slowly and deliberately. Her thoughts were in turmoil. *Maybe he's this way with everyone he meets. Warm, expressive. It's not the way he was described to me, though. Avital told me that he's on the reserved side.*

This. Is. A. Second. Date.

It's nothing. Stop analyzing, and just enjoy his company.

Yerachmiel watched Sheila come back toward him. *This is the one. I think this is the one. Ribbono shel Olam! Could it be? I think it is. I think that she is the one. My bashert.*

She was back. He smiled at her and moved the basket of rolls toward her. "Here you are. I prefer the whole wheat rolls, but the white flour ones are also delicious."

Sheila selected a white roll and took a bite, then chewed slowly.

"Now try the soup," he urged. "I waited for you."

"You didn't have to do that," she protested, secretly pleased that he had. "Gazpacho is cold. It's not as if it would cool down."

She took a spoonful as he watched. "Delicious!"

"Made it myself," he joked. "Tell me more about being a teacher."

"Are you sure you want to hear? Why? You aren't a teacher."

"I'm just interested."

"Um..."

"You know what? I know from everyone that you're an exceptional teacher. But are there any other dramas in your teaching career to match what happened to you today?"

"Dramas? That's a funny way to put it. Let's see. Drama? Maybe, in a sense. I would call them growth opportunities."

"Same thing," he told her.

"So, when I taught the first grade, there was plenty of that."

"You taught first graders?" He chuckled. "You don't seem the type."

"I'm not. I didn't do all that well," she confessed.

"So what? No one is good at everything. When you come right down to it, it's just a job."

"Nope," she said flatly. "It's *neshamos*. It's their whole school career. The first-grade experience affects their whole school career, and I…failed."

"I'm sure you're exaggerating."

"I'm not." She paused. "The parents complained about me."

"Their problem," Yerachmiel said instantly. "Their problem from A to Z. Not yours. I'm glad you quit. Serves them right. Their loss. I told you that parents nowadays coddle their kids to the point of pain. It's not the kids' fault. I'm not blaming them, but they think the world owes them a living. They have no idea how to adapt or rise to a challenge. It's Abba and Ima to the rescue." He folded his arms triumphantly.

"First of all, you're oversimplifying a complex reality, and second of all, I didn't quit."

"Don't tell me that you're still wasting your time and energy on them!"

"No, I was asked to sub for the seventh grade, so the first-grade hour didn't fit into my schedule. I wouldn't have quit. I would have stuck it out until the end of the year. Besides, it wasn't all bad."

"No?"

"It was an eye-opener. The whole experience was an eye opener for me. It taught me a lot about myself."

"Such as?" Yerachmiel was fascinated.

"It was the first time in my life that I failed even though I was trying my best to succeed. That was a first for me," she said softly. "I failed as a teacher, though I tried so hard. That's not how things usually turn out for me." *Except in dating.*

Yerachmiel was looking at her attentively. She wondered if he could read her thoughts. Perhaps he could.

"Even the most successful people in the world struggle with something. Some people give up, but the ones with guts"—he rested his hands on the table between them and leaned forward for emphasis—"the ones with guts, with grit, with...vision, they keep on trying."

"And in the end?"

"In the end, it's worth it."

"Worth it?"

"Worth it all. All of it. Worth the effort, and worth the wait."

Sheila looked up, startled, and more than a little overwhelmed. Then, deciding that she'd misinterpreted, she relaxed. *There's no way he meant anything about...us. It's only a second date. He was just talking in general, about the merit of grit, of being dogged in all areas of life.*

Wasn't he?

Yerachmiel regretted his words. *That was too much, too soon. I just blurted it out, which wasn't smart. At all. She looks uneasy. Time for damage control.*

"In all areas of human endeavor, effort is commendable," he declared. "It builds character. That in itself is worth it."

To his relief, she relaxed further. He cast around for an additional distraction. "If you don't mind my asking, what was the urgent call you were taking, the one that aggravated your mother?" He smiled.

"When you were waiting outside?"

He waved his hand. "Not a problem. I'm just curious. If you want to, call it nosy." He chuckled.

I owe him an explanation. It wasn't very nice of me to make him wait. He is being nosy, but at least he admits it.

Sheila described her conversation with Sarah.

"I don't see what the problem is, handing in assigned work in a timely fashion. How is she supposed to learn responsibility?"

"You sound just like me," Sheila told him.

"Thanks. I take that as a compliment. Why did she wait so long to let you know? When did you tell them about this project?"

"I told them about it months ago," Sheila admitted. "I warned them that I'd be very strict about keeping to a timetable."

"Then why are you making an exception? People tell me that children prefer firm, nonnegotiable rules. Theoretically, it makes them feel secure."

Sheila laughed. "I know. Theoretically, right. In practice, I can't say I've noticed that it's true. Still, it's my personality to be a more rule-oriented teacher."

"I personally respect teachers who don't allow the kids to push them around."

"It's not all black and white. Maybe I'm being too lenient, but I have a feeling that there's more to this particular situation than meets the eye."

"It's possible. Don't you feel like you signed up to be a teacher and ended up being a therapist? Or even, this may be stretching it, a mother?"

"I do feel that way, but I enjoy that part of my job. Who says the three roles are so different? I mean, they are, but there are definite overlaps. Life isn't black and white."

"How about healthy boundaries?"

"Oh, I have those. I want you to know that my rule about handing work in on time is generally nonnegotiable. If I make an exception for this student, it will be—"

"Exceptional," he quipped, and they both laughed.

"Because she needs it," Sheila said soberly.

"Let's eat our soup," Yerachmiel suggested. "The waiter's coming our way to see if we want anything else. We wouldn't want to insult the cuisine here, would we?"

"Never." She tried to relax and enjoy the delicious soup.

As Yerachmiel ate, he thought about the many meals he hoped to share with Sheila in the future.

How many meals would that be from age forty till one hundred and twenty?

Shabbos Invitation

"Do you want to go down to the dining room, or are you too tired for that?" Kayla asked her husband. "Should I call room service?"

"I'm not hungry."

"You aren't? I'm starving."

"We can order room service if you like. Whatever you want is fine with me, Kayla."

"Well, okay," she said uncertainly, reaching for the phone. "If you're not all that interested in food now, I'll get something light. How about a fruit platter?"

"Like I said, it makes no difference."

Kayla ordered a fruit platter and some light pastries as she sat in an easy chair opposite her husband, who was sprawled on the couch. "All that davening seems to have given me a big appetite. Probably the release from tension, wouldn't that make sense? Why are you looking so serious?"

"It was a very serious day."

"Yes. Very intense, but at the same time, I also feel happy, lighter. In a serious way, though. Happerious isn't a word, is it?"

"No, it's not." He smiled faintly.

"I just made it up. It means happy in a serious way."

"I know. You just told me."

"Do you like it?"

"Your new word? It suits you."

"Do you feel happerious?"

"Me? I don't feel that way, but I'm glad you do."

"Why are you depressed? I'm sure our *tefillos* today went straight to *Shamayim*. What's wrong?"

"For me, it was beyond intense. More like running a marathon." He paused. "Frankly? It was an ordeal."

"An ordeal? Sounds rough. What do you mean by that?"

"No, not ordeal," Avigdor amended hastily, recalling their immersion in heartfelt supplication in Meron. That hadn't been an ordeal. Sharing an experience of depth with Kayla was far from an ordeal. He knew his wife had dug deep into herself to replenish her stores of *emunah* as they traveled to the *kevarim* of Rabbi Yossi HaGalili, Rabbi Yonatan Ben Uziel, Choni HaMe'agel, Rabbi Shimon HaZaken, ending with Rabbi Meir Baal HaNess in Teveria.

"It's hard to shrink the experience into mere words," he said finally.

Kayla nodded her agreement, but she needed more. She had been the driving force behind their trip, but still. She needed him to be filled with hope, just as she was. Avigdor's hopes and dreams to build a Torah home matched hers, but he'd thought the trip unnecessary. They'd been married less than two years, and they'd just been in Eretz Yisrael for Elchanan and Estelle's wedding.

"To be honest?" He sat up and looked at her intently. "I made this trip to please you, and I'm glad of our time together. The bonus for me was a chance to reconnect with Elchanan, but he's gone. That's what's eating me. Being a good friend right now probably means backing off, but for how long?"

There was a knock on the door. Kayla opened it to find a young man holding a tray full of sliced summer fruits, rolls, butter, jam, pastries, and drinks. He deposited the tray on the coffee table, acknowledged their thanks with a nod, and left.

"I'm listening," she said to him.

"I expected Elchanan to be a part of this trip. I was sure that he and his new wife would join us today. Instead, it's as if we aren't even here, for all the contact we have with them."

"You and Elchanan talk on the phone every day. You davened for him and his wife, as he asked you to."

"Yes, but I can do that anytime."

"Not at *kivrei tzaddikim*."

"True," he acknowledged. "But today would have been far more meaningful to me if he had joined us."

"You mean if *they* had joined us. You wanted him to get married, didn't you?"

"Definitely."

"Neither of you are carefree bachelors anymore. Back off, Avigdor. It's the caring thing to do."

He nodded reluctantly. "Unless—" He cleared his throat. "I'm just kind of wondering if I shouldn't say something to him."

"No."

"Or to his parents."

"Don't you dare. You could cause terrible problems."

"He's having terrible problems already."

"No, he's not."

"Tiptoeing around his wife, afraid to defy her in any way. Is that what you call a good marriage?"

"Do us all a favor and stop exaggerating."

His phone rang. He looked at Kayla. "It's Elchanan."

"What are you waiting for?"

"I don't want to speak to him now. Let him leave a message."

Kayla eyebrows lifted in surprise.

The couple sat in silence. She plucked a bunch of grapes from the platter and offered them to him, then took some for herself and chewed in thoughtful silence.

"You're thinking that it wasn't nice of me to do that."

She spread her hands indecisively. "No, I'm thinking that I don't understand why you're reacting so strongly. Elchanan's your friend, not your father or your brother."

"That's just it. When my parents got divorced..."

"Yes?" she asked softly.

"My father moved out, and my brother and I fought constantly. Elchanan was there for me. I could call him anytime day or night. He always sounded happy to hear from me. He was never too busy. I spent a lot of time in his house." Avigdor stopped. "It's hard for me to go back to those years. They weren't good years for me, or for my family."

"Don't talk about it if it's hard for you…but, Avigdor?"

"Yeah?"

"He was so good to you."

Avigdor smiled bitterly. "He was the one bright spot in my life for a long time."

"So, now he needs you."

"He needs me to do what? Disappear?"

"He needs you to be a friend to him."

"It's not so simple. Whatever." He shrugged.

"How about listening to the message to see what he wants?"

He picked up his phone and listened to the message. "Yup, it's as I thought. He and Estelle are all-so-formally inviting us to a meal, or all the meals this Shabbos unless we have other plans."

"That's nice of him."

"Sure is, except that if it were up to him, we'd have an open invitation. Oh—wait. Kayla? Estelle's on the line. She left you a message."

* * *

"Strange." Elchanan frowned.

"What's strange?" Estelle looked up from the pile of clothing she was sorting. She'd owned some of the outfits for over fifteen years. The aqua jumper, for example, that she'd bought for her twenty-eighth birthday, and the peach-colored knit. That was a birthday gift from herself to herself at age thirty-four. They were in wonderful condition, but she never wore them. They were taking up valuable space. On the other hand, they were great quality, and so pretty. If she wasn't wearing them, someone else could benefit.

She held up the aqua jumper to look for stains or holes. If she did give it away, she wanted it to be in good condition. It brought back bittersweet memories of Menucha Shalom's wedding. *I may have looked good, but I felt horrible at that wedding,* Estelle mused. *My last mainstay, my only real friend who was still single, was disappearing on me.*

Eliezer was super possessive of Menucha, her time, and her space, not to mention that if I didn't find another roommate in two months' time, I'd have to move out of our shared apartment. I can't imagine how I dealt with the heartache and stress.

"Elchanan?" She held up the two garments for his inspection. "Should I give these away?"

"Huh? Why?"

"I need the closet space."

"So put them in storage."

"Good idea." She went into the laundry room and came back with two big bags.

Elchanan was sitting and staring into space. He looked up when she came back in. "Why didn't Avigdor answer the messages I left him yesterday?"

"You left him messages yesterday? About what?"

When Elchanan didn't answer, she reddened. "Sorry, it's none of my business."

"No, it's fine. Nothing private. I thought I told you, that's all."

"Told me what?"

"Today was their big *kivrei tzaddikim* day. I called yesterday to give them our names to keep us in mind. I called twice, and both times I left a message, but he didn't get back to me. It's strange. He knows I'd want to hear that he got our names."

"Not necessarily," she countered. "You left a message, so he got it. There's no need to play phone tag. For future reference, I would have appreciated being consulted before you gave my name to virtual strangers."

Elchanan looked nonplussed. "Avigdor? Avigdor's not a stranger."

"What is he then?"

"He's an old, close friend."

"You never told me that!" Estelle's voice rose in agitation. "You said he was your father's protégé. Didn't you say that? Didn't you tell me that he's your father's protégé who you spent some time with when he was in his twenties, and you were in your thirties? All you said was that you had some heavy *hashkafah* discussions. Why didn't you tell me that a close friend was visiting?"

Elchanan shifted uneasily from one foot to the other. Caught! "We were very close at some points in our lives, but not in the recent past," he backpedaled.

She sent him a suspicious glance.

"Don't look like that. It's no big deal. His parents got divorced. It was one of those messy, acrimonious things, and he was pretty broken up, even though he was already seventeen years old. I kind of...took him under my wing. He became a *ben bayis* at my parents' house. But now? Now he's married to a girl from a wealthy family, and he himself is a successful businessman. He's moved on in life. He doesn't need me anymore."

She was silent, mulling over what he'd said. "Makes no sense, Elchanan. That's crazy."

"What's crazy?"

"What a time to have low self-esteem. Closeness like that doesn't just die. You should have told me all this before. Now I feel like a total fool."

"Why?"

Estelle tried hard to make sense of her roiling thoughts, but clarity evaded her. "I can't explain it. I just do."

"Forget it," he said reassuringly. "Everything's fine."

"If you say so." She shifted an armload of clothing from a chair to a box.

"Should we invite them for Shabbos?"

"Yes. Definitely."

"Great!" He was already dialing, his face alight. After a moment his eager expression changed. "It's going straight to voicemail again."

"So leave a message."

"Hi, strangers. Where have you been? Did Estelle's burnt soup scare you off, ha, ha? We look forward to seeing you this Shabbos unless we hear differently, but just let us know as soon—"

"Give me that phone." Estelle dropped her armful of clothing and grabbed the phone. "Hi, Kayla. We miss you guys. Obviously, you're spending Shabbos here with us, even if we can't match the fancy stuff you'd get in the hotel."

She hung up. "It's going to be a ton of work. I'd better start making lists. We'll use china, not paper. I'll bet that Kayla never uses paper. She'd think it's tacky."

"They're coming for the company."

She looked at him as if she'd forgotten that he was in the room. "Elchanan, don't you understand? I'm not blaming you, but your low self-esteem—you'd better work on it, by the way—has landed me in a whole bunch of hot water."

"I don't see how."

"I can't explain. In any case, now's my chance to show your friends that you married someone they can feel happy with."

His shoulders drooped. "Excuse me, Estelle. I just remembered that I promised a client to find a cheap flight to Italy for him. I'd better get to work." He left the room.

Estelle trailed after him, feeling uncomfortable. "Don't worry. I'm sure that they got the messages, and davened for you, uh, for us. Thank you for giving them our names. I'm sorry if I sounded a little sharp before. I just have this thing about privacy. It's my *meshugas*."

"It's fine," he said, but he didn't look up from the computer.

"No, really," she pressed. "Now that I know he's your friend, I don't mind hosting them. I just wish you had told me sooner."

He gave a wan smile, still not meeting her glance. "Don't overdo anything, Estelle. A simple, homey Shabbos like you make for the two of us will be terrific."

Estelle felt unsettled. What was with him?

* * *

Elchanan trudged to Maariv that evening, his thoughts in turmoil. She didn't even realize how deeply she'd hurt him. It was all about her, always about her. It was never about how anything would affect him, how anything would make him feel. Suddenly, she was full of energy and good will, eager to host the Rubinoffs for an elaborate Shabbos, which was great, but her motivation stung. It was about her showing his friends that she was a good wife. Did she even realize how ridiculous that sounded?

Silently, he admitted the truth that he'd suppressed, that he'd kept hidden even from himself. He hadn't told Estelle that Avigdor was his close friend because he'd been unsure of her reaction. Or rather, he'd been only too sure of her reaction. She'd realize that the proper reaction to close friends visiting from the States was to spend a significant amount of time with them, perhaps even take a day off from work.

Did he think she wouldn't have done it? She would have. Estelle always tried to do the right thing.

She'd have done it, but she would have been resentful. She would have felt martyred. He didn't want that.

He didn't want it for her, but even more, he didn't want it for himself. He didn't want it for the way it would make him feel about himself, about his marriage, about his life.

What had she said? "You'd better work on your self-esteem?"

Another winning statement courtesy of his new wife that would be funny if it weren't so sad.

Consequences

Sheila woke up early in the morning feeling wonderful. How long had it been since she'd felt as energized, as lighthearted, as carefree as she did right then? Too long.

She caught a glimpse of herself in the mirror. She could definitely skip the blush today. Her cheeks were pink. She was smiling. As she moved swiftly through her morning routine, she noticed that she was humming. Well, why not? No one could hear her. She twirled in a wide circle, arms outstretched. It was so good to be alive.

She looked around her room, wondering how she'd allowed so many clothes to accumulate on the various surfaces. The room was messy. She'd skipped her usual *erev Shabbos* cleanup, and it showed. And yesterday, *motza'ei Shabbos*, she'd come home so late.

She'd been tired, but not anymore. Today…today nothing was too much. Nothing was too hard.

She dove into the task with a will. She made swift work of the pile of garments, hanging, folding, and putting away with her usual deftness. After a moment or so, she stopped what she was doing. She stood still, staring dreamily into space. Her heart was at peace.

Yerachmiel liked her. He liked her very much. He'd made that clear. She thought it was kind of him not to keep her guessing. At their stage in life, who had time for ego games? If she'd disliked him, it would be awkward and uncomfortable if things were one-sided. She certainly didn't want to cause anyone pain, particularly not the searing pain of rejection. On the other hand, if she had disliked him, they never would have reached a third date at all. At her stage of the game, with over a decade of dating behind her, she never gave a maybe situation more than twice. So, whether he realized it or not, by giving him a third opportunity, she was making a statement. She liked him too.

She could have agreed to Avital Salamonte's assumption that she'd be the go-between, Sheila reflected as she put neatly folded shells in her closet, but both she and Yerachmiel had decided they didn't want to involve a third party. Sheila wondered if his reason for doing so was the same as hers, which was that she didn't want any pressure or advice. And she absolutely did not want any pressure or advice from a blissful newlywed several years her junior.

As she put away the last items, she realized with a jolt that if she and Yerachmiel got serious, that meant Avital would be her sister-in-law.

Stop! She commanded herself. *You're getting carried away. Step by step. Easy does it.*

She pushed the thought out of her mind and surveyed her neat room with satisfaction. Pursing her lips, she opened her cream-colored book bag to verify that she had all her teaching materials with her. It wouldn't do to be absentminded. She ran a finger over the gigantic copper-and-blue flower embroidered on the bag. If they did have a go-between, there would be someone to inform Yerachmiel that for Sheila, a third date was no light matter.

She opened the window as wide as it would go. They'd made an adult decision, and everything would work out. Before he'd gone back to his car, Yerachmiel had suggested that he call her on Monday, to give her time to think things over. She'd thanked him, and agreed, all the while thinking that the gesture was really unnecessary. This time, she didn't have to think things over. Her mind was made up. She didn't tell him that, but it didn't make it any less true. She was looking forward to speaking with him. She was looking forward to saying yes when he asked for a third date. She was looking forward to getting to know him better. She was just…just looking forward, to a future that suddenly seemed brighter than it had in many years.

She left the house. Today, she'd walk to school. Why waste such a gorgeous day going by car? Besides, she had to work off her pent-up energy. There were two ways to reach school on foot. Both were uphill, but one way was a shortcut that featured a demanding climb that was practically perpendicular and culminated in a triple set of very steep stairs. The other was circuitous and took about ten minutes longer, but it was a much easier walk. Unhesitatingly, Sheila chose the former route. She walked uphill at a rapid clip, breathing in the refreshing morning air, gazing at the blossoming flowers and trees. How beautiful Hashem's world was!

Her elevated mood lasted until the first lesson of the day. On Sunday, she spent her first period in her homeroom class, teaching her seventh graders Jewish history. It was already ten minutes into the lesson, and Sheila was becoming concerned.

Something was wrong, but what could it be? She wasn't giving a frontal lesson. She never did on Sunday mornings, especially not after a long Shabbos that ended late. Who knew when most of her girls had gone to sleep the night before? She didn't think it was at ten thirty or even at midnight. No, absolutely no frontal lessons on Sunday morning. Why ask for trouble when there were plenty of other alternatives? Why teach in a way that would require her pupils to exercise the self-discipline they might not be able to muster coming to school after a long weekend and inadequate sleep?

As always, on Thursday night, she'd carefully planned and prepared a group activity, though it meant a lot more work for her. The girls usually appreciated group work, with its obvious opportunities for a little unrelated conversation, a chance to catch up and socialize a bit. Sheila understood their need to ease back into the school routine, as long as they didn't overdo it. It was a win-win situation all around.

Not today. Today, something was off.

What was it? On the surface, nothing. Subliminally though, she knew that something was up. Over a decade of teaching had taught her to trust her instincts.

She tried to analyze the situation objectively. The students had willingly divided themselves into groups. No one was left sitting on the sidelines, looking on forlornly, waiting to be chosen. They were reading and writing away. Good.

Still... They seemed cooperative but somehow managed to convey lethargy and edginess at the same time. There was a current of tension in the classroom. The constant low buzz of conversation, the many covert glances sent in her direction contributed to her unsettled feeling.

She was puzzled and more than a little irritated. What they were doing was wrong. Yes, they were barely out of childhood, true, they were simply acting their ages, but really. Where was it written in the Torah that it was the unalienable right of young teenagers to act out? What a letdown. She'd worked so hard preparing today's lesson to ensure their enjoyment and participation.

Don't let them see that you are angry. Bad behavior is not the way for them to communicate their needs. You're the grown-up here. Model the behavior that you want them to adopt.

Sheila forced herself to take several deep breaths. Her stomach was clenched in frustration, so it wasn't easy, but she persevered. Meanwhile, at the teacher's lack of response, the buzz of conversation grew louder. Sheila rapped on her desk and asked for silence. The talking stopped.

Good.

"Girls," she said, mildly, "is there something unclear about the instructions I gave you? Does anyone want me to explain what today's assignment is?"

From the sudden silence in the classroom, it seemed that there wasn't any problem with the instructions. She stifled a sigh. It wasn't that; of course not. She knew that her instructions were crystal clear, and besides, that would have been too simple a problem.

"Okay, then. Please continue working, but bear in mind that each group will be given a grade that will have a direct influence on your final grade. If anyone wants me to realign her group"—she smiled slightly to take the sting out of her words—"so that you actually get some work done, just tell me, and I'll be glad to help you out."

"Realign?" Mindy Lavie asked, unfamiliar with the term.

"She means, work with another group," Sarah Roth whispered.

"Oh, thanks." Mindy was already jotting down the new word and its meaning in the small notebook she kept on her desk. Sheila smiled at her fondly, reflecting that Mindy had come a long way in ten months. Mindy's early months in school as a new *olah* had been rough on her, and her family, but now she was settling in so nicely.

Sheila's smile broadened. Mindy's rapid adjustment was due in no small measure to Sarah Roth's loyal friendship. They were both such good girls. She was glad they had each other.

"Morah!" Halleli Shalom called out. "This chapter is easy, but the assignment is so boring."

The entire class stopped working, the better to hear what Halleli, one of the undisputed class leaders, had to say.

"Try to phrase yourself more accurately," Sheila said evenly, though Halleli's comment was jarring. "The word *boring* is inappropriate, and—" She paused. "It may not be the most mature way to express yourself. I'd like to hear what's on your mind. You can say almost anything you like, but say it respectfully." Another pause.

"One more thing, Halleli. Try to remember to raise your hand before you speak. Now, what did you want to tell us?"

Halleli turned slightly red. "I'm sorry, Morah. What I wanted to say was…was just that this chapter is, um…"

Osnat jabbed her with her elbow.

Halleli poked her back, stifling a giggle. "This chapter is not boring, but why do we have to know that in the Old Yishuv in Yerushalayim, it was a whole day's project to do laundry? As far as I know"—she looked around the classroom—"we all have washing machines."

There were murmurs of assent. Halleli smiled triumphantly. "Why waste valuable time learning about something that has nothing to do with us?"

"Way to go," Halleli's sidekick, Osnat, muttered sotto voce, smirking.

Sheila eyed her sternly, and the smirk disappeared. She breathed an inward sigh of relief. Halleli was easy enough to handle, or at least she was when her mother stayed out of the picture, but Osnat was a handful.

"It has nothing to do with our lives nowadays," Halleli continued. "Why do we have to know all this stuff? Like, who cares? Can we skip this chapter? I don't know why we even have it in our book."

"It's especially irrelevant to you," Osnat said in a loud whisper. "You don't even know what unfolded laundry looks like. Your live-in does all the laundry in your house."

A ripple of good-natured laughter swept through the room. A live-in maid was beyond the means of the majority of the class.

Halleli shrugged. "Sorry, everyone. That's just the way it is."

"I agree with Halleli, though we don't happen to have a maid at the moment," Bilha Kaplan added.

Another wave of good-natured laughter swept through the classroom. Bilha's family had thirteen children, both of her parents worked in *chinuch*, and everyone knew that the lively Kaplan family somehow managed on a shoestring budget.

"Still," Bilha continued, "we don't live in the olden days anymore. My *savta's ima* did laundry like that a million years ago. We all have washing machines and dryers. Mindy, is it true that everyone in America has a maid to fold the laundry and put it away?"

"A maid? We didn't have a maid in America, and most of my friends didn't either," Mindy answered in her accented Hebrew.

"No?" Osnat swiveled around to stare at her in surprise. "Isn't everyone in America rich?"

"No."

"I think it's interesting to learn about how other people lived," Sarah Roth said softly. All eyes turned to the class leaders to see how they should react.

Sheila sucked in her breath when a beat later Osnat whispered, "Teacher's pet..." Now it was Sheila's turn to see if anyone would come to Sarah's defense. That would be far preferable to the teacher's intervention. However, no one did.

"Enough," Sheila said. "Let's get back to work. Anyone who doesn't contribute to her group's progress, and I will know who those individuals are, will get a zero in this class," Sheila declared so loudly and firmly that everyone obeyed.

She was fully aware that there were all kinds of educational opportunities in this exchange. She could initiate a discussion about the relevance of Jewish history in the girls' lives. She could speak about the value of knowing about the way their great-grandmothers had lived, in the not-too-distant past. But she preferred not to do that just now. Hopefully, the major project she'd assigned them at the beginning of the year would accomplish that.

The girls were expected to interview a relative or neighbor at least two generations removed from them. The second stage, the one many of her pupils were currently struggling with, was to write a short story, poem, or play using the information they had learned. As a finale, the girls would present the information to their classmates. In addition, each girl was to extend a formal invitation to her interviewee to attend the presentation.

The process was often grueling, this year perhaps a bit more than most, but Sheila wasn't fazed. In all her years of teaching, she'd never encountered a class that hadn't benefited greatly from the experience. In addition to the information they acquired, the close intergenerational relationships that often resulted were heartwarming to see. In the final analysis, the parents were extremely grateful to Sheila for affording their daughters the experience, which went way above and beyond the requirements of the seventh-grade Jewish History curriculum. Over the years, it had become a Machon Atara highlight.

Now, for Osnat's comment. Insulting Sarah was something else again. It was inexcusable. Osnat had to apologize. In public. On the other hand, perhaps the best course was to let things go. Sarah didn't seem too upset by the comment. It was hard to know how to react.

Sheila was used to being a specialty teacher, but being a homeroom teacher was a whole different story. Normally, she'd speak to the regular homeroom teacher. Well, guess what? Now *she* was the homeroom teacher, and she wasn't at all sure what to do. Seventh graders were so volatile. She didn't want to make things worse. She decided to consult with Nechama Rotter as to the best course of action to take in the future, so that should the incident or behavior repeat itself, she'd be better prepared.

There was a brief lull as everyone worked industriously, cowed by their teacher's wrath. Unfortunately, all too soon the whispered conversations started again. Twenty minutes into the lesson, Sheila gave up trying to snare their elusive cooperation. Time for another show of force. Sometimes, nothing else worked.

I prefer the term "exercising my authority." I think he would approve. Sheila hid a smile as she turned to the whiteboard. *He would tell me not to allow them to walk all over me.*

Ignoring their vociferous protests, she wrote down the contents of the lesson in question-and-answer form.

"There will be a pop quiz on the material next lesson. I strongly advise you to curtail your social lives for the duration of the class, and concentrate."

The girls grumbled, but she didn't care. Halleli bent studiously over her page. Osnat stared defiantly at her teacher, but Sheila matched her gaze for gaze until the girl picked up her pen and began copying the work, not before letting out an exaggerated sigh.

He might approve, but it's not the way I like to operate.

Sheila rested her head on the palm of her hand. Why were they so restless today? They were usually so cooperative. What could the problem be?

Maybe it was end-of-the-year-itis. Many teachers were complaining that in this last month of school, the students were much harder to manage. Whatever it was, the hostility she sensed in the atmosphere couldn't be allowed to continue. By ten fifteen, she was longing for the bell to ring. When it did, she was as relieved as her pupils were to take a break. Discreetly, she approached Sarah, who offered a shy smile.

"It's fine, Morah. I don't care that they said that."

"But why did they say that? I don't show you any favoritism in class."

Sarah shrugged again. "It doesn't matter."

"Aren't you entitled to have an opinion?"

"Two girls are just upset because you allowed me and Mindy one more week to do the project when no one else got permission."

"For that, the whole class was in an uproar?" Sheila demanded incredulously.

Sarah shrugged.

"Who told them that I allowed the two of you another week?" Sheila demanded, trying to keep any accusation out of her words and tone. "Didn't we agree that our agreement would be private?'

"I don't know who told them. I didn't tell anyone, only my mother, but somehow when I got to school today, everyone already knew, and…everyone was talking about it.

"I did. I told them."

"Mindy?" Sheila recovered her voice first. "You did? Why?"

"I had to." Mindy tugged agitatedly at a long blond curl.

"Why did you have to?"

"Because…because some girls were talking. Some girls were saying things about you, about Morah Sheila, that weren't so nice, how ever since you became our substitute you're so strict, and I wanted to show them that you aren't. I wanted to tell them that you're nice." Mindy looked down. "Sorry."

Sheila left the classroom feeling deflated. Where had her bright morning mood disappeared to?

She sought out Nechama in the teachers' room, but it was Nechama's free day.

I'll just have to tackle this on my own, and hope for the best.

* * *

Halleli and Osnat strolled around the periphery of Machon Atara's courtyard, arms linked, deep in discussion. More than one of their classmates watched them admiringly, enviously, longing to know what they were discussing so seriously, but no one had the temerity to approach them. Osnat and Halleli were a twosome. That's the way it always had been for as long as anyone could remember. Osnat and Halleli were in charge of the class, and everyone did what they said to do, even, sometimes, the teachers. Morah Yocheved, for example, often deferred to their wishes. It was just the way things were.

"It wasn't very nice of you to call Sarah a teacher's pet," Halleli told her friend. "You should go over to her and apologize."

"Why?" Osnat demanded. "It's true. Sarah's always been the teacher's pet. Remember how even Morah Noa loved her in first grade? What a goody-goody."

Halleli stopped walking and detached her arm from Osnat's grasp. "But Morah Noa loved all us. She was the nicest teacher."

"Why should I apologize to Sarah? Who asked her to be annoying?"

"You should. You should because..." Halleli said mysteriously.

"Tell me."

"It's a secret." Halleli lifted her long black hair off her neck. "It's hot today. Let's go back inside. At least it's air-conditioned in there."

"Stop changing the subject."

"I'm not."

"Yes you are. Anyhow, Morah Sheila is in there. I don't want another lecture."

"You'll get one anyway when you come back to class," Halleli said pragmatically.

"She got so mean!"

"Who did? Morah Sheila?"

"Yeah."

"That's *lashon hara*."

"Now you sound just like Sarah."

"So what? I don't know what you have against her."

"I told you, she's a goody-goody. I don't like goody-goodies. We need to be united. Us against the teachers."

"Mmm. You have a point. Morah Sheila was a lot nicer before she took over for Morah Yocheved. Even my mother says so."

"See?" Osnat said triumphantly. "I can't wait for Morah Yocheved to come back."

"Me neither."

"Maybe she'll cancel this dumb project."

"You wish," Halleli answered gloomily. "She won't."

"Maybe she will."

"Forget it. Rabbanit Sudri loves this project."

"How do you know?"

"I heard my mother tell my father."

"I hate this school," Osnat grumbled. "Whatever. You're the only reason I stay here."

"I know."

"Tell me what your mother said about Sarah."

"No." Halleli turned to face her best friend. "I really, really can't tell you anything."

"Yes, you can. You just don't want to."

"Well…"

"Yes?" Osnat stood still, her eyes gleaming.

"If you knew what Sarah has to put up with, you'd be glad that she has Morah Sheila on her side."

"That's all?" Osnat waited, but clearly, Halleli was determined to say no more.

The two girls resumed walking. Osnat took Halleli's arm once again.

"Fine, don't tell me what your mother said, but is it anything new? I know that she's an orphan, and all. Is her…is her mother remarrying? Does she dislike her new stepfather? Is she taking it hard? Is it that? Hey! Just shake your head yes or no if I guessed right. You didn't tell me, I guessed."

"No, it's not."

"Do you even know what the big secret is?" Osnat stopped walking and put her hands on her hips.

"No, I don't," Halleli admitted. "But I can tell you that my mother told me, in strictest confidence, that nobody in our class should feel jealous if Morah Sheila favors Sarah and Mindy. They are both *chesed* cases, and we should be very nice to them, and you should apologize to Sarah."

"If it makes you happy." Osnat tossed her head defiantly.

"So you'll apologize to her?"

"I said I would, didn't I?"

26

I'll Give You a Call

Yerachmiel woke up on Monday morning with a sick feeling in the pit of his stomach. He hoped he hadn't blown his chances, but he was afraid he had done just that.

He'd made his liking for her far too obvious, and she was going to get cold feet. He couldn't take the risk of that happening. He was a man of his word, no question about it. Fine. He'd keep his word, but at the same time, he'd give her all the time and all the space that she could possibly need to arrive at any decision she wanted to.

Damage control. He'd play it cool, the way he had all the years he'd been dating. Had it been nearly twenty years? It had. Playing it cool, that was always the best way to do these things. They hadn't fixed a time that he'd call her, just Monday. That meant at least eighteen hours for her to wonder if he was interested in continuing. Monday was Monday, all day long. Let her take all the time she wanted to decide. He wouldn't jump the gun, no siree.

This time, there was too much at stake. Way too much at stake. If a terrific girl like Sheila wasn't married, it wasn't for lack of opportunity. He wasn't about to put her off by any show of overeagerness.

Why had he said he'd call on Monday? What would have been wrong with a vague, suave statement like, "I'll give you a call?"

He hadn't been thinking clearly.

So, Monday it would be. She'd have plenty of time to think, plenty of time to realize that he had no intention of begging.

His distress was exacerbated midmorning when his sister-in-law, Avital, conveyed a message to him through Menachem: Sheila hardly ever granted anyone a third date.

He supposed he should be grateful to Avital for giving him the information. Forewarned was forearmed.

At six o'clock, Rina-O-Mangina was playing at a bar mitzvah, but they were scheduled to stop at nine thirty to make time for some type of family presentation. There was no reason, absolutely no reason that they shouldn't be through by ten, or ten thirty. He'd call her then, but not a moment sooner.

At ten thirty, the celebration was still going strong. Yerachmiel shook his head in dismay, but there was nothing to be done.

On second thought... It was *bashert*. If she was just a tiny bit unsure, a little tiny bit thrown off balance, it couldn't hurt, could it?

He'd call her tomorrow, during her ten o'clock break.

* * *

Tuesday morning, tensions were still running high in the seventh grade, but their substitute homeroom teacher took it well in stride. Now that she knew the reason why, she had zero intention of backing down. She could weather adolescent storms with the best of them. The main thing was that Osnat had apologized to Sarah in front of the entire class. The girls were being sulky adolescents? That was fine, just fine. As long as they didn't pick on Sarah or Mindy, it was fine. She wasn't dependent on being a successful teacher just to hold on to her self-esteem. *Baruch Hashem,* other people thought highly of her, she hoped. That being said, the way Osnat Portal was glaring at her didn't feel all that comfortable. Once again, the ten o'clock break couldn't come soon enough. As the bell rang, and the classroom emptied out, Sheila pounced on the phone.

There was a message. There was. There was.

It was him. Finally.

"Hello?" A pause. "This is Yerachmiel Kantor calling. I'd like to speak to you."

That was it.

What a letdown. Was that all? Just that cryptic message, with no indication of what he wanted to say? Not even a hint? After she'd waited for this call all day yesterday?

He'd dropped her off at home on *motza'ei Shabbos*. He'd gotten out of the car to open the door for her, and walked her to the lobby of the building. He'd told her that he'd had a "wonder—a very good time," and she'd smiled and nodded in agreement. He'd thanked her and said he'd call on Monday.

Monday morning had come and gone without a call from him. When Monday afternoon crawled past without any call, she checked her phone two or three times, to make sure it wasn't on silent. Unfortunately, the phone was in fine working order and not on silent. So then why hadn't he called?

"Have you heard anything from the young man who took you out on *motza'ei Shabbos*?" Professor Leipzig asked her, that evening, while she was setting the table for supper.

"Not yet."

"No?" Her mother shook her head in dismay. "Too bad."

"It's only been two days," Sheila protested.

"True. It does no good to worry, that's for sure. Are you eating with us? Should I set a place for you?"

"No thanks, Ima. I'm not hungry. I'll have a sandwich later on."

"I'm sure he'll call soon," her mother said. "You told your father that you had a good time. I'm sure he did as well."

"Thanks."

"That being said, I do think that you should learn a lesson from this."

"Learn a lesson from what?"

"You did keep him waiting while you spoke to your student. That may have conveyed to him that marriage isn't your top priority in life."

"I'm sure he's not thinking about that."

"Hopefully, he's not."

"*Ima*."

"Probably he isn't, but all the same, if I were you, I'd keep it in mind for the future."

"I will."

"Good."

Later that night, unable to concentrate on anything, she'd hovered over the phone, trying to think of a thought-provoking question or interesting activity to open the next day's lesson. It was no use. She couldn't concentrate. Her mind was blank. Creative thinking? Individuated lesson plans?

Had she put school at the center of her life? Was he thinking that? It wasn't so. Teaching was important to her, but thinking that she centered her life around it? What a joke. Marriage was her life. Building a home was her life.

Sheila forced herself to concentrate on the lesson she was planning. She owed it to the girls. A commitment was a commitment, and in any case, when he called was completely out of her control.

Just before ten thirty, she'd determinedly put on her Nikes and gone for a brisk hour's walk around Neot Yaar. She'd deliberately left her phone at home. When she came home, she allowed herself to check for incoming calls.

Nothing.

Maybe she'd misheard what he'd said? Maybe. Perhaps he'd said that he'd call later on that week, and she'd been so tired that she'd heard him say Monday because that was what she wanted to hear?

Not likely.

Could it be that in her fervent wish to have finally met someone with real potential, she'd misinterpreted the entire conversation, inserted her own meaning when he'd meant to convey a different message entirely?

Maybe it was all a figment of her imagination. After all, she hardly knew him. It could be that he was a cordial, outgoing individual who exuded warmth toward everyone. As the leader of a successful band, he was accustomed to dealing with all kinds of people. The open, flowing communication she'd thought they'd shared might be nothing more than good people skills; the friendliness and interest he'd displayed, a matter of professional habit.

She didn't think so. She thought not, she hoped not, but you just never knew. He had managed to reach the age of forty without anything more than a broken engagement. When all was said and done, she hardly knew him.

And here she'd told him so much about herself. Nothing really personal, but still.

She'd gone to sleep late Monday night, reassuring herself that it had been a good meeting, a meeting of the minds, if she wanted to put it that way. She was positive that she'd never fall asleep, but to her surprise, she slept very soundly. Tuesday morning, right after *netilas yadayim*, she'd checked her phone. Perhaps he'd called while she was asleep? After all, musicians did keep odd hours. Hadn't he mentioned something about a bar mitzvah on Monday night? Or was that a wedding?

Nothing.

Why wasn't he calling?

No walk to school that morning for her. The uphill hike was far too daunting to contemplate. So was facing a hostile class of angry girls.

Sheila punched in her sister's number and told her what was going on.

"Unreal," Michal said. "It sounds like you like him."

"Maybe."

"No maybe. Hey, stop worrying. There could be at least ten reasons why he didn't call you yesterday."

"Such as?"

"Anything. Don't worry, Sheila. He'll call you today, for sure."

"What are you, a prophet?"

Michal chuckled. "Hardly, but I just know he will. I'd bet my very last shekel on it."

Sheila felt better. "I don't know why I should believe you, but I do."

"Good."

"Give Batya a gigantic hug from her Aunt Sheila."

"Will do."

Now she was ready to enter the fray. She never brought her cellphone into class, but today was an exception. She compromised by leaving it on silent. That way, she wouldn't have to endure the three-minute walk between her classroom and the teachers' room, wondering if he'd called.

Now, now, *now* he'd finally called.

And left her in the dark.

She listened to the message again.

Sheila put the phone down on her desk for a moment, frowning in concentration. She was unaware of the many pairs of seventh-grade eyes fixed on her curiously. Then, she made up her mind.

I'm calling him back. Now.

She hurried out of the classroom into the hall. The noise level was unbelievable. There was a heated game of what looked like dodgeball taking place. Fourth grade versus fifth grade. The competition between the two grades was fierce. Sheila wasn't surprised to hear the captains of each team yelling excitedly at each other. There seemed to be some contention about who exactly had caught the ball last, and who exactly was winning.

She hurried past the groups to the lower floor where the first and second-grade classrooms were located.

There were groups of second and third graders jumping rope. There were first and second graders playing house. There were first and second graders trading stickers. There was a first grader wailing loudly, while some of her classmates attempted to comfort her. There was no place to have a conversation, especially not a private conversation.

What had she been thinking? It was recess, after all. She poked her head into the teachers' room.

Out of the question. It looked like every teacher in Machon Atara was there and talking at once.

The schoolyard was the most spacious place in Machon Atara. It was also the quietest location, even during recess, and afforded relative privacy. She'd go there.

Outside, a group of sixth graders spied her. They seemed to be headed in her direction. Sheila half turned away, punched in Yerachmiel's number, and held the phone to her ear. The students were getting closer. They'd see that she was busy on the phone.

She heard the number ringing and then it went to voicemail. She hung up without leaving a message. The first pupil in the group was standing at her side. Sheila smiled, pointed at her phone, and turned around further so that her back was to the group. There was a different teacher on yard duty. She'd take care of whatever needed to be taken care of.

Go tell that to the students, she thought in frustration ten minutes later. How many students had approached her to tell her something, to complain, to arbitrate quarrels, to share, to bask in her attention? She'd lost count, and it was hot. The midday sun beat down everywhere and left no patches of shade. She turned to retrace her steps back to the building.

Why wasn't he picking up?

I'll call him next break if he doesn't get through to me first. I'll go sit in my car. I should have done that in the first place.

"Morah!" An insistent little hand tugged on her sleeve. "Morah Sheila, look! Look what I got. *Looook.*"

Elianna Rosse. Elianna, who had been the bane of her existence when Sheila had struggled through her hour on famous people in Jewish history in the first grade. Elianna! How could the small child in front of her have been the source of so much trouble? How could it be that the young person standing in front of her, spilling out a rapid stream of words, was the one responsible for so much soul-searching and self-doubt?

The fact was, she had. Though, to be fair, it wasn't Elianna who was the source of the trouble. It was the fault of the adults surrounding her. Elianna's mother had complained bitterly to Noa about Sheila's lack of rapport with her daughter, and about Sheila's abysmal teaching skills in general. She'd demanded that Rabbanit Sudri replace Sheila, pronto, with a softer personality, who would simultaneously build the children's confidence, and manage the classroom far more effectively than Sheila did. Elianna's mother hadn't been the only parent to complain. Sheila realized with a start that most probably Noa had protected her from the worst of the claims against her.

Nice of her, but that didn't mean that Sheila had to be a quitter and allow anyone to take over for her. Especially not Aviva. If Nechama Rotter had been suggested, or even Estelle, she would have given the suggestion serious consideration. Diplomacy was never Noa's strongest point.

"Morah Sheila!" Elianna's tugging on her hand escalated. Her eager, gap-toothed grin broadened. "I lost two teeth. Two! See?"

"I see!" Sheila replied. "What a big girl you are."

"My mommy bought me real jewelry. Look!" Elianna proudly displayed a pink pearl necklace and matching bracelet. They were drugstore purchases, to be sure, but Elianna's face shone with joy.

Never one to stand in the shadows for long, a fellow first-grade classmate, Sherry, tapped Sheila insistently on her elbow.

"I lost *three* teeth. And one of my teeth is all wobbly."

This is supposed to be my time.

She had to talk to him. Now.

She glanced at her watch. Twelve minutes till class started, which left four minutes to race outside to her car, four minutes to hopefully connect, and four minutes to race back upstairs to her classroom. Turning thought into, she sprinted toward the gate. Luckily, the school's long-time guard was sitting in his booth.

"I'll be right back," Sheila told him. Her heart was pounding now, and not because of the run.

She tried to calm her hammering pulse. *He either wants another date, or he doesn't.*

The phone rang. He was calling back. Wait, the caller ID showed it was Menucha Shalom.

I don't want to speak to her now, Sheila thought. *Besides, the whole issue of getting my own place may be redundant if…if things get serious.*

I'm being ridiculous. This is ludicrous. I don't even know if we're going out on a third date. What was that I told Ima about not putting my life on hold? It's just that I hate being single. Hate it, hate it. HATE IT.

* * *

Sitting in her husband's real estate office located in an elegant building in downtown Jerusalem, Menucha Shalom bit her lip in frustration. *I call her with the perfect place for her and get her voicemail. How annoying is that? Doesn't she ever pick up her phone? Is she never, ever available? Is she trying to show me how super-duper busy she is? I'm not impressed.*

With no other choice, she left a message: "Hello, Sheila. There's a couple who left here not five minutes ago. I tell you, they have the perfect home for you. Grab it before someone else does. Can you believe this *mazel*? They are friends of your parents named Bellinson. Moving for half a year to their daughter's community. Their apartment is five blocks from your parents' house. Two rooms, fully furnished, nice building, good directions. Call me. I told them about you. CALL ME."

* * *

Sheila let Menucha's call go to voicemail and then listened to it. *Oh, my. I'll deal with this later.*

Then she dialed Yerachmiel again.

"Sheila? Sheila Leipzig? Is that you?"

She laughed, enjoying his surprise. "Yes, it's me. I got your message." She stopped, unsure of where to go from there.

"Thanks for calling back." He cleared his throat. "Would you like to meet sometime this week?"

"Yes. Yes, I would. Listen, Yerachmiel, I'm sitting here in my car. I'm playing hooky, but seriously, I have only three minutes till I absolutely must be back in the building. I just wanted to tell you that I got your message." She was babbling. Since when was she so inarticulate? What would he think of her?

"I appreciate that," he said sincerely. "I really do. Can I call you, say around six? I hope it's not too early, but I'm playing at a wedding tonight."

"Six is very convenient. Okay, bye."

She raced into the building, reaching the classroom breathless, with seconds to spare before the bell rang.

During the next break, she'd call Menucha Shalom back. It seemed pointless, but it was the right thing to do.

She floated through the rest of the day. So this was what it was like. This indescribable feeling of being special to someone who… was also special.

Next time, she'd tell him about her dreams. She wanted an open home, where she could have students over anytime. Sarah and Mindy for example. And Rita. Rita would see that she really cared. Her family. She'd finally be able to host them for Shabbos meals, and during the week, they could drop by. His family would always be welcome as well, Menachem, and—

Yes. Even Avital.

27 Going Home

"I don't know what the best decision for me might be," Sheila told Geula Leibowitz the following day. The two were seated in a far corner of the schoolyard, enjoying the unseasonably cool day. "I saw the place Menucha called me about. I went right after school because it's supposed to be better to see a place in the daytime."

"So they say," Geula agreed. "Did you like it?"

"Did I like it? I feel like none of the options are good. My parents don't care if I keep living at home forever, so why am I putting myself through this…torture?"

"Torture?"

"Uprooting myself for no reason," Sheila explained. "Causing upheaval in my life when I don't have to do it."

Geula looked puzzled. "It sounds like a dream come true to me."

"It does? Why? To me, it's some kind of sad compromise at best."

"Depends on your attitude," Geula retorted. "Your parents are paying for it, so you'll move into a nice practically new apartment and buy gorgeous furnishings. Two"—Geula squelched a small surge of envy—"no one's pushing you out of the nest. You can take your time, move when it suits you. Look how incredibly it all worked out. You wanted to try out a place for six months and then perhaps buy. I thought you were looking for the impossible, and look how everything fell into place. I'd say, go for it! Look at me. I'm still renting, and not a palace either, just to be able to live in a good neighborhood. Not too many people are in your position. They rent, they get roommates, not all of whom are, uh, a good fit, shall we say? Thousands of girls live in shabby places if they move out to rentals. That's not what you're facing at all. Your parents are buying you a home! All you need to do is be willing to stretch your comfort level just a tiny bit. You can decorate it beautifully to your own taste, turn it into your own cozy niche. Why are you getting cold feet now? Do you know how many women would love to be in your position?"

"Do *you* know how many women think that my position is their worst nightmare ever?" Sheila shot back, stung.

"Why?" Geula asked. "Nightmare? Oh, please. Give me a break. A challenge, granted. A difficult adjustment, sure. But a nightmare?"

"Okay, so maybe it's not a nightmare. But in any case, I'm still ambivalent about the entire idea when I'm not even...while I'm still..."

"Single," Geula supplied. This show of vulnerability was a side of confident, reserved Sheila Leipzig few ever witnessed. *Stop feeling sorry for yourself. The move you're considering is fairly common in this day and age. No pity parties necessary, though it is hard.* "Mark my words: this is only temporary. I know you can't believe you're house hunting without a husband, but you're only thirty-two. You're a baby."

"Hardly." *She doesn't know about Yerachmiel, Sheila thought, and it's way too soon to say anything to anyone. Limbo. How am I supposed to act normal when my whole life is in limbo?*

"So, do you have a date for the end-of-the-year evaluation with Rabbanit Sudri?"

"Huh?"

"Earth to Sheila," Geula said. "You know, that little issue the entire teachers' room will soon buzzing about? Evaluations?"

"Buzzing about? Why?" Sheila asked blankly.

"Boy, are you out of it. I can't believe you don't know what I'm talking about. I thought you're all buddy-buddy with Rabbanit Sudri. Come on, don't deny it." Geula wagged her finger playfully.

"Me?" Sheila felt the first stirrings of annoyance. Sometimes, Geula's sense of humor got under her skin. "She's not my friend. She's a friend of the family, and let me tell you, I have no say in any decision-making process, no more than any other member of staff. I'm not in on any secrets, and I don't want to be."

"Hey, chill. Take it easy. I was just kidding around, changing the subject because the other stuff we were discussing was upsetting you too much. I'm really sorry."

"Forget it," Sheila said shortly. *She doesn't know about Yerachmiel.*

"I said I'm sorry. Don't go all stiff and formal on me now."

"I have to get going." Sheila got up.

Geula sighed. "Sheila, sit back down."

"What?" Sheila remained standing.

"Have it your way," Geula said ruefully. "I didn't mean to upset you."

"It's okay."

"Aren't you even curious to know what Yonina Nachum told me, in strict confidence?"

"If she told you something in strict confidence, of course I don't want to know."

"Sheila, Sheila. I was just trying to make you curious. It's no big deal. Just that in a week or so, everyone's going to have to schedule a date for a meeting with Rabbanit Sudri."

"Why?"

"End of the year evaluation. You, obviously, have nothing to worry about, because you're the administration's darling, but—"

"I really want to ask you not to talk like that. It's not even true." Sheila's cheeks flamed.

"Sheila, you're very gifted. It's nothing to be ashamed of. I'm no slouch myself, but I'm new on the staff, so naturally, I'm apprehensive about the outcome of the meeting. You, however, can expect a *nachas* report from A to Z.

"You have nothing to worry about, either," Sheila retorted automatically, her thoughts in turmoil. "Everyone knows you're a complete professional."

Is it even possible that the entire staff of Machon Atara is unaware of how badly I messed up in Noa Lewin's first-grade class? Week after week, I failed in front of everyone. Kids refusing to come in from recess, so that Avital Salamonte, the guidance counselor, had to bribe them to enter my classroom. Kids who had accidents because I never knew if or when I should excuse them for a trip to the restroom. Anyone passing by that room heard loud and clear that I couldn't control the class. It was a miracle that I got the seventh-grade substitution so that my entire schedule had to change. Geula thinks I have nothing to worry about? Could it be that she doesn't know?

Why don't I just go to Rabbanit Sudri and tell her the truth, that first graders aren't my area of expertise, and could she please let me drop this hour? Let her give the hour to someone else. I don't need the money.

Is it because I don't want to be a quitter? Because I'm afraid Rabbanit Sudri will think less of me if I drop out when the going gets tough?

I think it's the second reason. Sheila flinched. *Aren't I a little too old to need approval so much? Maybe Geula has a point. Maybe...maybe I am too stiff and closed.*

Sheila sat down.

Geula heaved a sigh of relief. "Me and my big mouth. One day I'll learn tact."

"You're fine the way you are. I need to ask you something."

"At your service, ma'am."

"How do you cope with Noa's class?"

"With difficulty."

"No, tell me how you manage. I need your help," Sheila persisted. "Seriously."

Geula looked surprised. "I am being serious. We all struggle with three, four girls in the class, the same three or four girls who are really too young to be in first grade. Either that or they have real problems, poor things. Though I have to tell you that first and second grades are my favorite ages."

"Why? They're such babies."

"Babies? Yes, I can see that for someone like you who is accustomed to teaching the junior high school students, they do seem very young. Plus, it's not as if you have your own children who have gone through first grade."

Sheila kept her expression neutral.

"I'm just lucky, I guess," Geula continued. "I enjoy the way they're so open, and not sneaky or secretive. What you see is what you get. No masks. They tell it like it is, the way they see it, but they don't have an agenda. Most kids this age—first graders, second graders, even third graders—are still so innocent." Geula looked into the distance. "School isn't always the best place for it, but when you come right down to it, the thing they want most is our love."

"You sound like Aviva."

"She happens to be right on the money. Listen, Sheila. I also get overwhelmed by the demands of a class of first graders, but individually? They're a pleasure to deal with and a pleasure to have around."

"It's not as if you have children of your own..." How true! Would it change her approach to teaching? Would she ever have a chance to find out?

My Brother, Menachem

"Menachem! Menachem, where are you?" Avital Kantor, née Salamonte, stood in the tiny foyer of her apartment. "Menachem! Come fast! Hurry! Where are you?!"

She clapped a hand over her mouth, fighting back nausea, and ran out into the hall. As the door swung shut behind her, she heard a faint groan from the depths of the apartment, followed by her husband's weak voice.

"Avital? Where are you? Where did you go?"

"I'm going out. Outside, downstairs to the garden."

She hurried to the small patch of fenced-in lawn fronting the building. Now, surrounded by fig trees, shaded by the large leaves, she took deep breaths. She felt better, much better. Here, far from the smell of whatever food her husband of six months was heating up, she felt her queasiness abate.

"I'm out here," she called.

"Avital?" He stuck his head out the window of their first-floor rental. "Sorry. I forgot that you can't bear the smell of chicken. *Oy vey*. I was warming up the chicken soup Ima sent us. I'm turning it off. Be right down."

"I'll wait out here."

Outside, Menachem sneezed violently into a gigantic wad of tissues he held clutched in his fist. Avital looked at him properly for the first time that day.

"Menachem, how are you feeling?"

A violent sneeze followed by a fit of coughing was her only response. She waited, trying to curb her mounting impatience.

"It's this cold. I felt like death warmed over this morning. Do I look like death warmed over?" he asked, clearly hoping for her sympathy.

"Nope. You look like you have a bad cold."

"So, anyhow, I dragged myself to shul, and when I came home, I was shivering my head off. I thought maybe some chicken soup from Shabbos would warm me up."

I'm throwing up all day, every day for a month, and he's going on and on about a cold.

"Come, let's go upstairs."

"I'll see if I can manage with the smell. Otherwise, I'm going to have to wait downstairs till it goes away."

"Poor you," he said contritely. "Do you want me to open all the windows?"

"No, you're shivering as it is. You know what, Menachem?"

"What?" He groaned.

"Keep the windows closed. I'll go out to the balcony. It's summertime out here, by the way. Just, could you please bring me some salty crackers and iced tea from the kitchen? I don't want to go in there. Eat your soup. *Refuah sheleimah*. Tell me when you're finished."

"No, I'll also have crackers, but with hot tea."

"But soup's good for you."

"It's okay."

Avital smiled her gratitude.

Seated on the stone ledge of the balcony, she closed her eyes, marveling at her good fortune. Menachem was such a nice, considerate guy.

I'm a lucky woman.

Her husband soon joined her, carrying a tray that held a glass of iced tea, a cup of hot lemon tea, and crackers. Placing it carefully on the ledge next to her, he sat down.

"Peach flavored tea, complete with ice cubes. Thanks, Menachem. So, this morning, I happened to meet Menucha Shalom. You know, the real estate agent who's also head of the PTA? I asked her if she knows about properties outside Yerushalayim that are within our price range, and she does."

"Great!"

"So, we're going to have to start looking pretty soon. This place"—she waved her hand toward their tiny apartment—"is barely big enough for one person, forget three. Did you speak to Yerachmiel yet about cosigning on a mortgage for us?"

He shook his head. "Nope. Soon." He took a cautious sip of his hot tea.

"You didn't? Why not? Didn't you plan to do that last night?"

Menachem took another sip of tea. "Ah, that feels soothing. I'm waiting for the right moment. It's not going to be an easy yes, Avital. He's frugal with his money, and he knows that I'm, let's just say, more happy-go-lucky in that area."

"Frugal? What makes you say that? He just got himself a new car!"

"Not new, second-hand," Menachem said, to set the record straight. "He bought that car second-hand, and what's more, he got it at a discount, because—did I ever tell you this story, Avital? It's just pure Yerachmiel. See, there were these classy people who were looking for a different kind of band for their youngest daughter's wedding. They wanted violins, silver flute, even a harp."

Menachem waved his hand, inviting her to picture it. "All those orchestra instruments."

"But Rina-O-Mangina doesn't have a harp."

"No, they don't, but other than that the band fit the bill. They wanted a classical sound. Rina-O-Mangina was one of the only bands both sides would consider."

"Nice."

"The customers were thrilled with the band. Everyone who hires them is because they only hire top musicians, and boy, do those guys practice." Menachem chuckled. "I think I told you this story while we were dating. Stop me if I did."

"Go ahead."

"This was around, oh, let's say around five, six years ago. The band was advertising for a second singer, and I thought, why not? I came to audition as a singer, and this guy, Zev Schwartz, he's the manager, *knew* I was Yerachmiel's brother. I didn't tell Yerachmiel I was planning to audition. It was going to be a surprise."

"So the manager told you that you have a great voice, but you aren't polished enough. He said you should take voice lessons and get some job experience and then come back," Avital broke in. "And you asked him not to tell Yerachmiel, so he shouldn't feel bad about it. Very impressive indeed."

"So I *did* tell you."

"You did."

"Anyhow, those two clients I was telling you about? The other side—not the *kallah's* side—had a barely used car they wanted to sell. Is that *siyatta diShemaya* or what? To make a long story short, Yerachmiel happened to mention that he wanted a car more suited to his image, and right away—"

Avital broke into his flow of words. "Why should someone who can upgrade like that be concerned about cosigning on a loan—for his only brother, no less?"

Menachem looked at her questioningly. "Tali, he lent us his old car on a long-term basis. Because of his generosity, we have unlimited use of a car. He bought the new car because of his, um, his image, you know, which is fine."

"I never thought otherwise. I didn't say that it's not okay. Let him spend his money any way he likes. All I'm saying is that you shouldn't feel like you're asking him for this huge favor."

"I know you think that presenting an image is shallow, but it matters to him," Menachem explained, despite her comment. "Yerachmiel is used to admiration. He was a child prodigy, as far as music goes, and he's very good looking and self-confident. It's just the way he is." He paused. He needed to say this. Not that it was easy. "And the truth is, Tali, that he's cautious when it comes to money and me. When I was younger, I borrowed money from him a bunch of times planning to pay him back, and then… Long story, I couldn't. He would never borrow money and not pay it back, get it?"

Menachem fell silent.

Avital sensed he had more to say, so she waited.

"He did something very impressive the day we got engaged," Menachem said. "He gave me a gorgeous set of *Chumashim* and told me that all my loans were null and void. I tell you, I was so touched and so impressed."

I admire the way you worship your big brother, but you're the impressive one here, loyal brother that you are. No jealousy, no sibling rivalry at all, when he's clearly your mother's favorite.

"What are you thinking, Tali?"

She smiled at him sweetly. "I'm just thinking over what you said."

"Good." He stretched. "I'm sweating."

"I should think so."

"Do you think it's the fever breaking?"

"Nope. I think it's the fact that you're sitting outside in the summer heat wearing heavy winter gear and drinking hot tea."

He felt his forehead. "I don't know."

"Maybe get a thermometer?" she suggested. "That way, you'll know for sure."

"Great idea." He hurried inside.

Avital lapsed back into thought. *Yerachmiel's whole image issue is his business. It doesn't bother me one way or the other. What does bother me a lot is that he's just a touch unapproachable. His father is too, but here's the difference. His father tries to put me at ease by keeping the conversation going, by asking me questions I feel comfortable answering, and then seeming interested in the answers, but Yerachmiel doesn't bother to do that. I feel like just because I'm not working in a high-powered career, he thinks I'm beneath his notice.*

You tell me he's shy. I don't buy it. Nope, I identified his aloofness for what it is when I met him and your parents that first time. I was scared out of my wits, but I have a sense of people, and I'm usually right on the mark.

Arrogance. Menachem, I hate to say it, and I never will, but your brother Yerachmiel is full of himself. Maybe it's not his fault, but he is. It makes it hard for me to feel sympathetic toward his plight. I set him up, I try to help, but both of them—he and Sheila—make me feel like they're doing me a favor instead of the other way around.

Menachem was back, wearing normal summer clothing.

"I take it you don't have fever."

"No, but I hardly ever do. I still don't feel so great. I need a nap."

"Go right ahead."

Menachem sat down. "It's his money, you know. He's a generous guy, but he doesn't owe us an income just because we need more than we have."

"How did you know I'm still thinking about that?"

"I just assumed. Look, we do host him for Shabbos whenever he needs it, but let's not mention that."

"So are you saying that we owe him when and if he's in need of help but he doesn't owe us anything?" Avital asked. "You may accept that, but I don't. The way I see it, each individual is obliged to contribute what he can, and what's more, to do it willingly."

"Plenty of people think the way you do, but I know my brother, and I know that he hates, really hates being forced into positions in which he feels he has no choice. He can't stand feeling taken advantage of."

"We won't be taking advantage of him! No one's suggesting that he pay our mortgage. He won't have to fork out a single shekel."

"Yerachmiel will come through in the end, but he'll do it reluctantly because when it comes to finances, we see things differently." *He doesn't trust me to be responsible with money, which I understand. Wish I had someone else to ask.*

"Speak to him soon, all right?"

"I will, just as soon as I feel a little stronger," he promised. "Then again, why the rush? Why don't we wait until we actually find a place and then ask him?"

"I read that it's better to know your financial options before you go to a realtor."

"Okay." He drank the rest of his tea. "I'm going back to bed. I hate feeling sick."

"You poor thing. I'll make you another cup."

Her husband smiled at her, blew his nose vigorously, coughed for good measure, and shuffled back into the bedroom.

Such a fuss about a signature. Menachem may be happy-go-lucky with his money, but I'm not. I'll ask Menachem to tell Yerachmiel that I'll be handling the budget once we have a mortgage to deal with.

He owes us for convincing Sheila to meet him. She didn't really want to, but I persuaded her that he was an extraordinary guy who was just held up by not finding the right woman. He is pretty special. Super talented, that's for sure. As for the rest of what she wants... Doesn't she realize that at this point in her life it's time to make some compromises?

Avital hoisted herself to her feet, taking the tray with her into the kitchen. All the windows had been thrown wide open. The offensive pot of chicken soup was nowhere in sight. She checked the water in the electric kettle. It was still hot. She could hear Menachem in the bedroom, coughing away.

He's a prince of a guy. Funny how two brothers could turn out so different. Yup, Sheila's a good match for Yerachmiel. She won't be overawed by him. I'm not comfortable with her, either, but not because she's a snob. She's not. She can't help being intimidating. She doesn't mean any harm.

It's just the way she is. I think that if we do become sisters-in-law, we'll be fine together, as long as I give her plenty of space and privacy.

Avital poured a generous amount of honey into a fresh cup of tea. She climbed up on a chair to reach the top closet, where the whiskey was kept.

Cognac. That ought to help his cough. He'd better see a doctor before it turns into pneumonia.

The coughing came closer, and Menachem shuffled into the kitchen. "What are you doing up there? Tali? Should you be climbing now?"

"I'm not an invalid. Here, just take this bottle."

"Cognac?"

"For your cough. I'm calling the clinic right now to make you an appointment with Dr. Kravorski. Put two teaspoons of cognac in your cup, and give me back the bottle. No, on second thought, we'll leave it down here for later."

"It's nothing. I don't need a doctor. I'll be fine by tomorrow," he insisted, but Avital was already on the phone, speaking to the doctor's secretary.

What a wife, he thought. *Yerachmiel, please. Please be more flexible. If Sheila's not the one for you, don't give up. You don't know what you're missing. I want you to have this too.*

"Menachem?"

"Yes?"

"Two things. One, you have an appointment for tomorrow at noon, and two"—a big smile illuminated her face—"when you feel better, don't you think it's time to tell our parents our news?"

* * *

"I'm not going to be here this afternoon for rehearsal," Yerachmiel told Zev Schwartz, his assistant bandleader who doubled as assistant business manager. "You know what to do."

"Remind me," Zev said around a gigantic yawn.

Yerachmiel treated him to a sharp look. "What's really going on, Zev? What's with you lately? I haven't said anything because I figured anyone's entitled to have a couple off days or even weeks, but it's months now since you've operated at top capacity. This time, you won't give me the brush-off. I may be your boss, but I'm also your friend."

"It's my daughter," Zev admitted, yielding to another face-splitting yawn. "My six-year-old, Chaya. She's been having nightmares about her mother, poor kid. Screaming, carrying on. Every time I thought she'd calmed down so that I could grab a little sleep, she woke up again."

Yerachmiel's look changed to one of concern. "How long has it been?"

"Almost two years."

"You need to—"

"I know. I need to get married again."

"Yes. Chaya needs a mother, and you need a wife. Frieda would want you to be happy."

"No way. I'm still too raw. Frieda and I... Frieda was my world. No one can replace her. I know she's gone." He swallowed hard. "But to me, she's alive. There's no way you can understand."

"In a way, I think I can," Yerachmiel said softly.

"How can you?" Zev looked skeptical. "With all due respect, there's no relationship in the whole world like that of a husband and wife.

"Never mind. Forget it."

Zev allowed Yerachmiel to drop the subject.

"About tonight's rehearsal," Yerachmiel said. "The new cellist has to work on the slow Yerushalayim medley. It was a little sloppy last time."

"No it wasn't."

Yerachmiel raised his eyebrows.

"The word *sloppy* is harsh for a guy who missed his cue once or twice," Zev countered. "We need to be realistic. Gedalya came highly recommended, but he's just a kid, really. What is he, nineteen, twenty years old? He had stage fright."

"Stop right here," Yerachmiel commanded. "Why are you assigning me the role of the big bad boss? Did I say anything about firing him?

"I'm just stating a fact."

Yerachmiel narrowed his eyes. "I'm listening."

"According to most people's standards, he did a phenomenal job." Zev held up his hands. "I know, I know. You don't need to say it. Rina-O-Mangina is in a class of its own, and we have to keep ourselves cutting edge. I agree. But on the other hand, have you noticed that the average age of our band members is late twenties, early thirties? Other than the two of us forty-two-year-old fogies."

"For your information, I'm forty," Yerachmiel said stiffly. "What's more, you know as well as I do that it's our policy to hire family men whenever possible. Those are the kind of people who stay put in one place, and what's more, they take earning a living very seriously because they have to. I didn't object when you hired Gedalya, but I can't say I wasn't surprised. We took a risk with him, and he has to keep to our standards."

"Rina-O-Mangina needs fresh blood." Zev stifled another yawn.

"Are you sure you'll manage to keep yourself awake this afternoon, or should I put someone else in charge and let you go home and rest?"

"Thanks for your concern," Zev said dryly. "Don't worry, a couple of extra-strength coffees, and I'll be a ball of fire."

Yerachmiel relaxed. "Right. Thanks. I know I can count on you." He headed toward the door.

"Good luck on your date," Zev called after him.

Yerachmiel swung around. "How'd you know I have a date?"

"It's written all over you. We all notice it. What number date are you up to, if you don't mind my asking?"

"Only the third."

"But you're ready," Zev stated.

"Yes," Yerachmiel admitted. "I am. I can't believe it, but I am."

"That's the way it was for me and Frieda, too."

Yerachmiel swallowed hard. He retraced his steps and put an arm around Zev's shoulder. "I'm sorry, Zev. I'm so sorry."

"Don't be sorry. I wish you well. It's high time you got your show on the road." He smiled, reminiscing. "When it's the right one, all the details fall into place. Don't get caught up on the trivial."

"I try not to. That's why we're having an afternoon date, even though I personally find it inconvenient. Tomorrow's wedding is a biggie, and I want us to be note-perfect."

"You're making the right choice. Make her happy. Do what makes her feel good. A good supportive wife is worth almost any sacrifice. I met Frieda when I had almost given up hope. We had seven unbelievable years together. I'm not complaining. Give this relationship your all."

"I'll try," Yerachmiel said in a low voice. A wave of pity for the lonely man sitting in front of him engulfed him. Yerachmiel longed to help him. "Are you"—he tried to find the right words—"are you okay?"

"I'm managing. Day by day. I don't look further than that. Don't feel bad for me, Yerachmiel. It's okay. I had my turn."

29 Third Date

When Yerachmiel reached his apartment early that afternoon, he was in a pensive mood. Though he'd met with his client at the opulent wedding hall he was going to play at the following night, the conversation with Zev wouldn't leave him.

What Zev had said just didn't sit right with him. It was all so sad. The entire situation was tragic, but he was so lonely. Shouldn't that provide him with ample motivation to try and fill the gaping, aching hole his wife's death had caused? How long could he suffer? What good did it do anyone?

However, Zev had sounded so adamant that Yerachmiel doubted he could be the one to change his mind.

Wait! Maybe someone else would succeed in doing so? That could be an idea. But who?

As he made his preparations for the early afternoon date, he thought hard. The irony of his situation made him chuckle. Until he'd met Sheila, it was he who had to be coaxed, persuaded, *forced* into agreeing to give any suggestion at all a try, and here he was, plotting to rescue Zev for his own good. The irony of it.

He paused in his search for an appropriate tie, one not too formal, yet not too casual. Aunt Eva! Yes, if anyone could get Zev to move forward it was her. He doubted that he could convince Zev to call her, but what if he were to give Aunt Eva Zev's number? Should he? It might be underhanded, but then again, it might be a kind and caring act.

He'd run the idea past Sheila. Why not?

Why not? Because it's a third date, and I promised myself to keep it low key. She doesn't have to know that I'm ready to propose to her. Crazy. It's been all of two dates. And I want to know what she thinks. What are we supposed to do, make small talk all afternoon?

Monday was Sheila's short day in school. Though initially he'd been reluctant to leave more than a week between dates, Sheila had wanted an afternoon date for a change, and Monday was her only free afternoon. Yerachmiel had agreed, sufficing with a phone call *erev Shabbos* to touch base.

At precisely one fifteen, he picked up Sheila a block away from Machon Atara, as she'd requested. He fully understood her wish that they not meet in front of the school gates.

"Thanks so much for being punctual," she said, sliding into the passenger seat.

"Good day?"

"Yes, *baruch Hashem*. Better."

"Great! I'm glad to hear that."

"Thanks." Sheila smiled. "It's a big relief not doing battle with them."

"As I told you on Friday, I can't understand how they dare to do battle with their teacher, but I imagine it was tough. You must be thrilled it's over."

"I am. It was. They were so convinced I was out to get them." Sheila buckled her seat belt. "Thankfully, most of the seventh graders seem to have forgiven me for my chutzpah in daring to exercise my judgment as a teacher. One or two kids are still manning the barricades, but on the whole, peace has returned to my domain."

He chuckled at her choice of words. In the course of their phone conversation on Friday, Sheila had filled him in on her current struggles with her students.

"How was your Shabbos *shiur*?"

"Good. That kid, Rika, the one giving me a hard time, has been staying away. I hate to say it, but we get a lot more accomplished when she's not around."

He started the car. "Why do you hate to say it? It's the truth."

Sheila looked at him, her eyes troubled. "It is, but you know what they say."

"What?" He glanced at her for a second, then hastily turned his attention back to the road.

"That the kids who give us the hardest time are so often the ones who need us the most."

"You can't rescue everyone. You can't even reach everyone."

"But I want to," she said plaintively. "I wish I knew how."

"I know that you want to," he told her. "Sheila, I'm taking you to *Something Fishy* for lunch." He pulled into a spot close to the entrance.

"Wow! Thanks. I'm always famished after I teach, and I love fish. But it's so expen—" She bit her lip.

Yerachmiel laughed. "Yeah, it's upscale, but that's fine."

They walked inside, were escorted to a table with a view, and sat down.

"Do you like sushi?" Yerachmiel asked, looking up from the menu.

She made a face. "Not really. I know lots of people are nuts about it, but I'm not. Are you?"

"Nope," he declared. "Can't stand the stuff."

It was Sheila's turn to laugh. "If you don't like sushi, what do you like?"

"Cholent."

Sheila giggled in disbelief. "Cholent? Really?"

"Why do you look so shocked? Thursday-night cholent, Shabbos cholent, leftover cholent, whatever." He cocked his head to the side. "What could be bad? Flank steak, potatoes, real stick-to-the-ribs stuff. My mother's thrilled. Every *motza'ei Shabbos* she sends me home with a huge container. Win-win. It's my brother's recipe. Menachem was our official cholent maker until he got married, and I've retained my title as our official cholent eater par excellence."

Sheila smiled. "Are the two of you close?"

"We've grown close. There's a big age gap, so it wasn't automatic." Yerachmiel pursed his lips. "At the moment, though, I'm a bit..." He hesitated, choosing his words carefully. "...at odds with him. He asked me to do him a favor he knew I wouldn't want to do. I'm surprised at him."

"What did he want? Something big?"

"I'd say so. He and Avital are looking to buy their own apartment, and he wants me to cosign for a mortgage."

"Which you'll do," Sheila half asked, half stated. "I mean, he's your brother. I cosigned for all my brothers and sisters."

"Yes, but you're living at home with your parents."

"So? It's all theoretical anyway."

"Not always," he said briefly.

"I hear."

There was an awkward pause.

Yerachmiel was dismayed, and irrationally, very annoyed at Menachem. "Thing is, I don't want to be stuck holding the bag if Menachem can't keep up his payments."

"That makes sense. But, look, people cosign all the time without reaching that point. Why would you assume otherwise?"

"Uh..." *I'll never let you know that he has any faults whatsoever.* "He's working, teaching computers in a program for *kollel* guys, but it's not full-time because he's studying to become a male nurse. It's not exactly a high-paying profession, and I don't need to tell you that

Avital isn't exactly raking it in as a guidance counselor. So, in my humble opinion, he ought to have a more realistic idea of what his financial position is and budget accordingly, but—"

"It's fine. You really don't owe me any explanations."

Yerachmiel found himself growing angry at Menachem. Why did he have to be the cause of an unpleasant conversation with Sheila, who, though she'd been as tactful as possible, was missing crucial facts that as a loyal brother, he, Yerachmiel, couldn't supply? Could he tell Sheila about the two thousand shekels Menachem had borrowed from him while he was dating Avital that was somehow never repaid and never mentioned? And the loans before that? Could he tell her that the night of Menachem's engagement, he'd told him that he forgave all the loans that hadn't been repaid?

No, he could not, no matter how good it would make him look. Instead, Sheila now thought he was a skinflint.

"What made him decide to go into nursing?"

"He wants to work with the elderly. He feels terrible when he sees an older person with a caregiver he can't have a conversation with." Yerachmiel smiled. "My brother the idealist."

"Well, good for him!"

"What?" He looked her questioningly.

"Being an idealist, seeing a need and sacrificing personal comfort to do something about it."

"It's not a sacrifice. I told you, he likes old folks. He'll probably find a job in the field. There's a shortage of nurses in general, especially male nurses. It's not on top of the glamour list, but who cares?"

She was silent.

Yerachmiel drummed his fingers on the table. "Sheila."

She looked up.

"Listen to me. I don't want you to think I'm ungenerous. I can't afford to have my brother let me down, especially when… Especially when I may be soon buying a place of my own."

"You are?"

"It depends. Look, I'm a self-made man. Do you realize that

most *simchah* bands come and go? Rina-O-Mangina is in a different league. I hire real musicians who are also settled as far as their personal lives go."

"What do you mean?"

"Married guys, or people settled in one place for a long time. We're solid. We've been around for twenty years. We deliver a product that discerning people—the kinds of clients we want to attract, clients who have money and want a certain sound—are willing to pay for. It's *parnassah,* Sheila. Idealism's terrific, but don't knock a good, dependable *parnassah.*"

"I'm not naive," she protested. "I know that money is important."

"And yet you're an elementary school teacher. I'm sure your parents were willing to pay for you to study for a more lucrative career choice."

"They were. I wanted to become a teacher. I wanted to make a difference in people's lives. In case you were going to tell me that the average professor easily makes twice, if not almost three times the salary of a teacher, I know that. Who cares? Teaching is real. It's touching lives. It's connection, and influencing the next generation. Nothing can match that for importance," Sheila said passionately. "Nothing."

He looked at her with admiration. "When you put it that way, when I listen to you, I think that many of the teachers I've encountered over the years ought to be fired."

She shook her head in disagreement.

"You don't agree?"

"There's idealism, and then there's day-to-day reality."

"Go on."

"Not everyone is as fortunate as I am, to have discovered a way of living that fits them so well. I think that teachers who do a good job, even if they don't love it, who show up to work loyally and do their job well, minute after minute, hour after hour, day after day, month after month, year after year, for decades, even if they don't have the luxury of feeling my level of motivation…"

"What about them?"

"I've learned to give them a lot of credit."

"That's very kind of you." He gave her another admiring look. "Please, tell it to me straight. You think that a person who sees himself as average in the *middah* of *chesed* would just sign, no second thoughts?"

"I didn't say that. I have no idea what the relationship between the two of you is. Besides—"

"I have a very close relationship with Menachem. He's my only sibling. Tell me what you think. It's always interesting to hear what you think. To hear another point of view."

Sheila hesitated.

"Come on," he cajoled.

* * *

Yonina Nachum, who had been the secretary at Machon Atara since the school's establishment, entered the teachers' room. It was empty save for Estelle, bent over a *sefer Tehillim,* oblivious to her surroundings.

Shanah rishonah is quite a stretch, Yonina reflected. She hoped it wasn't too rocky an adjustment for Estelle. Yonina had been concerned about Estelle during her engagement period. Somehow, she hadn't had the *kallah* glow, though she had seemed content. At least she hadn't been a volatile bundle of nerves like many.

Estelle sensed her glance, looked up and smiled, and then bent back over her *Tehillim.*

In that moment, Yonina saw the tears glistening in her eyes. But Estelle had always been a sincere davener, and besides, there was no desperation or bitterness in her demeanor.

"Sheyitkablu hatefillot bivrachah," she said softly into the silence. Estelle smiled faintly, once again.

Tefillah had its place in every circumstance, and Estelle's personal situation had undergone a significant upgrade, as far as Yonina was concerned. Marriage, by and large, was a vast improvement over singlehood and, in any case, she'd come to do a job.

She taped two average-sized pieces of paper to the refrigerator door. Each teacher would receive an e-mail containing the identical information, but Rabbanit Sudri knew that many of the teachers in Machon Atara didn't check their e-mail messages unless they were at school. On the other hand, everyone approached the fridge at some point during the school day.

These were two announcements no one would ignore. One invited each teacher to the principal's office to summarize the year and to discuss plans for the following year. The other contained a list of dates on which either Hadassah Noleman, the assistant principal, or Rabbanit Sudri would view a model lesson and evaluate the teacher's performance.

Yonina added an extra piece of tape to make sure the papers wouldn't fall off when the teachers signed up. She knew the two innocent-looking notices would elicit—depending on the staff member—a storm of comments, anticipation, and apprehension as well as worry, anger, and fear,

One more glance at Estelle, and Yonina left to return to her office.

* * *

Nechama Rotter was the first teacher to fill in her name, the date, her preferred time for a visit, and her preferred time to meet. She did so almost absentmindedly because her daughter's wedding was only four days away and there was so much to do. Besides, Rabbanit Sudri would probably be forced to change one or both dates due to a last-minute emergency of the type that always seemed to come up.

Latest challenge, being evaluated. Hmm. The class given had to incorporate the school's uniform teaching goal for the year. Fine. Only...

Let's see, what *is* this year's buzzword? Not group work. That's old news. Having the children explain what they'd learned at the end of the lesson, that was last year's innovation. Hands-on, tactile stimulation?

"I'll ask one of the teachers, someone who attended the teacher enrichment course, to fill me in on the details, and I'll put together a couple of lessons that conform to the requirement."

Nechama had no doubt that whatever the demand, she'd rise to the occasion. Just one more thing to cross off her endless list. However, in keeping with Yonina Nachum's expectations, few teachers reacted to the news with that degree of equanimity.

Cash Flow

Today was the day.

Geula began setting up her display of handcrafted jewelry on a side table in the teachers' room of Machon Atara. She'd hoped to obtain Rabbanit Sudri's permission to use the center table where everyone would be sure to see her wares and hopefully be tempted to buy them, but the principal had been friendly, yet firm.

"I didn't realize you make jewelry. How interesting!" Rabbanit Sudri had exclaimed when Geula had approached her hesitantly the week before.

"I love doing it. I guess you could even say that I'm passionate about it. Um, I actually wanted to ask you if I could, that is, if it would be okay if I displayed some of my pieces here, at Machon Atara, in the teachers' room." The words came out in a rush. "You know, to sort of celebrate the end of the year?"

The principal had smiled. "No one ever asked me for permission to hold a sale before, but I don't see why not. Celebrating the end of the year? Good idea."

"Thank you."

Rabbanit Sudri thought for a moment. "Just don't let whatever you put out take over the public space."

"Fine."

"As it is the room is small, and many teachers complain that it's messy, crowded, and cramped," the principal had explained. "Good luck with your sale."

"Thanks."

Now, Geula held her breath as her first prospective customer headed her way.

"This is stunning! I love it! This is so my mother's taste." Aviva Lavie picked up an intricately woven beaded bracelet. "Where did you find these earth-toned beads?"

"I shop around in all kinds of places. I keep my eyes open."

"My mother is crazy about just these colors, brown and gold and copper. What a find. This matches everything in her wardrobe. And it's so cheap. Fifty shekels for hand-crafted jewelry? That's nothing." The curly headed twenty-year-old spoke with her characteristic friendly bubbliness as she held out a fifty-shekel bill.

"It's so nice of you to buy something for your mother. You're a good daughter. How about, um, how about, uh... Do you see something for yourself here on the display? How about some earrings? I notice that you're very into earrings."

"Well. I am, but—" Aviva was at a loss for words. "I do like earrings, but that's just it. I already have so many pairs, and I only have one pair of ears, so—" She stopped again.

"Forget it. I didn't say anything."

Aviva tried again. "Geula, don't get me wrong, all handmade, just unbelievable, but no offense, I go for um, simpler, you know, smaller? Not that your stuff isn't gorgeous..."

"Gotcha. They aren't your taste." Geula congratulated herself on her nonchalant tone of voice. She was feeling anything but nonchalant. The opposite was true. She was desperate to make as many sales as possible. After she'd gotten permission to use the teachers' room, she'd received yet another winter electric bill that had somehow gotten lost in the mail, and she needed eight hundred shekels to pay it. The sum seemed as far away and inaccessible as the moon, but she had to start somewhere. She'd embarked on a marathon of jewelry making, working as swiftly as she was able every spare moment, trying her best not to compromise on quality or workmanship. If she earned, let's say six, seven hundred shekels today selling her wares, and then lived frugally until the end of the month, somehow she'd scrape up the other one or two hundred shekels. She hoped.

Aviva was eyeing her anxiously, sensing that Geula was upset. "Your feelings aren't hurt, are they? You know why I like smaller stuff? Because I like real gold, real diamonds. My *zeidy* was a diamond dealer, so my Bubby Beatrice used to give me jewelry gifts when we lived next door to her. I got used to real, and small. It's not that the other kind isn't beautiful. It is. It's just that I have this silly quirk. I only like real stuff. Real stones, real diamonds, gold. I don't even like silver."

"It's not a silly quirk to like the real deal. I appreciate your honesty."

"You do?"

"I sure do. It's okay. I shouldn't have put you on the spot. I can see that what you're wearing is a lot smaller than the pieces I made. Besides, you're entitled to your own personal taste. I just thought that you might enjoy putting on something different, broadening your horizons."

Aviva wavered. "I do, well, um..."

Geula felt uncomfortably guilty. *Liar. You just need to sell this stuff. Why do you land in this situation time after time?*

Stop it. Now's not the time for self-recrimination. Now is the time for action, and besides, in my opinion, she would look even nicer if her jewelry were more interesting. She's not a bas mitzvah girl or a bubby.

I'm not lying, but I feel so dishonest.

"But that's just my take on it. Plenty of well-dressed women go for understated accessories."

"You must have worked so hard."

"I did."

"How many pieces are you displaying?"

"Twelve. Four bracelets, now three, thanks to you, four necklaces, and four pairs of earrings. It took me ages to make it all."

"I'm sure it did. How do you have the patience to string all those tiny beads and deal with all the itty-bitty details?" Aviva mock shuddered. "Better you than me. I'd go nuts. The results are gorgeous, though."

Geula pulled a wry face. "Actually, I find that aspect of jewelry making…how'd you put it?"

"Itty-bitty." Aviva giggled

"Right, that. I find that aspect of it very satisfying."

"Why?" Aviva asked.

"It's the creativity, taking potential beauty, and creating real, functional beauty out of it.

"Wow! You're an artist."

"Oh, please. Anyone with hands and eyes can do it. It just glorified craftsmanship."

"Oh, totally," Aviva mock agreed. "Any two-year-old could make this stunning stuff."

"Not a two-year-old, but any competent adult with time and patience. It demands a lot of concentration, you're definitely right about that, and it's very time consuming. Very. The materials aren't cheap, either." Geula smiled humorously. "Time is usually not a problem. I have a lot of free time in the evenings. But I'm sometimes strapped for cash, and that's a fact."

"You want to borrow money?" Aviva offered instantly, still eager to make amends for what she viewed as her faux pas in not buying something for herself.

"Borrow money from you? Borrow? Nah, I'm good."

"You are?"

"Yes."

I can't borrow money from a kid half my age living with her parents! She hardly makes any money. I haven't come to that. Why, why, WHY do I do this to myself?

"Okay. But if you need to, let me know."

"Thanks, Aviva. I will. I began saying, money can sometimes be tight, but I'm hardly ever strapped for time. Making jewelry is great that way. It keeps me busy and out of people's hair."

Aviva bit her lip.

"Yup, a person in my position needs an absorbing hobby to keep her busy and satisfied," Geula continued. "For me, making jewelry is the secret to being in a good mood. If I'm feeling blue, or lonely, it's the answer. That in itself is a big bonus for someone in my position. Plus, it earns me some spare cash. Plus the items I create are really nice, in my opinion anyhow. Why are you looking at me like that? What in the world did I say?"

"Nothing," Aviva stammered. "You didn't say anything special."

"Tell me. It's far from nothing. I know you far too well for that."

"Really, it's nothing."

"Tell me about it. That's why you look like a tomato."

"I do?" Aviva put her hands to her flaming cheeks.

"Yup. Makes your eyes an intense shade of blue. Very becoming," Geula said matter-of-factly. "Let me find you a matching bag for that bracelet. Don't just stick it in your pocketbook. The bag is the finishing touch." She rummaged in her copious carry-all. "Let's see now. I put gold, silver, and copper bag material. Where did they go? I thought I stuck them in here just this morning. Aha! Here they are." She pulled out a package of gauzy copper-colored bags and ripped open the package.

Aviva watched her silently.

"Is it that I praised my work? Did I sound boastful? Sorry about that."

"You should praise yourself. You should praise your work. You do great work."

"Don't you know it's bad manners to toot your own horn? You're supposed to wait for other people to do that. Do you want me to have bad manners?" Geula teased.

Aviva shook her head.

"*Nu*, tell me. Don't keep me guessing. That's not fair. As a woman who is old enough to be your mom, I deem it disrespectful of you not to tell me."

"There you are. You're doing it again," Aviva blurted. "Saying stuff that no one else says. Why do you make yourself sound pathetic? Why do you put yourself down?"

"Huh? What did I say? Old enough to be your mom? That's putting myself down? It's true."

"That doesn't mean you have to go out of your way to emphasize it."

"Emphasize it? Is that what you think I do?" Slowly, Geula reddened. "Call attention to it?"

"Yes. When you say all these things."

"All what things? Back up, Aviva. I'm having a hard time following you." Geula sat down, still clutching the delicate gauze bag. "I certainly never meant to upset you."

"Things like having time on your hands and keeping out of people's hair—"

"That's true too. It's the way things are for me. People are very busy, very busy with their lives, so it's up to me to make myself busy with my life too."

"That's horrible. It sounds horrible."

"It's just the way things are," Geula said. "Nothing personal against me."

"I don't get the way that you just, that you just…" Aviva struggled to find the right words. "That you just accept something that…that hurts. People don't think that you're important enough to make time for? That hurts so much..."

Geula looked at Aviva hard. "Listen, sweetie. If I accept it, it doesn't hurt so much. That's the secret."

Aviva shook her head vehemently. "I don't get it."

Geula handed Aviva the bracelet in the bag. "Here. Tell your mother to wear it in the very best of good health and spirits."

"Thanks," Aviva said automatically, looking miserable.

"Aviva? What's eating you? I'm so sorry if I stepped on your toes."

"It's not you." She tried to smile. "Thank you so much, Geula. The bracelet is super stunning. I'm really pleased to have found her such a great present right here in school. I can't wait to see the expression on her face when I give it to her."

* * *

Sales were slow. No, more accurately, other than Aviva's purchase, sales were nonexistent.

How will I manage to pay that bill if I don't sell anything? What if they cut off my electricity?

Geula paced the length of the empty teachers' room. Back and forth, back and forth. Wasn't the teachers' room always crowded with far too many people? Where were they now? And Nechama Rotter, where was she? Didn't she come in first period on Tuesdays? Geula had used up her entire stash of the expensive beads she'd bought as a pick-me-up along with her ring to fashion a one-of-a-kind bracelet-and-earring set for Nechama. She winced. If she'd spent less on any one of the purchases of that day, she'd be in a better position now. Where was Nechama?

It's only second period, Geula encouraged herself. *She'll be here any minute. I hope she's not going to be absent today of all days. It would be ultra tacky to bring it to her house.*

She took out the necklace. The blue-green beads shimmered in the sunlight, reminding Geula of the ocean, sun shimmering on the waves, and cool breezes, relaxation.

Lots of teachers aren't in school yet. Soon it will be the ten o'clock break. Then, people will come in to wash and eat their sandwiches, and they'll see my stand. I'm sure that sales will pick up then.

Helen Tauber entered the room. At last, a real, live human being.

"Hi, Helen. Did you happen to see Nechama Rotter around?" Geula asked, anxious but trying for a nonchalant tone. "I thought she comes in early on Tuesdays."

"She does start earlier, but as you know, she's making a wedding." Helen paused and seemed to remember who she was speaking to. "Soon by you," she added.

For once, Geula didn't bristle at Helen's well-meant comment. She was far too anxious for that.

"Thank you."

"Say Amen."

"Amen."

"That's better." Helen took a foil-wrapped package out of her bag. "I took over her first two periods today." She unwrapped her sandwich. "Nechama, bless her, went running to a *gemach* at eight thirty this morning. A gown *gemach*. Can you imagine her doing that at this late date? She had the perfect dresses for all her older granddaughters, but then, guess what happened?"

"What?" Geula forced herself to look interested though her stomach was tight with nerves. *Get to the point. Is Nechama coming to school today, or isn't she?*

"One of the younger set had a bas mitzvah, and wouldn't you know, she decided she wanted to wear what the older girls are wearing."

Helen went to the sink, removed her rings, and washed for bread. Geula waited tensely for her to finish. Helen dried her hands meticulously and replaced her rings. She took a bite of her sandwich, chewed it thoroughly, and swallowed.

"She'll be in any minute now."

Geula breathed a sigh of relief. She shouldn't allow herself to become so worked up. Show a little patience, and many things did eventually work out in the end. Some things didn't, but in most cases they did.

The two teachers sat in silence. Helen continued eating. Abruptly, she put down her sandwich. "I don't approve of allowing children to blackmail us!" she exclaimed.

"What?" Geula blinked.

"Yes. Nechama's granddaughter, the one I was just telling you about? She called the *kallah*. She called her and told her that if she couldn't have a dress like the big girls, she wasn't coming to the wedding."

"Oh, my."

"So, Nechama to the rescue, as usual. I don't approve of what she's doing, but that doesn't mean I won't help her in any way I can. What do you think?

"Of what?" Geula had put hours of work into designing and creating the braided loop of the varying shades of blue and green Nechama had requested. She was going to receive 350 shekels for the finished product—a unique earring and necklace set. Some of the stones she'd used were semi-precious, and the crystal beads were the far more expensive kind. Maybe, just maybe when Nechama saw the finished product, she'd like it so much that she'd offer to pay more. Maybe she'd urge other teachers to buy some jewelry. A woman always needed more jewelry, didn't she?

Four hundred fifty shekel will be the minimum amount I'll make today. Three hundred fifty from Nechama, fifty from Aviva. I'm sure I'll make more. I'll be more careful about spending from now on.

"Of giving in to teenage blackmail."

"Oh. Well, obviously, in general, it's not a good idea, but there can be unique circumstances."

"How diplomatic." Helen finished her sandwich and patted her lips with a napkin. "Who put that jewelry stand here in the teachers' room?"

"I did."

"You received Rabbanit Sudri's permission to do that?"

"Yes."

"Well, good for you. Where did you buy all those pieces?"

"I made them."

"You made them! That's wonderful." Helen beamed proudly and came to stand next to Geula. "How marvelous. We have our very own on-staff artist, right here at Machon Atara."

"Do you want to see what I made for Nechama?" Geula asked. Despite her anxiety, Geula felt more than a touch of justified pride.

"What an unusual design. Unusual and attractive. It will accentuate her lovely bluish-green eyes."

"It's my original design."

"You don't say! That's terrific. When I was just a girl I dabbled in crafts, but now the children and grandchildren, bless them, swallow up any free time I have. As well as the not-so-free time." Helen chuckled. "Good for you, making time to pursue a hobby. Maybe someday I'll get back to such things. How much do you charge for a piece like this?" She indicated the necklace.

"Three-fifty."

"That much?"

"In fact, I'm undercharging her. For an original, handmade piece, my price is on the lower side of the spectrum. It would cost her at least five hundred shekels in town."

"Perhaps, but she has so many expenses now that she's making a wedding, you simply cannot imagine. Maybe as a colleague, you might give her a discount?"

"I put a lot of work into this, and in any case, that's the price we agreed upon."

"Look, if the two you agreed, you agreed. Just a suggestion, that's all, for further sales. The teachers in Machon Atara aren't wealthy, so if they see a bargain…" Helen lowered her voice and leaned closer conspiratorially. "It will make good business sense to drop your prices."

"I'll think about what you said. Thanks for your advice."

"My pleasure."

Geula steeled herself and asked. "Do you, um, that is, do you see anything here to your taste?"

Helen eyed the pieces.

Geula's heart sank, even before Helen responded.

"Oh, no darling. An old lady like me needs something far more conservative. Less ornate. I'm sure you'll have better luck with the younger teachers." She looked up, and her eyes met Geula's for a moment.

The door to the teachers' room opened. Helen's face lit up. "There she is! I'm sure she'll love your work."

Nechama entered the teachers' room talking on her phone. Geula hurried over to her. Nechama gave her a polite smile and continued her conversation. Geula waited as patiently as she was able to for the conversation to end, but when the other woman turned to leave the teachers' room, she could hold back no longer. She hurried after Nechama, clutching the necklace. It was tacky, she knew, but she had no choice. She tapped Nechama on the shoulder.

"Just a minute, and no, they don't have a size minus-two for her. Her parents just have to reason with her. What? No, she won't miss your wedding," Nechama said into the phone. "Hold on. Stop panicking."

"Nechama? I have your order."

"My order. My order?" Nechama said distractedly. "Remind me?"

"The jewelry you asked me to make for you?"

"I did?"

Geula's heart plummeted. *Degrading doesn't begin to do this experience justice.* "When you told me that the colors of the wedding are all or any shade of blue or green? When you said that the wedding is for the parents because they're the ones paying for it, so you chose your favorite color, blue, and your *machateiniste* wanted green, and the *kallah* didn't care, so you all compromised? I told you I'd design you something really special? Remember?"

Nechama's eyes cleared in comprehension. "I'll call you right back," she told the person she was speaking with. "Five minutes tops. Take something to eat or a drink."

Geula heaved another heartfelt sigh of relief.

"Now I remember. Certainly. It slipped my mind. Sorry, dear, marrying off a daughter is an unbelievably complicated process. Helen, did you see what Geula made me?"

"Isn't it fabulous? Can you believe she made it herself?"

"She's fantastic." Nechama slipped on the necklace and went to look in the mirror.

"This morning, I really thought I'd lose my mind," she added over her shoulder.

"I told you not to go. You look fantastic."

"You're very talented, Geula. Thank you." Nechama smiled with pleasure.

"Wear it in good health," Geula said sincerely, holding out the bracelet. "Would you like me to help you with the clasp?"

"No, I must call the *kallah* back." Nechama opened her phone.

Geula cleared her throat. "By the way, I just wanted to ask, Nechama, is there anyone else in your family who needs anything? Earrings or something else from my"—she swallowed—"my collection?"

Helen stared at her again, then turned her gaze to Nechama.

Nechama smiled abstractedly and punched a button on her phone. "It's sweet of you to ask. No, thank you. I think we're all set. My daughters wear clip-on earrings exclusively."

"Why?" Helen asked. "Clip-ons get lost so easily. They're also very uncomfortable. You should get their ears pierced."

"My husband disapproves of pierced ears. How much should I write out the check for? One fifty? One seventy-five? Please remind me, how much did we say? I should have written it down. I'm so forgetful lately.

Geula took a deep breath. "Three hundred."

"Didn't you tell me three-fifty?" Helen said sharply.

"Staff discount."

"It's unnecessary in this case. I'm sure that Nechama appreciates the door-to-door delivery. This way, she doesn't need to squander valuable time searching through the shops. Isn't that right, Nechama?"

"Yes, it's much appreciated," Nechama said, oblivious to the undertone. "Hello? Now, where is she?" She left a message for her daughter and closed her phone. *I can't believe I agreed to pay more than two hundred shekel for what is—when all is said and done—costume jewelry, even if it is very pretty. Well, we took out a loan, so for now, at least, the money is available. What's three-fifty when I'm spending tens of thousands?*

She went over to the table and wrote the check. "Here you go, Geula." She ripped out the check. "Thanks so much for remembering my request, even if it slipped my mind. I look forward to seeing you at the wedding."

I can't tell her I need cash. It's just too humiliating. This check will take three days to clear. Three more days of this torture.

I did this to myself. Why don't I remember how this feels?

I do. But when I do need a pick-me-up, I really need it.

"Mazel tov, Nechama. Wear it at your *simchah*, in the best of health. Nechama? You have a moment?"

"I do need to return a phone call—" Nechama wavered.

"I just want to show you what I made. This will take two seconds." Geula walked over to her display with Nechama following.

"It's too bad it's not before a *chag*," Nechama said. "People are far more likely to buy extras then. This is skilled work. The results are lovely."

"Thank you so much." Geula tried to hold back a sigh. "I thought the end of the year…"

"You're absolutely correct," Helen intervened. "I think the teachers' committee should sponsor this sale, don't you agree, Nechama?"

"Sponsor the sale?" Nechama repeated blankly.

"Yes." Suiting action to word, Helen grabbed a thick black felt-tipped pen and a big piece of white paper, and began printing big block letters: The end of the year is near! / You owe it to yourself! / Exclusive, original handcrafted pieces / From our Machon Atara collection / Ten-percent discount to the first five customers / Buy while the supply lasts!

It was signed: The teachers' committee of Machon Atara, where our teachers are our jewels.

"There we go," she said, taping the sign to the refrigerator. "That should help. Almost everyone goes to the refrigerator a couple of times a day. *Nu,* Nechama? Did you find anything to suit the exclusive tastes of our little blackmailer?"

31 Miscommunication

Three hundred fifty shekels and no agorot. Geula stuffed the check from Nechama into her purse just as Aviva came into the room, looking far more cheerful than she had before.

"Those kids! I could eat them up, they are so delicious. They're a breath of fresh air. All they want is love. No shtick, no games, no ego. I wish everyone was like that. It's so easy to make them happy."

There was a soft knocking on the closed door of the teachers' room.

"Must be a pupil," Geula commented. "Don't they get that the teachers' room is off limits?"

Aviva looked troubled. "I don't see why it should be. We're supposed to be here for them."

"Teachers are human. We also need space."

The knocking continued.

"Maybe it's an emergency."

"I doubt it."

The knocking persisted, grew louder, and turned into outright pounding.

Geula exchanged a bemused look with Aviva, shrugged, and went to open the door. Elianna Rosse was standing there, fist poised to knock again.

"Elianna? Why aren't you in class? Did Morah Noa send you to get something? Do you feel okay? Next time, please don't bang on the door of the teachers' room or any other door."

Elianna ignored her.

She doesn't seem like the shy first grader I teach at all, Geula thought.

"Is Morah Aviva here?" Elianna asked urgently, peering into the depths of the teachers' room. When she saw Aviva, she darted in. "Morah! Come! I need you right now!"

Geula was shocked. She waited for Aviva to usher the impulsive first-grader out the door, but instead, Aviva led her to a chair and sat her down. "Elianna, honey," she said softly, "how can I help you? You look very upset."

"Everyone hates me!" Elianna burst out. "Sherry's telling all the girls to hate me."

I can't believe this! Geula thought. She can't just barge in. It's the teachers' room. Maybe I'm an old fogey. Should I say something? Elianna's just a first grader who doesn't realize how inappropriate her behavior is, but doesn't Aviva know how noneducational her actions are? Not just noneducational, anti-educational.

"Elianna." Aviva enfolded the sobbing youngster in a maternal hug. "You must be so hurt."

"Punish Sherry! Punish her for being mean to me! She's always mean to me, and Morah Noa doesn't do anything. She only likes Sherry."

"First of all, dry your eyes." Aviva handed Elianna a wad of tissues from the dispenser. "Good. Now, this will calm you down," Aviva said, pouring Elianna a cup of cold water. "Say *shehakol* and drink. Morah Geula and I will say Amen."

Elianna complied, muttering a *shehakol,* which was followed by a ringing Amen from Aviva. She turned to Geula. "Wasn't that a beautiful *brachah*?" she asked proudly. "It's so nice that Elianna's conquering her shyness, isn't it?"

At least three rules disregarded for no particular reason I can see. Why? Is Aviva unaware, after almost a year working in the school? Not very likely, especially when she's a protégée of Noa Lewin. Noa's a stickler for school protocol.

A. No students permitted in the teachers' room during school time.

B. Pupils may not sit on a chair from the teachers' room.

C. Pupils are not permitted to drink from the cups designated for teachers.

Maybe Aviva's convinced that because Elianna's so upset, she should make an exception just this once. Fine, there are many places in school for her to sit privately with a pupil. I'll just remind her of them. That way, I won't sound rigid or hardhearted, will I?

"Um, Aviva. I need to make a private phone call without any little ears listening in to the conversation. There are a couple of private nooks and crannies in the hallway, with chairs and paper cups. Sorry to ask you to move, but…"

Aviva was so absorbed in Elianna's saga of woe that she didn't respond. An increasingly perturbed Geula struggled to excuse the fact that neither Elianna nor Aviva paid her the slightest bit of attention.

When I was a beginning teacher, I was absolutely intimidated by my more senior colleagues. Ages ago, when I was a student, we avoided the teachers' room as much as possible. Never mind, Geula decided, feeling defeated. *Let someone more assertive tell Aviva what's what. I know I'm well within my rights, but how does that help me when the world's such a different place? If I didn't mind what she was doing, that would be a different story, but it does bug me. No limits. No boundaries. No place to relax.*

After a moment or two of intense conversation punctuated by Elianna's sobs, Aviva looked up, seeming to notice Geula for the first time. "Sorry, did you say something?"

"Yes. Elianna, it looks like you're feeling better now. I think Morah

Noa must be worried why you aren't in class. Do you want me or Morah Aviva to walk you back to class?"

Elianna didn't even deign to dignify Geula's comment with an upward glance, while Aviva didn't seem to pick up on the hint.

That child didn't even glance in my direction. Please don't let this be the new normal.

The door opened, and Noa Lewin peered in. "Aviva, I need you to look for Elianna— Oh, *there* you are. You disappeared to go to the bathroom ten minutes ago. Get back to class this *instant*."

Before Noa's sentence ended, Elianna was out of the teachers' room, presumably headed back to class, followed by her teacher, who gazed at Aviva keenly for a moment before shaking her head slightly.

Aviva blushed furiously. "It's so hard to know how much extra attention to give Elianna. I'm still so new at this, and I'm constantly getting something wrong. After almost a full year as teacher's assistant, you'd think I'd have the hang of it, wouldn't you? No? I'm getting better at setting boundaries, though. At least, I think I am. I learned from Sheila that setting boundaries and keeping to them isn't harsh. I used to think that way, but I'm starting to see that there's definitely merit in making one set of rules for all the kids and enforcing those rules. Even if the kids are unique individuals."

I'm so glad I didn't reprimand her, Geula thought. *If this is progress for her, it must have been very stressful for Sheila to have her in class, particularly in Noa's challenging class.*

"Can I vent here for a minute?" Aviva continued. Tears started to flow. "Everything's so stressful. No one's talking to me about a job for next year, and here it is, almost the middle of June."

"If anyone's going to be hired for next year, it's you, Aviva. You've made a sparkling impression."

Aviva shrugged and sniffed. "That's so nice of you to say."

"It's what everyone knows."

"Still… Everything's so up in the air. Everything."

"Everything?"

"Not just work."

Geula waited.

"I'm almost twenty years old. I know, I know, that's not so old. Six girls in my class are already married."

Noa Lewin rushed into the room. "Aviva! There you are! Come on, quickly, I'm testing on *kriah* now, taking the kids out one by one. I need you to hold the fort. They have a *parshah* sheet. Come on, I've just left them alone for the second time today and you know that's not great even if the classroom *is* right next door.

"I'm on it." Aviva hurried to the sink and dashed cold water on her face. "Do I look like I was crying?"

"Yes. Should I go in instead of you?"

"Nah, it's okay. I'll be fine. The kids will cheer me up."

"What if they notice that you were crying?"

"I'll tell them that someone was mean to me." She gave a crooked smile. "Thanks for listening, Geula."

Aviva rushed out of the room.

The door to the teachers' room swung wide open once again. Geula's pulse quickened at the sight of Nechama, followed by Estelle. Estelle usually stopped to chat. She and Geula were friendly. This time, other than a distracted nod in Geula's direction, she seemed to be completely in her own world.

Wow! She must be really preoccupied. Too bad. Will she buy anything? Maybe not. Maybe as a new kallah, Elchanan buys her jewelry. I wonder if he knows her taste.

I wanted to ask her—without mentioning names, naturally—what her take is on what Aviva just did with Elianna. I'm glad I didn't say anything to Aviva. Poor kid, she's really suffering.

However, I don't want her to do the same thing again. Unless there's some Machon Atara rule that I'm not familiar with? Estelle's been teaching here forever.

Estelle took something out of her cubby and went to a far corner of the room. She hunched over a small book and started writing.

She looks sad. I told Aviva that marriage isn't all fun and games, but she thinks I'm just trying to make her feel better. It happens to be true, especially at Estelle's stage of the game, but it's never easy.

* * *

"Hello? This is Menucha Shalom."

"Hello. How are you?" Yonina Nachum asked politely, regretting that she'd answered the phone. School was never a particularly tranquil place to work, but she usually thrived on the human interaction. However, the frenetic, crazy, utterly impossible pace that characterized the end of the year was something else entirely. Event followed event, with no pause for breath. Inevitably, as school secretary, she was the first address for all frantic last-minute requests. Demands. They never ended.

She sighed soundlessly. She had no time whatsoever for lengthy phone conversations. However, Menucha didn't seem to appreciate brevity any more than Yonina favored it. Someone would have to give in.

Poor thing, with only one single child to occupy her time, and no real reason to work. It's a chesed to chat with her for a couple of minutes.

Time must hang heavy on her hands.

Having made her mind up to be kind, Yonina smiled into the receiver. "How are things with you, Menucha? I must tell you that the teachers all appreciated the Pesach gift certificate you organized, and so do I."

"You're all very welcome," Menucha responded distractedly. "Is Rabbanit Sudri available? I absolutely must speak with her about something super urgent. She's not answering her cell phone."

"Her door is closed."

"Knock."

"I'll check to see if she's available."

"Please do."

Yonina knocked on the closed office door, reflecting that there was no way that Menucha realized how imperious she sometimes sounded. When there was no answer, she opened the door the smallest crack. Rabbanit Sudri was typing away industriously. She lifted her eyebrows in surprise at the interruption.

"I'm sorry. It's Menucha Shalom on the line."

"Can't it wait?"

"She says it's urgent."

"I really wanted to leave on time today, for a change," her boss said. Yonina waited, her expression neutral. No one had asked for her opinion. "Put her through."

"We were all very excited when Sheila Leipzig took over for Yocheved," Menucha began.

"I anticipated you would be." Maya Sudri hadn't missed Menucha's usage of the past tense.

"We knew she's professional and dedicated and all that, but there's such a thing as too much."

"I'm not following." The principal frowned. "How can a teacher be too professional or too dedicated? Could you explain that to me? What exactly is your concern? Didn't we discuss Sheila Leipzig's educational policies a couple of weeks ago? I told you, Menucha, I don't believe in breathing down my teachers' necks, and furthermore, let me remind you that Sheila did Machon Atara a favor when she took this subbing job on practically a day's notice."

"She did," Menucha admitted. "And what's more, in the beginning, I for one was very pleased with your choice."

"Has anything significant changed since we first spoke?"

"No. An educator of Sheila's caliber is a gift to our girls. But…"

"But?"

"I tried to tell you then. Believe me, I'm speaking for more than half of the parents. Sheila's way too hard on them. She expects them to perform like college students."

"In what way?"

"Well…in the strict way she treats deadlines, for example. Why, for a week's lateness, a student could have as much as ten points deducted from her grade."

"Do you find that to be unreasonable?"

"I certainly do. We all do." Menucha warmed to her theme. "Our girls aren't just students. They are daughters and sisters. They're expected to help out at home. They have chores and babysitting responsibilities, besides which, they have lives."

"Lives?"

"Social lives, and choir, and art and ballet lessons—you know, the whole nine yards. They're only young once."

"When was this assignment given?"

"At the beginning of the year," Menucha admitted.

"Then"—Maya Sudri paused significantly—"I don't think it's in the girls' best interest to be soft on them. Not in this instance."

"I see," Menucha said slowly. "I see. Well, thank you for your time and patience."

"If it's any comfort to you, Yocheved Sutton will be returning to school next week, which means that Sheila will be returning to her original position as the Jewish history teacher, and as such, she may feel less responsible for molding the girls' characters. Not that I'd consider that to be an advantage, not at all, but when a teacher has a class for only two hours a week, she can't be expected to invest as much in them as their homeroom teacher does."

Menucha put the phone down feeling dissatisfied. Rabbanit Sudri certainly didn't mince words, did she? She wondered if the principal was aware that Sheila was no longer the same incredibly effective teacher she'd been just a year or two before. The proof was in the pudding. As head of the PTA, Menucha had been apprised of Sheila's struggles in Noa Lewin's first grade. Too bad Rabbanit Sudri was playing favorites. Or perhaps she was in denial.

There's nothing more I can do for Halleli. She'll just have to hang in there until Yocheved takes over. Menucha frowned in annoyance. She hated feeling helpless. Should she consult Eliezer, and see if there was an avenue of action she'd overlooked?

Eliezer would tell her to stop coddling Halleli and let her deal with the consequences of her actions. But Eliezer didn't understand.

He didn't understand how guilty Menucha felt for not providing Halleli with a houseful of siblings.

No, forget a houseful. Menucha wiped away the tears that always came to her eyes whenever she permitted herself to dwell on this excruciatingly painful topic.

Just one sibling would be a gift. A sister or brother for Halleli to love.

No, when it came to parenting their daughter, she and her husband didn't always see eye to eye, and in any case, Eliezer had been grouchy and out of sorts lately.

Menucha wondered why. Maybe he needed a vacation.

* * *

Who am I fooling? Geula thought later that night. *I have a hole in my heart, not physically, baruch Hashem, but emotionally. Spending, and spending, and spending money I don't have, getting myself into horrible situations like I did today. Trying so desperately to fill the emptiness.*

People need people. I need people. And not just any people.

Geula wandered over to her bead box and opened it. Nothing spoke to her. Maybe it was the nonstop beading marathon she'd just engaged in, but instead of feeling inspired by the vivid hues of the sparkling, glowing piles of beads, she felt listless.

She washed the few supper dishes. Her apartment was neat. It was still too early to go to sleep. She was feeling too restless to study anything on her own, and she'd never gotten around to setting up study partners after her move to Yerushalayim.

It was just after eight. Some of her contemporaries, those with younger children, were still contending with bath time and bedtime. Others, with older children, were dealing with homework, teenage angst—or maybe not? Maybe they were simply enjoying family time together? That concept still existed, didn't it?

She also could visit family, but she just wasn't in the mood, which sounded infantile, but she was deeply, viscerally not in the mood to...

To what? To seek companionship that never sated, never filled, never touched the core of things? To have the same conversations, and be left with the same questions?

Why am I feeling so restless? So discontented? What is with me tonight?

Maybe it was a result of the tough day she'd had. Probably it was that. Though, she admitted, she'd been having this growly, down, desolate feeling more and more lately.

Besides, today hadn't been *that* difficult. Helen Tauber had helped. She'd helped a lot, going from teacher to teacher to advertise Geula's sale. Thanks to her efforts, Geula had sold every single one of her creations. She'd even received one or two commissions for more. She should be so grateful that Helen had helped extricate her from the hole she'd been in. She should call to thank her again. She should get to work on the orders she'd received. She should be feeling so good.

What's with me?

She knew exactly what was with her.

I'm wrenchingly, painfully lonely for—

Forget it.

She drifted into the kitchen and took out a jumbo bag of potato chips, the one she'd bought for the end-of-the-year teacher's party, the one she'd heroically resisted for an entire week.

She pulled it open unceremoniously and poured a gigantic portion into a big soup bowl. She stared the mound of potato chips. If she started eating, she wouldn't stop until it was gone. If she ate so many potato chips, she'd become physically ill.

So what? She didn't care.

I need comfort, and I need it now.

She had absolutely no sweetened drinks in the house. It was a matter of principle, not an oversight. She did have grape juice for Shabbos. She placed four ice cubes in a big cup, poured grape juice over them, and put the entire treat on a tray.

She paused. What would she have told herself that morning, had she known this would be her mood tonight? What would she have said to herself?

I won't grab junk food, just because I'm alone in the house.

But morning was long ago and now was now.

Oh yeah? Try and stop me. Alone in the house, alone in life, alone, all alone.

The phone rang. Geula ignored it, and after a moment, it stopped ringing. That was fine with her, absolutely fine. There was no one she wanted to talk to, anyhow. She was utterly, completely depleted.

It was only nine. She was still dressed. She'd go to the supermarket down the block and buy a big gooey chocolate bar. Yes, and maybe a pint of vanilla ice cream. They'd go well with the potato chips.

Was she going to make such a poor choice?

She was.

I deserve a break. I need it.

Something felt off about that statement, but she couldn't figure out what. She tried to think past the all-encompassing loneliness she was feeling, past the restlessness and emptiness that gnawed at her soul.

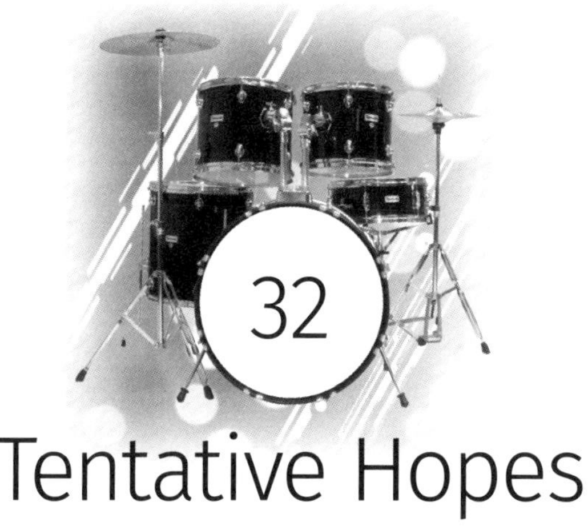

32
Tentative Hopes

Elisheva Kantor was having a vivid dream. In the hazy way that dreams operate, this one had begun with a visit from her married couple—her younger son, Menachem, and Avital, his wife. They'd been married for just under a year. No sooner had she absorbed the earth-shattering news that she and Shlomo were about to become grandparents in a few short months, than a smiling Yerachmiel had incredible news of his own to share. To have the joy of impending grandparenthood compounded by Yerachmiel's broad hint that he and Sheila Leipzig were on the verge of engagement was making her cry. A glance at her husband's face showed that he too was sniffling, and blinking rapidly.

After so many years of waiting—while her peers already had teenaged grandchildren, as her sons dawdled their way through *shidduchim,* as even her perennial optimism groaned with the strain of sustaining hope, year after year—who could have imagined this moment? Now their younger son was soon to present them with their very first grandchild, while simultaneously, their older son, senior by more than a decade, so eminently eligible, yet inexplicably, *impossibly*, still single, was going to get engaged to a good girl from a good family. That put the finishing touch on their joy and gratitude. It was almost too much joy to encompass. All at once, all her cherished dreams were coming true.

Well, it literally was a dream. The front door creaked open. Elisheva slowly surfaced back into reality, still smiling. Dreams could come true, couldn't they?

Elisheva was still only half awake. Her mind drifted to the conversation she'd had earlier that day with her older sister, Eva Goldenberg. Yerachmiel's rented apartment was located one short block away from his Aunt Eva's home. He was a frequent guest for Shabbos. Elisheva knew that her sister knew more about the day-to-day minutiae of her son's life than she did. She was grateful for Eva's involvement because Yerachmiel tended to be very closed when it came to sharing anything personal. But Eva just ignored his reticence and somehow extracted information from him, whether or not he intended to share it.

The two sisters had been on the phone, discussing Yerachmiel's newest relationship, and not for the first time. Eva had taken to calling her sister after every date.

"Yes, Elisheva, dreams come true. You know when that happens? When a person's smart enough to have realistic dreams, that's when. And, in addition, when he pursues the dreams he professes to have."

"He is pursuing his dreams." Elisheva hated speaking on the phone without anything to keep herself busy. Anyhow, she knew what Eva was going to say. Her sister's opinions on this matter were very predictable. Elisheva began sorting through a pile of magazines. It was a chore that demanded minimum concentration, and it kept the magazines from piling up.

"Is he? He claims that his most fervent dream is to get married. I asked him, if that's what he wants, a mature man of forty, then why does he go barreling off in any crazy direction, the better to shoot himself in the foot, and distance himself from the very goals he claims to cherish so dearly?"

"Why do you say that?" Elisheva cradled the phone under her chin and went to search for a pair of scissors. She'd spied an interesting article on care for the elderly that she thought Menachem would appreciate.

"A younger girl, again. Much younger, and the cream of the crop. What's he thinking? Does he think she's looking for a father figure?"

"She did agree to go out with him a third time, you know." Elisheva cut out the article carefully. "She seems to like him."

"Yes. She seems to like him, and he's ready to propose. Who does he pick to give his heart to, as if hearts grow on trees? Sheila Leipzig! Yes, no more and no less will do for Yerachmiel, and I shudder to think what will happen if he proposes, and she turns him down. Who'll pick up the pieces then?"

"You're such a pessimist. Pieces. Why should there be pieces?" Elisheva reached for the next magazine in the pile.

"Tell yourself the truth, darling. Can you guarantee an unqualified yes when he proposes to her? How? And, by the way, is he even ready to get married?"

"What?" Elisheva had dropped the magazine she was holding. "What kind of a crazy question is that? Of course, he's ready."

"I'm not referring to his chronological age. His sister-in-law, Avital, just called me. She's very distressed."

"About what?"

"Yerachmiel's taking his own sweet time about cosigning for their mortgage."

"She called you about that? What's wrong with calling me?"

"She didn't want to place you in an uncomfortable position," Eva explained.

"So why are you telling me now?"

"I'm trying to indicate areas in Yerachmiel's character that I think could use improvement."

"He's going to be a wonderful, caring husband to the right person. All the self-absorption you're hinting at? With the right person, it will all disappear. He'll be inspired to give to his wife."

"Yes, at least in the beginning. What will happen, though, after the stars in his eyes fade? It's a question he needs to ask himself now, before—"

"You know, Eva, it's hard for me to hear so much criticism every time we speak about Yerachmiel. You make him out to be a monster of selfishness." She picked up a magazine and began leafing through it, then put it down. It was no use. She couldn't focus enough to perform even a mindless task like this one.

"I don't think that about him at all. However, from my information about Sheila, the type of life that she envisions for herself will be a stretch for him."

"So, he'll stretch, and so will she."

"There's something else."

"What?" Much as she loved Eva, she needed this conversation to end.

"Are you aware that Sheila's looking for her own apartment? Apparently, Menucha Shalom has shown her several properties, but none she liked. That girl's very particular."

Sheila was looking for her own apartment? That wasn't good news. "And if she is?"

"How close do you think she considers herself to being engaged if she's going with real estate agents to look for her own place? Does that make sense if she's serious about Yerachmiel? Does he even know that she's planning to move out of her parents' house in the near future?"

"I don't know. How do *you* know?"

"I've been making some calls."

Now Elisheva was completely awake.

The dream had felt so real, mirroring her deepest, most heartfelt desires. Well, at least the first part about Avital and Menachem was true. The part about Yerachmiel? It was too soon to know. Neither she nor her sister was omniscient. It was all in Hashem's hands.

She peered at her bedside clock. Just past eleven. Menachem and Avital had visited that evening, ostensibly to pick up some of the wedding gifts they'd left in the guest room, but the mother and mother-in-law in Elisheva had sensed something hidden beyond the pedestrian request. It wasn't simple, not being able to ask outright, but that was part and parcel of being a mother-in-law.

Menachem and Avital were both nearing thirty. Time to start a family, please Hashem. No pressure.

Her daughter-in-law had been wearing looser clothing for at least three months, as opposed to her usual tailored look. It could mean a mere change of style or even different eating habits now that she was cooking supper every night, but as usual, Elisheva had leaped to the most optimistic conclusion possible, while waiting to be told the good news. In any case, her younger son had asked if his father would be home when they dropped by, which could simply mean that he wanted to see him. But it could also mean that he had something important to tell both of them. Couldn't it?

That very evening, at eight thirty, Menachem and Avital had exuberantly told them the wonderful news.

It was true!

Shlomo had driven the couple home with their packages, and caught a minyan at the Kosel, while she, exhausted by all the emotion coming at the end of a packed day, had called it a night.

Who was that humming just outside her room? No, not just humming, actually singing in a very melodic voice. Yerachmiel! And he had been out on a date that evening with Sheila, their third in less than two weeks. Along with the ever-vigilant Eva, Shlomo had cautioned her not to get her hopes up. Well, she couldn't help her dreams, could she? And who said she should?

Imagine, Yerachmiel singing after a date! Yerachmiel, her beloved *bechor*, aged forty, singing after a date.

She swung her door open. "Yerachmiel?"

He jumped. "Ima! Did I wake you? I tried to keep the noise level down."

"Don't worry, I wasn't sleeping, just drifting off. Daydreaming, actually. Did you have a good time?" *Don't pry. No eagerness. He's been burned too often.*

"I had a very good time. Yes, very good." He sat down on a kitchen chair.

"You did?" He was actually sharing dating information with her. "You were singing, you know?"

He grinned. "I know. In the middle of the date, a song just came to me. It burst into my mind, two thematically related *pesukim,* melody fully formed, first stanza, chorus, second stanza, finale. A song that works, that's easy to sing, but not so predictable that it's boring. The perfect balance. It's got that special something that just gets to you when you hear it. Know what I mean?"

Elisheva was astounded by Yerachmiel's unexpected burst of loquaciousness. Is this what he would have been like had he married and started a family in his twenties? Was the reserve bordering upon taciturnity when he was alone with his parents a result of simple loneliness?

"That's only happened to me three or four times, you know?"

"Is that what you were singing now? It's beautiful."

"Yes. I sang it during the date three or four times and recorded it on my phone."

"You did? I hope she wasn't put off."

He shrugged. "Not the world's most conventional action, but Sheila took it in stride."

"Well, she knows that you founded Rina-O-Mangina," Elisheva reassured herself. "She wouldn't want you to forget a song. It's your *parnassah,* after all."

"That's what I thought. It made for some interesting conversation too. No one told me that she took piano lessons for ten years. I can't imagine why anyone thought that was an irrelevant detail. I do run a *simchah* band."

"I think Menachem did tell you that she's musically inclined."

"There's musical, and there's musical. Ten years of piano lessons mean that music's a very important part of her life. She appreciates music and musicians. We definitely have that in common."

"So it would seem."

"Anyhow, my determination not to lose a song wasn't out of left field as far as she was concerned. Not at all."

"As a matter of fact, I bet she was impressed," Elisheva ventured, catching his enthusiasm.

"Not to boast, but I think she was."

"Did she say anything?"

"She liked the song. I thought she'd be a little more enthusiastic, but she did like it."

"She may have felt shy. What happened next?"

"Do you really want to know?" he teased.

Elisheva was shocked by the change in her son. He was almost giddy. "I most certainly do."

He took a deep breath. "Sheila wanted to know if songs often come to me, out of the blue, as it were."

"What did you tell her?"

"The truth. That any time it's happened, it was because I was experiencing a feeling of heightened emotion and connection."

"You actually said that? Tell me you didn't say that. I cannot believe that you put her under that kind of pressure. Why take unnecessary risks?"

"It's been three dates, Ima. I already felt this way two weeks ago. I thought it was time to let her know."

"I think it was much too soon."

Yerachmiel's face crumpled. "Do you think I ruined it? Will she back off? What should I do?"

His mother took pity on him. "Don't panic."

"How can I not panic?" He stood up and began pacing.

"It's not so bad."

"No?" He looked at her hopefully

"No one ends a relationship because someone's going fast unless the second person is plain old uninterested or maybe afraid of commitment."

"You think?"

"You were there with her, and you thought she was ready to hear such a strong statement, but in the future..."

"She's a big girl, and she's dating for a reason. I'm almost sure the two of us are more or less on the same page."

"The age difference between the two of you doesn't bother her?"

"Nah. Why should it? She wants to marry an accomplished guy she can respect, which, with all modesty, I am." Yerachmiel chuckled. "She knows I have a full-time career running one of the most successful *simchah* bands around. I have *semichah*. I learn every chance I get, plus I swim and jog. I know personal fitness is important to Sheila. Why am I listing my credentials? Ima, what's going on with you? Why aren't you happier for me?"

"I just don't want to see you hurt, that's all."

"Thanks for the vote of confidence."

"Let's just say that if she's not discerning enough to appreciate you and want to marry you, it's on to the next one."

"I can't believe the way you're talking. I finally like a girl. I'm planning to propose, within the next couple of times, if you want to know, and I wouldn't do that unless I thought she'd say yes. What's the story here, that you're questioning my ability to read the signs in a relationship?"

Once again his face shuttered, but this time she read the signs correctly. He wasn't nearly as confident in the relationship as he wanted to be, poor thing.

Elisheva looked at her son in dismay. *Who am I to crush his dreams after all the years of emptiness? What kind of a mother am I to imply that he can't tell if Sheila is interested in him or not? Or tell him that he's misleading himself with false hopes? Who says I'm right?*

"I don't think that at all. I'm being protective. That's what mothers are supposed to do, Yerachmiel. You know that, don't you?"

The look of relief that crossed his handsome face didn't calm his mother's doubts completely, but she'd made her decision. No more second-guessing his judgment. Yerachmiel didn't need that.

"Let's have a midnight snack," he suggested. "All this emotion is making me hungry."

"Good idea. I'll make us both grilled cheese and cocoa."

"I'll make it, Ima. You sit and relax."

Yerachmiel puttered around the kitchen fixing the snack.

She sat quietly, trying to think of a way to reopen the subject in a way that wouldn't erode his confidence in the growing relationship. There should be a course on it.

"Tell me one thing the two of you have in common," she said finally.

"We're both successful at what we do," came his prompt reply. "We both set goals. We set our sights high and are willing to work hard to reach the top."

"So you're both perfectionists?"

"You could say that."

"And you're both leaders," his mother continued. "But, digging just a little deeper, do you want to run a similar household? Have you spoken about that?"

"No," Yerachmiel admitted. "You mean like china versus paper plates?" He set a grilled cheese sandwich in front of her. She pushed it in his direction.

He pushed it back. "I think Sheila's going to want an open home. Lots of guests, students visiting. The fact that she values community projects means that when people turn to her for all types of assistance, she won't want to refuse. Given that she has a leadership type of personality, she'll probably be the head of more than one committee. I think it's very admirable."

"Yes, it is. Now let me ask you this. I know that you value your privacy, your peace and quiet. When you come home, will you want to see all kinds of people in the house?"

"So she'll send everyone home before I come home. She's teaching me to be more aware of the needs of the *tzibbur*. That's good, isn't it?"

"If it's what you want, it's wonderful. But, here's another example. Will you mind her going out night after night after the two of you are married, to attend the bas mitzvah of a child you've never met? More than not minding, will you be proud of her? Will you support her efforts? Will you even encourage her to grow in the areas she excels in?"

She braced herself, knowing that she'd probably hit a raw nerve, but her son's reaction surprised her.

"Ima, it's a moot point. You and I both know"—he flashed his charming grin—"that she only does those things because she needs to fill her time, because she has no one to share her day with. Once she's married, she won't need all these artificial distractions."

"Yerachmiel Kantor. Listen up, and listen well. If you value this relationship, and I believe that you truly do..."

Her son nodded vigorously. His handsome face turned toward her.

"If you don't want to lose Sheila, you had better believe that these activities aren't extracurricular nonsense intended to fill a void in her life. Never utter a sentence like that in her presence, or she'll drop you. I mean that. These activities are a reflection of her deepest values."

"I hear you, Ima," he said soberly. "It's good that we're talking."

"Your role in her life will go beyond what you may envision. You may wind up shouldering childcare and housekeeping tasks you didn't imagine because she's become a sought-after public figure. Is that how you visualize your marriage, your future home?"

Yerachmiel was aghast. "Don't tell me that you're implying that Sheila's irresponsible. It sounds like you're saying that she has mixed-up priorities. Is it fair to suspect her of being one of those women who have room in their hearts for the entire universe but not for their own family? Why take an asset and turn it into a liability?"

"Yerachmiel, slow down." Elisheva was unfazed by his outburst. Yerachmiel had always been quick to anger and quick to forgive. For a fleeting moment, she allowed herself a selfish thought. *If Yerachmiel got his way, he'd have to work to curb his temper.* Somehow, she doubted that Sheila would be as tolerant of the occasional outburst as she, Shlomo, and Menachem were. His close family members attributed his somewhat high-strung nature to an artistic temperament, but would Sheila?

She had better! Elisheva thought vehemently and smiled inwardly realizing that she was contradicting herself. She counted to ten, and sure enough—

"Sorry, Ima. I'm just a little stressed here, but I apologize for yelling."

"A little stressed?"

"Extremely stressed. Please understand that I've never met anyone like her in all my years of dating, and I never will again. Sheila's my last chance. She's my last chance to get married. So, all the stuff you said, I'm going to learn to live with it."

"She'll need you to do more than just tolerate her passion. Can you support it?"

"If that's what it takes to marry her, yes." He got up from his place and washed for bread.

As she watched her son eat, she wished with all her heart for a way to convince Sheila not to hurt her son.

This is not the time to remind him that there are other fish in the sea.

Poor boy. I'm definitely not going to ask him if he knows that Sheila's planning to move out of her parents' home. Anyhow, who says it means anything?

Who are you fooling?

First Fight

"Okay, we're almost there. Shut your eyes."

"Where's the surprise destination, Elchanan? And would you mind letting me in on the big secret? What's the occasion?" Estelle asked impatiently. "And I'm opening my eyes. It's enough."

"We're almost there," he promised. "No peeking now, or you'll ruin the surprise."

Estelle pursed her lips. "This is silly. I'm not in third grade anymore. And I just so happen to hate surprises. You ought to know that by now," she grumbled, still keeping her eyes shut.

"You're going to love this surprise." He hoped so, anyhow. "Where's your sense of fun?"

"Who says I have one?"

"Of course you do. Hold on. One more minute." Elchanan expertly maneuvered the car he'd bought when he officially made aliyah into a parking space, muttering to himself, "This is a tight spot."

He quickly got out of the car and went around it to open Estelle's door with a flourish. "Now! Open your eyes, Estelle."

She opened her eyes and got out of the car. "About time. This had better be worth dragging me out of the house at nine thirty at night when I have a packed day in school tomorrow. I tell you, Elchanan, every day in the last month of school feels like three days during the rest of the year." She sighed dramatically. "Some people begrudge teachers their two-months' paid vacation. I tell them that the last month of school is the equivalent of teaching three months. Not that it helps."

"This way, please, Madam," he said with a mock bow, and led the way. "Don't you start at ten thirty on Tuesdays? That's what the school schedule you left for me on the fridge said."

"Usually I do, but tomorrow I'm accompanying the first graders on their end-of-the-year class trip. I have to be in school at eight thirty. I know I told you that."

"Oops, you did. Sorry. I completely forgot. Hey, that's great!"

She frowned. "What's great?"

"It means that we're already establishing routines, like a settled married couple. I'm used to your starting late on Tuesdays, so I forget if you tell me something else."

Estelle's eyes widened. "You know what?"

"What?" he asked hopefully.

"You have a point."

Elchanan smiled. "I guess that proves that we're both creatures of habit."

"Most people are," she asserted.

"Come, we're heading this way," Elchanan said. "Did I lock the door?"

"Yes, you did."

They started out, feet crunching along the gravel path. In the silence, the sound of their footsteps was audible. It was just after sunset. A cool breeze was blowing the heat of the day away. Estelle relaxed.

"One second," Elchanan said. "Didn't you already accompany a class trip this year? Do you have to do more than one? I thought one was enough, considering how uncomfortable you were last time."

"When did I tell you I already went on a class trip this year?" she asked after a moment.

"When we were dating, remember? You told me all about a day trip you went on with the sixth grade, and how frightening you found the climb. You did it anyhow. I was impressed. What's more, I remember your telling me that you went as a favor to another teacher, and I was impressed by that too."

His wife of three months fidgeted. "That's only somewhat accurate. I did take over last minute, and I do have a small phobia as far as heights go, so I figured I'd do a little exposure therapy on myself."

"Good for you."

"Stop with the compliments. Didn't I tell you that I hate compliments?"

"No, you never mentioned it. I'd remember if you had. You do? Why?"

She shrugged. "They make me uncomfortable."

"Why?"

"I don't know. They just do."

"All right then, I'm simply stating a fact. It was kind of you to do a favor for another teacher. Was that pareve enough?"

"Yes, it was. Stop worrying. In any case, it was a one-time thing. It's all in the past."

"You're doing it again now for another teacher," he pointed out.

"It's not as big a deal as it sounds. Teachers do these kinds of things for each other all the time. Last time, Avital Salamonte was supposed to go, but she had her engagement party that week, and Menachem's mother needed to take her shopping or something like that, so she woke up with an upset stomach from nerves. Typical *kallah* behavior, I suppose."

"Did you have upset stomachs from nerves while we were dating?"

"Nope. Other than the occasional bout of insomnia, I was pretty grounded, because I never knew until the last three dates if our relationship was going to lead anywhere. I wasn't that emotionally involved, whereas Avital spent their entire engagement period worrying that Menachem would change his mind.

"Besides," she went on, "I hadn't yet accompanied a class that year, so I figured I'd just get it over with. So you see, I'm far from the *baalas chesed* you imagine me to be. Sorry to burst your bubble. I can't imagine that I told you about the school's policies regarding the various staff obligations. Not when we were dating. Did I? You must have been passing out from boredom."

"Not at all. I found your conversation interesting. I don't know all that much about girls' schools, and especially not girls' schools here in Israel. Anyhow, you didn't tell me about school policies," he explained. "I asked Menucha Shalom why Machon Atara couldn't just hire a substitute to go with the sixth grade instead of that teacher who couldn't make it. Why put you in the position of having to refuse another teacher's urgent need? Menucha informed me that on the contrary, you wanted to go, to face down your fears. She told me I shouldn't feel so bad for you, that each teacher only had to go once each year, and that in any case, a lot of teachers enjoy the break from routine."

"Hmm. They do. Not just the break, the scenery, the climb, Eretz Yisrael, historic spots. I do too, just not when I need to climb up and down mountains."

"No rock climbing this time, I hope."

"Thanks. No, there isn't. This time we're going to the bee farm."

His eyes widened. "A bee farm? Better you than me."

"Why do you say that? I'm *davka* looking forward to going. Bees are apparently fascinating."

"I'm sure they are, but…I'm allergic to bee stings."

She stopped walking to look at him. "Elchanan! You're unreal."

"What's wrong?"

"What's wrong? You're allergic to bee stings. You never told me that. Do you realize how many picnics we've gone on together? Why didn't you tell me?"

"It just never came up in conversation."

"You should have brought it up.

"I don't see why," he said, perplexed.

Estelle crossed her arms. "Don't tell me you're serious."

"It's not as if it's some deep, dark secret I was keeping from you. All that happened is that I had a pretty serious reaction to a bee sting when I was two. I can't say I have any memories of what happened, but my parents sure do. I haven't been stung since."

"You should have said something to me," she insisted.

"What for? I had an EpiPen in my pocket, just in case. Why would I want to make you worry? Nothing happened."

"But it could have."

"I don't think that way. I do my best to be prepared, and Hashem does the rest. What's the difference? Now you know."

"Now I'll worry."

"That's the reason I didn't tell you. Forget it. That's not why I brought you here. Do you know where we are?"

Estelle looked around the crowded, nondescript parking lot. All she saw were numerous parked cars, with the occasional pedestrian passing by. "Where are we?"

"Don't tell me you don't recognize this place."

"I don't. What am I supposed to recognize here? It looks like a regular parking lot."

"I'll give you a hint. It wasn't here three months ago. Soon you'll recognize the very special location I'm taking you to tonight. Let's go. We have a reservation for five minutes ago."

"Wait! Give me a second. Got it! Yes, this is the hotel I first met you at, right?"

"Bingo!" he exclaimed, gratified. "You remembered. I knew you would, once you got your bearings."

Estelle smiled in spite of herself. "Well, naturally, once I saw the name of the hotel, Homestead Hotels. I always thought that name was corny, to tell you the truth."

"Could be. So what? You know what they say, clichés become clichés because they're true. I happen to think it's a nice name for a hotel. Brings back nice homey memories. Homey memories—hey, not bad." He laughed.

She groaned. *Maybe for you, but not for me. What a horrible date that was.*

All at once, Estelle was overcome by a wave of annoyance. "I want to tell you that it's obvious, both from your expression and from the fact that you brought me here, that this place holds special memories for you, but I don't feel the same way. Now, had you taken me to the rose gardens, where you proposed, that would be a different story."

At his crestfallen expression, she altered her tone, not without an effort.

Why does he constantly insist on being secretive? I'm not a baby. I feel...manipulated. Why can't he be straight with me? Why's he still insecure about our relationship? We're married! It's been— What is it? Almost three months? His need for reassurance is wearing at me, and it's never enough for him.

"I do remember the date, every moment of it," she added, which was more or less true, though not the way he wanted it to be.

"So do I." He looked at her and smiled, mollified.

"Lead the way, Elchanan. You mentioned that we have a reservation?"

"I did." Elchanan straightened his shoulders and held the lobby door open. "Can you believe it? Isn't this miraculous, Estelle? We're back in the hotel lobby where we first met each other exactly ten months ago. It's our ten-month anniversary since we met the first time."

That's why we're here? Sweet, but... Aren't wives supposed to be more into anniversaries?

"How in the world do you remember things like that? The exact date?" she marveled. "Were you looking at your calendar from last year?"

"I remember what's important to me," he told her, looking at her very seriously. "Just like everyone else. I'm sure you remember what made a strong impression on you."

Estelle squirmed. *Oh no, all this mushy stuff! I hope he'll realize someday soon that I'm just not the type to wear my heart on my sleeve. I know he wants me to, but I can't. Maybe I'm supposed to try.*

It doesn't mean I don't think he wants to be a good husband, and sometimes, occasionally, he even understands me though not with the whole Avigdor-Kayla fiasco. So glad they went home before I lost it. How is it that he tries to be understanding and close, but he seems to know so little about what pushes my buttons?

I'm letting bygones be bygones. I promised myself I'd do that. I do give him credit for doing his best, I definitely do, but we're so different from each other.

I have no one to ask if the way I feel is normal. I have to translate myself into his idioms, and we speak different languages or at least different dialects. I never had to do that with Menucha.

I can't talk to her about this. She always takes his side. Some friend.

Take Avital, for example. Now there's a classic starry-eyed newlywed. She literally worships the ground Menachem walks on. Why am I not like that about Elchanan? I'm sure it would make him very happy if I were. Then he'd probably get all the reassurance he needs.

I can't not be me, just because now I'm married.

Happily Ever After

Estelle and Elchanan entered the spacious lobby of the hotel. She shivered, a combined result of the icy air-conditioning and gratitude for the undeniable fact that the years of countless, hopeless evenings spent in similar lobbies were behind her, forever.

He noticed, of course. "See? Told you this place would bring back memories. Yes, here I am folks, Elchanan Hacohen, mind reader extraordinaire."

"Lower your voice, Elchanan. People are staring at us."

"Just kidding." He lowered his voice as he led her to a table. "I made reservations for two to commemorate the time we first met, and this time, we'll actually get to finish our dinner, I hope, without having to flee in the middle because you see someone you know. You do recall that small detail of our first date, don't you?"

"Don't be like that. They weren't just people I knew. They were an engaged couple."

"Avital Salamonte and Menachem Kantor. The contrast must have been excruciating."

"How did you know that?"

He looked surprised. "It's an obvious conclusion."

"And then— Do you remember how you acted?"

"Remind me."

"You acted as if it was the sixth or seventh time we were meeting each other. I barely knew your name."

"So? Why is that a problem? Who made up all those silly dating rules, when each and every couple has their own dynamic?"

"You don't know me very well if you can ask that," she retorted.

"I know, you told me. The dating protocol made you feel safe, and following rules, in general, makes you feel safe. I was a little unconventional at the time, I admit, but we wouldn't be sitting here if I hadn't been. Right? Tell the truth."

"Who knows? Could be. You may be right. Or, maybe not. Who knows? There were a million different factors involved in the fact that we got married."

"*Baruch Hashem.*"

A waiter approached, and they ordered an entrée.

"Now we're an old married couple and so are they."

She nodded. *Except that our relationship is so dismally different than theirs.*

Later, as they ate the minestrone soup, Elchanan cleared his throat and said, "I'm very grateful for your hospitality to Avigdor and Kayla."

"Some hospitality."

"It made it a big difference to their entire stay in Israel. It was okay for you, wasn't it? Despite all the school pressure, after all's said and done, it was a worthwhile experience, wasn't it?"

"Mmm," she commented noncommittally, casting around for a way to change the subject. She didn't want to talk about it.

"I want you to know that Kayla liked you a lot," he persisted

"I'm glad they enjoyed their visit," she said blandly. "That's good."

"They did. I give you a lot of credit for stretching the way you did, what with it being grading period and all the school pressure. I never asked you. Did you tell Rabbanit Sudri why you were late handing in grades for the first time in your entire life?"

"No, what was the point? The grades were late, I caused her inconvenience, I put her under pressure, she had to remind me twice, as if I forgot. What does it matter what my excuse was? I think she was a tiny bit put out. Certainly, she hasn't been smiling at me much lately."

"Why assume it's about that? Or about you at all? She's a busy woman."

"I'm not assuming, I know. I just hope she won't bring it up at the end-of-the-year evaluation."

"You're human."

"Yeah, but she's a superwoman. She doesn't understand how ordinary mortals function."

"Oh, come on. She's a mature woman."

"She keeps reminding us that she gave us plenty of notice. It's true. She did."

He ate a couple of spoonfuls of soup, mulling over what she'd said. "Sorry, then, but she'll have to get over it. I'm sure you're blowing it out of proportion, Estelle. I'm not going to convince you to think differently, but theoretically, even if she's really put out with you—"

"Not theoretically," Estelle insisted stubbornly. "And that's far from the point. *I'm* put out with me. I dropped out of choir, I handed in the grades late. I can't do anything well anymore."

"Not true. Listen! This is your first time being a newlywed, juggling a home and, me, wonderful as I am. I think you're doing a fabulous job.

She made a face. "A husband and a home? That's nothing."

"Do you really think that?"

"I do. Look how well everyone else manages."

"Why compare yourself to anyone else?"

"How do they manage? I wish I knew the secret."

"Do you live in their homes? How do you know they're managing so well?"

She ignored his question. "Do you know how much stress other teachers deal with on a daily basis? Do you know that Nechama Rotter patted my shoulder as I looked for my name on the list of those who had handed in their students' grades, even though I knew it wouldn't be there? She told me that it takes time to get it all together. Can you imagine? I was ready to crawl under the table, I was so embarrassed."

"Nice lady. You weren't the only one not on the list."

"Yeah, along with the usual ones who never have their act together. Believe me, it's no great honor."

"Now you see it's not so simple," Elchanan pointed out. "People struggle. I'm sure they all have good reasons."

"I don't think there's ever a good reason to inconvenience others. I should have started much earlier, and this past week was a bad time for company."

There. I said it! I guess to avoid future misunderstandings, I'm going to have to spell out everything.

He was silent and then said, "I guess the timing was off."

"It was."

"But you're glad you got to meet people important to me, part of my past, aren't you, Estelle?"

"It was challenging, and hard, even if it was important, which I'm not saying it wasn't, but couldn't you have protected me a little bit? Told them we'd meet them at the hotel? A little luxury wouldn't have hurt for a change instead of having to scrub the house from top to bottom in addition to everything else I have to do."

"Estelle, I wanted to welcome them to my home, as a married man. Do you know how long I waited to be able to do that?"

"But why weren't you straight with me? How can I trust you when you don't tell me the truth?"

"I always tell you the truth."

"Then why did you tell me that Avigdor is your *father's* protégé when he so clearly worships the ground you walk on? Why didn't you tell me that he's a virtual younger brother to you? Do you realize it made me look like a witch?"

"What made you look like a witch?"

"Was I welcoming the way I would have been to a dear friend of yours and his wife? No, I was not. The way I acted that first time they came! It made me look like a cold, unfeeling, self-centered person who cares for nothing other than her own comfort and space. Do you know how humiliated I was, once I realized we were dealing with people who are an important part of your past?"

"They said only good things. Other than that first evening, you were super welcoming to them. I don't even know where to start. Where should I start? I'm sorry you were hurt, Estelle. I'm sorry you suffered. I feel so bad."

"First, you feed me misinformation. Then—why did you bring them into my messy kitchen and put them to work while I was sleeping? Does the entire world have to know I'm not managing? Don't you care about me?"

His shoulders drooped. "I'm trying to digest that I had such good intentions and they so backfired on me." He slapped his forehead. "*Oy*. Send me to husband school. I want to do this right. Tell me I did something right. I tried so hard to please everyone."

"Stop fishing. I'm not in the mood," she snapped.

His face closed up. His cheeks reddened. "It would be great if you would be *dan lekaf zechus*, you know?" he said tightly.

"You're angry?"

"Yes, I am."

Estelle was shocked.

"A little less hurtful honesty would be nice sometimes. Fake it till you make it, and all that. Maybe you don't remember that we met here tonight ten months ago but why not leave it a little cloudy?

Maybe I was fishing for compliments just now, but why call me on it? Maybe I made a mistake, but can't you be a little nicer?"

"Flattery and mushiness are not my thing. You know that."

"Maybe you could incorporate them into your repertoire. Maybe it would be a good idea."

"You want me to pretend to be someone I'm not? Pretend to act differently than I do?"

"No, not at all."

"What then?"

"You've heard of the male ego, haven't you?" he joked, trying to drown out the clamor of his hurt feelings. "So, pander to my ego. Why not? It would be a *chesed* on your part. You like doing *chesed*."

"Stop putting yourself down, Elchanan. It's not ego. I'm not being nice when I say that it's not ego for you to want me to remember our first date. One thing you are not is arrogant. I'll try to be more *dan lekaf zechus*."

Instantly, his expression cleared. "Estelle?"

"Hmm?"

"*Mazel tov*."

"On what?"

"We just had our very first fight. We're a real married couple."

"That wasn't a fight."

"Hey, don't burst my bubble."

"It was more of a disagreement."

"I say it was a fight. Come on, Estelle. Make me feel good."

"Make you feel good? Okay, have it your way. It was a fight."

From the diary of Estelle Bruner

Here I am sitting in the nearly empty teachers' room, the picture of a blissful kallah reveling in shanah rishonah.

Why didn't anyone warn me it would be so hard?

Is it just us, Elchanan and I, or is this par for the course?

I'm also not too hopeful that writing will help, but in any case, I'm sitting here, in a far corner hidden by two closets, writing in the diary I never threw out but haven't written in since my marriage.

Marriage! What's my take on marriage?

I'm married, but am I happy?

Marriage in Hebrew is nissuin. And that about sums it up. Carrying burdens. Schlepping along another person, with his endless, ever-present expectations, and all of society's never-ending expectations.

That's not why I got married. This is not what I signed up for.

I wanted connection. Belonging. But not with him. Not with Elchanan. I don't feel that I want to share with him or get to know him better.

There. I said it. I'm saying it.

So...wonderful, great. Plenty of people have told me that marriage is about building something together. Building what?

Is this what the hype is all about?

Is this what I davened for, hoped for, cried about?

Is this what everyone pushed me toward?

Is this all?

My husband is such a special human being. But so what?

For the record, despite everyone's mistaken shallow assumptions that I'm living happily ever after—

I'm not.

Even if he's a treasure, which he is, what does it help me if he's a buried treasure, completely inaccessible to me?

Elchanan's better at being a husband than I am at being a wife.

What can I do to improve things? No idea.

It's not fair. It's not fair!

First, I had to work so hard to get married. Now, I have to work so hard at being married.

When does the rewarding part come?

One more thing. All the articles say that healthy married couples fight, disagree, and all that. Well, I think that if the issues are small, like who takes out the garbage or leaving around socks, Elchanan and

I are good at that. But the big stuff, like discussions, communication. Hah!

What if I were to say, just for example, "Elchanan, do you have a moment? I want your opinion on something that's been bugging me."

"Sure, Estelle. What's on your mind?"

"Not much. Just wondering."

"I'm with you."

"Nah, forget it."

"Now I'm really curious. Come on, not fair."

"Forget it. Okay, but remember, you asked."

"I'm all ears. Sit down. Why are you standing?"

"Here goes: Should I have waited to get married to someone I liked more than you, even if we were both in our early forties? Want to talk about it?"

I don't want to picture the look on his face. Why should both of us be miserable?

Or how about this one?

"Elchanan, what do you think? I can't seem to figure this one out."

"Well, I'm no genius, but two heads are better than one. Go ahead."

"If you were my last chance at marriage, given that I refused to become a stepmother, and no other kind of suggestion was coming my way?"

"What are you trying to ask? I'm not sure where this line of thought is going."

"It's not going anywhere. I'm just babbling. But enough about me, Elchanan. Now it's your turn. Poor you. Maybe you could have done better. Maybe you should have dropped me after you started meeting with Dr. Schiff? He helped you figure out how to look less shlumpy and present yourself better. You could have started all over again! After all, you had no commitment to me. We'd gone out only twice? Three times? I certainly didn't give you a lot of encouragement. Hope I'm doing better now that we're married, but I'm not sure I am. You could have found someone who'd adore you, who'd be really happy to see you when you come home every day."

Strike that last remark from the record.

"Your mother would be pleased, and your father would be a lot happier with your choice."

"I chose you, Estelle. I'm a big boy."

"Well, thanks. Thanks, but these questions give me no peace of mind. Is there any place we could look this up?"

"Look up what, Estelle?"

"Does the statute of limitations for being ecstatic about someone stop after thirty, let's say?"

You know, Elchanan, when I write this stuff, I realize that I do kind of like you. You're a nice guy. For both of our sakes, I hope that's enough for me. Good enough to be, maybe not happy with, but content enough to be nice to you.

Wish it were true!

One more thing. Not his fault, but I feel like a total fool. All those times on dates he was sitting there with an EpiPen in his pocket, and I had no idea. Yup, and it would have been my fault completely because I stipulated no more hotel lobbies.

What if a bee had stung him?

I would have been devastated if anything had happened to him. I would have been much more than devastated, because—

Elchanan was my last chance. He was so much more than I dared even to daven for at my stage of the game.

I ought to be treating him like a king.

How much can I force, cajole, persuade myself to feel something I don't, just because I really should? Everyone else thinks I should feel that way, so who am I to disagree?

Why isn't that funny? I meant that last remark as a joke.

35
Shanah Rishonah

"Estelle? Take a look at this." Elchanan held out an open circular published by the Neot Yaar community.

Estelle got up from the couch, where she was relaxing with a book.

"So many different courses," she marveled, taking the small booklet from him and turning to the section for women's classes. "Let's see… I should sign up for some movement class, I guess. Question is, what? Pilates? Israeli dance? It would be great if they offered a beginners' class. Is there a beginners' class? As usual, all the dance classes are for advanced groups. What about the klutzes among us? I guess it will have to be Pilates."

"Do you want to take a Pilates class? It doesn't seem like you do."

"Nope. I don't want to. I hate all these yoga, Pilates stuff."

"Hate them? Why?"

"Because they're hard and boring. And super healthy, so that I feel guilty for not signing up this minute."

Elchanan laughed at her vehemence.

"It's not funny," she said, but she was smiling too. "I'm not joking. Unless you happen to be one of those fit, dancer types who flock to these classes, the I-started-ballet-classes-when-I-was-three-years-old type. They're the only people in the class who can actually locate all the muscles the instructor tells us about."

He laughed again.

"I'm never sure if I'm doing the exercises correctly or not, so who knows what benefit I'm getting? Dancing is a lot more enjoyable. I love dancing. The music is so beautiful. Not that I'm a good dancer, but over the years I've taken so many classes that I can sort of follow the teacher. Sometimes."

"Good for you."

"When's the Pilates class? Tuesday night? Right after my longest day at school too. Fine. I'll give them a call and register before the class is full. It says there are a limited number of places left." She started to dial the number.

"Slow down. Why on earth would you drag yourself after a long day at work to an activity you dislike?"

"Because it's good for my core muscles." She put down the phone.

"Forget Pilates. That's my advice. Everyone knows dancing is good for the heart and soul."

"I wish. My heart and soul are one story, but my core muscles are another. Unfortunately." She turned a page. "Aerobics? With teenagers? No way. Zumba? Riiiight." She handed the booklet back to him. "Too bad there's no beginners' dance class. The advanced one is way beyond me. I always want to be able to dance at weddings and all the rest, but everyone goes so fast. I finally get one of the steps and then another complicated one starts up. Forget it."

Elchanan listened appreciatively to her outpouring and felt her enthusiasm.

"I never knew you love to dance. You have so many talents,

Estelle. Drama, writing, and dancing too? I learn something new about you every day."

"It's nothing," Estelle said, flushing at his obvious fascination. "A lot of people like to dance. Why is something so common interesting? Besides, I told you, I'm not good at it."

He raised his eyebrows. "A lot of people aren't my wife. You are. I like learning new things about you."

"Thanks. That's kind of you. It's a moot point, though. They aren't offering a beginners' class." She made a face. "That's all I can handle, even though at this point, I should be very advanced."

"Who says? Isn't the main point to enjoy yourself?"

"Maybe it is, but I like to be good at what I do."

"There must be others in the community looking for an enjoyable activity. Why not ask around? If there are enough interested parties, they'd probably hire a teacher."

"Should I be that much of an activist?" she asked doubtfully.

"Give it a try. What do you have to lose?"

"Time? Wasted effort?"

"Or not."

"Maybe. Sounds like a lot of work, though. We'll see. Right now, I'm frustrated. Why isn't anything ever smooth and straightforward? Always a catch." She sighed moodily. "Did you want to show me something? Sorry I went on and on about myself."

"Yes, this." He pointed to a colorful full-page ad.

She glanced at the page and read aloud: "'Clowns for Kids—a new medical clown course that will change your life!'"

"This is right up my alley, Estelle. What do you think about my participating taking this three-month course to train as a medical clown?"

"A medical clown? Doesn't speak to *me*." Estelle plunked herself back down on the couch. "But if you think you want to look into it, why not?"

"Children in hospitals have always broken my heart," he explained. "When I think of doing something to cheer them up, something that can really help, I'd like nothing better."

"Well, if that's how you feel, naturally you should look into the course," Estelle said generously. "But why can't you just go visit the hospital on Shabbos afternoons? The next two months, Shabbos doesn't end till late."

His face brightened. "Yes, maybe I'll do that too. I think it's a marvelous opportunity to give in an enjoyable way. Did you ever think of how frightening a hospital must be to a child? I'd love to get a kid to smile during a scary medical procedure. Don't you wish you could do that?"

"No. I feel terrible for the kids and their parents, but hospitals are just not my thing at all."

"I hear you." He nodded understandingly.

"On the other hand, if you're thinking of taking a course, why choose that? If you want to move on from being a travel agent, maybe you want to pick up another marketable skill. There are men's classes in technical writing, computer programming, translation. You're good at languages, and you like to write. Why not try one of those?"

"I'd love to make someone's hospital stay even a tiny bit easier."

Estelle wrinkled her face, noting—too late—the way his shoulders had slumped at her instinctive response. He was so sensitive. She berated herself for her reaction, but—what should she do? Wasn't she entitled to an opinion? If he wasn't interested in what she thought, then why was he asking her advice?

"Elchanan? Do you want to know what I think, or do you prefer a sounding board?" She left the couch to sit opposite him at the table.

He shrugged. "You're entitled to your opinion. But what's wrong with a medical clown? Do you know how much good they do?"

"Nothing's *wrong* exactly."

"But?"

"I'm not giving a *psak* here, Elchanan. Don't go getting all hurt just because we aren't clones of each other."

"Nu? Go ahead, I won't melt because my *ezer kenegdo* is doing her job, being a *kenegdo*."

"All right. Remember, you asked, so don't be upset if I tell you what I think, okay?"

Elchanan chuckled. "Thanks for trying."

She simultaneously bristled, thinking, *Who is he, to condescend to me?* and blushed, pleased at his acknowledgment of her efforts. *I have been trying to respect his choices more, to judge favorably and assume they're coming from a worthy place that takes both of us into consideration. It hasn't been easy for me, either, so I'm glad he notices.*

"I have an idea. Why don't you offer to teach a course in marriage counseling or in counseling older singles?" she suggested, trying to think of a choice that would please them both. "It doesn't have to be *davka* in the community center if they don't want to offer it there. When we were dating, you wanted to study marriage counseling. It would be a great field for you to specialize in. I happen to think that your list of commonly held beliefs about older singles is very enlightening and very relevant, and what's more, anyone you show it to thinks the same thing. It's a dignified, mature way to give people encouragement and hope. How about it?"

"Wow! Thanks for the compliment. Medical clowning is respectable too, Estelle. This isn't out of left field. I've always been interested in doing something to alleviate the suffering of sick people. In any case, I am already counseling a few older singles, informally, of course."

"You never told me that!" Estelle felt a slight tug at her heart. "Why didn't you share that with me?"

"I don't know. Maybe because it's really no big deal. Nothing official. Remember how I told Dr. Schiff that I thought I could help chronic daters get unstuck?"

"Sure."

"So, he's been giving my number to certain of his clients. A success story, so to speak."

"You're doing it for free? Is it taking up a lot of your time?"

"Not always. Sometimes."

"Then I think you should ask for at least a symbolic fee," she said. "The people who call will take your advice more seriously if they have to pay for it. And they won't call you with every little issue if they know you charge for your services."

"I *want* them to feel free to call me," he protested. "People gave me advice when I was dating, and I'm just passing on the kindness, so to speak."

"Nope. I happen to know that your Dr. Schiff wasn't cheap."

"Worth every penny." He smiled at her. "He's a professional who specializes in dating and marriage issues, so he's entitled to charge a fee. I have no training in this field whatsoever."

"You experienced prolonged singlehood. In my opinion, that's worth much more than tons of theory from a guy, who, as I recall your telling me, married at age twenty-three."

"Thanks, Ess, but what can you do? A degree is a degree. I just have the benefit of my years and years of dating. Besides, I want to do something new. But if you're against it…" He paused. "I wish we were on the same page here."

"I'm not against it. We're not the same person. Do what makes you happy."

Elchanan tried to contain his disappointment. *I guess that's the best she can do. I wish she'd be proud of my ambition. That would feel very good. I'm ready to spread my wings, learn something completely new. I guess she is who she is.*

Estelle fidgeted in her seat. *I'm glad he can't read my mind. He's already not the most dignified-looking individual. There are too many moments when already he seems like a clown, at least to me. He'd be devastated if I told him that. Does he have to make things worse by turning himself into an actual clown? I've never liked clowns. Boy, am I glad he can't see my thoughts!*

Looking at his face, she felt her heart lurch with remorse.

"Elchanan, I never heard you mention this before now. I want to explain my reaction. You're forty-five years old, so I would have thought that you'd have already done something in a field you were interested in. In this case, acting, clowning, visiting sick people on a steady basis. You know what I mean?"

"Good point. But isn't liking a field, being drawn to it, often a sign of aptitude?"

"Sometimes." Estelle sighed in relief, as the relaxed, peaceful atmosphere returned to the room. Heading back to the couch, she opened her book again eagerly. It had been a long day, and some time to chill would feel good.

"It's to your credit," Elchanan said meditatively.

"Mine?" She looked up from her book. "What's to my credit?"

"I was busy all these years with lots of survival issues."

Her mouth fell open. She bolted upright. "What survival? Elchanan? Are you trying to tell me something?"

"Not physical survival. I didn't mean I hid some illness from you. Emotional survival. Now that I'm married, something's happened. Inside, I've sort of expanded. I feel more inner possibilities. Does that make sense to you?"

He was looking at her expectantly. Oh, my. I hope he won't ask me if I feel the same way.

"You're asking if it makes sense that a person would feel inner expansion after marriage? You often mentioned that idea to me when we were dating."

"You remember my saying that?"

She leaned against the arm of the couch and put her book carefully on the end table, trying to buy time. "You said it, and it's common knowledge. A lot of people told me that when I was dating, to make marriage seem more tempting."

"And?"

He wants me to tell him it's the same for me, that I feel the same way, but is it? Do I feel part of a unit? Expanded? I never thought of it that way. Mostly, I feel that I've lost independence. So much of the time, I'm frustrated beyond belief at so many trivial details of sharing my space with another human being. I've gained the status of being a married woman, plus the peace of mind of knowing that I didn't turn down a good opportunity. That would have haunted me.

He's still waiting.

"Of course I remember, and—"

"And?"

"As very frequently happens, you had a valid point."

"A valid point?"

Just say it. Maybe saying it will help me feel it. In any case, it's the only kind thing to do.

"It's mutual."

Her husband actually stood up and did a joyous jig. "So, see any aptitude for medical clowning?"

"Let me just ask this: do you really want to be involved in the medical field? Life-and-death dramas? Don't you find the responsibility terrifying? What if you make a mistake?" After she said it, she realized how foolish that sounded. What kind of a mistake could a clown make?

"If everyone gave into fear, the world would be a dismal place," he responded. "And sickness is an unavoidable fact of life. I wish it weren't, but since it is, I want to help."

"That's certainly commendable."

Elchanan was silent. After a moment, he began to speak. "Estelle," he said slowly, feeling his way, "I feel very strongly about the course in medical clowning. It may seem like a trivial ambition, but it's close to my heart. I don't know how to explain why that's so, I wish I did, but I don't. I'm signing up for the course."

"As you wish."

"It's right here in the neighborhood."

"Do what you want." Estelle picked up her book. Of course, she'd lost her place.

Her husband picked up the phone. "Hello, is this Clowns for Kids?"

"Speaking. How can I help you?"

"I was thinking about signing up for the course." He held his breath, trying to ignore Estelle's stare, and let it out when she left the room.

"We're starting our next course two weeks from Sunday. You have two options, either twice a week for three hours each session for twelve sessions, or our accelerated course, four hours twice weekly from five to nine in the evening for a total of nine sessions."

"How much does it cost?"

"The first meeting is an introductory one, and it's free. The full three-month course is 950 shekels, and the accelerated course is 1190 shekels."

He took a deep breath.

"Sign me up for the accelerated course."

* * *

"Doesn't he care? Shouldn't he respect my wishes?" Estelle never made private phone calls from the bus, but now, she was too upset to wait. The middle-aged woman in front of her turned around pointedly.

Estelle lowered her voice.

"Estelle, Estelle. Aren't you blowing something trivial way out of proportion?" Menucha asked.

"No, I'm not. I expressly told him that I wanted him to choose something more respectable."

"What's not respectable about being a medical clown? They do a lot of good."

"I'm happy they exist and do good. But he's my husband, and he, uh, isn't that impressive looking anyhow, and what he does reflects on me, okay? Now, do you get it?"

"Estelle, I'm starting to get really worried about you."

"Don't tell me you're on his side again."

"There are no sides here. Estelle, please. He's showing you that his patience isn't endless. Don't you see that?"

"So I should just erase myself."

"No. I didn't say that at all."

"Yes, you did. That's what you just told me to do. You want me to say, 'Yes, Elchanan, dear, do as you please. Make yourself into a fool in front of an audience. Go to hospitals where people know that we're married and make yourself look silly. Anything you say, dear. You know best, so please, go make a fool out of yourself in front of as many people as you can, Elchanan.'"

"Estelle, stop!"

36 Deadline

It was almost four. She was supposed to be in the office until five, but one of the perks of being employed in her husband's real estate business was that she made her own hours.

Menucha yawned and stretched. The warm Thursday afternoon felt more like spring than summer. It was a day made for being outdoors on their shady patio, breathing in the fragrance of the many flowers she and Halleli had planted the previous summer. It was not a day to be shut up in an office, however attractively furnished and temperature controlled.

It was a day for...for...

For a family barbecue! Eliezer enjoyed manning the grill. *If* she could convince him to leave early and stay off his phone and computer.

Not happening.

Then maybe at least during supper. Maybe he'd unwind enough to tell her why he was so out of sorts.

Menucha grinned. It was a plan.

She looked at the to-do list she'd compiled at the week's beginning. Most of the items had a neat checkmark next to them. Yup. This week, as always, she'd achieved most of her goals. It felt good. Very good. There was nothing like success. It was all about organization, and about facing up to unpleasant tasks.

She hummed contentedly. She knew she wasn't perfect, no one was, but she prided herself on the fact that she hardly ever permitted herself to procrastinate, no matter how daunting the job. It was hard, it was often inconvenient, even scary, but the rewards of her policy were clear. An impressive lineup of accomplishments smiled at her. She smiled back triumphantly.

Eliezer sometimes complained that she never slowed down, but here was her justification, black on white. Now the burning question was, how could she best pass on these essential life lessons to Halleli?

Her smile faded. It was downright embarrassing the way Halleli was making her look like an inept parent in front of Sheila Leipzig, of all people. Sheila had high standards; she wasn't exactly the soft, forgiving type. Not that she had a right to judge since she wasn't a parent herself, but still.

Her face clouded. That one unfinished project, the reason she was going to have to remain in the office, was none other than Sheila Leipzig herself. Sheila still hadn't called back about renting the Bellinson property. She was acting irresponsibly. It would serve her right if the Bellinsons gave up on her and rented to someone else or even better, sold their apartment.

I'm being vindictive.

Most annoying was that Halleli was going to be penalized for not meeting a deadline, but Sheila thought she could get off scot-free for the same type of thing.

Poor Halleli.

Not that she didn't agree with Sheila about the girls' obligation to adhere to a schedule, meet deadlines, and hand in their assignments in a timely fashion. Menucha bit her lower lip in frustration. If she asked Sheila to extend the final deadline of the seventh-grade history presentation, she would refuse. Then she could casually mention that everyone was human, and everyone missed deadlines occasionally for perfectly legitimate reasons. Why, even the most organized, considerate adults had been known to let other people down by not getting back to them when they said they would.

That ought to convince her not to take off ten grade points for not making the deadline.

As if. She was talking about I-never-make-a-mistake Sheila.

That approach would be very effective with some personalities. Estelle, for example, would fall all over herself apologizing. Then again, she'd avoid all confrontation in the first place.

Sheila would listen politely and then explain, ever so persuasively, that the girls were at an important age to learn responsibility, and that a lower grade was a relatively painless way to learn that priceless lesson.

Menucha frowned. Sheila was no soft touch. She couldn't be intimidated, um, persuaded. It wouldn't be easy to get her to change her mind. However, she planned to do just that. She'd pull rank if she had to. She'd tell Sheila that a lot of parents were displeased with her overly strict approach and that she needed to lighten up. And besides, she was just a substitute.

She'd texted her repeatedly about both the deadline and the Bellinson place but the week had gone by with no response whatsoever. Did Sheila think Menucha had nothing better to do than play phone tag with her?

Menucha felt her head tighten with anger. Not good. That meant that her blood pressure was rising. A rise in blood pressure was a sign that once again, where Sheila Leipzig was involved, she, Menucha Shalom, was becoming too emotionally involved.

Too bad that Sheila was too arrogant to accept advice. Was it insecurity? Maybe. She understood where Sheila was coming from. She too was once an older single. Teaching was probably the only area where Sheila still felt in control. That said, she could not be permitted to vent her frustrations on the kids. Let her go to therapy to work out her issues.

Menucha bit her lower lip in irritation.

She'd gone the extra mile for Sheila Leipzig. Make that the extra miles. As soon as the Bellinsons told her they were apprehensive about selling their home and moving near their daughter, she'd thought of Sheila. She was the one who steered them in the direction of opting for a six-month rental. Then she'd contacted Sheila to notify her of the rare opportunity that had come her way.

And this is the thanks she got.

Menucha tapped a pen absentmindedly against her teeth. At first, Sheila had seemed enthusiastic, ready to sign a contract with the Bellinsons that very week and move out of her parent's home later that month. Now she was holding up the entire process by making herself incommunicado.

If she'd changed her mind, all she had to do was say so.

Menucha decided that this time instead of texting she'd call and leave a message on Sheila's voicemail.

"Hello, Sheila. This is Menucha Shalom—again. This is urgent. The Bellinsons are waiting for your answer. Please call to let me know your decision regarding their apartment. We'll be in touch. Also, I wanted to consult you about another urgent matter that concerns school, so please call me as soon as you can."

Menucha took a sip of coffee. Too black, too bitter. She put down the mug and opened the small office refrigerator to take out the milk.

"Cup of coffee?" she asked her husband.

He shook his head.

She added milk to the coffee. Her phone beeped, and she pounced on it triumphantly. *Sheila. Finally.*

But no, it was her new cleaning lady calling to confirm her arrival the following morning.

Menucha gritted her teeth. She was leaving early, and too bad for Sheila.

"Eliezer?"

He looked up from his computer. "Yes?"

"I'm going home now. I'm through for the week, and guess what?"

"What?"

"You're coming with me."

"I am?" He looked amused.

"Yes, you are. Look at this glorious weather we're having. You need a break. You've been looking—"

"I know how I've been looking," he said. "Sit down, Menucha. We need to talk."

Apprehension flooded her. He looked so serious. "I'm listening."

It took fifteen minutes. Fifteen life-altering minutes. When he finished, Menucha said quietly, "This has been on your mind for some time, hasn't it."

"Yes, it has."

"Why didn't you say anything until now?"

He smiled sadly. "We have Halleli. I tried to tell myself that that was enough, but it's not."

"And?" She knew there was more.

"I didn't want to hurt you."

Adoption!

You're a failure! her mind was screaming. *You're failing where it matters the most. Your husband wants another child, and you can't give him one.*

"I'm sorry to have failed you," she whispered.

"Menucha, that's not it!" He spread his hands in a gesture of helplessness.

"What then?'

"Halleli is the joy of my life, but—"

"But?"

"I want a son, Menucha. I want a son."

"I know." Menucha tried to smile at her husband, but her lips wouldn't obey. Draining her coffee in one long gulp, she found that despite the milk, it had a bitter aftertaste.

Sheila

Judgment Call

I should have dealt with these questions much earlier, instead of hoping that the issues would become clear while we were dating. Too late.

She seized a pen and wrote.

How would Yerachmiel react if, G-d forbid, I were to become handicapped or disfigured?

How would Yerachmiel react if my family lost its money or social standing?

This isn't helping me. A picture of his hurt face asking why she didn't trust him to be a *mentsch* was enough for her to crumple up the paper and toss it, with unerring aim, into the wastebasket in the far corner of her room

She had started a list of pros and cons after the second date. Where was it?

She dug through her desk drawer, finally emptying it out onto the burgundy carpet, uncharacteristically disregarding the mess. It didn't matter. Nothing really mattered.

Am I really going to do this to myself? Am I going to break off a promising relationship with a person who cares about me and wants to take care of me forever, just because I don't think he asks enough of himself? Because I'm afraid that I'll stop respecting him and that will ruin our marriage?

Sheila smoothed the paper. It was divided into two columns and dated around a month ago. She read the words she'd hurriedly scribbled late that night: "Con: I'm not sure if he'd still like me if my resume were less impressive. What if only the essential me was left? What then?"

She'd never felt more bewildered or more alone in her entire life. Tears rolled down her cheeks, staining the paper.

She got up and looked at herself in the mirror, at her eyes, now puffy and bloodshot. Just outside her closed bedroom door were people ready and willing to give her advice. The problem was, she knew her parents thought she was being ridiculous. Her mother especially felt she should seize with both hands the opportunity Hashem had sent her way.

"We don't share the same basic values," she said aloud. "I know he thinks my feelings for the girls I teach, like Sarah, for instance, are just a pathetic substitute for the real thing, my own kids. Is he right? I hope not, but who knows?"

She forced herself to continue. "I'm ambitious. I'm an ambitious, goal-oriented woman. I never realized how much I admire ambition in another human being, but I do. I like him too much to see him objectively, but that feeling won't last if it's not strongly backed by building together. He lives solely for himself. He doesn't seem to connect to the concept of sacrificing for something bigger than himself. At his age, he won't change.

"How can he be content to go through life the way he is? So small, so trivial, so self-centered? I can't respect a guy with such narrow goals. I'll end up despising him."

Five blocks away, there was a man who was convinced that he was her *bashert*. He was almost definitely thinking about her. Not almost. He *was* thinking about her. She'd just follow his lead.

I can't. Sheila sank down on the plush rug and sobbed.

She tried to start from the beginning, back to their first phone call. He'd called after the time and venue for their first date had been finalized, and she'd been surprised.

"Yerachmiel Kantor speaking."

"Hello."

"I want to make something clear before we even start."

Oh, my. Physical illness? Mental? "Yes?"

"I want you to know that my fortieth birthday was last week."

"Mazel tov."

"Thanks. So, to make a long story short, on the off chance that anyone shaved a decade or so off my age to get you to meet me, those are the facts."

"Well, thank you. I appreciate your honesty, but I already knew how old you are more or less."

"I'm wondering why you agreed to meet me then," he'd said bluntly. "I'm quite a bit older than you are. Don't tell me that the pool of guys closer to your age is all used up because I won't believe you."

"Why did I agree to meet you? I liked what I heard about you."

"Which was?"

She'd felt a twinge of pity, which she'd suppressed. She didn't think he'd appreciate pity.

"For starters, let's see, you are Jewish, *frum*, never married—"

"You haven't told me anything you heard that would tilt the scales in my favor."

Someone took the wind out of his sails. I wonder if he knows how obvious he's making that fact? "You had the ambition and drive to start your own band and build it into one of the most successful ones around. Plus, I was told that you're kindhearted and generous with your possessions and time. I liked those facts, so I'm planning to meet you tomorrow night, a block away from school. Good enough for starters?"

Yerachmiel had chuckled. "Good enough."

"See you tomorrow then."

"Yes, *b'ezras Hashem*. I'm looking forward to meeting you, at long last."

Sheila appreciated directness; she liked sincerity. The relationship, she'd decided, was off to a good start, and she'd been determined to match his honesty with forthrightness of her own. She'd been telling him the truth. His age made no difference to her. She had begun the relationship intending to discover what made him tick. She was determined to discover the rich inner world Avital Salamonte had adamantly claimed he possessed. What were his life choices and why had he made them?

My eyes are wide open now. We both stand to lose so much if I say no, and if I say yes, then what?

If she said yes to another date, and then yet another, in one short month, give or take, she'd be Mrs. Yerachmiel Kantor. Was that really so terrible?

If I say no…

The phone rang. Her eyes blurred with tears.

I need to do this. I'll ask him all the questions I've been avoiding until now, all the questions I've been terrified to ask him. Yerachmiel, you hate being pressured, but I'll do it for both our sakes.

The phone was still ringing. Julia Yanavov. "Hello? Sheila?

"Yes, this is Sheila. How are you, Julia?"

"*Baruch Hashem*, all is well with me personally."

"Good, good."

"And yourself?"

"I'm doing well, *baruch Hashem*." Sheila waited for Julia to get to the point.

"So." Julia cleared her throat. "Rika stopped coming to the class, but she asked me to convey her sincere apologies for the way she spoke to you."

"It's fine," Sheila said listlessly.

"She's a troubled little girl. We do our best." Julia sighed. "I'm calling to ask you for a favor."

"What?"

"I convinced Rika's mother to celebrate her bas mitzvah."

"Good!"

Another sigh. "But now her mother just called me, and she's very upset."

"Why?"

"They have very little money. Rika has her heart set on having a band. She issued an ultimatum: no band, no bas mitzvah. You told me that the young man you've been seeing has a band, so I thought that perhaps you might be able to help out."

"I hear you, Julia. I'll speak to him and let you know as soon as possible."

"Thank you."

Yerachmiel, I can't marry a man whose main goal in life is to preserve his own comfort. I'll never respect a man like that. You see that, don't you?

38
Fault Line

Travel conditions weren't optimal at six on a Thursday evening, but Yerachmiel doubted that the traffic jam was adequate reason for Sheila's pensive mood and subdued demeanor. The quiet in the car was making him feel uneasy, for reasons he couldn't pinpoint. Usually, he and Sheila had no problem maintaining a smooth flow of conversation, but today, she wasn't herself.

"You're very quiet, Sheila," he said. "Why?"

"Just thinking."

"Care to share?" He took his eyes off the road briefly to smile at her.

"Okay. I want to ask you a favor."

"A favor? Sure, ask away."

"It's not for me.

"All right."

"It involves Rina-O-Mangina."

"Okay. What about the band?"

"You know the class I give on Shabbos?"

"Yes."

"Did I tell you about Rika?"

"You did."

"She's having a bas mitzvah next week."

"Mazel tov."

"No, not mazel tov."

There was an edge in Sheila's tone that made Yerachmiel slow down.

"What are you doing?"

"Parking." He parked the car. "What's on your mind?"

'"Let's say that someone vulnerable asks you to stretch yourself, and you find it inconvenient in terms of timing, or money, or whatever?"

"Yes?"

"How would you react?"

"Sheila, could you just ask straight out?"

"Julia Yanavov asked me if you could come with the band and play at Rika's bas mitzvah. Gratis. They can't afford to pay for a band. It would mean so much to her."

"And to you?"

She crossed her arms. "Forget me for a second. Rika needs the help. She's gotten a very raw deal in life so far."

"From what you've told me, I agree. But you're asking for a very big favor. I would do it for you, on a one-time basis, or for a family member, gladly. I'd pay the other musicians out of my own pocket. But this is a *parnassah,* Sheila. Rina-O-Mangina is booked solid months in advance. There are cheaper bands out there."

"I'll pay you."

"Don't be ridiculous."

"I'm not being ridiculous at all. If the band is all about money, about turning a profit, I'll pay you for your valuable time."

"I didn't say that. You can't be serious, Sheila." Yerachmiel looked angry, for the first time since she'd met him. "I do my best, Sheila, but I'm only human. Why do you want me to be larger than life?" His voice broke. "I'm not you, Sheila. I'm just me. I wasn't brought up to be responsible for the welfare of the entire Jewish people. You know… there's another possible reaction, if you wanted to make another normal, decent human being feel supported instead of constantly on probation."

"Is that how you feel? On probation?"

"About this issue? To be honest, yes. Very much so."

"I didn't know." Her face turned pale. "What's the second option, the one you prefer?"

"You could tell me that you understand my reaction, that you don't condemn it. Or, better yet, and I hate buzzwords, but you could validate my judgment."

"Don't you want to do something great with your life? Don't you realize that the more people you care about, the bigger a person you become?"

He took a deep breath. "I'm sorry, Sheila, but no. I don't. I'm not wired that way. I don't object to your wanting me to grow in that area. Maybe, with you at my side, I could learn to see life from a broader perspective and reach out a bit further than I do at present. What I do object to is what you're implying now."

"I'm so sorry," she whispered.

"I'll give my all to support my wife and children, but the entire Jewish people? That's a different story. If you wanted me to, let's say, contribute toward her bas mitzvah celebration, I could see that."

"No, forget it."

"Okay." He started the car.

The silence was thick with tension.

"Where would you like to go, Sheila?"

"I'm not sure about anything anymore."

"Should I choose a place?"

"No. I think… Yerachmiel, could we drive back home?"

39
Broken

"I'd like to give that girl a piece of my mind," Elisheva said. "How dare she tell Yerachmiel that his lifestyle choices are too narrow, shallow, and self-centered? She's lucky she's not here, or I'd give her a good telling off. Who does she think she is? Yerachmiel is worth ten of her. She's not serious about getting married, that's all."

"You can't know that." Shlomo was determined to see things rationally. One of them had to do that, and it clearly wasn't going to be his wife. "She explained that she's not as positive as she needs to be that they're suited to each other. And you know what? I don't think it's about any of those things you mentioned."

"Then what?"

"He's too laid back for her, Elisheva. He's just not driven enough. He's satisfied with what he's achieved with his band, and now he's finally ready to look seriously for a wife. She wants to marry someone high-powered, someone who'll take the world by storm."

"She needed so many dates to ascertain that? Each date was three, four hours long. What is she, an eighteen-year-old? Don't you dare defend her, Shlomo Kantor. Did you see the look on his face when he came over yesterday? A three-month break?"

"Her recommendation was that they take a break and date other people for a couple of months. I'm not saying it's easy, but it might not be such a bad idea."

"Our son begged her for that tiny concession, and she agreed. Throw the dog a bone. But you and I both know that she's just trying to let him down easy."

"Not necessarily. I believe she meant what she said when she told him she needs perspective. I think it shows how much she cares for Yerachmiel because she doesn't strike me as the type who has a hard time saying no."

"Why is she playing with him? A flat-out no would be better, if you ask me. He's better off forgetting he ever met her. Deep down, Yerachmiel realizes that too. He's just putting a good face on things. He's broken, that's what he is."

"Elisheva, be fair. Would you prefer that he pressure her into an engagement she'd eventually break?"

"No, but he won't meet anyone else. He'll wait for her. I know him too well." Elisheva slumped down in her chair and buried her face in her hands. "Yerachmiel will turn into a cranky old bachelor who tries to hide his heartbreak from the world, but at home, he won't succeed. He'll be snappish and irritable because he's lost hope."

"Dismal picture," Shlomo said. "Remember, time heals all wounds. It's only been a week since they decided to take a break."

Her head snapped up. "*They*? Excuse me, but *she* decided to stop."

"Admit that that's one possible outcome when people go out. He'll have to get over it."

"She sprang this on him with no warning. Not even a hint. She didn't let on in any way that they weren't going to get engaged, never mentioned any doubts. One possible outcome? How can you speak so coldly? He'll get over this? If you think that, you don't understand him. He feels very deeply. He was committed to this relationship. I'm afraid for him."

"If she decides that she wants to stop altogether, he'll have no choice." Shlomo sighed heavily. "He'll have to make peace with his situation and move on. I believe, trust, and hope that eventually, he'll find the strength to do so."

The phone rang.

"If it's for me," she said, "tell whoever it is that I'll call back."

He nodded sympathetically and picked up the phone. After he'd listened for a moment, he held it out to his wife.

"I told you—"

"It's Eva," he said. "She's calling with a *shidduch* suggestion for Yerachmiel. The same one she suggested last week."

Elisheva shook her head but took the call. "Eva, I'm really sorry, but it's too soon. His pain is too raw."

"You can't give in to his pain any more than you have. You aren't helping him that way. Time to move on. Sheila's had time enough to change her mind. If she hasn't called by now, she's not going to."

"He can't. He'd just be going through the motions. It's unfair to the girl. Devora Levin, you told me her name is?"

"Yes. I'm going to check her out."

"I should do it. I'm his mother."

"You've just sustained a blow."

"Thanks," Elisheva managed to choke out before she hung up the phone.

40 Finished

"It's Yerachmiel Kantor."

Miriam Leipzig stood in the entrance to her daughter's room holding the house phone.

Sheila's eyes teared. "Tell him I'm not available," she whispered.

"I won't lie," her mother said. "You *are* here, and you *are* available, and I won't say anything different."

"But, Ima, we broke up. We're taking a break. I've told him that every day for the past week. It's enough. If we talk on the phone every day, how is that called taking a break? Tell him that I ask that he not call until the three months are up, and then, maybe Avital will contact him."

"Tell him that yourself. I'll have no part in encouraging this immaturity."

Sitting in his small living room, ear pressed to the receiver, Yerachmiel froze. She wasn't coming to the phone.

"Yerachmiel?"

It was her mother.

"Sheila will call you back in five minutes, all right?"

He grasped at the lifeline. "It's fine. Thank you." *I can't take much more of this.*

"Why did you tell him that?" Sheila asked her mother. "Why encourage him? It's cruel."

"You owe him that much, and you owe yourself that much too. For once in your life, realize that someone may be smarter than you."

Sheila waited until she was certain her mother was out of earshot and then called him.

"Yerachmiel, we had an agreement."

"Sheila."

"Yerachmiel, we agreed to take a break for three months. If you are unable to abide by the terms of our decision, then—"

"*Our* decision? I don't remember arriving at any decision at all; I was just along for the ride." He paused. "Laugh, Sheila, that was a joke. We were in the car when you made the decision, so I was along for the ride, get it?"

Her voice was chilly. "If you refuse to abide by our decision, then forget about three months."

"Forget?" His voice lifted in hope. "I was hoping you'd see how silly it was to stop a…promising relationship over some random discussion."

"Forget, as in not after three months, either."

"You can't mean that."

"I do."

"But why? Sheila, please, just tell me why you're so upset with me? I wasn't thinking straight. Look, I'll come to Rika's bas mitzvah, and I'll bring my keyboard with me. I'm sorry, I just don't take well to being pressured."

"She already had her bas mitzvah."

"Was it nice?"

"It was fine. I told you that already. I told you that I don't want you to do these kinds of things for me. I want them to evolve naturally from the person you are, or at least from the person you aspire to become. Otherwise, I won't be able to respect you. You already promised that your decision has nothing to do with me, but please, let's be honest with each other: We don't share the same goals."

"We can work on that. We can discuss it."

"Yerachmiel, I need to get off the phone."

41

Alternate Route

Yerachmiel felt cheapened. He'd offered Sheila the best he had to offer, and she'd turned it down. He'd shown her all that was best and biggest in himself, and it hadn't been good enough. He felt ugly. When he looked in the mirror, he saw a downward turn to his lips, to his eyes, that hadn't been there. What was the point of anything, really? There was no point. Was she thinking of him? Did she ever think of him? Who cared if she did? No was no. As soon as he was able, he'd gather the broken shards of who he was. Yes, and then what? He didn't know.

* * *

Sheila leaned her aching head on the door of her home, reliving her day. She couldn't face her mother's disapproval just yet.

Going on was hard enough. Going on was hard and painful. Going on when the people closest to her didn't understand was unbearable.

Yerachmiel would have tried to understand. He'd have offered her his support. She could just call him, and—

Plunge back into the same sea of doubts.

She'd done the right thing. It would get easier.

Maybe. No guarantees.

I've changed. People are living entire lives while trying to cope with a feeling of something crucial missing. Just missing. How did I never see that before?

Osnat Portal had come over to her with a confident smile just two hours previously, Halleli Shalom at her side as usual. It was a week before the history project was due. Osnat was holding a signed note from her mother, which she placed on her teacher's desk. Sheila looked at her questioningly.

"You see, first my brother had a bar mitzvah, and then, my oldest sister got engaged, so that's why my mother is giving me permission to hand in the history report late. Me and Halleli."

It was most definitely the wrong way to put a request. Sheila's temper flared.

"Did you happen to mention that this project was assigned over two months ago?"

Osnat's smile flickered, then disappeared. She snatched the note off the desk.

"Give me that note, please," Sheila commanded. "I'd like to tell your mother when you were told about this assignment since you seem to have forgotten to tell her that fact. I'm sure that if she'd known, there's no way she'd try to force me—to ask me—to agree to an extension."

Halleli Shalom pulled urgently at her friend's shoulder. The two friends conferred hastily. This time, it was Halleli who approached her teacher, fiddling nervously with the end of her long black braid.

"Morah, we started on time. We really, really did. We worked together every night all last week." Behind her, Osnat nodded her vigorous agreement. "It's just that we got stuck, and my mother couldn't help us because she was very busy at work, and, um, then Osnat's mother couldn't help us either because of the bar mitzvah and so…"

"And so, maybe I ought to give your mothers grades."

"We just get our mothers to help out a little bit so it should be perfect."

"I'll think about it."

Both girls were perfectionists. Sheila knew that. Their request was just one of the many she'd been bombarded with in the week prior.

It was unfortunate that she caught Osnat's triumphant smirk, and her too-loud whisper, "Good for you, Halleli. You know how to get the grown-ups to do things. Teach me your secret."

Halleli's response sealed their fate.

"I overheard my mother on the phone last night."

"Really?"

"Yeah, explaining to your mother that Morah Sheila's having a tough time and that the parents should be extra sensitive and careful with her feelings. She said that teaching's the only stable thing in Morah Sheila's life now."

I've turned into an object of pity. Forget chinuch, forget teaching the kids responsibility. If they can't push the teacher around, it's because the teacher can't cope with real life. How twisted can people's thinking get before they realize that they're ruining good kids with misplaced indulgence?

Sheila exited the classroom, furious.

* * *

"Many pupils requested extensions on the date the history project is due. Some pupils even brought in notes from their parents," Sheila stated the next day in a tone she tried to keep neutral.

An excited rustle swept through the room.

"No extensions whatsoever," she announced, staring Halleli straight in the eyes.

Halleli lowered her glance, as rebellious muttering swept through the classroom.

"There will be absolutely no exceptions whatsoever."

"Not true! Sarah Roth and Mindy Lavie got an extension," someone hissed.

Sheila glared forbiddingly around the classroom. "All you girls need to get something straight," she stated icily. "It seems that unfortunately, a number of you managed to convince one or two grown-ups that you are helpless and incapable of coping in the real world."

Osnat whispered behind her hand to Halleli.

"You can't have it both ways. Either you are on the way to developing the skills all grown-ups need, or you can hide behind your par—, behind people who aren't used to the fact that you're well on your way to maturity."

The classroom was utterly silent.

"The person you'll affect the most is none other than yourself. Sure, you can keep taking refuge behind a convenient adult. Or, you can face the music. It may be uncomfortable, but there are benefits. If you stop evading responsibility for your actions, you'll develop a crucial skill for lifelong success. If you stop looking for the easy way out, you grow as a person. The choice is yours."

* * *

"Speeches are all very well, but grades trump bravery most of the time. I sincerely pity any parent who calls me tonight to pull *shtick,*" Sheila said to Estelle later in the teachers' room. "I can't tell you all the details because you'll guess who I'm talking about, but the mood I'm in, I don't care what anyone says to anyone about my teaching skills or lack thereof."

"Good for you," Estelle said. "I'd be quaking in my boots. By the way, I'm sure that many of the girls took what you said to heart. I think you'll be very pleasantly surprised at how many parents will respond positively to your message."

"I hope. I'm too angry. Nobody, and I mean nobody gets away with trying to manipulate me. Never have and never will." She paused, breathing hard.

"I'm rooting for you," Estelle said, encouragingly. "I admire your guts."

I wonder if you'd sing the same tune if you knew who I'm referring to. Everyone knows you and Menucha Shalom are very close friends.

* * *

Zev Schwartz picked at his microwaved baked potato. He could put some cottage cheese on it to make it more nutritious. The last remnants of the container of salad his mother had sent with him after Shabbos were long gone. Another royal repast of baked potato and salt awaited his dining pleasure. He was always welcome to eat supper with his parents, but paradoxically, being his parents' perpetual house guest made him feel even more alone. Besides, his only daughter, six-year-old Chaya, needed the stability of her own home and her own bed, with a consistent bedtime routine.

Tonight, he'd eaten supper together with Chaya, but he hadn't had much appetite at five thirty in the evening. Listening with half an ear, and half a heart, to her chatter about her day in school, he half regretted his choice to feed her dinner at home. If he were to tell the truth, Chaya, deeply as he loved her, didn't provide much in the way of company. Her stories of teachers and friends weren't all that interesting to him. Her long-winded way of telling them did little to enhance their content. Listening to her high-pitched prattle, he'd stifled his boredom, smiled, and asked all the right questions, while waiting longingly for her bedtime.

Zev was feeling too low-spirited to cope well with any additional emotional discomfort, even one as trivial as boredom. He was doing his best to be an involved, attentive parent, even if he often felt that he was pushing an unbearably heavy heart uphill, with no respite in sight.

In the final analysis, how he felt was irrelevant. Chaya was his daughter, and he was her only surviving parent.

Now, she was asleep. As he listened to her even breathing, he wondered how to survive the rest of his life.

His wife had reveled in motherhood, never uttering a word of complaint about sleepless nights spent pacing the hallways with a colicky baby who was only content being held. She'd willingly exchanged her job as a buyer of women's clothing to stay at home, telling stories, building Lego towers, dealing with repetitious activities, noise, mess....

She'd passed away two years previously. He and his young daughter were left bereft. Physically, they were managing, surrounded as they were by devoted family and caring neighbors, but emotionally?

Chaya seemed to be going on with her life; her father was another story. Zev couldn't remember the last time he'd laughed or felt content, though he wore a happy face at work. As he cleared the table, he wondered bleakly if it was possible to choke on loneliness.

Here in Neot Yaar, where they'd relocated after Frieda passed away, surrounded by her grandparents, aunts, uncles, and cousins, he could almost fool himself into thinking his daughter had everything she needed to thrive. He could almost convince himself that she wouldn't notice his absence. In two short months, he had a commitment to be a *chazzan* for a community in Scotland. Didn't his commitment to his daughter come first, though? Maybe he should cancel. Then again, maybe not. He was longing to get away, breathe different air, air that he and Frieda hadn't shared. Air with no memories.

42 Fresh Start

"Menucha? Hi, it's Sheila, Sheila Leipzig. I owe you an apology for keeping you hanging this week." Sheila swallowed hard. "There was...a lot going on in my life."

"Sheila? Is that you? You sound like you have a bad cold. I'm sorry, I didn't realize you were under the weather," Menucha said. "Halleli didn't tell me you were absent—though, you're the type to come to school no matter what."

"I don't have a cold. I'm fine," Sheila said. *And if I'm plagued by doubts, and if Yerachmiel keeps pleading with me to change my mind, and if my father keeps telling me to reconsider, and my mother's snapping at me, that's the name of the game, isn't it?* "I'd like to take the apartment. Is it still available?"

"Yes, it is."

"Then I'd like to rent it for the six-month period they suggested. If you could just let the Bellinsons know about my decision..." Her voice faltered. "I'd like to sign a contract as soon as possible."

"I'll speak to the Bellinsons and get back to you." *Halleli had told her that something happened to Morah Sheila. Did Sheila really think that a group of sharp-eyed seventh graders wouldn't notice her red-rimmed eyes? Did she really think they bought her excuse about seasonal allergies acting up? They might have, but not after Osnat Portal saw Sheila sitting in her car in the school's parking lot last week, reading her text messages and sobbing. The girls hadn't stopped talking about it, and she couldn't blame them. Obviously, Sheila had broken up with someone.*

Poor thing. She wasn't getting any younger. Who broke it up, Sheila or the guy? It must have been Sheila. No man in his right mind would reject her.

She had piles of work on her desk, emails to answer, calls to return, but Menucha ignored it all. Instead, she thought long and hard about how life was so unpredictable.

* * *

Geula speaks:

Something's up with Sheila, and that something has removed the bounce from her step, the verve from her speech, and the radiance from her smile. At her stage of the game, it's only natural to assume that the some*thing* is some*one*—someone very significant, someone who mattered to her a lot, someone she admired and respected and liked.

I wish she'd confide in me. Not because I'm nosy, but because she looks so forlorn. It's hard to see her looking so bereft, poor thing. At least, that's what I tell myself.

It's hard for me to say "poor Sheila" as sincerely as I should. She keeps me out of her life with an invisible barrier that's far more effective than temper or rudeness, which is too bad. I've been through a thing or two, and I could help her get through this intact. If her need to maintain a perfect image is more important than simple human warmth and the feeling that we're all in it together, that's her choice to make.

In my unsolicited opinion, she shouldn't have turned him down, whoever he is. Anyone impressive enough to make an impression on Sheila must have a lot going for him. There can't be too many men like that around.

I realize I'm building a mountain of assumptions here. One, that she's so devastated because of a guy. Well, come on. What else could it possibly be? Two, that she was the one to break things off. But then, what normal, thinking person would turn down Sheila?

What's certain is that something happened and that something is big.

Poor Sheila. My heart goes out to her despite myself. I wish I could help.

It's not only about Sheila if I'm being honest here. Witnessing the raw pain that she tries so hard and so unsuccessfully to hide brings back memories I wanted to bury forever.

I still can't say his name without doubling over, so I won't. It happened this past summer, the last year I taught in the other school. We were very compatible, and things were moving in the right direction. I couldn't believe it. I couldn't wrap my mind around the incredible fact that someone so perfect for me even existed at our late stage of the game.

I didn't believe it, but it was true. Until it wasn't.

I was thrilled to hear his voice whenever he called. We'd just gone out on our seventh date the week before, and I was ready to move on to the next stage. Ready to get engaged.

He was too, but, as he told me on that seventh date—which was also our last date ever—he needed a favor from me.

I have a small mole, some might call it a beauty mark, just above my lip. I think it's kind of cute, if I think about it at all. Turns out that he wanted me to have it surgically removed. Turns out that it was standing in his way. In our way.

I was more than shocked. I was insulted and deeply hurt. I felt diminished in ways I can't even begin to explain. Most of all, I was taken aback. I happen to be very nice looking. I'm not boasting, that's just the way it is. Quite honestly, I was baffled. Sure, I liked him a lot, more than anyone I'd ever met, but did that mean he was perfect? No, it definitely did not mean that *at all*.

"No way," I said incredulously.

To give him credit, he looked wretched.

"I'm so sorry, Geula," he said, and I could tell that he was very sincere. "You're such a special person. But this has been on my mind since our first date."

"It has?"

"Yes. I've tried to overlook it, but it's impossible." He looked even more miserable. "I just can't do it. It's getting in the way of how I feel about you." He swallowed hard. "How I want to feel about you."

"You can't mean that."

"I wish I didn't."

I don't know what we talked about next. I don't know how I got home. What I do remember, acutely and piercingly, was how our conversation went flat after that bombshell. I had nothing more to say to him.

The pain is still fresh, and seeing Sheila like this brings it all flooding back.

* * *

"Hello, am I speaking to Yehudit Sapir?"

"Speaking. Who is this please?"

"My name is Eva Goldenberg. I'm calling on behalf of my nephew, Yerachmiel Kantor?"

"The head of Rina-O-Mangina?"

"None other."

"Yes?" *For me? To go out with me?*

"I received your name as a reference for a young woman by the name of Devora Levin. I understand that the two of you have shared an apartment for a number of years?"

"Yes, we're very good friends." *Oh, yay! Devora hasn't had a normal suggestion in two or three months. Wow! I didn't know that Yerachmiel Kantor was single. I wonder why no one ever suggested him to either of us before.*

"Then you probably know her well. I've been told she's an attractive woman with above average social graces."

"She's very pretty and charming," Yehudit said. *I like this lady.*

"Speaking of age, how old is Devora? I couldn't get a straight answer from anyone I asked. You may fudge by a year or so, but please, no more than that."

"Rebbetzin Goldenberg, we are talking about someone who's honest to a fault. She never says anything that's not 100 percent accurate. Speaking in her name, I can tell you that she just celebrated her thirty-sixth birthday five months ago."

"Around thirty-four years old then," Rebbetzin Goldenberg decided.

Didn't you hear what I said? On second thought, silence was the better part of discretion in this case.

"I'm going to come straight to the point. I've heard lovely things about her. She's apparently an accomplished musician, just as he is. It seems that she possesses many of the attributes my nephew is looking for in a wife." Eva paused.

"I think she'd make some man a wonderful wife," Yehudit said with emphatic loyalty.

"I'll tell you this in confidence. Yerachmiel just endured the painful dissolution of a relationship with a girl he hoped to marry."

"I'm so sorry to hear that."

"That's why I want to be very careful with whom I set him up. I'm veering in the direction of setting the two of them up. They do sound well matched."

"She's a real catch, I'm telling you. She'll make some lucky man very happy."

Eva cleared her throat. "She's fortunate to have loyal friends. As I said before, in general, I've heard only good things about Devora, other than one small point I'm hoping you can clarify for me."

Yehudit's heart was pounding. She gripped the phone tightly.

"Many musicians have intense personalities. They take things to heart, they are sensitive, and in general, perhaps more temperamental than the rest of the population."

"Um, could be."

"Does Devora exhibit—please forgive me, but I must ask this question: Does she exhibit any behaviors that would make it difficult to be married to her?"

Yehudit took a very deep breath. "It depends on who the guy is. On his personality. I think that the best kind of husband for Devora would be, um, someone not too intense. I don't think someone too demanding would be a good match for her."

Devora. Please forgive me. I just murdered this shidduch, but you wouldn't want me to lie.

Would you?

"Thank you for your candor," Rebbetzin Goldenberg said. "You've been very helpful."

Fallen Star

Yerachmiel had a new schedule.

Machon Atara, where Sheila taught five days a week, was out of his way, but he had to see Sheila. He had to speak to her in person. What could be accomplished on the phone? Nothing at all. It had been a huge mistake on his part to call her. On the phone, all she could hear was his voice. She couldn't see his facial expressions, and he couldn't pick up on her nonverbal cues.

It's not too late, Hashem. Not because I deserve anything, but please help me. She's my bashert. Please help her know that as clearly as I know it. It can't be too late. It can't be!

At seven thirty that morning, he parked a block from the school and waited. If the first face-to-face conversation with her didn't work out, he'd keep on trying.

He refused to think beyond that. He couldn't imagine a future without Sheila. As for her wish for a three-month break, they could discuss it. Maybe she'd relent.

He sat in the car watching and waiting for her to show up. Phone calls went unanswered. He didn't care how much business he was losing. He didn't want to miss her.

Sooner or later, she had to show up, but when? It was already the third day he'd been sitting there.

Sheila had described her schedule to him on one of their dates, even pulling out a written copy so he could follow it more clearly. Too bad he hadn't paid more attention.

He should have taken the copy from her and saved it. He should have shown her how interested he was, let her know that what was important to her was doubly important to him.

It wasn't too late.

He should have realized how much of herself she gave to her students and the school. He should have realized how much of her identity was wrapped up in being a successful teacher, instead of assuming her feelings were a poor substitute for the real deal, kids of her own.

He should have done a lot of things, thought a lot of things, and said a lot of things, fool that he was.

But it wasn't too late to change all that, he comforted himself on this third morning of his stakeout. She had to show up one of these days. And then, he'd just call out to her, and they'd make a time to meet and iron things out. He'd apologize for being shallow and unambitious. He'd state his intention to change his priorities. She'd be his guide and teacher. They'd learn from each other.

She'd learn to accept him for who he was.

Just don't let it be too late.

* * *

Rabbanit Sudri was surprised to see the same silver car parked a block away from the school for the third day in a row.

The driver was a *frum* man who looked vaguely familiar. Was he the father of a student?

She felt uneasy but knew it could be nothing. The man might work nearby or daven in one of the many shuls in the neighborhood. There could be numerous entirely legitimate reasons for his presence in this very spot, just one block away from her school.

But it bore further investigation, just to make sure. She had a responsibility to the school.

On her way into the building, she described the car and its driver to the school guard, who nodded in comprehension and promised to check into it.

* * *

Osnat Portal bolted out of her seat without a backward glance. As one, the seventh graders stopped what they were doing and stampeded out of the classroom. Their homeroom teacher, Yocheved, still on maternity leave, had come with her newborn to visit.

Sheila whirled around from the whiteboard where she'd been writing the goals for the following two classroom hours, but it was already too late.

"Girls!" she called instinctively but then stopped. What was the sense of entering a lost battle? None. It would be both pointless and beneath her dignity. She was just grateful that she hadn't been addressing the class because then their behavior would have been inexcusably out of line.

The fact that they hadn't asked her permission, that they'd all left her for Yocheved stung, but that wasn't the issue here. Right?

Not quite all, Sheila amended, still gazing after them in open-mouthed hurt. Mindy Lavie looked confused, clearly unsure of whether she should join the throng of girls swarming around their homeroom teacher while exclaiming loudly and eagerly over the baby. Halleli Shalom glanced imploringly at Sheila, who nodded her permission. Halleli shot out of the room. As Sheila watched in fascination, Halleli effortlessly made her way through the girls jockeying for a place close to Yocheved. When their teacher took her baby daughter, beautifully dressed in pink, out of her Silver Cross carriage, the girls' excitement and the decibel level in the hall soared to new heights. Would Yocheved quiet them down, or was she waiting for Sheila to do so?

The eighth-grade classroom door opened. Nechama Rotter stepped out, looking annoyed.

"Sheila, could you please have the girls move elsewhere for their debate— Oh. Yocheved! Mazel tov. When are you coming back? Oh, is she precious. Nothing like a newborn." She took the baby from her mother's arms, cradling her close. Sheila noted wryly that not a single eighth grader emerged from her seat to see what was going on in the hall. Nechama had them well in hand.

We all have our strengths, even though I thought I'm fairly authoritative. Let Yocheved bring them back whenever she likes. I'm not getting involved. Should I join the girls? I can't. I'm not ready emotionally.

Sarah Roth was conversing quietly with Mindy Lavie.

Sheila forcibly quelled the tears doing their best to force their way to the surface. *That could have been me in a year's time. I could have said yes. I could have told Yerachmiel that I want to be his wife. He didn't ask, but it was just a matter of time.*

How was Yocheved supposed to know that she'd cause pandemonium just by opening the door? Why should anybody even think to have the sensitivity not to appear in the one safe place, the one place I'm still successful, the one place where my achievements are still relevant, with an infant in her arms? How can she know that I feel erased?

I'm too raw. My feelings are way too close to the surface. She's not superhuman. What she's doing now is well within the norm, not at all insensitive… I should be out there, too. Soon. Not yet. I'm not ready yet.

The tears were a giant lump in her throat.

Give. Give to Sarah. Don't concentrate on yourself. Channel your pain toward something constructive, she commanded herself.

She made her way to Sarah, who was still sitting in her seat. "Don't you want to join everyone outside?"

"Nah." Sarah waved her hand dismissively. "How about you, Mindy?"

"No. She won't notice the two of us anyhow. She's surrounded."

"She's too busy with the kids who always know how to get noticed."

Sheila noted the shadow of sadness that fell on Sarah's face.

"'Morah Yocheved,' not she," Sheila corrected. "'She' is a disrespectful way to speak about a parent or teacher. Besides, she will definitely notice you, even if she doesn't have a chance for long conversations with everyone. She cares about both of you very much. No one can give an entire class attention all at once. I think both of you should go out to greet her, even if just for a moment."

Sarah shrugged. "Maybe soon."

"She— I mean, Morah Yocheved, could be leaving any second."

"Morah Sheila, we wanted to ask you for something," Mindy said in her accented, though impressively fluent Hebrew. "My Bubby Beatrice, who lives in America, was the person we interviewed for the project. She told us all about how hard it was for a Jew not to work on Shabbos when she was growing up, and how her Abba and Ima had to take the hardest jobs in the world because they both got fired so often."

"Is your Bubby coming to Israel to visit you this summer?" Sheila guessed.

"Yes, and she wants to see our presentation."

"Hmm. Both of you girls realize that I allocated two presentation days on which the girls who are chosen can invite one family member. Why don't you just tell your Bubby Beatrice when the dates are so she can choose?"

"Because," Mindy said, "those are the days she's taking our entire family to the Galil and the Golan. She already made reservations at a hotel and everything. But she really, really wants to see the presentation."

"You're telling me two things then. One is that in any case, you, Mindy, won't be here for the presentations. In addition, your Bubby wants me to make an exception for her. I understand her point of view. She must be so proud of your progress."

"Then it's okay to ask her when she can come?" Mindy's eyes shone.

"Not so fast. I already made an exception in your case when I permitted the two of you to choose your topic and give me your initial outline a couple of weeks past the deadline without taking ten points off your grade. In addition, I informed both of you, ahead of time, in strict confidence, that you'll be presenting your topic. You're the only students I've told, so far." Sheila stopped.

What am I afraid of? I want to agree. I want to grant Mindy her request. She's come so far this year, and a lot of her progress is to Sarah's credit. I want to give her Bubby nachas.

What's stopping me?

I'm permitting myself to be dictated to, long distance. I'm allowing Menucha Shalom to dictate how I run my classroom when it's my obligation to run my classroom as I see fit.

"Ask your Bubby Beatrice when is the best day for her to come to school and see your presentation," Sheila said to a beaming Mindy as Sarah smiled in relief. "We'll work around her schedule."

* * *

Yerachmiel was parked right in front of the school. He checked his watch again.

Who was he fooling? Sheila could have arrived at school early. She could have come from another direction or used a different entrance he knew nothing about. The adrenaline driving him fizzled out.

Sheila could be in another city, on another planet, for all I know.

For all the right I have to know, he amended, a bitter taste filling his mouth. *She could be far away. Or, she could be right here on this block, and I? I'm cut off from knowing. I have no rights here.*

Who was I fooling these past couple of days, pretending that she's accessible to me?

Why?

Just too bitter. Three months means forever. Forever. It can't be. I won't let it be!

There was a tap on the open window of his car. He looked up to see a uniformed security guard.

"Shalom. Are you waiting for someone?"

"You could say that," Yerachmiel said, too startled to think up an excuse.

"Okay, then." The guard peered at him more closely. "You look familiar. I never forget a face. Wait! Don't tell me." He held up a hand. "It'll come to me."

Yerachmiel had absolutely no intention of revealing his identity.

The guard snapped his fingers triumphantly. "I know who are, you're that band leader. Rina-O-Mangina! That's it. You played at my nephew's wedding. You guys are the best."

"Thanks. Thanks so much. I appreciate that. Well, I guess I'll be going now."

"What about the person you're waiting for?"

"Maybe I'll try a different time."

So much for that plan.

Smiling through numb lips, Yerachmiel started the car, faking a friendly wave to the guard as he drove away.

He had never been more miserable.

44
Sad Clown

Their suitcases were packed. Estelle had gingerly placed her cream linen suit, the most elegant outfit she owned, at the very top of the pile. She wanted to look her very best—poised, collected, a woman with her act together—at this first Shabbos as a married woman in Menucha and Eliezer's home. Had she remembered the forest-green chiffon blouse she'd purchased especially for this occasion? Yes, she had. Her Shabbos *sheitel*? Ditto.

I did my best with my outer appearance, and as for my insides, that's more complex. A lot more complex. Why is it so important to me to prove to Menucha, of all people, that I have my act together? She knows I don't. Is it because she set me up with Elchanan, and I want to show her that she did something unbelievably beautiful and life altering for me? I wish it were that. I'm not sure what my motivations are, but it's not that.

Elchanan was all packed. He'd packed for himself, a small overnight bag. She hoped he hadn't forgotten anything essential, but was she supposed to pack for him? He was her husband, not her son. So many questions. She had so many about the most mundane areas of married life. Maybe she should have offered to pack for him? Was that one of the countless ways that wives showed caring? She schlepped her suitcase into the foyer. Elchanan jumped up in dismay.

"What are you doing? Your back. Let me put that in the car for you."

"No car this week," she reminded him. "Not till early Sunday morning."

"Right." He slapped his forehead.

"You forgot?" she asked incredulously.

"Would you believe that, yes, it slipped my mind for a moment?"

"How could that be?"

"I'm excited that you're visiting your best friend forever as a married woman."

"You're that excited?"

"Definitely."

Momentarily, she registered that it was kind of him to feel that way, but then, practical considerations took over. Too bad about the car. It would have been so convenient to just pop everything into the trunk of Elchanan's car—oops, their car—and leave, let's say, forty-five minutes before candle lighting. It was strange how quickly she'd become reliant on the convenience of having a car, after many years of managing well with buses, supplemented by the occasional cab. Now, though, with Shabbos in two hours, if they wanted to catch a bus, they'd have to get a move on.

"What are you thinking about, Ess?"

She told him, and he grinned ruefully. "For sure. What a time for the car to break down, when your back hurts, and I have to get to Tel Aviv twice a week for my clown course." Now it was his turn to look pensive. "At least that's one thing that's given you gain without pain."

"What?"

"The car we were able to purchase with my *oleh* rights."

"Would you stop that, Elchanan?" Estelle flared. "I hate when you sneak those side comments in. They make me very uneasy. Be straight. I can't take hints today when we're in a rush to get going. Say what you have to say. Don't force me to guess."

"Take it easy. That comment was just my feeble attempt at humor."

"Ha. No, it wasn't. You meant it."

"It was. I promise."

"Okay," she yielded. Her back was hurting again. She'd take two more Advil before they left for Neot Yaar.

"Sorry about the word sneak. It was harsh. How's the course going?" she asked after the pause had grown too long.

"I like it."

"What do you like?'

"Lots of things. For starters, it's nice to have official permission to be goofy. It's a pleasure to give free rein to my inner goofiness. In the context of the course, even failed attempts at humor are commendable."

"Was that a dig?" Estelle asked frostily.

He looked startled. "Not at all."

Should she believe him? Probably. She knew that Elchanan didn't hold grudges.

"In general, the entire atmosphere of the course is completely nonjudgmental."

I suppose that wasn't a dig, either.

"For example, last session, we all were supposed to pick a clown persona and a name."

"A persona?"

"You know, happy, sad, scared, goofy, the entire spectrum of human emotions can serve as a persona." He paused. "My clown is sad." Elchanan's heartbeat accelerated rapidly. The words were out.

"Sad?" Estelle was appalled.

"Yup," her husband affirmed.

"But why a sad clown? You're an upbeat person, Elchanan. I mean to say, really, truly an upbeat person. You don't just see the full half of the glass. You're one of the few people I know who feels that his glass is full, because half is enough for now, and Hashem will always fill it up for you as needed, which is why I think you're a true optimist. That's unusual." Estelle paused uneasily at the inscrutable expression on her husband's face. "Am I wrong?"

"No, you aren't wrong."

"The way I described you—the way you think, your attitude, and the way you approach reality— are you trying to tell me that I'm off target?"

"No, you're not. You're pretty perceptive, as usual."

"Then what's wrong? Why sad?" Estelle felt the first stirrings of dread.

"It's not such a big deal."

"It is. We're at the beginning of *shanah rishonah*. If you're sad, then it's probably connected to me, and I have a right to hear how and why I make you sad."

"It isn't exclusively about you."

"I knew it. Please don't make me pull teeth. Come on, Elchanan, have a heart. Everyone in the entire world speaks their mind to me without thinking twice. What is it that makes you tiptoe on eggshells around me? Don't you trust me?"

"I trust you not to lie to me, ever. I trust you to give me an honest opinion. I don't necessarily trust you to—" He fell silent. "Leave it alone, Estelle. What's the difference?"

"Stop manipulating me. Must I always guess what you're thinking? Haven't you ever heard of communication? Of respectful disagreement?"

"Sure, if the foundation is there. And if you could maybe just keep away from words like *manipulating*, I'd appreciate it."

"Sorry. Not manipulating. Just hoping for a certain outcome without heading toward it directly. You know what, Elchanan Hacohen? No more games. This time, I'm not going to speak for you and have you confirm my answer. Say it yourself. What foundation is our marriage missing?"

"I told you to forget it."

"No, I am not forgetting your accusations, that I make you sad and that our marriage has a shaky foundation."

"I never said any of that."

"Sure you did. I can take a hint."

"It's not the right time to have a heavy discussion like this, Estelle. Why initiate a discussion like this on a Friday afternoon half an hour before we have to leave? If we had the car, it would be different, but since it's being repaired, we need to get going."

She knew he was right, but. "We'll get a cab. This is way more crucial. I'm not going to play the blissful newlywed in front of Menucha and Eliezer unless it's true. We have to get to the bottom of this once and for all. If necessary, I'll cancel on them. This is way more important to me. To us."

His face lit up. "It is?"

"There you go again. Of course it is, but I can't stand this…this… this bottomless need for reassurance. Why do you need so much reassurance that our marriage is important to me?"

"That's not in doubt. Not for one second. I believe you're glad not to be single anymore. I know you hated being single."

Now the dread was a lump in her throat.

"What I don't completely believe, Estelle, is that you married me because it was me you wanted as a partner for life."

"Why do you say that?"

"You see?" He smiled at her sadly. "You could have said, 'Of course I wanted to spend the rest of my life with you,' but you're too honest to say what's not true."

"It is true. Really. I promise. I wouldn't say that unless I felt it, you know that."

"Why *did* you marry me?" Beads of sweat shone on his forehead.

"Because—oh, please, Elchanan, now?"

"It's fine. We'll catch the last bus."

"Because, you're upbeat, like I said, and brave."

"Brave?"

"You work with what's in front of you. You don't kvetch. You don't let life get you down."

"Thanks."

"So, I liked that, and I wanted that in a husband, and—"

He took pity on her. "That's terrific, Estelle. I appreciate your telling me all that."

"Elchanan, this discussion isn't over, not by a long shot."

He shrugged, then looked at her searchingly. "Stop feeling guilty, Estelle." He dug deep into his inner resources. Estelle had probably dreamed of her first Shabbos visit to Menucha as a married woman over endless lonely years. He wouldn't ruin it for her now.

"What I said about foundation—"

"Yes?"

"It takes time. And effort. And patience. And—"

"And?"

"So we're doing well," she insisted.

And hope, he thought. He'd hoped for so much more by this point. It was more than three months. Was it really just a matter of time?

45

Shifting Gears

As Estelle watched the last bus before Shabbos pull away, she clenched her jaw in irritation. She couldn't help but remember that as a single woman, she'd never, ever allowed herself to miss the last bus. Why waste hard-earned money on cabs because of poor planning?

What person in his right mind initiated emotionally charged discussions on erev Shabbos? she berated herself. *Why did I do that? But what happened to him? Where did he disappear to?*

Elchanan emerged from the house and carefully deposited their suitcases on the sidewalk. As he locked the door, he smiled ruefully. "That was my father. He sends his best regards and wishes us a good Shabbos."

Estelle counted to ten. "Thanks. How are your par— um, how are Mommy and Abba?"

"Great! Abba specifically asked that I remember to thank you for treating Avigdor and Kayla so well."

"Oh. Thanks for telling me."

"That was the last bus?"

"Yup."

As she watched him serenely dial taxi company after taxi company, she could no longer restrain herself.

"Forget it, Elchanan. We've been standing out here for almost fifteen minutes. Let's go home. Menucha will understand. I'll just pull a chicken out of the freezer and defrost it in the microwave. Shabbos is in an hour and a half."

"It's fine, Estelle. Please stop panicking. Truth is, it's gorgeous outside. If your back wasn't aching, and we didn't have suitcases, we could even walk there. Wait! Do you see what I see? Hashem loves us."

A cab pulled up, and they got in. Elchanan used the fifteen-minute drive to calm down and refocus on the vast blessing of their first visit to Menucha and Eliezer's home as a married couple.

Though she tried hard, Estelle was unable to master her agitation.

* * *

"Morah Estelle!" Halleli exclaimed as she opened the massive carved wooden door of her elegant Anfei Ilanot home. "I need to tell you something about Shabbos. Something very important."

"Can't it wait a moment?" Menucha's mild rebuke was accompanied by an understanding smile. "I know you've been waiting all afternoon to ask her, but be patient for a couple more minutes. Give Morah Estelle a chance to catch her breath. I've reminded you too many times to count that—"

"That I shouldn't jump at people the minute they walk through the door. But Ima, Morah Estelle doesn't mind."

"She does mind. She's just too nice to tell you. I'm not as nice. Now, can I see some manners? How about a hello for Rav Elchanan, and why don't you take their suitcase and Morah Estelle's *sheitel* box to the guest room?

"I'm not a rabbi," Elchanan protested, as Halleli gave him a shy smile.

"Why do you say that? You have *semichah,* don't you?" Eliezer said as he gave Elchanan a welcoming handshake.

"True, but I'm not a head-of-a-*kehillah* rabbi type like my father and *zeidy* were."

"So what? You could be. You have the halachic knowledge and the people skills."

"Hmm. Maybe," Elchanan said doubtfully. "They're tall, imposing fellows. People seem to like that."

"Oh, come now. There are tons of short *rabbanim* who garner tremendous love and respect," Eliezer asserted, clapping Elchanan reassuringly on his shoulder.

"Come on into the kitchen. Shabbos is in just under an hour," Menucha said, ushering them all into the large room, newly remodeled in shades of crème, mint, and lime. Maria, the Filipino live-in, had laid out cold drinks, cheese bourekas, carrot muffins, and apple pie.

No fruit this time? Estelle was starving. All she'd had that day was a cup of coffee—no, two. Bad planning. She could ask for some fruit, but why make Menucha feel bad for not having thought of it herself? Better not to say anything.

Halleli returned to the room, looking at Estelle expectantly.

"I'm all ears, Halleli." Estelle refrained heroically from taking even a tiny sliver of pie. And she'd heard there was no such thing as a diet muffin. She watched Elchanan help himself to a heavenly looking, steaming-hot cheese boureka, and frowned. *Bad choice. He just had a cheese omelet at home not two hours ago.*

At Elchanan's guilty sideways glance, she rearranged her features into a smile. *He's a grown man. He doesn't need a policewoman. Poor guy, I'm sure he lived on those before he met me. And I'm sure he buys himself plenty now too, any chance he gets.*

"These are a special treat." Her husband chewed appreciatively.

Estelle tensed. *Don't you dare say that you never get them at home. I never told you not to bring them into the house. Maybe I did imply that I'd prefer not to have to fight with that type of junk, but it was your decision.*

Eliezer pushed the tray closer to Elchanan. "Try the potato ones."

"Can I have another one, too?" Halleli asked plaintively.

"No way, young lady," her mother said. "These are terrible for your skin and your waistline. One was more than enough."

"I also had enough," Elchanan said. "Uh, Menucha, could I ask you for something?"

Menucha turned to face Elchanan. "Sure, what?"

"Estelle's ready to keel over from starvation. Her back's been bugging her all week long, so all *erev Shabbos*-related activities took a lot of time, and she didn't eat anything all day."

"Of course! I feel terrible. What's wrong with me? How could I have forgotten?" Menucha leaped to her feet.

"I'm a big girl," Estelle protested. "I can take care of myself. But, thanks, Elchanan."

After their discussion, she had a feeling that once again she needed to demonstrate that she was glad they'd gotten married. It got annoying, but if he needed it, she'd do it. Why did he need it, though? She'd promised him that she was glad they'd gotten married to each other. How long would the effects of that reassurance linger? Probably not too long.

What else could she do, send him roses?

"Elchanan, for your information, Estelle *always* forgets to eat on Friday. When we were roommates, she was always a complete grouch by the time *kabbalas Shabbos* was over. She didn't rehumanize till after the soup course." As Menucha spoke, she removed a tuna platter from the refrigerator and placed it in front of Estelle. "Thank your husband for reminding me," she teased.

Estelle blushed crimson.

"Is rehumanize even a word?" Menucha ignored her friend's embarrassment. "Come on, Ess. We're all family here now. I get to tell Elchanan your deepest, darkest secrets. Eat. What's with your back?"

"She's stressed because of the end of the year, so her back went. At least, that's our theory," Elchanan said. "Makes sense, no?"

"That's the way she is, super-conscientious," Menucha agreed. "Ahh, good. The color's coming back to your face," she told Estelle. "Thanks for not canceling on us."

"Wouldn't dream of it. I love coming to you for Shabbos."

"And we love having you. Halleli, let's tell Morah Estelle our news. Good that it's a long Shabbos afternoon. Your back needs to be rested and healthy by around five thirty."

Halleli took a deep breath. "A whole bunch of girls from the class are coming over on Shabbos, in the afternoon. Um, Morah Sheila is also coming, because Morah Yocheved is coming back from maternity leave, and we're making her a goodbye party. Other people are coming too." She paused. "Is that okay?"

"Why shouldn't it be okay?" Estelle said. "Morah Sheila and I are friends, and as for you girls seeing me on Shabbos, they'll either see me in my Shabbos *sheitel* or in a snood. Why are you asking? I've come here for Shabbos tons of times, and you had kids in the class over." *I'm not saying that when I met my pupils, I didn't feel self-conscious because I did.* "People? Which other people?" Estelle asked.

"Morah Sheila asked if the kids from her *shiur* in Anfei Ilanot can come to her goodbye party, so naturally we said yes."

"Oh. Fine. I guess. Wait—are you expecting me to speak? Give a *dvar Torah*? Not my speed. Isn't Sheila giving one?"

"Stop panicking," Menucha said. "You just need to be your personable self and help me host."

* * *

It was just before candle lighting. Eliezer and Elchanan were in the living room, learning. Halleli was in her room.

"Menucha?"

"Hmm?" Menucha looked up from the interior of the fridge. "Could you put this on the counter?"

"Yes. Menucha, am I nice to Elchanan?" There. The question was out in the open. She'd said it.

Menucha straightened up and closed the refrigerator door very gently. "Estelle. Let's sit down."

"What's wrong with a simple yes or no?"

"Then, no. You could be nicer to him."

"No? How can you say that? I'm not a nice person? I'm not nice to my husband?"

"You aren't as nice to him as he deserves because you don't see him for the dignified individual he is. You don't respect him. You're very nice to him in actions and words."

"Not always in words," Estelle admitted painfully. "He wants… or needs…a lot of positive feedback. I don't appreciate it. I don't always come through for him."

"I'm not talking about that. That's a matter of style. It's not your style to be effusive."

"Then what are you talking about?"

"You still don't respect his essence. He, on the other hand, thinks the world of you. Look what he gave up to move here to Israel where you live. His whole family, who he's super close to, lives in Flatbush."

"He moved to Israel to date."

"Once the relationship became serious, he could have asked what your feelings were about moving back, at least for a short while. He didn't want to put you in the position of feeling that you'd deprived him of anything, so he never brought it up."

"I never thought of that." Estelle twisted her hands. "I never thought about how much he misses his family."

"I'm not blaming you, Ess. I know you do your best to be a good wife. I know that he's still the short, shlumpy guy you married because you thought he was your last chance, but I wish it was easier for you to make your peace with those things, and start enjoying all the phenomenal qualities he brings to the table." Menucha's eyes filled with tears.

"It's almost Shabbos. Don't cry. Look, I'm not crying," Estelle sobbed.

"For both of your sakes, I daven all the time that you'll get beyond it. He really is gold, Ess. No, not gold. He's a diamond."

"I know that, but I can't feel it. And if I can't feel it, I can't act on it. Menucha, what should I do?"

"Estelle, let's light. And then? And then, I need *your* advice."

Estelle's eyes widened. "*You* need *my* advice?"

"Yes."

"Just give me a hint. About what?"

Menucha closed her eyes. She took a deep breath.

"What is it, Menucha?"

"I'm… This is so hard for me. I'm making a big deal about nothing. It happens all the time. People do it all the time."

"What is it!"

"It's Eliezer. He wants us to—"

"What? Tell me." Estelle took her friend's hand. "I'll support you no matter what."

"He wants us to adopt a child."

Estelle's jaw dropped.

"It's still a complete secret. I just can't go a whole Shabbos without telling you, but please, Estelle, don't tell anyone. Not even Elchanan."

* * *

Estelle, pleading exhaustion, had gone upstairs for the night as soon as the meal was over.

Menucha, Eliezer, and Elchanan were still at the dining room table. Eliezer kept throwing meaningful glances at his wife, hoping she'd take the hint. He too was at the end of a long, tiring week.

But Menucha ignored him. It was obvious to her that Elchanan had something on his mind.

"Menucha, I'm sure our guest is tired," Eliezer said finally.

Elchanan, at least, knew how to take a hint. He stood up. "Thank you for a delicious, out-of-this-world meal, not to mention the wonderful company. I speak for Estelle as well."

"You're welcome. Elchanan, what's on your mind?" Menucha asked bluntly, taking pity on her husband.

"Um. Just this. A small question is all."

"Yes?" Eliezer yawned widely.

"Forget it. It's not important."

"Oh, yes it is, Elchanan, if a nice guy like you has kept the two of us up while you try to figure out how to say whatever it is on your mind," Eliezer teased.

"Stop it, Eliezer. Don't mind him, Elchanan. It's just his twisted sense of humor. Take as long as you want."

"Just… Is it Estelle's nature to be unusually reserved?"

"No," Eliezer said in surprise.

Menucha kicked him under the table and said, "She can be when she feels shy or unsure of herself."

"I see. How about when she's not feeling shy or unsure?"

"She often feels that way in new situations," Menucha said hastily.

"And I'm a new situation to her."

"Yes. You are."

Elchanan heaved a gigantic sigh of relief and gave Menucha and Eliezer a heartfelt smile. "Whoa. Thanks for saying that. You've put my mind to rest."

"Let's put the rest of ourselves to rest also." Eliezer chuckled at his own wit.

Once Elchanan had left the room, though, Eliezer's expression rapidly grew sober. "Menucha, I don't like the sound of that question at all. Speak to Estelle."

"What do you think I've been trying to do all along?"

46

With All Due Respect

On Sunday morning, Estelle woke up to a backache that was impossible to ignore. Stiffness in her back and legs. Sitting down hurt, standing was somewhat better. Elchanan wasn't home. He'd davened at the earliest minyan and gone to get the car from the garage. When he came home, she was leaning against the kitchen counter trying to do some stretching exercises that had been helpful the last time her back went out. This time seemed worse. Her cup of extra-strong coffee, abandoned after a tentative sip or two, was still hot.

"Don't go to school today," Elchanan urged. "Nothing will happen if you're absent once in a while. You have plenty of sick leave left."

"I need to go teach today." Estelle straightened up for a second and winced. "My back's killing me. I took two painkillers. Extra Strength Advil. I hope I won't need Voltaren. That stuff kills my stomach. I'm just waiting for the Advil to kick in so I can leave."

"Why must you go? You, at least, get paid absence. When I compare paid absence to what a travel agent does—hours of work, and then a customer can back out. After what happened on Wednesday with the Glas— never mind who they are, I wonder why *I* didn't become a teacher."

"I think you'd be good at it." Estelle tried sitting down but had to close her eyes against a wave of discomfort. After a moment, she opened them cautiously. Ahh, better.

"You do?"

"Why not? You're intelligent, personable, you love people. What happened on Wednesday?"

He sighed. "Do you remember my telling you about the couple who wanted information on booking a ticket for a kid who would be turning two during their trip to the States?"

"Yes. I'm sure you spent hours getting the pertinent information for them."

"Yup, you got that part right." He sighed again. "I'm sure they thought that for me, it was just a click of the mouse. In the end, they booked their tickets elsewhere."

Can't you be more of a go-getter? Stand up for yourself more? Don't tell me this happens to other travel agents too. Estelle bit back the words forcibly. *He is who he is.*

"Elchanan, listen. That's their problem, not yours."

"No. I don't know how to demand my due."

"The world is full of people who demand their due, who push for their rights. It's not full enough of the kind of people who are willing to go the extra mile because that's just who they are, or who they put a major effort into being. If you think you did the right thing, if you did a *chesed,* if you grew in the direction you want to grow in, their reaction is really not your responsibility."

"Thanks, Estelle. I told myself the same thing, but when you say it, I believe it. When I told myself all that, I felt like I was just making excuses."

Do I mean what I just said? Maybe. In a way, I do. I know that bravery and charisma wear many faces, but I wish my heart knew it too.

"Excuses for what?" Estelle asked.

"For the way I sometimes let people step on me. Estelle, you're white. Stay home."

That last, innocent remark about people stepping on him hit too close to home for comfort.

"No. I can't do that to Hadassah. I can't tell her at seven thirty in the morning that I'm going to be absent. I teach six hours straight on Sundays. She'll be going crazy all day long trying to find someone to take over for me."

"It happens. You won't be the only teacher in history to feel okay in the evening and suddenly feel a lot worse in the morning."

"I'm giving myself five more minutes."

"I still don't understand why you have to push yourself so hard."

"My attendance record used to be perfect," she explained. "Maybe I was absent one or two days a year, but look, I took off for an entire week before our wedding, for three days afterward—"

"Yes, and you see? Machon Atara managed to survive without you."

"It took me a full three weeks to reteach my students. Unteach, I should say."

And undo the damage three different teachers who filled in for me did. If only Machon Atara would employ one or two full-time subs, maybe I would stay home. Oh, my, I have Noa Lewin's first grade at three. What a bunch. I don't think I can manage them today.

"Reteach? Unteach?"

"After the three subs who took over for me, I realized how individual my methods are. Each sub did her best, but none of them knew the strategies I employ to make sure that each kid absorbs the material. Sure, I left detailed instructions and personalized worksheets, but in reality, it didn't work out all that well."

"Why?"

"Why? That's just the way it is. Nothing like a human being, the human touch."

"That's for sure. Let's see how far the people I helped would have gotten if they'd googled the information I got for them. Even I, who knew what I was doing, spent at least three hours until I got precise answers."

"A lot of people say computers can replace teachers, but if you ask me, I think that's just another way to make teachers feel inferior. Just another putdown to make sure we don't demand too much."

"Why would anyone want to put teachers down? There's nothing like a steady teacher who knows his stuff and cares about the kids."

Estelle chuckled and stood up gingerly. "Schools are a microcosm of society, so if anything goes wrong, the people in a position of authority always take the blame. That's one answer. I'm feeling better. Gotta get a move on." She opened the refrigerator and bent down to the fruit bin. Her back rebelled, and she retreated with a gasp of pain.

"Let me do that." He took out some apples, cheese, and a yogurt. "Anything else?"

"If you don't mind…?"

"My pleasure."

"Maybe a carrot? There are peeled carrots and cucumbers on the third shelf down."

"Great. You were saying—"

"I also think that some adults never got over being furious at their teachers. Now, if they're ever in a position of strength, they attack. Boy, do they attack."

"I hope that no one has ever attacked *you*."

"Nah. Most of the parents I've worked with are full partners. We all do our best. The parents I was talking about are the exception. Unfortunately, *they* demand far more than their due share of attention, and give parental involvement a bad name."

"As long as you were never on the receiving end," her husband said protectively.

Estelle opened her mouth to say that she was a big girl who could take care of herself and then closed it, noting with surprise that today, at least, she found his coddling of her less grating than usual.

"What happened in the end, the one time you were absent?"

"The result was that the more talented students progressed, but the weaker ones just got some sort of a confused idea of what was going on, with plenty of errors I had to struggle to uproot."

She got up. "See. I'm a lot less stiff than I was. I can sit on a chair without pain from my lower back stabbing me. I stood up in a single movement."

"Yup, you're altogether the picture of health. I'll drive you to school."

"I'm going to try to walk. It's so beautiful outside today. It's only twenty minutes from the house, and all downhill, except for the last two blocks."

"Estelle."

"No, really. Walking makes me feel better. The fresh air will wake me up. Look at the time. Everything took me so long this morning. Don't worry about me, Elchanan. I'll be fine. I'm sure the kids will make me forget all my woes."

"Call me when you're finished. I'll come pick you up."

"Um, okay. Elchanan, the linguistic staff has a meeting scheduled after school."

"Skip it."

"You know what? How about I call you in the afternoon to let you know how I'm feeling?"

"You do that."

* * *

At first, the fresh air revived her. Estelle set out cautiously, rejoicing in the double blessing of an activity that combined health and enjoyment. After a block or so, her right leg began to complain. She slackened her pace. A glance at her watch told her that she'd have to take a cab or be late to work.

A car pulled up alongside her and beeped.

"Elchanan!"

"Hop in."

"I could get used to this. You spoil me, but thanks."

"We can still go home. If you want, I'll call in for you."

"I don't have fever. I want to go in today."

"Okay."

"Um, Elchanan, could I tell you something?"

"Go right ahead."

"There are a lot of ways to be tall, you know?"

"You sound like my mother. Sorry, but I speak from bitter experience. The best way for a guy to be tall is just to be tall. Or at least not short. Few people take a short man seriously. And Estelle? I know you feel bad about what I said on Friday, but really, everything's fine. I'm happy, don't worry. Everything's great. Just take care of yourself, and call me during the day. Don't try to be a heroine. Take painkillers during the day, as needed. They aren't addictive if you take them for a day or two."

They pulled up at the school gate. Elchanan got out of the car and came around to open the door for her. She thanked him and got out, giving her husband a discreet wave as he drove off.

Despite her achiness, Estelle noticed broad smiles on several faces, both colleagues and students, as she joined the stream of people entering the building. She wondered what they were smiling about.

47 Better Nature

What a beautiful tune. Yerachmiel ought to take his beautiful singing a step further. He's definitely as talented as the singer on the radio. Let him try. Let him go for it. It's a matter of emotional survival, no more, no less. He thinks his personal life is in shambles, fine. I can't change his nature, and I don't want to, but, if one door is locked, let him try to open another one.

As she got out of her light blue Toyota and locked the door, Elisheva became increasingly convinced that her idea would serve to extricate her oldest son from his funk. There really was nothing like an absorbing project to rekindle a person's zest for life. The problem here was that Yerachmiel was likely to get insulted by her belief that the terrible disappointment of Sheila's rejection could in any way be mitigated by additional recognition and fame. Too bad.

She wasn't going to permit him to outtalk her, not this time when so much was at stake. She'd discuss ways to present her idea to Menachem, who apparently had arrived early for their Wednesday afternoon lunch, let himself in with his key, and turned on his favorite station while waiting.

Between the two of them, they'd persuade Yerachmiel. Wait! That sounded like a real piano being played, not a radio. Menachem was playing a difficult piece. Good for him. She hadn't realized that his technical skills had reached that level. Both her sons were musically inclined, though in this area, as in many others, Yerachmiel's natural abilities outshone those of his younger brother. Good thing the birth order wasn't the other way around. Not that she ever compared one son to the other, but sometimes she wondered if Menachem hadn't found his handsome, talented, charismatic brother a tough act to follow. The age difference helped a lot, as did Menachem's accepting, placid nature, much like her own.

That nature is a blessing, equivalent if not more valuable than all Yerachmiel's visible and impressive attributes. Look how the tables have turned. Menachem was happily married, his wife was expecting, and Yerachmiel was searching, searching, stumbling, falling, his need to settle down growing ever more desperate now that he'd come so close, and—

"Who's there?" The music stopped, and the door swung wide open.

"Yerachmiel."

"Hi, Ma. I hope it's all right if I stand in for Menachem today. He left a message that he and Avital have an appointment."

"Oh, dear. That must have been the message he left on my new cell phone. I can't figure out how to access my messages on this thing." Elisheva brandished the phone.

"Am I such terrible company?" Yerachmiel said lightly.

"Not at all. I'm enjoying every minute. I just wish he and your father wouldn't keep trying to advance my technological skills. What's that you were playing before? It sounded very familiar, but

I couldn't quite place it."

Yerachmiel reseated himself at the piano and pointed to the sheet music. "I actually wrote it out for four hands, if you're interested."

She hesitated. "I'm a bit rusty as far as sight reading goes."

"Don't tell me you're embarrassed in front of me!"

"I am, just a bit. You're such a true professional. I actually had an idea I wanted to run by you."

"If I am, the credit goes to you and Abba for all the years of expensive lessons."

Elisheva was touched. Once again, she wondered how Sheila had allowed herself to be blinded to Yerachmiel's virtues. Did she think that diamonds like her son grew on trees?

I'm mixing my metaphors, but how could she take the risk of losing him? Whoever said that a parent is only as happy as their unhappiest child told the unvarnished truth.

I hope she won't grow to regret it bitterly. Maybe I don't hope that. Maybe I hope she'll realize what she did. I was always the optimist who was convinced that troubles were just a passing phase, and now… I see no light whatsoever at the end of the tunnel. I know my son. I'm afraid. What if he decides that either it's Sheila, or—

Or no one.

I can't bear the thought.

"Come on, Ima. I don't bite. I want to hear how the two parts sound together," he urged.

Elisheva started.

"Ima?"

"Okay. Let's give it a try."

The two played in tandem for a moment before Elisheva stopped and placed her hands on her lap.

"What's wrong? You were doing well. You aren't at all rusty."

"This piece. I know this piece. It's the one you sang to Sheila on your date." His mother looked at him in dismay. "I thought…I hoped you'd gotten over it. Such a joyful tune. I assumed it reflected your mood, but now I realized it's your way of reliving that date again."

"Is that a problem?" He avoided her gaze. "I enjoyed that date very much. It's all I have left. Can you blame me for trying to revisit that time, when I was happy, and I thought I'd finally found the one?"

"No, I can't blame you, but you're drinking poison. It's not healthy for you to wallow in memories. You have to pick yourself up and move on."

"That word, *wallow*. There's no way you would use that word if you knew how much it hurts me."

"I'm trying to shock you awake. It's been three weeks already."

"Three weeks, two days, and one night," he corrected his mother, who bit down hard on her lip.

"The sooner you go on with your life, the sooner the pain will fade."

"I *am* going on with life. Two bar mitzvahs, one wedding, one choir performance. I haven't exactly been sitting around moping since Sheila, and I…since Sheila told me that she—" He stopped.

"It's too much emotion. You can't even say the words. Say, since she turned me down."

"Would you rather I be a stone, without feelings? I thought she'd be my wife, my future, and so, I don't think that a couple of weeks to grieve over a lost dream is too much. I can't believe I need to explain all this to you, Ima. Shouldn't it be obvious?"

"Don't reopen the wound. It's pointless." Elisheva turned away before her son could catch sight of the tears welling up in her eyes, but he'd noticed.

"I'm really sorry you have so much *agmas nefesh* from me. I have no one to talk to about this. Sure, I could go to therapy, but I honestly don't feel that my reaction is exaggerated. I know it's hard for you to see how broken I am, but should I go live in a cave until I can paint a smile on my face?"

"If therapy would be helpful to you, I'd push you to go. No one's telling you not to be sad, even though the two of you weren't engaged."

"I need to heal at my own pace."

"The healing has to include some action, don't you think?"

"Nope." Yerachmiel closed the piano.

"There's this lovely girl, Devora Levin, for example, who happens to be free at the moment," his mother plunged on desperately. "One evening, and you'll feel much better."

"Poor little Yerachmiel. Did someone take away your lollipop? Here, have a toffee instead."

"Don't be cynical. I'm just trying to help."

"You can't help me."

"You'll never know if you don't try."

"I don't think it will work that way for me. It's a waste of my time, a waste of her time, but I don't care."

"Sheila's dating." Elisheva braced herself.

"So what?"

His mother winced at the raw pain in those two words.

He paused, rubbing his eyes hard with his hands.

Her heart contracted. "It hurts a lot to hear that, but less than I thought it would," he said reassuringly.

That's why you're hiding tears. I'm so proud of you. You *are comforting* me. *Sheila Leipzig, you're a fool. You have no idea what you turned down.*

"I'm trying to find my better nature here, Ima," he said, to her surprise. "If I cared about her, and not just about myself, I ought to be wishing her success. *I'm* not her *bashert*. Right?"

Elisheva managed to give the barest of nods.

"She clearly needs to get married, so I want to be in a place of letting go. Letting go with a full heart."

He was never this open with me in the pre-Sheila era. She *was* good for him. In that way only.

"Some generosity is in me, someplace, buried under all my… pain and frustration. I'm trying to find my *emunah* here, that all this was meant to be, but I'm not doing too well."

"I think you're coping as well as anyone who's had high hopes frustrated."

"High hopes?" He tasted the phrase and tried to laugh.

Elisheva's fury at Sheila resurfaced. "Aunt Eva has a suggestion for you."

"Nope."

"How long will you put your life on hold?"

"We dated for two months, and nothing came of it. Dating and marriage don't necessarily have anything to do with each other."

His mother struggled to mute her resentment. *I'm also trying to find my better nature. For you, Yerachmiel. I want you to have a life.*

"I'm not too pleased with Sheila, but, I see that something in the relationship made you…softer? Better at communication?"

"Could be."

"Sheila gave you that gift. You'll be a better husband."

"I can't sit through another date."

"Do you want to just hear about Aunt Eva's suggestion?"

"No." He shrugged in resignation. "Okay, if you like."

"If I like? Okay, here goes." Elisheva reached excitedly for the phone and punched in the familiar number.

"Ima, when I go out, I want you to do me a favor. No expectations. I'll go through the motions, but it's not in me to marry anyone just because it makes sense."

All at once, Elisheva found herself enraged, though there was really no one to blame. Perhaps frustrated right down to the marrow of her bones was a better way to put it, she thought briefly, before the words bubbled out of her, words she'd suppressed, but felt deeply. She put down the phone.

"Yes. You can't be anyone but who you are. But you can follow advice for a change."

"I am. I just agreed to go out."

"And basically warned me that it's all just an act."

"I didn't say that at all."

"What's going through the motions supposed to mean?"

He was silent. Elisheva felt his pain, felt it in the pit of her stomach, and in her throat. How must he be feeling?

"I told you," she blurted out, against her better judgment. "I told you when you came in from singing that tune on the date, a fourth date, not after an engagement, just a fourth date, that you'd frighten her off."

"I never thought my own mother would hurt me when I'm down."

"I'm hurting you for a reason. I know, even if you don't, that there are many possibilities out there, a thousand times better for you than Sheila Leipzig. Next time, make sure you don't repeat the same mistake."

"I don't understand. It was going so beautifully. I was there. The entire world can have the best advice in the world, but I was the one on the dates." He pulled himself together. "Ima, what was your idea?"

"My idea? Oh." All at once, she found herself stammering. What was recording all his original compositions in a studio and marketing them compared with what he'd lost?

Worst-case scenario, he'd accuse her of trivializing his loss.

Elisheva outlined her idea quickly before she lost her nerve.

"You think my stuff is good?" he asked her.

She was shocked. Where was his self-esteem?

"Good? It's exceptional. Some of it is really inspiring, like this song, because you wrote it from your deepest self," she added honestly. "Some of your compositions are less wonderful than this one, but it's all at least as good as what's out there."

"Does the Jewish music world need another CD? Especially if only one or two songs are really special?" The bitterness was back.

"Not necessarily." Elisheva never lied to her sons.

"But I do."

"Yes."

"Ima, that's pathetic."

She shook her head vehemently. "It's not pathetic. It's the furthest possible thing from pathetic."

"What is it then?"

"It's courageous."

Yerachmiel looked down at the piano keys and shrugged. "You're my mother, so that's what you think. The world out there isn't anywhere near as kind or as tolerant."

"Why, what do people say?" his mother asked, though she was pretty sure she knew. Talking should help him move forward, shouldn't it? Talking the episode through would help him get over it, get all the bitterness out of his system. Wouldn't it?

"Get over it. Plenty of fish in the sea. You ought to be ashamed of yourself, a healthy young man with your whole life ahead of you. Go to a hospital and volunteer. Go to a prison or an old-age home. Then you'll see people with real problems. Snap out of it. Think of something besides yourself and your own little world. Someone was finally the address for your hopes and dreams? Someone was going to go forward with you, build a life together with you? Someone special, who you could talk to, be yourself with, and—"

"Could you really and truly be yourself with her?" Elisheva broke into his monologue. "Didn't you have to pretend to be bigger than you really are just to keep her respect?"

"And if I did?"

"Marriage is about being your best self, but it's not about being someone you aren't. If Sheila could only respect the ideal image of who she wanted you to be, then—"

"Then what?"

Elisheva fell silent.

"Then I'm better off without her. Well, I'm not. This isn't a math equation, Ima. I'm not a ledger, where all the pluses and minuses neatly add up."

"Does it help you to hurl bitterness at me? If it does, I'm willing to be the address, but only if it helps you feel better. If not, spare me, please."

He looked at her with hollow eyes. "No, it doesn't help."

"It doesn't?"

"Nothing helps."

End of the Road

Elisheva Kantor was the fortunate possessor of an inborn optimism, an innately positive view of people and events. Her most heartfelt wish was to spread her happiness far and wide, to share her sincere enjoyment of Hashem's world with as many people as possible. She hated to see anyone in pain. Human suffering tore at her.

She found herself envying her husband, Shlomo. He, too, was helpless to alleviate Yerachmiel's agony, but his sympathy was tempered by anger. Shlomo staunchly maintained that Yerachmiel had brought the suffering on himself by being picky and wanting perfection, and now, by aiming his sights too high.

"He set himself up for this, Elisheva," Shlomo said on their after-dinner walk, a practice they'd instituted years before as their safety measure against high blood pressure, cholesterol, and other midlife demons. The steep hills of Neot Yaar provided them with a natural workout, as well as a chance to discuss various issues. Their usual route led them downhill from their home in the beginning, which meant that the way home was one long uphill climb. Elisheva wondered if the heavy spirits that had become her constant companion were making tonight's walk a form of torture instead of the usual pleasurable outing.

"I wish you'd stop saying that."

"Why? It's the truth. Tonight's date with this girl, Devora, is a far more logical choice for him, age-wise. And otherwise."

"Why otherwise?"

"Come on, Elisheva. The Leipzigs are such a prominent, well-known family, not to mention well-to-do. How do we match them? We don't."

"That's not why Sheila ended the relationship. Could we walk a little more slowly?"

He slowed his pace. "I hope Yerachmiel plays his cards right tonight. If he's smart, he'll do his best to find a way to like what's accessible to him. In any case, he'll be doing this young woman a service if he puts his best foot forward."

"Which young woman? Devora? I'm sure he'll be a perfect gentleman." Elisheva sank down on a convenient bench. "Why a service?"

"Devora's thirty-six. About time to end her search, don't you think? I imagine she's had her share of disastrous dating experiences. I'm sure she's quite excited to have landed a date with someone as eligible as our son. I'm sure she'll try hard to be good company. He liked what he heard about her, so I'm sure that if he actually tries to get to know her instead of going through the motions, this could be the start of something good."

Elisheva rose wearily to her feet. "I wish it were that simple."

They continued walking.

"Maybe it is. Maybe he's finally ready to learn that no is also an answer, even for him."

"Shlomo, it's cruel to put it that way. He's had to accustom himself to receiving no as an answer since he started dating seriously when he was twenty-two years old."

"He created those nos."

"Let's drop the subject, shall we?" She plodded upward. When had the hill become so steep?

* * *

A quarter of an hour into the date, Devora Levin was getting up the courage to ask Yerachmiel a direct, though potentially uncomfortable question. She was angry enough, hurt enough, and feeling fed up enough to risk confrontation, though ordinarily, she feared conflict more than anything else. But this time… Enough was enough.

From the moment he'd arrived at the date, he'd been giving one-syllable answers to most of her questions. He hadn't initiated any conversation at all. Why was he there if he didn't want to work at making the date a success? She didn't have to put up with it.

Heart pounding, hands clammy, Devora forced the words out. "Do you want to go home?"

He looked startled, but at the same time, it was impossible to miss his look of relief.

"Home? Go home? We only just got here. Why do you ask? Is something wrong?"

Her nerve failed her. "No, everything's fine."

"Why did you ask?" Yerachmiel straightened up for the first time since the date had begun.

"Nothing, it's just that, um, I hope this isn't too rude to mention, but, um, never mind. Nothing."

"It's not nothing. I'm sorry. I'm the one who's being rude here."

Once again, she steeled herself to ask. What did she have to lose? Nothing, that was what. Oddly, her sense of humor began to bubble to the surface. With difficulty, she suppressed a giggle. He looked at her in surprise.

"What's funny?"

"It's just that you remind me of myself a couple of years back. Hashem works in funny ways."

"What are you talking about?"

"So, I was engaged to be married, and two weeks before our wedding, the guy got cold feet."

"*That's funny*?" he asked incredulously.

"Not at all." A giggle escaped. "No, it's just that not more than a week later, I was sitting in a hotel lobby opposite some guy and I was actually supposed to start again. Crazy."

"You know about me and—?"

"Nope. I don't. But you have that hollow look, and what can I say? I know hollow." She picked up her evening bag.

"Where are you going?"

"I told you. Home. I wish you and whoever she is all the *mazel* in the world together, if that's what Hashem wants."

And then she was gone.

* * *

He was in the forest, just down the road from his home. Dusk was falling. He got out of the car.

"Sheila?" He began speaking, very softly. "Sheila, do you want to hear something strange? I think you're more of a serious musician than you ever let on. I get the oddest feeling that you're even a composer. Why did you never tell me?" He began edging down the gravel path that led deeper into the forest.

"Sheila, I wish I could get your take on this. My mother, who I really thought you'd be meeting any day, but now it's different. Now, I don't suppose that's too realistic. So, anyhow, she wants me to put out a CD with my songs. You know, to cheer me up, and provide me with a new interest in life. Thing is, I know that only two or three of my songs are worth hearing, so... I know how disappointed I am when I have to plow through seven or eight boring songs just to get to the real meat and potatoes. The soul-satisfying stuff. I think

I should wait until I have a bunch of magnificent songs that really do what music is supposed to do before I put myself out there."

Now, he was standing among the trees. It was getting darker.

"You know what bugs me most, Sheila? That I don't know how you'd react. I don't know what you'd think. I spent so many hours with you. I could have gotten to know you so much better."

Yerachmiel looked up at his car, parked directly on the road above. No use being foolhardy, putting himself in a risky position, alone in the forest, in the dark. He'd lost so much already. He began climbing back up to the car.

If that's what Hashem wants, Devora had said. Yerachmiel stopped short.

"Hashem. *Ribbono shel Olam.* I want. I want! I've never wanted anything as much as I want this! What do You want for me? Do You want this for me? You can give me anything, anything You want. Do You want me to keep on trying in the direction I so desperately want to take?"

He was at the car.

"If You want something else for me..."

He choked.

"If You want *someone* else for me…"

He couldn't say the words.

"Free me, *Ribbono shel Olam*. Free me to go on."

Last-Ditch Effort

"Leipzig isn't that common a name," Rabbi Henry Eisenberg muttered as he pulled the Jerusalem phone directory closer. Whatever small part he could play in Yerachmiel's future, whatever he could do to contribute to his happiness, was worth any amount of effort.

Relatively speaking, Rabbi Eisenberg was a fortunate man. Relatively speaking. So, was it poor judgment or poor management, or perhaps a combination of the two that had left him without some very important relatives, namely a spouse and children, not to mention grandchildren, at his age and stage of the game? Who could be sure? No one in the world, that was who.

When all was said and done, he had nothing to complain about. His health was good, all things considered. How many gentlemen in their mid-eighties could make that claim?

He continued counting his blessings, a habit he practiced frequently.

His vision was still sharp enough to make out the relatively small print in the directory. How many people of his age could still do that, even without reading glasses? He was still living in his own beautiful home, managing just fine, with minimal assistance. Yes, Hashem was with him, and always had been, even if pain still knifed through him from time to time at all the missed opportunities he'd perhaps allowed to slip past him, at all the fullness and richness he was missing.

He jotted down the ten phone numbers that appeared under Leipzig. Good thing Yerachmiel hadn't set his heart on a young woman named Levy. Ten calls would take time, but free time was one commodity he had in abundance.

Momentarily, his spirits flagged. He was a useless old man. Who said Professor Leipzig would even be willing to listen to him? And even if Sheila's father did take him seriously, who said the man had any influence on his daughter in today's day and age?

The girl obviously had a mind of her own, perhaps too much so for her own good. If she'd turned down Yerachmiel without blinking an eyelash, she needed to be told just who she was rejecting.

But why would her father listen to an old man? Why bother making himself look like a well-meaning old fool?

And as far as Yerachmiel was concerned, what guarantee was there that he'd be pleased if he found out that his mentor had meddled in his private affairs?

It took great determination on his part to dismiss that line of thought. Growing old wasn't for the faint of heart. No, not at all. Using his old-fashioned rotary phone so as not to make any mistakes, he dialed the first number on his list.

"Hello, Miriam Leipzig speaking."

He started. That easy? He'd reached Sheila's mother on his very first try? But, then again, the *Ribbono shel Olam* was involved here, helping Yerachmiel find his *bashert*. Sheila was on Hashem's *shidduch* list too, for that matter, and he, Henry Eisenberg, was merely a *shaliach*, so why should he be surprised when his efforts went smoothly? He shouldn't.

Where's your emunah peshutah, you old man? he scolded himself. *Your simple faith that Hashem is a loving Father who looks out for His children? If you still don't automatically realize that, at the age of eighty-four, when are you planning to internalize the simple reality that even a five-year-old is aware of?*

"Hello?" Miriam repeated, puzzled by the silence. "Did we get cut off?"

He roused himself. "Hello, am I speaking with the mother of Sheila Leipzig?"

"Correct."

"I'd like to introduce myself. My name is Henry Eisenberg, and I'm a close friend of a young man named Yerachmiel Kantor. We have a relationship that spans a good thirty years, at least."

Miriam started. "Oh? A friend of Yerachmiel's? Did he ask you to call?"

"No."

"How can I help you?"

"Actually, it's I who wish to be of service to you," he said. "I know that Yerachmiel and your daughter were dating seriously and that things were moving along nicely. I believe I can help both of them overcome this temporary snag they seem to have encountered."

Miriam thought rapidly. Despite his denial of the facts, this elderly gentleman was obviously an emissary sent by Yerachmiel to convince Sheila to change her mind or, more likely, beseech her to give him another chance. She couldn't blame him for trying. She herself was furious at Sheila for rejecting such a promising opportunity.

Sheila had told her she was thinking of going out with Adam Goldberg again, their second date.

Miriam was against the idea, most emphatically so. What was her daughter thinking, going out with a bereaved widower with a young son? Sheila had at least four, five, even six years before she fell into that category, which just went to show how mixed up and in need of guidance she was.

Sheila had been a shell of herself this past month. Apparently, Yerachmiel was also having a hard time moving forward. Sheila hadn't dismissed the *shidduch* on a whim. She'd gone through agonies making up her mind. Angry and frustrated though she was at her daughter's decision, Miriam knew that what she was about to say was true.

"It's far more than a temporary snag. They've broken up."

"I know it seems that way, but it needn't be. I can tell you the most wonderful things about his character, which ought to put your daughter's mind at rest."

"I'm not sure Sheila wants to revisit the issue. Maybe it's more beneficial for them both to move on. Less painful. Especially for Yerachmiel. The more time that passes after their breakup, the more he'll heal."

"Or maybe not," he countered.

"I think that for him, seeing Sheila again will reopen the wound."

"Who said anything about Yerachmiel seeing your daughter again? Tell me, what do either of you have to lose by visiting an old man one midmorning or late afternoon, and spending a couple of minutes listening to what he has to say?"

It was time to end the conversation. Gently, graciously, so as not to offend Yerachmiel's well-meaning friend, but—

"I assure you that Yerachmiel has no idea whatsoever that I called you," he went on. "This is my own idea entirely. There will be no ambush, no surprise visit while the two of you are in my home, with Yerachmiel accidentally on purpose dropping by for our learning session."

Miriam smiled at his perceptiveness. "In terms of both of us visiting you, Sheila would never agree. Please don't imagine I can convince her, either. My influence on her is quite limited, and has been for years."

"I wouldn't be so sure of that."

"Why not?" Miriam found herself asking the elderly gentleman on the line, who was, essentially, a perfect stranger.

"Girls always want their mother's approval."

"Sheila's far from being a girl," her mother countered. "Besides which, as you just may have realized, she's very independent."

"Girls always crave their mother's approval," he repeated. "Even if they don't show it. Even if they don't demonstrate that need, it's there. At age ten, at age twenty, and at age thirty as well."

"Is that something you've seen in your own home?"

"I saw that with my sisters," he replied. "Before you say something that will make you feel badly afterward, I want to let you know that I've never married."

"Oh."

"I see so much potential in this match. Yerachmiel is like the son I've never had. Though I've never had the privilege of meeting your daughter, I can tell you that he has become softer and more compassionate by far since they began to date. It was obviously a salubrious combination of joy and your daughter's influence. I cherished hopes of hearing of an engagement within a month."

"Thank you. In confidence, I want to let you know that I…" Miriam swallowed hard. "I, too, as you so eloquently put it…" She strove for a light tone, but her voice wouldn't obey. "I, too, cherished hopes."

"I truly feel that I am in possession of information that could alter the course of events. If it's difficult to arrange a meeting in my home, it would be my privilege to come to your residence instead, at a time when your daughter is present."

"Oh no," Miriam said hastily. "I'd never dream of putting you out that way."

"I'd do far more for Yerachmiel."

"What exactly is your relationship with him?"

He told her.

When Miriam put down the phone, she'd agreed to host him at her table that Shabbos.

He put down the receiver, overcome by a wave of exhaustion. *What have you done? Put yourself out on a limb, that's what. You have no wife. No daughters or granddaughters. What does an old man like you possibly have to say that will convince a sophisticated, decisive, determined young woman like Sheila to change her mind?*

Another thought crossed his mind, and he buried his face in his hands, feeling ancient and very, very tired.

If, in my efforts to make this sorry situation better, I end up making matters worse, I will never forgive myself. If my well-intentioned meddling ends up ruining Yerachmiel's chances…

He might never find out, but I will always know. If the situation further deteriorates through my intervention, it will be difficult for me to live with the guilt.

* * *

"I'm reminding you that I'm not planning to be home this Shabbos, Ima."

"Oh, did you tell me that? It must have slipped my mind. Where are you going?"

"To Renée."

"How is she? I want you to be here for the afternoon *seudah*. Renée's place is within walking distance."

"But it's going to be so hot this Shabbos."

"So? Don't tell me you were planning to cancel your *shiur* in Anfei Ilanot because I know you aren't going to do that."

"I'm not, but it's closer from Renée's house. It makes absolutely no sense for me to walk half an hour here, in the opposite direction from where I'm supposed to be."

"As far as I'm concerned, you are supposed to be right here at home."

"Why?"

"There's someone I want you to meet. To meet, and to listen to."

"Ima, does this have anything to do with Yerachmiel?"

"Yes."

Sheila was silent and still for a long, long moment. Finally, she raised a tearstained face to her mother.

"I'll be here."

Estelle

50

That's That

So that's that. Either I swallow my deep disappointment—no, make that my grief, okay?—at the way that things have turned out for me; swallow, accept, trust in Hashem, and go on, minute by minute, hour by hour, day by day, doing my best with what's in front of me, or, I can continue living life as I have up until now. And, before anyone objects to the word *grief*, well, how else would I define the final death throes of a hope I held from my teenage years, to be married to a husband I cherish and adore?

I distinctly recall telling Menucha when I turned thirty that if this dream wasn't realized, I didn't want to go on living. I meant that this hope, wish, dream, longing is situated at the very core of my being and is the motor that keeps me going, to put it inelegantly.

I'm not going to merit the only thing I've ever wanted with my entire heart. I'm not going to get the one thing that would make my life so much smoother, easy, and more enjoyable.

I'm forever stuck trying to be happy, trying to be whole, dragging my heavy heart from place to place.

Maybe that was a little melodramatic. It's hard to verbalize something so deeply felt.

I can't cherish Elchanan. I can't adore him. I can't, and I don't. I don't care if Menucha deplores my lack of maturity, because she *did* marry the man of her dreams, so how can she judge or understand what I'm going through? I don't care how many times she tells me that what she felt for Eliezer before they got married, and for the first couple of years until she got all obsessed with not having a family, was infatuation. Who cares what she called it? I was there to see how she sparkled, how people were drawn to her carefree joy, how nothing, but nothing, bothered her or got under her skin. I was there to see how beautiful she suddenly became, how she effortlessly shed twenty pounds, and how the burden of selfhood grew so light. I was there when people praised her courage and patience in holding out for what she wanted until she got it. With me, they didn't call it that. They called my attitude stubborn and inflexible. That's because she got what she wanted. It made people feel good. My unmet needs made people feel helpless. Then they blamed me for not accepting whatever they had to offer.

This is all old. I've thought these thoughts countless times, many times, too many times. No one, no one but Hashem can look into my heart, gaze into my soul to see, to feel, to support the intensity of my disappointment. No one truly understands, and maybe, just maybe that's the way it's supposed to be. Just me and my Creator. Just me and *HaKadosh Baruch Hu*.

There's a problem though, named Elchanan. If I were Geula Leibowitz, had I made her choice and opted to remain single, it would really be just me and my Abba in Heaven. But I couldn't make that choice. I couldn't live without the thought of at least trying to live the life I've always dreamed of with a good, decent, normal man who so much wanted to marry me. I thought that he cared enough to make it work for both of us. It didn't work out that way.

If I lived on a deserted island, with no one to compare him to, with no one to compare our marriage to, then maybe, just maybe our marriage would have a fighting chance to become the type of union I know is out there.

Maybe if I lived on a deserted island, then I'd realize that traits my husband lacks aren't crucial to my growing to see him the way he wants me to see him. The way other people see him.

I don't live on a deserted island.

I'm no heroine.

I'm not into *mesirus nefesh*. Or maybe the better way to put it is that I don't believe in lying to myself on such a basic, fundamental level. That's not *avodas hamiddos*. It's not the way I'm wired. I would need an *adam gadol*, a true *gadol B'Yisrael* to tell me that it's my *tafkid* to work on myself in that direction, and even then it would be excruciatingly hard, but at least I'd have the deep comfort of knowing that I'm a partner in Hashem's plan for me. As things stand now, though… If anyone tells me to live for Elchanan, for the children I teach—no. No. NO! NOOOOOO.

Stop erasing me and putting a puppet in my place. Hashem didn't do that and neither should you. I'm smart enough to think of those answers for myself, and they don't work for me. They won't work for me.

What then?

Minute by minute, hour by hour, day by day, I'll try to make good choices for myself. For myself and the man I married. Choices that will bring me joy. Choices that will bring us joy.

Choices that will build me and grow me into the Estelle bas Chana that Hashem created me to be.

How does Elchanan put it?

It's an *avodah*.

51 Awakening

Estelle surfaced momentarily from a deep sleep. Was that a phone ringing? Or was it part of her dream? She turned over and went back to sleep.

The phone rang again. This time she woke up fully alert. Was it her imagination or did the shrill ring have an accusing tone, as if to say, "Where are you, Estelle? Come on already. Pick up the phone!"

She got out of bed and shuffled over to the phone.

"Where were you all day, Estelle? Why haven't you been answering the phone? I've been calling and calling."

"Sorry, Ma. I came home from school and crashed. I haven't been sleeping very well at night for"—she yawned—"for I don't know how long. A week at least, and you know me, I'm a Bruner through and through, and we need our sleep."

"I was worried."

"Why?"

"I've called at least five times without getting through."

"I was teaching, Ma. You know I don't bring my cell phone to class. I'm so sorry you had to try so hard to reach me. Did you leave a message? I didn't get to check my messages, either. You know I usually call you right back. I'm really sorry."

"Is everything all right?"

"Sure. Why shouldn't it be?"

"Because I got no fewer than three frantic phone calls from Menucha Shalom this afternoon."

"Oh."

"The third time, she was calling from school."

"What was she doing there?" Estelle walked into the kitchen and sat down, feeling drained.

"She went to school to see if you were okay."

"She didn't have to do that."

"We're going in circles." Fear sharpened her mother's voice. "I'm your mother, Estelle. I've known you for more years than you've known yourself. Do you think I haven't noticed that you're not as happy as I hoped you'd be, finally married after all these years and what's more, to a wonderful, caring person like Elchanan? I couldn't have wished better for you. What's going on?"

"Nothing, Ma. Really. Nothing at all. I'm just"—she put her head down on the kitchen table—"adjusting."

"It's taking too long," her mother stated bluntly.

Tears pricked Estelle's eyes.

"Estelle, you need to go for help. For counseling."

"Ma," Estelle choked out. "Ma, this is just too hard."

"*What's* just too hard?"

"Please don't yell at me, Ma. I'm having such a hard time."

Mrs. Bruner softened her tone. "I'm very concerned about you. What's too hard, sweetheart?"

The tears were flowing freely. "He wants me to really, really like him. He wants me to be really, really fond of him. He wants me to look forward to spending time with him."

"Of course he does," her mother said blankly. "He's your husband."

"But I can't."

"You can't?" her mother echoed.

"I can't force myself to feel that way. That's not how I feel about him. I can't!"

Her mother gasped. There was a long, heavy silence as Estelle wept helplessly.

"Estelle…why did you marry him?"

Why *had* she married him? The question hung in the air. She groped for an answer. She had married him, because…because…

"I don't know. I just did."

"That's not an answer."

"I married him because"—Estelle reached blindly for a tissue—"because he thought it was a terrific idea." She started to sob again. How could she still have tears left? "He was just so sure we could make it work. I was already forty-two, and intellectually, he was right for me. I was kind of getting used to having him around. Everyone I knew thought I'd be a fool to let him go. Everyone I knew told me to go for it. Everyone I knew told me I'd never find anyone like him."

"Don't play the blame game." Mrs. Bruner felt her heart sink.

"I'm not. I'm trying not to."

"Ultimately, the choice to marry him was yours. You chose to marry him because you thought it would be better for you than what you had." Her mother hoped fervently that what she was saying was true.

"I guess."

"You guess?"

"What would you have done in my place? "

"He liked you a lot, Estelle."

"I know." Estelle hiccupped. "You think I don't know that? You think I like the way I treat him?"

"Do you?"

"Like the way I treat him? Not really. Do I like him?" Another bout of sobs shook her. "Sort of."

Mrs. Bruner groaned.

"It's not as bad as I'm making it sound. I do admire him, kind of. I admire the way he handles himself. I respect him for that."

"Is that all?"

"I know, Ma, it's not enough."

"You seemed so happy in the beginning," her mother said, wonderingly. "During your engagement, you seemed so content. Not in the clouds, not floating, but…tranquil. You were so at peace with yourself."

"I know." Estelle blew her nose. "Everybody was just so thrilled, and so pleased for me. Everyone made an enormous fuss about both of us. And, besides, I *was* in the clouds."

"You were? It didn't look like it."

"Never to have to go out on a date again? Never, never, *never*?"

"What are you going to do, Estelle?"

"Do?" A terrible pit of fear roiled within her. "I'm not getting divorced and starting all over again. Forget it."

"Go speak to someone."

"Can't I just give it a little more time?" Estelle begged.

"You need to do whatever it takes. Whatever works for both of you must be done, and fast. But something has to change."

"Something has to change," Estelle repeated, closing her eyes.

* * *

Paradoxically, that evening Estelle experienced the tranquility that had eluded her for so long. Was it because she'd finally told her mother the truth and the sky hadn't fallen in? The implicit permission to step out of the role that had been choking her for three months, that of a blissfully happy *kallah*, was liberating. She could stop pretending and stop feeling guilty. Maybe she would go to a therapist. Most probably, she would. She planned to check out the options, but in the meantime, it was good to feel better.

Elchanan was at his clown course and wouldn't be home until at least ten thirty. She curled up on the sofa and began writing in her diary. She started with her argument with Menucha and continued with the conversation with her mother, not leaving anything out. More than once she had to stop to wipe away her tears.

At some point, she dozed off, the diary still open on her lap, the pen fallen from her hand.

Elchanan turned the key in the lock. The house was eerily silent.

"Estelle?" he called softly. "Estelle?"

"I'm here, in the living room."

He walked into the room.

"How was your course?" she asked.

"Good. Were you sleeping just now?"

"I guess so. I must have dozed off for a minute."

"You've been working hard."

"Mmm-hmm."

"What are you reading?"

"Reading?" She blinked. "I was journaling."

He sat down nearby. "I didn't know you still did that. I thought that was for when you were single."

"I still write in here from time to time."

"Oh. Were you in the middle?"

"Yes."

He stood up. "I'll give you some privacy then."

"No." She held out the open diary to him. "No, read what it says."

He looked at her intently. "You want me to read what you wrote?"

"Yes."

"Are you sure?"

She took a deep breath. "Yes, Elchanan, I'm sure."

Elchanan took the diary from her hands. Still standing, he began to read. She watched his face as he did so.

When he gave the diary back to her, his eyes were moist. "Quite a document you have here."

She nodded.

"Estelle? Listen to me." He pulled over a dining room chair and sat down close to her. "It's going to be good. *We're* going to be good."

"We are?"

"Yes, we are."

"Why?" she demanded. "Because you say so? Because you want it to be so?"

"No." He shook his head. "Not because I say so. Because *we* say so. Don't we, Estelle?"

"Yes," she told him. "Yes, we do."

52

Next, Please!

It was late Sunday afternoon, the day after Rabbi Eisenberg's visit. She was standing in line at the supermarket, waiting for her turn to pay, when the phone rang. Sheila rummaged in her pocketbook and pulled out the phone without bothering to glance at the screen.

"Hello, Sheila," a very familiar voice said.

She froze.

"I hope I'm not reaching you at a bad time."

"Next, please," the cashier said.

"Sheila?" the voice said into her ear, sounding a bit less self-assured. "Are you there?"

Her throat was tight. Where was her voice? "It's…it's nice to hear from you."

"Same here," he retorted in a valiant attempt at a nonchalant tone.

"Next, please," the cashier repeated impatiently.

Sheila pointed helplessly at her phone.

The cashier glared at her. "Next, please!"

The people on line behind her began to grumble. She couldn't think straight. She couldn't have a potentially life-altering conversation with Yerachmiel while distracted. He deserved better.

They both deserved better.

"Yerachmiel? I'm glad you called. Just, I can't talk right now. I'll call you in five minutes, okay?"

"Not a problem."

They hung up.

Yes a problem! What was so important that she couldn't talk more? He wasn't asking for much. Just two seconds longer, to put his mind at ease that his call was welcome. He needed that, after her repeated rejections.

He tried to come up with a valid reason, any reason at all why she couldn't spend two seconds longer on the phone, but his mind was blank. He was too panicked to think.

Who said she'd be calling him back at all? And, if she didn't—his panic mounted—was he supposed to call her back or just pretend that nothing had happened? Nothing, except that he'd made a fool of himself. Again. That wasn't so terrible, because, really, what was the shame in her knowing that he still thought about her sometimes? Okay, constantly, ceaselessly, but there was no way she could know that from one short casual call. No way at all. No, the lump in his throat was from finding her and losing her all over again.

He never should have called. Why had he reopened the wound, which had never really closed in the first place? When Rabbi Eisenberg told him that Sheila seemed receptive to hearing what he had to say, that he'd definitely call her if he was in Yerachmiel's position, was that adequate reason to bring the conversation with his former mentor to a hasty close and call her right then and there?

Why had he done it?

Because he wanted to. Because he had to? She was his *bashert,* and if any chance existed for her to see that, he had to take it.

Calm down, Yerachmiel. Try to think. What really happened just now?

Twice she'd said his call was welcome. True, she could have expressed herself more warmly. She could have said, "It's great to hear from you," or, "I'm so happy to hear from you." She even could have said, "I missed you." That would have been nice. Heartwarming. Reassuring.

He paused, struck by a realization that should have been obvious to him by now. *But then, the speaker wouldn't be Sheila.* It would be Yerachmiel, and he'd better get used to her more reserved style if they were going to start dating again.

No, not dating. As far as he was concerned, they were through with dating. One or two more meetings, if that was what she needed to feel sure enough to move forward, and then...

He couldn't think that far ahead. There was no future without her, but no more dating. Did that make sense? Nothing made too much sense anymore except—

The phone rang.

"Hi? Yerachmiel? I'm so sorry about before. About just now. I should have explained. I was in the supermarket, paying, so I couldn't talk to you. I should have told you that."

"It's okay."

"No," she insisted. "It's not. You were probably biting your nails off, obsessing about whether or not I was planning to call you back."

"Well," he said cautiously. After all, a man had his pride. "Maybe I was just a little anxious there."

She laughed. "I couldn't think straight for a moment. I know that you probably would have just left your purchases on the counter and left the store, right?'

"Yup."

"I was on automatic pilot."

"It's fine."

There was a pause while both searched for words.

"Yerachmiel, are you free now?"

"Am I free?"

"Could you possibly meet me in like, half an hour in the pocket park between both of our houses?"

"I could."

"So... I'll see you pretty soon."

"Sheila?"

"Yes?"

"Don't laugh, but—wow. Just wow," he said fervently. "Know what I mean?"

She didn't laugh.

"Yes," she told him. "I know exactly what you mean."

* * *

She had fifteen minutes to prepare for a date with Yerachmiel.

What should she wear?

She stopped rifling frantically through her closet as a realization hit her full force. She wasn't preparing for date number 315 or whatever the number was. This meeting with Yerachmiel wasn't going to be a date exactly. Not in the way dating had been. There was no need for her to put her best foot forward. No need for her to impress him. He already liked her a lot, and probably would find her attractive no matter what she wore. Who knew? He might even propose to her today.

Would he? Or had she burned him too badly for him to trust her as he had before?

She shivered. She'd had only the best intentions in stopping their relationship. She'd only been trying to do the right thing. It seemed, though, that despite her intelligence, experience, and purity of intention, she'd been mistaken.

Had she been mistaken? Even now, she wasn't entirely sure, but she couldn't allow Yerachmiel to slip between her fingers again. That, and…

And she couldn't hurt him anymore. He was so convinced that the two of them were meant for one another.

So, she decided, closing her closet and heading out her front door, no, this wasn't a date. This was going to be an attempt at a meeting of the minds in the truest sense of those words. She and Yerachmiel needed to ascertain, once and for all, if… If what?

If they were on the same page as far as their life goals were concerned?

If they were willing to support one another while heading toward those goals?

It sounded like a business merger.

Why were they meeting now? Shouldn't she have clarity before they saw each other again?

Was the purpose of this meeting? To see if they valued each other? If they respected and admired each other? It wasn't that.

Why were they meeting today?

To pick up exactly where they'd left off?

She sighed in defeat. It was all too much to puzzle out on her own. Maybe that was the point. Maybe a person needed a partner. Maybe two people who cared about each other, who respected and trusted each other, who—

Trusted each other.

Suddenly, she very much wanted to speak to Yerachmiel.

She quickened her pace until she was practically running, and then, she *was* running. She flew through the streets she'd run down as a sixth and seventh grader, late for school, because after all, she lived only two blocks away, so there wasn't any reason to get up early, was there? She ran past the former homes of close friends from high school and beyond. They were long married, and she?

She was going to marry Yerachmiel Kantor. She was going to become his wife. They would build a home together.

Sheila smiled exultantly as she reached the main avenue and waited for the light to change. She'd be the best wife in the world to him.

If he proposed to her, at this meeting, or one soon after. *If* he was still interested. But she knew that he was.

Sheila's triumphant smile softened into a far gentler and more thoughtful expression. In his loyalty, constancy, and single-mindedness, her *chassan*-to-be was someone very special.

She'd never tell him that, but maybe he'd pick up her vibes. Or maybe she would tell him, one of these days. Anything was possible, wasn't it?

She retraced her steps and ducked into the lobby of the nearest building. Making sure the coast was clear, she pulled out her lipstick. Two seconds, and then she'd be on her way.

She replaced her lipstick and rushed out of the building.

Yerachmiel stood waiting for her at the park entrance.

"Hi."

"Hi."

"I hope you weren't waiting long."

"No, not at all."

They both looked down in confusion. Sheila knew it was up to her to reopen the conversation, but her mind was blank. Yerachmiel had always been the one to take the lead. He was the one who spoke straight from the heart, while she allowed him to do so, but now, the silence stretched. What should she say?

"You're here." It was the only thing she could think of.

"Yes. I'm here."

"You're here, and...and..." She couldn't continue. She looked at him helplessly.

"Why don't we find somewhere to sit?" he suggested.

Sheila looked around. "Where?"

It was a good question. The park was teeming with children of all shapes, sizes, and ages. Children running, jumping, screaming, eating. Children fighting, crying, laughing, complaining.

"Mommy! He's bothering me."

Children swinging, sliding, tumbling, and digging.

"Mommy! Look at me! See what I can do."

"See how high I can climb."

Mothers, sisters, and babysitters occupied all the available benches. There was nowhere to sit.

"How about over there?" Sheila pointed to a stone ledge at the far end of the park. It was partially shaded by overhanging bushes and compared to the rest of the park it was an oasis of quiet and peace.

"Looks great."

They walked over and sat down. Yerachmiel pulled a bag out of his pocket.

Her mouth dropped open. *Not yet. Please, not yet.*

He laughed at her appalled expression. "Did you think I was about to propose to you?"

"Yes," she told him quietly. "I did."

"I want to." His tone was equally quiet. "I want to, but I can't be on probation anymore, Sheila. I want to grow as a person as much as anyone else, but I can't be pushed into a role that doesn't fit me. Even," he smiled crookedly, "by you."

Sheila didn't answer. "Look!" She pointed. "We have an audience."

They did. A small towheaded boy, perhaps three or four years old, was staring intently at the bag in Yerachmiel's hand.

Yerachmiel looked at the child and laughed.

"What's so funny?"

"He has healthy instincts, that's all."

"What do you mean?"

"It's a chocolate bar," he explained. "I don't know how he knew."

"They say kids know."

Yerachmiel held out the bar to the little boy, who stared gravely with big gray eyes. After a moment, he ran off.

Yerachmiel shrugged. "I guess his mother told him never to take candy from a stranger."

"Could be."

"But if I would have?"

"Would have what?" she asked, distracted.

"Proposed?"

"Then I…" She closed her eyes tightly. When she opened them, he was still there. "Then I…"

"Then you…?"

"Yes."

"Yes?" Yerachmiel repeated, barely daring to breathe. "Yes, Sheila?"

She nodded, smiling very slightly.

The little boy was back, leading an even smaller child by the hand.

"That must be his little sister," Sheila remarked, inconsequentially. "They look alike, don't they? Yerachmiel? Do you see the family resemblance?"

Yerachmiel thrust the chocolate at the startled children. The little boy drew back slightly, but his sister had no reservations about accepting the unexpected gift. She flashed Yerachmiel a radiant smile, grabbed the chocolate from him, and ran off before he could change his mind. Her older brother stared at the grown-up couple for a moment longer before giving them a more thoughtful smile of his own and setting off in pursuit of his sister, intent on claiming his share of the prize.

"Or maybe you need some time to think about it?" he asked.

"Why do you say that?"

"I ought to be older and wiser than that little girl at my advanced age, don't you think so?"

Sheila gave him a long, steady gaze.

"Don't you think so?" he repeated.

She tilted her head. "Don't I think so? Maybe I do, and maybe I don't. But Yerachmiel?" She smiled at him.

"What?"

"I'm happy you asked. Yes."